The Girl With a Thousand Interviews

Giorgi Lebanidze

BookLocker
Trenton, Georgia

Print ISBN: 979-8-9906171-0-0
Ebook ISBN: 979-8-9906171-1-7

Published by BookLocker.com, Inc., Trenton, Georgia, U.S.A.

The characters and events in this book are fictitious. Any similarity to real persons, living or dead, is coincidental and not intended by the author.

Library of Congress Cataloguing in Publication Data
Lebanidze, Giorgi
The Girl With a Thousand Interviews by Giorgi Lebanidze
Library of Congress Control Number: 2024908957

BookLocker.com, Inc.
2024

Dedication

Dedicated to Elena Ferrante, whose works inspired me to pursue my own path in storytelling.

Special thanks to Linda Kleinschmidt, whose keen insights and expert guidance proved invaluable in the creation of this book.

Table of Contents

Prologue

Stars that wander from their constellations teach us that even in the expanse of the universe, choosing your own path is the truest way to shine - Just like many of you, my mom always pegged me as the 'could-do-better' type, 'she's talented but lazy' It's like moms worldwide get a script called 'Classic Mom Lines'. Ask, how did I see myself in this mom-scripted world? Was I talented? That was up for debate, especially on days when I felt more washed out than my botched home hair dye job. On those days, 'talented' felt more like 'Hina fail in progress'. But on the good days? Oh, I'd strut around thinking I was the hidden genius of my generation.

Life sure knows how to throw curveballs, doesn't it? As I flip through the pages of my past like some quirky comic book, I can't help but chuckle at the unexpected twists and turns. Even those 'end-of-the-world' moments now seem like they were just trying to add some dramatic flair. It's one of those peculiar human quirks, you know? We look back, have a laugh, and think, "Well, guess it wasn't the apocalypse after all." But it's those very moments that give life its value. I mean, what's life without its ups and downs? If there's no pulse, there's no life, and a pulse means experiencing both highs and lows. If it's all just one or the other, it's like a straight line—and a straight line means stagnation, even death. But I'm far from being dead; I'm writing this book because I want my pulse to resonate with countless readers. I want them to understand the joys and struggles of youth, and most importantly, I want to challenge those who have wronged justice—not the laws written by the state, but the sense of fairness held by the people themselves. This story is my way of signaling that I'm ready for whatever comes my way.

As I delve into my old notes, a flood of memories rushes back, tucked away in the corners of my mind. It's both humbling and exhilarating to revisit the story my life has written so far. And why am I spilling all these beans, you might wonder? Well, my journey has been anything but ordinary. Recent upheavals have turned my narrative on its head, forcing me to rethink what I reveal and conceal. So, I've decided to lay it all out there, for better or worse. Buckle up, because this book is venturing into uncharted territory, all thanks to the rollercoaster ride my life has become.

****

Consistency is born from a pattern of inconsistencies, yet everyone interprets it in their own way. As for me? Well, I've often been tagged as 'not your average.' But let's get one thing straight—I'm not about to slap any conventional labels on myself. But if there's one thing you should know about me, it's that I have a soft spot for the extraordinary.

Although—not everyone's jazzed about hanging with the extraordinary. It could be envy, or maybe just a nervous tick, when things stray from the mundane. I've had my fair share of critiques lobbed at my offbeat choices. But, borrowing a line from my very first ex (yeah, he's getting a shoutout here—consider it a rare honor), he'd say:

"Criticism? Think of it as free confetti for your own party." And guess what? That snippet, out of all the things about him, actually stuck with me... Okay, so picture this — life's not just about dodging bad dates, trying out that spicy Taco truck everyone's raving about, or y' know, impulse buying that glittery thing you want but (totally) don't need. For me, it also involved a lot of... Appointments, "Not everyone wants to be saved" moments, meetings, sit-downs in places ranging from swanky to "is that actually a raccoon there in the corner?" The people I regularly encountered? A real motley crew! Some were like walking soap operas, and others were so quiet you could hear a pin drop around them. Every gathering still had its own unique flavor and soundtrack, but then, we were all part of the same strange symphony called life, or perhaps... job screening.

Right in the middle of a hilarious mix-up and a deep dive into the merits of llama yoga (yep, it's a thing), Cupid decided to take aim at yours truly. But hold up, we're not diving into the mushy stuff just yet. Let's rewind and dish out the deeds on these quirky encounters that oddly became my scene. Now, looping back to that burning question—am I a talent, an oddball, or just a danger-seeker? I'll toss that big question over to my favorite armchair judges–to dear readers. If we gave my mom a buzz right now, (Which we cannot) (she's supposed to be enjoying a piña colada in the Virgin Islands with husband number four — quite the charmer, but unfortunately, she is not.), she'd belt out a confident "Absolutely, darling!" But catch her in a quiet moment? I bet her answer would be a tad more reserved. But leave mom aside for now, we're diving into my early journey, from the rollercoaster decisions I've made to the interesting and for some dangerous paths I've walked, and how quickly life turned from a comedy to the darkest thriller.

On my path, I've dived into hobbies that aren't just off the beaten track—they're off the map, underscoring that 'ordinary' is a label you'll never stick on me. My tale? It's unique, peppered with light-hearted moments that'll draw you in, yet it packs enough punch to ruffle some feathers. And for those who might want to challenge my narrative or take issue with my choices, especially after publishing 'the whole story,' my door's open—come and have a chat. For the skeptics out there wondering, "Why should I listen to her or her advice?"—you absolutely don't have to. But here's a fun fact, a small reminder for friends, foes, and everyone in between: I've been through more job interviews than the average soap opera has episodes. So, grab your popcorn or glasses—it's going to be a long story to tell.

PART I

Chapter I:

Holding Fast to This One

"You're fresh from academia's embrace, so what makes you think the corporate world is ready for you?" Mr. Knowitall began, a sly twinkle in his eyes.

My nerves were taut. I cleared my throat and answered. "Well, my student job taught me a lot about..."

Ms. Sharpnose just smiled benignly. "Oh, those quaint student jobs! They're rather like preludes, aren't they? Important, yet hardly the main performance."

I resisted the urge to raise an eyebrow. "True, but those preludes have given me great insights into..."

Mr. Knowitall then gently interrupted, "Insights? Interesting word choice. Don't you feel that real-world challenges might differ a little from... just college-level insights?"

Struggling to retain my composure, I replied, "Absolutely, but they provide a foundation, a starting point to..."

Ms. Sharpnose now looked genuinely curious after interrupting again - "And how do you suppose these foundational experiences will transition to our setting here?"

I felt a knot of frustration and self-doubt tightening in my chest. Words failed me—three points, no, four—yet they slipped through my grasp like sand. Was this interview meant to break me down, to strip me of my confidence? Was the corporate world always so merciless? Had I somehow misstepped, or was this just the harsh reality? My previous student job interviews had been straightforward, nothing like this. But here I was, feeling small and inadequate. Choosing silence, I shifted my focus to my body language, unable to shake the sense of unease settling over me–I started moving instead.

As I fumbled to gather my belongings, Mr. Knowitall continued, this time in a contemplative tone, "You know, it's truly eye- opening when we encounter someone so... so steadfastly anchored to their collegiate days."

Ms. Sharpnose, adjusting her glasses and sharing a subtle glance with Mr. Knowitall, further mused, "Indeed, it's somewhat endearing. Like watching a child clutching their favorite toy on the first day of school, uncertain of the bigger playground they are entering."

I hesitated at the door, their comments echoing in my mind. Were they offering help or just poking fun? The embarrassment pinched at me. I quietly said, "Thank you," quickly exited, eager to leave yet feeling the burden of their remarks linger as I stepped out into the corridor, trying to shake off the unease and confusion that clung to me.

Outside, it felt like the city turned up the volume just to laugh at my newbie blunders. The sun was throwing down heat like it was going out of style, but the real sweat? That was courtesy of that intense interview room vibe. And about those nicknames, Mr. Knowitall and Ms. Sharpnose? Yeah, they might sound like rejects from a Disney cartoon, but trust me, they're spot-on. In the grand lineup of quirky characters I've met, these tags are more real than their actual names.

That evening, I was tempted by the charm of ballroom dancing—a fresh adventure for me, straying from my usual cozy house parties. Lilly, always chasing unique experiences, had sold it to me as something glittering with potential. But post-interview fiasco, my excitement had definitely cooled off. Looks like the dance floor would have to wait.

After the grind of another day, I stumbled into our flat, my heels chattering against the tiles like a Morse code message for "S.O.S.". Michael, my flat mate, glanced up from his video game, a raised eyebrow asking his lips didn't dare to.

"Did the world chew you up and spit you out, or what?"

"It spat alright," I replied, heading to the sink. If only the day's disappointments could be scrubbed off like last night's mascara.

Interviews,
HR Departments,
Talking,
Jobs,
Can my head think about different topics?

Dinner was a plate of mushroom risotto, as comforting as a hug from the inside out. I plopped down in front of the TV, hoping to drown my sorrows in the fickle currents of StreamScape. Halfway through some crime drama, my room started winking at me from the corner of my eye. Michael, ever the empath, gave a knowing nod as I trudged off. Once tucked away in my solitude chamber, my ears picked up the TV's muted chatter, and I found myself reaching for my phone.

Whipping through social media felt like attending a masquerade ball, everyone wearing "my life is perfect" masks. My interview faux pas suddenly felt like a wardrobe malfunction on the red carpet. I shifted gears and tapped out a few key phrases into the search bar: "Surviving job interviews, " "What NOT to drop in an interview like a hot potato, ", and "Do all interviewers have a master's degree in sarcasm?" Tips, tales, and pity parties flooded in, as if I had opened the floodgates to the 'Land of Failed Interviews'.

After a long day of job hunting and dance video binging, I slumped into dreamland to the soundtrack of the city. My cozy bed and I became one as I let the day's drama dissolve. But then, morning sunshine, like a spotlight, rudely interrupted my peaceful slumber. Groggily, I realized it was market day. I shimmied into my trusty old jeans and a tee that should've retired ages ago, then whipped up a smoothie that hinted at today's fresh produce. Michael, my bill splitting mate and resident coffee-addict, was already brewing his morning lifeline.

"Going to dazzle 'em at the market today?" he teased, with a wink. "Oh, please grab me some of that basil, will ya?"

"Ja natürlich," I responded and quickly ran.

As I cycled to the market, Sacramento's streets stretched out wide before me. Tower Bridge was a familiar sight, its silhouette towering in the distance, and an early-bird street musician strummed a tune, the notes floating in the air like a morning greeting.

Once I arrived at the market, my to-do list unraveled. My stall, a patchwork of colors, was a reflection of both the bounty of nature and a college student's budgeting skills. Unrolling the canopy, setting up crates, and artfully displaying produce — every tomato, every leafy green, was placed with precision and a dash of pride. The market wasn't just about sales; it was an exchange of stories, recipes, and sometimes, life advice. My regulars would often linger, discussing the best way to sauté zucchini or the secret to creating a hearty salad.

Surrounded by the captivating aroma of fresh strawberries and the jovial atmosphere created by my fellow growers, the mishaps from yesterday now felt almost funny. Everywhere I looked, I heard another exchange of laughter or a teasing joke, reminding me that life often has its ups and downs.

The day's first task was always the small mountain of apples that needed sorting. I'd always pick each one up, checking for bruises or imperfections, brushing away any dirt with a cloth, and then place it into one of the three wooden bins that said: "Perfect", "Slightly Blemished", or "For Juicing".

As I became engrossed in my apple-checking, Mrs. Henderson, one of our regulars, approached with her characteristic swagger.

"I swear, every week you're here trying to hide the best ones from me!" she accused in jest, a smirk on her face.

I laughed, "Well, Mrs. Henderson, I've got to keep you on your toes." I reached for a particularly rosy specimen. "This one's just been harvested. Perfect for one of your legendary pies, I'll wager."

She squinted at the apple, then at me, playful suspicion in her eyes. "Hmm, looks almost good enough. But remember, my pies are only as legendary as the apples that go in them. So, no skimping on quality, young lady!"

I saluted mock-seriously, "Understood, Ma'am. Only the best for Mrs. Henderson's pies."

After Mrs. Henderson completed her apple transaction, I returned to my task of carefully arranging all the apples in a neat line. The work was normally tedious, but it was moments like mine with Mrs. Henderson that made it enjoyable. Given the cheerful interaction between vendors and customers, the labor was more than worth my time.

After pocketing my day's earnings, I sauntered through Sacramento's bustling streets, letting the city's rhythm wash over me. Then the serene moment was broken by my phone's insistence. It buzzed, it rang, and judging by the "Abigail-calling" tone, it seemed like it had been doing so for at least an eon... or maybe it was just eighteen seconds. Dread filled me, not because of the call, but because that jingle was the unofficial anthem of our 'Workout Evenings.' Abigail's fervent dedication to fitness was infectious, so under normal circumstances, I'd be gearing up to break a sweat. But today was anything but 'normal.'

As I took a deep breath and swiped to answer the call, a borderline hysterical voice screeched from the other end,

"HINA!!! I've been circling the cafeteria like a hawk for the last fifteen minutes. Where are you?!" Instead of embarking on the treacherous path of explanations and justifications, I opted for brutal honesty.

"Abby, I'm bailing on today's burpees and squats," I declared.

Then, in a voice dripping with faux tragedy, she sighed, "Fine, traitor. But don't think you're escaping me completely. Meet me downtown, later. Michael's tagging along." The deal, of course, sealed. I continued my leisurely stroll, wondering if the universe would throw any more curveballs my way this day.

For two hours, I strolled around the park, my phone practically glued to my hand as I mulled over self-help articles and interview tips like a broken record. By the time the sun decided to clock out, I joined Abby and Michael for dinner. Our meal felt more like a sprint than a chill gathering, as everyone seemed to have places to go and food to digest. Amidst the food marathon, Michael, ever the comedian, dished out his usual blend of self-tease and complimenting others. His specialty? Joking about his love life. But his current love, Dan, was a tough nut to crack.

Dan was a trifecta of sophistication, smarts, and sportsmanship (yeah, one of those football hotshots). Tough to make fun of someone when they're a hair's breadth away from being an action figure. But we had faith. Michael's wit was like a bloodhound, always sniffing out the laughs. And sure enough, he delivered.

"The hardest part about going out with Dan?" Michael started, his face twisting into a mock pondering look. "It's keeping up with his morning face ritual. Seriously, it's like he's prepping for surgery. I get moisturizing, but this guy's skincare regime is more complex and guarded than the secret formula of a cola brand!" Amidst our howling laughter, the nearby tables seemed divided between annoyance and amusement at our little comedy club.

Even in the intense realm of modern skincare obsession, Michael had found his comedic gold. It was a real talent. How could he turn the mundane into something so hilariously noteworthy? I suppose in some way, it was his way of coping–finding humor, even when things seemed humorless. And today, of all days, I needed that laugh more than ever. Our escapade through downtown unfurled as neon lights played across the towering monuments of corporate might.

Looking at the buildings, I blurted out, "Ever think about how some folks up there in high-rises might just be getting paid for looking busy?"

"A what?" Michael replied, raising an eyebrow as if I'd told him I'd seen a UFO. Abby just rolled her eyes like she was watching a rerun of a show she didn't like.

"Isn't it wild?" I continued, making my best impression of a dramatic TV host. "Some kid's working two jobs, running around like a headless chicken, earning just enough to cover rent. Then there's Mr. Big Shot, in his fancy office," I pointed straight up to emphasize, "makes a few calls, taps on Excel, and voila! He's swimming in money."

Michael just looked at me, completely baffled, while the only response from the city was a distant car horn. I could see the wheels turning in their heads, debating whether I was on to something important or just having another of my strange 'moments'.

Michael sighed, giving the towering buildings a long look. "It's not just about the surface," he mused, "Hard work doesn't always equal big bucks yes, but" After a brief pause, he switched gears, "Anyway, how was bowling with Adrianna and Derrek? Was Adrianna cool?"

"She was... sympathetic about Martha's ordeal, but love's a tricky beast," I replied.

Michael snorted, "Love my ass. It's barely been a month!" Then, circling back to our original discussion, he added, "And those execs up high? They've got their own battles. Not physical, sure, but the stress of decisions, office politics, it's a different kind of weight."

Abby, now drawn into the conversation, nodded. "It's a bit like apples and oranges."

Michael grinned. "More like comparing apple pies to orange juice. Both take an effort, but they're not the same beast."

"But isn't more paycheck always better?" I challenged.

Michael, after a thoughtful silence, ventured, "Maybe it's about finding the right formula after all."

"A Formula?" Abby giggled. "Oh, not the infamous 'formula' again!"

Michael playfully scolded her, "Okay, okay, madam, life isn't math, but maybe it borrows a formula or two from it."

His typical jest was laced with an unexpected gravity. "You see, the world doesn't come with an instruction manual for fairness. There's no universal tutorial for fairness either," he explained, a thoughtful furrow forming on his brow. "We're left to navigate this on our own, wrestling with questions of equitable wages and what it means to be genuinely decent people. It's all about finding the right formula, discovering that elusive balance that harmonizes our personal ethics with the broader societal scales. That, my friends, is the crux of the matter."

Our eyes met, Abby's and mine, sharing a look of mutual discovery, as if we'd stumbled upon something entirely new.

Fairness,
Formula,
Balance,
Paycheck? How are these interconnected, along with success?

As the evening's conversation mellowed into the night's serenity, Abby, true to her role as my personal cheerleader, made me pledge, "Gym, no bailing out the day after tomorrow." She declared the upcoming day a "Slacking Day," a golden opportunity to delve into the world of comic books, a newfound curiosity of mine.

Yet, amidst this laid-back planning, a persistent notion lingered in my mind: the concept of 'the right formula.' This notion shadowed my thoughts, even as I pounded away on the gym's treadmill, sparking a deep internal dialogue. "*How do I evolve from being merely another employee to someone wielding genuine influence, without transforming into one of those uptight, those who have lost their true selves, those execs we often criticize?*"

Chapter II: Belle Epoch Envy

Post workout. As the bright city lights streaked past the window on our ride home, my brain was in overdrive: *There's got to be a way to skip the mortifying interviews and sidestep the pitfalls. A way to reign over my destiny.*

As I flung my shoes off, preparing to dive into the enticing world of StreamScape, a thought struck me with the force of a lightning bolt:

'Hold on a sec... maybe the answer isn't finding someone else's path but creating my own. Entrepreneurship.' The idea of crafting the 'right formula', or at least stumbling upon it, began to resonate more and more. I mulled over this revelation, turning it over in my mind again and again, trying to piece together what this meant for me. It wasn't just a onetime epiphany; I revisited the thought, scrutinizing it, challenging it, and gradually, it began to solidify. That was it! My own path. The concept didn't arrive fully formed; it was honed through repeated contemplation, each iteration bringing me closer to a definitive direction.

Ah, life. It's a bit like a sitcom without a laugh track, isn't it? Here I am, 24 days in (Yes, I'm keeping a tally.)—you'd expect some grand revelation, some earth-shattering epiphany about my next big move. I've been on a quest, a deep dive into the murky waters of self-reflection, trying to figure out my 'What Now?' You know, those moments of profound thought squeezed in between binge-watching sessions on StreamScape (hey, a girl needs her downtime). But guess what? I'm still out here, playing detective in the mystery of the 'right formula.' It's elusive, like that last piece of pizza you were sure you had in the fridge but can't seem to find.

The days morphed into a seamless blend of moments. Work. Stroll. Sweat it out at the gym. Crash at home. Gab with friends. And occasionally sprinkle in a few oh-so-enthusing discussions about impending graduation with my fellow students. Glamorous, wasn't it? Two job interviews winked at me from my calendar, but I promptly cancelled them. Why? Because the siren song of entrepreneurship was suddenly proving too seductive to ignore.

Now, before I lure you down the rabbit hole of my endless contemplations, let's fast forward, shall we? Social media was taking the world by storm. Everywhere you looked, someone was trying to 'influence' something. Some parlayed their newfound fame into shilling products, while others crafted their own unique merchandise. '*AHA*!' I thought, *'That's my ticket.'* Enter ClipClock: the hub for zippy, time-crisp video clips that had the masses hooked. Some of my 'well-intentioned' buddies even suggested I lean into my... let's say, 'physical assets' to lure the 'less cerebral' portion of the male populace. But really, they had instead just meant, 'Drop the sweater, show more skin, and watch the likes roll in. 'Oh, the depth of male predictability!' So, picture this picture. I skyrocket to fame, amass a whole million followers - I'd have brands slipping into my DMs, begging me to pose with their new lip gloss or fancy water bottle. Heck, I might even launch my own line of... cute cat socks? But before I got completely carried away with those daydreams...

I gave ClipClock a whirl. Big mistake. Within seconds, I realized it's the dumpster fire of an app. Who are these people getting their kicks from watching endless, mind-boggling 60-

second videos? And the very thought of me contributing to this madness? A hard pass. I am not committing any sin against humanity! - Deleted -!

But here's the twist - I couldn't ghost social media entirely. Like it or not, I had to set up camp on Facebook and Instagram. Every job, hobby, side gig, or Grandma's knitting club had a page these days. So, even if I don't become the most famous person on the Internet, at least I won't disappear into a void. It was time to create some precise, high-level Hina content... without any extra embellishments. The quest for that 'next big thing' had me burning the midnight oil and practically inhaling volumes of market trends. The public domain data, although fascinating, felt like I was only scratching the surface. So, in what can only be described as a "spur of the slightly mad moment," I forked over a whopping 780 smackers (yes, from my savings!) for specialized data from those ever-secretive data collection moguls.

The information sprawled before me like a cryptic jigsaw puzzle, demanding expert eyes. But who needs experts when you have the audacity of ambition (and a knack for winging it)? Armed with my self-proclaimed analytical prowess, I deciphered, deduced, and finally had the lightbulb moment I was seeking. I saw the breakthrough of creative-sales-on-demand and their potential...

It was vintage women's lingerie. Now, don't twist your eyebrows just yet. We're not talking here about picking up any ol' lacy number. My mission? Sourcing them from the farthest corners of the digital world and the mustiest aisles of local thrift shops. From kilo shops (where the loot is weighed, and the joy of thrifting is taken to an economical paradise) to exclusive boutiques. My hunts often culminated in treasures like bras, bralettes, panties, corsets, and the elegant, yet saucy, bustier. The lineup also boasted of teddies, babydolls, camisoles, garter belts, and slips. That was just half the fun. The real magic started when I began to tweak them. Some received delicate knitting accents, while others got a splash of paint. Some bore evocative messages, taking the lingerie from mere attire to a powerful statement. The goal? Marry Edwardian elegance to a touch of modern audacity and vulgarity. Think Jane Austen meets Lady Gaga.

And so, my darling reader, what happened to this eccentric endeavor? It didn't just change my closet. It changed my life. Transforming mere lingerie into wearable art was no walk in the park. From refurbishing to recoloring, every piece became a canvas of creativity. Then came the digital frontier—establishing a social media presence and setting up an online store. My savings? Well, they bore the brunt of this endeavor, dwindling faster than a double dip ice cream cone on a summer day. But hey, what's the point of having savings if not to pour it into chasing one's passion and goal?

Michael, with his uncanny knack for strategy (and a seemingly endless reservoir of patience), also pitched in. He'd toss ideas about digital marketing while I'd furiously jot down notes, the two of us crafting an online empire for my revamped lingerie. Still, even with all the hustle and bustle, I still had to maintain my regular job. Those savings weren't going to replenish themselves, after all, and I had other bills to pay.

The clock ticked away, and thirty-seven industrious days later, my first collection made its online debut. No stone was left unturned in marketing my masterpieces. I became a one-woman publicity machine, distributing posters, curating digital ads, and even sidestepping details like my long-past graduation. But hey, let's put a pin in that for now. Juggling the demands of my job with the burning ambition of my venture soon wore real thin. So, with a heavy heart, I handed in my notice. I could almost visualize Mrs. Henderson's vexed face, knowing she'd lost her trusted hand in curating the finest picks and her go-to hide-and-seek partner. Yet, as one door closed, new windows of opportunity flew open and sales notifications began trickling in, first in Sacramento, then throughout the county, and before I knew it, all across the Golden State.

So, with a mix of astonishment and pride, Michael remarked, "Wow, Hina, you're actually pulling it off!" And pull it off, I did.

It became my full-time job. My beloved word, sales, skyrocketed in a way that even my wildest dreams hadn't foreseen. Each passing day saw me diving headfirst into a whirlwind of creativity, giving my social media a facelift, and constantly refining my online store. In a matter of three months, I saw my bank account begin to expand, indicating that I was likely on the path to constructing a real empire. Mine.

Despite achieving this success, a nagging feeling remained. Have you ever felt like something is unfinished? Like you've left a puzzle incomplete? One missing piece and it's driving you nuts? That was me. My victories seemed hollow, and anxiety's familiar sting prickled at the edges of my mind. So, I did what Hina does best–I faced the music. It might sound like a move from the playbook of the deranged, but hey, that's just how I roll.

Given that I wasn't in dire straits hunting for a job, I didn't cast a wide net. But a ghost still haunted me — that woeful job interview from yesteryear. With renewed determination, I hunted for openings at the very company that housed the illustrious Ms. Sharpnose and Mr. Knowitall. The plan? Land the job, and then on day one, waltz out. A poetic exit! But lady luck had other plans. There were no openings.

Undeterred, I widened my net. Similar companies. More interviews. Crafting my resume became an art form. Initially, the specter of my past failures weighed me down. Although I had made a name for myself as an entrepreneur, the idea of sitting in a sterile corporate interview room still gave me anxiety. After several rejections, I was shocked when a job offer finally did arrive in my inbox. However, it didn't take long for me to remember that I had moved beyond this kind of career path. I was not just another candidate fresh out of college.

No way was I going to dive into the 9-to-5 grind again. So, I did the logical thing. I accepted the job and never showed up. Closure? Not quite. An insatiable hunger had been awakened in me. Applications flowed out like water, targeting every conceivable job in and around Sacramento. Interviews became my pastime, sandwiched between business meetings. Fast forward to 13 months post- graduation, and I was the interview veteran Sacramento had never asked for. The number of interviews I'd racked up? Staggering. The valuable knowledge of the people and businesses I had acquired were now all combined? Invaluable.

Life, as they say, is a whirlwind. Since launching my small lingerie and writing empire, there have been many plot twists and not only there, but in personal life as well.

Notably, my venture had evolved, bringing me a steady, albeit not lavish, revenue stream. This financial stability gave me the freedom to explore other industries and expand my knowledge. Abby and a group of my friends were continuously pushing me to pursue pricey certifications. Yet, I remained steadfast, laser-focused on my dual passions — the booming business and my newfound hobby of interviewing.

My company had grown so much that I now had a pleasant mid-sized office downtown on J Street. With seven to nine employees working in the office and two operating from a distance, we ran like a finely tuned engine. There was nothing like the comforting aroma of my morning coffee, now delivered promptly to my desk. And our morning briefs? Well, they had attained something of legendary status. It was an unspoken rule that no one started to work without the daily brief. The fun part? Anyone, from intern to manager, could helm these sessions. It was empowering, motivating, and often a tad chaotic. On the eve of my 24th birthday in August, as another fulfilling day wrapped up, my checklist was nearly all ticked off. But then, just as I was ready to call it a day, Mark, or Tyrese, you may call him, my ever-so-punctual assistant and adviser, breezed in, handing me a document. It detailed an upcoming business meeting—a potential partnership with a company that could bolster our writing division.

Ah, I seemed to have skipped a beat! Amidst all this activity, I'd delved into writing and publishing. But it wasn't the age-old traditional type. It was avant-garde, novel, and refreshingly different. I had already gone through a crazy number of 999 job interviews by that time, and this next one wasn't just any other. This upcoming meeting was expected to be my final job interview - at least for me personally. Wrapping up, Tyrese and I headed out, rendezvousing with Michael, (But he never showed up) who by now had moved in with Dan (Probably was spending time with him). We geared up for that monumental meeting. Reflecting on the sheer magnitude of my journey—a fledgling lingerie line turned Stories told by interview collector that had conquered Sacramento and sensing not only, the relentless hum of those near-thousand job interviews, helming two thriving businesses, and finding solace in a hobby, I felt the weight of every choice, every twist, and every turn. There was more going on than it seemed. Hidden stories and even darker secrets were about to come to light, showing me worlds I never knew existed. I was stepping into a new place full of opportunities and risks, emotional stress, and happiness. So, before we launch into the song of my life, let's go back a few years and take in every moment of joy, pain, and drive wild moments up to this culminating point. I invite you to join me on that journey beginning at the very beginning.

Chapter III:

Entering GSU

You know how they say life's a circus? Well, let me tell you, mine feels more like a comedy club in the middle of a startup fair, with a dash of thriller drama. Balancing career chaos, entrepreneurial escapades, and love-life lunacy is like attempting a grand plié in a sandbox. I've face-planted (metaphorically, of course) so often, I could qualify as a professional diver. But hey, each laughable and depressive stumble has been a steppingstone. Remember, if Hina, the girl who once thought a 'bull market' was a petting zoo event, can find her groove amidst the gaffes, so can you? Stuck in the shadows? Just wait for the punchline. It's always lurking around the corner.

I might have mentioned I graduated from college, but that's not entirely accurate. I spent four fulfilling years at Golden State University, Sacramento, chasing that always elusive bachelor's degree. However, my crew and I had a little quirk. We referred to universities as "colleges." That might sound odd, especially since colleges traditionally offer two-year programs that act as a springboard to the universities. But come on, doesn't college sound a lot more laid-back and fun? Back in 2019, when my college adventure started at Golden State, everything all began in September with the start of classes for the Fall semester! But as a freshman, I had to roll in a bit earlier, late August to be exact, for all those boring orientation sessions that give you a little heads-up on what to expect, where to go, and how many coffees it takes to survive a lecture.

Well, walking into that vast campus, I kept my fingers crossed, hoping to see, maybe even bump into, a familiar face. Perhaps someone from high school, middle school, or even that kid who used to steal my newspaper back in the old neighborhood. But luck was taking a break. I was alone in the midst of a sea of unfamiliar faces. I felt totally alone.

You might chuckle at this rendition, but I actually majored in Anthropology - with a focus on Archaeology and Biological Anthropology. Yep, I'm the same girl who now juggles a lingerie and interview stories, imaginative tales to inspire folks to do... well, "something." A strange combo, right? It's like I majored in 'digging up old bones' to eventually sell, well, bras and stories at the time, though it wasn't comical. It felt like one of those puzzles was the pieces in three different boxes.

For a good decade, Mom and I called Stockton our home. What was our history before that time? Let's just bookmark it for another novel. Now, with college calling loudly, it was time to hatch a plan for my own Sacramento nest. GSU graciously offered me student housing, but I said "nope" and optioned right out of it. Living with a random flat mate? The thought made my skin crawl. What if we didn't mesh? Would I have to put on my big-girl pants and actually deal with college authorities or take the rogue route and evict flat mates myself? So, the life hunt began. Apartment searching is no child's play, especially when you have some real specifics in mind. My mother was willing to help out, but she had her hands full with the aftermath of her third divorce. That husband? He was so strange, it almost defied comprehension. If 'weird' could be measured on a scale, he would have broken it five times over.

Before I knew what happened, I was sharing an apartment with Louise, or as I like to call her, my 'Semi-Friend from Childhood'. Not exactly BFF material, but her family and mine used to rub elbows back in the day. I figured teaming up with a half-known entity was better than rolling the dice on some campus stranger. Our tiny abode in Rosemont was very 'charming-Ish.' The walls were pleasant. A few half-decent pictures hung here and there around the room, and just enough unexpected surprises kept your interest going.

How long was the honeymoon phase with Louise? Shorter than a goldfish's memory. By the start of the second semester, our interactions had evolved into artful eye-slides. It's almost poetic, if you think about it. So, the apartment hunt was back on my list, this time for a non-eye-rolling cohabitant. Enter Martha, my freshest catch from GSU. Boy, was she a charmer. Adorable to the power of infinity.

She was close to flawless, except for her endless complaints about her love life. No matter how much sage advice I gave her, she'd just keep going back to the same song on repeat. It was like feeding coins to a broken jukebox. What truly ground my gears? The fellas who've mastered the dark art of exploiting a girl's loving nature, then make her feel like she's got two left feet in the dance of love. This type of guy, from my imaginative experience, has a real predatory streak. They probably cornered a girl at a party once or twice or took liberties they weren't given. But pointing that truth out to Martha would be like telling someone their favorite song is out of tune — not my place, even if my gut was humming a wary tune.

The first semester? Okay, don't let anyone ever sell you that it is like 'stepping into a dream' narrative. It's more like stumbling through a fog of self-discovery, unless you're one of those turbocharged extroverts that hits the college ground sprinting. While the classes did spark some interest, many of my classmates seemed like they had been plucked from a monochrome palette. Still, Martha was different, an outlier. Every time she raised her hand, her answers were not just correct, but filled with insight. So, when we planned a simple meal out, it took an unexpected turn. Out of nowhere, her boyfriend showed up, assuming he was part of the plan. He whisked us away to Lemon Hill.

When I dropped the hint about potentially ditching Louise and scouting for a fresh flat-mate, Martha's eyes sparkled with mischief. Sneaking over one day while Louise was probably outsourcing another abstract art piece for the living room, Martha whispered her own escape plans to me. Our combined wanderlust saw us relocating to a roomier dig in Florin. Seriously, the place was really massive! I was lodged deep in boredom watching an infomercial when Martha came lunging into my room, beaming with enthusiasm.

"Hina, are you ready? Brad's pursuing a career as a DJ now. He's been mixing some music tracks or something." I raised an eyebrow, holding back a chuckle.

"A DJ? Sweetie, these days, everyone and their dog want to be a DJ. It's like the new-age existential crisis. If you're lost in life? Become a DJ!"

She plopped down on my bed, her face a mix of hope and doubt. "Is it... you know, really a terrible idea?"

I paused, chewing on my words, resisting the urge to unleash a torrent of sarcastic wisdom. I settled with just saying, "Life's an odd tune, Mar. Perhaps they'll find their rhythm in this DJ jig." Martha's eyes shimmered, now on the brink of tears but desperately holding them back. "You always have a way with words, Hina. But Brad... he's different, right? Maybe he could be that one-in-a-million DJ who actually stands out?"

I lounged back onto my bed and leaned against the pillows. "If Brad was a track, he'd be an unexpected remix in a world of overplayed songs. Things are never certain though. He might end up a hit or he could just become another forgotten B-side."

Martha sighed, a soft, heart-tugging sound. "I just want him to be happy, you know? But I also don't want him to dive headfirst into something and then face a ton of disappointment."

Reaching over, I patted her hand reassuringly. "Mar, life's a record. Sometimes it scratches, skips, or plays the wrong tune. But every so often, it surprises you with the most beautiful melody. Let Brad play his set; you might both dance to beats you never imagined existed."

She smiled weakly, nodding. "Thanks, Hina. I always feel better talking to you, even if you do wrap your advice in a blanket of metaphors and wit." I pulled out a book from my shelf that practically screamed 'pop psychology.' Its flashy title was something along the lines of "72 (or was it 99?) Tips to Make Six Figures." Who even writes this stuff? But, in a twisted way, it was perfect fodder for our group roasts.

As the days rolled on, college life was surprisingly, becoming more vibrant. New friendships, fresh dramas, and occasional unexpected turns. Like when Abigail, the very same gal I'd hinted at earlier, approached our usual hangout spot. Now, under any other sky, I'd have mentally swiped left, but there was something about her infectious energy that was intriguing. In no time, we were chatting away, and she was sharing her ambitious dream of becoming Sacramento's top fitness icon. It was actually refreshing to see someone so passionate about... well, passion.

I'm tempted to dive into more tales of campus romances like the guys who tried their clichéd pickup lines and those I may have thrown a wink or two at a few times. But honestly, that's neither here nor there. Let's just say freshman year was a rom com of sorts, with me obviously not being the problem, nor being particularly interested. My last relationship had wrapped up about a year ago, and I was in no rush to trade in my newfound independence for romantic chains on my neck.

By the time my sophomore year dawned in 2020, things had taken an intriguing turn. It was like I'd swapped a soap opera for a blockbuster movie.

Mum, meanwhile, had emerged from the shadows of her third marital misadventure, now living life with the zest of a teenager at a summer festival, while also engrossed in her role at a budding media firm. Seeking her counsel on student jobs ended with me getting a dissertation on dating instead. Classic Mum!

In the end, a chat with the top brass at Golden State sent me to the human resources wing, a hub that was actively linking students with job opportunities. And, before I knew it, the date was set for my very first job interview. FOR THOSE WHO DON'T KNOW IT YET, there's a world of difference between a university-facilitated job interview and going rogue in the wild jungles of employment. You see, when the university's got your back, there's this comforting illusion of having one foot already in an open door. It's like going to a party with a plus-one; you've got some backup. But diving into the job market solo? That's akin to entering the gladiator arena. You either shine in your armor or face the swift sting of a confidence blow via a quick exit.

Rolling into my first job (student part- time) interview, I was all sparks and shine. No sweaty palms, no heartbeat drumming in my ears. I sauntered in like I'd been doing it for years. Perhaps that's what gave birth to my lofty notion that every interview would be a cakewalk. I slipped into my killer heels and the dress– the one that screamed confidence and whispered charm. Martha was my sideline cheerleader although I made it clear Brad's good wishes could wait till... well, never.

Hopping on the bus, I soon stood in front of a five-story building. The Sacramento Farmer's Market headquarters. The branches that could potentially be signing my paychecks was perched on the fourth floor. After an excruciating fifteen-minute thumb twiddling session, a gentleman who seemed to have a few butler-esque qualities ushered me into a modest room. There, a poised woman with reading glasses looked up, appearing like she'd weathered many a job interview storm. "Miss Strubel, am I right?" She began.

Dazzling her with a smile, I replied, "That's me. It's a pleasure!"

She then did that age-old move of lowering her glasses before reclaiming them and murmured as she scanned a paper, "GSU student, correct? Your major?"

"Biological Anthropology," I answered, chin high.

A hint of a smirk appeared, as she probed further, "Ever been intrigued by the organic treasures of the world?"

I paused for a moment, then declared with major enthusiasm, "Anything made from the Earth that humans have interfered with? That's my passion!"

She quickly followed up with, "And what about selling those products or guiding people to the right choice?" Her eyes twinkled with a hint of mischief, obviously probably accustomed to throwing newcomers off balance. "So, Miss Strubel," she leaned forward, "Let's imagine for a moment that a customer approaches you, absolutely livid because they believe they've bought expired produce. How would you handle it?"

I took a breath before speaking, picturing the situation in my mind. "Well," I started, "my approach would be to lend a listening ear. Listen to them and take their message into account. Then, I'd look at the product carefully and explain that organic items can look scruffy even if they are still usable. If the product truly is expired, I'd apologize sincerely and ensure the customer would get an immediate replacement or refund."

She nodded, scribbling something down. "Impressive response. And tell me, what drew you to a role here at the Farmer's Market, particularly when your academic pursuits seem... a tad different?"

"Well," I hesitated just a moment, my inner snark itching to jump out, "much like anthropology decodes human history, understanding food and its market helps decode current human behavior. Plus, I love the idea of promoting a healthy, organic lifestyle. It feels... grounded."

She smiled, seemingly entertained. "Last question. Where do you see yourself in five years, Miss Strubel? And no, 'doing this very interview' isn't an acceptable answer," she added with a playful smirk.

I chuckled, "In five years? Probably waist-deep in research, deciphering some fascinating human behavior, while sipping the organic green tea I had bought from my favorite Farmer's Market." Her eyes grew wide as she listened, and her face broke out in a broad grin.

"That's a unique answer, I must admit. Thank you, Hina. We'll be in touch soon."

Heading for the door, I thought I was free to go. But as my hand touched the cold metal handle, a voice filled the silent room and detained me with one final question. After an initial cough to clear a male throat, it began, "Excuse me, Miss Strubel, might I ask where you're originally from?" I paused, my heels pivoting on the carpet. My eyebrows rose in bewilderment; I hadn't noticed anyone else in the room. Then, in the dimly lit corner, I spotted a figure, all suited up with a pen poised over paper and legs crossed in that classic 'I'm-important' fashion.

"California. Born and bred," I quipped, still taken aback.

He adjusted his glasses. "No, I meant your roots, your heritage."

Caught off guard, I responded, "Well, I've been a state girl through and through. Mind if I sit again?"

"Of course," he motioned to the chair.

The lady now interjected with a soft-spoken introduction, explaining his role. He was the Chief Decision Maker or Chief Disturber; I wasn't quite sure which.

Settling into the seat again, I replied, "Certainly, I was born and raised in Berkeley, California. My mother is originally from Pakistan, while my father comes from Virginia." He nodded, scribbling. A tiny voice inside me whispered, "*Does every interview here come with a mini genealogy dive? Or perhaps it was just my enchantingly ambiguous looks. Go figure.*"

The man continued, "Do you still live with your parents?" I blinked a couple of times. That question felt weirdly personal for a job interview. I went for a half-truth and shuffled into my seat. "Well, I'm a student, so I bunk in the university dorms,"

He nodded, maybe getting the hint that he'd ventured off-script. "That's cool. We need fresh, energetic folks like you, Miss Strubel. Hope to see you around here more often."

Finally, the oddball Q&A was over, and I needed a coffee. Badly. I made a beeline for Jade's café. I took a sip of my usual latte and caught sight of Michael. We had spoken a few times before and shared some laughs, and yet we were still in the 'hello acquaintances' stage. I had this strong intuition that he could become a really good friend if we continued catching up over coffee. So, there I was, mindlessly stirring my latte when Michael popped up next to me.

"Same order today? The latte and cinnamon combo?" he inquired with a slight smirk. Before I could react, he was back with the latte and another piece of news. "Guess what? I'm graduating this year. And I'm dropping this barista gig too. Got a fancy finance job lined up." I tried to recall the company name, but it escaped me. What did stick, though was my surprise.

We'd exchanged pleasantries in university corridors, the usual nod-and-smile routine thanks to mutual friends. But this? A full-blown life update in the middle of a cafe? It was... unexpected. But hey, I'm a fan of odd stories, especially when there's a splash of ambition tossed in. Given his recent success on the job hunt, I thought he'd be an ideal person to chat with about his interview experience. So, amidst the clatter of cups and chit-chat, I grilled him on his own interview journeys.

The minutes went by quickly, and the cafe was soon bustling with customers. Realizing it was time to take orders, Michael motioned to the people forming a line at the counter. "Duty calls," he said. But not before we made plans to hit the bowling alley that night, Martha in tow. Who would've ever thought? A shared love for oversized shoes and knocking down pins would definitely cement our budding friendship.

I mentioned I loved odd things and weird people. I mean positively weird or positively odd, because I have almost zero tolerance for unethical weirdness and passively rude folks. That evening me and Martha had one hell of a fight, which I thought would lead to one thing, but it went in an absolutely other direction.

Back then, while Martha, Mikey, and I were getting hyped up for our inaugural bowling night out, strolled Brad. He strutted in with those clown-like bowling shoes as if he had orchestrated the entire event earlier.

I glanced around, waiting for someone to claim responsibility for this surprise visit. Nothing. So, I couldn't help myself.

"Looking lost there, Brad?" I asked, trying to coat my voice with salt, but it was hard to hide my irritation. "Didn't think you were on the guest list." Assuming Martha would echo my sentiment that men shouldn't automatically think they're invited everywhere that their girlfriends go. Instead, she just threw a curveball ...

"Actually, I invited him," she said, her tone shifting, suddenly aligning herself with him, and challenging my claim on him.

Was she for real? This wasn't the first time Martha had sidelined our plans for Brad. Movie nights, brunches, even our spa dates. He'd become a sudden and consistent inclusion in what used to be 'our time'. It wasn't just his unexpected presence, but rather the shift in Martha whenever he was around. She became more distant, defensive, different. I often wondered if she even noticed the change herself. Had she genuinely invited him tonight, or was this another case of Brad nudging his way in and her covering for him? Either way, a bit of heads-up would've been nice.

My pride wasn't about to be trampled on, though. Not after the countless times I'd bit my tongue, keeping the peace, ignoring the growing wedge that Brad was driving between us. Tempers flared, past resentments surfaced, and words were exchanged that night. Our long-standing bond now seemed fragile, hanging by a thread. And just like that, our bowling session crumbled, too. I stormed out, with Mickey trailing behind me.

Some of my friends argue I can be a tad headstrong. And maybe they're right. Perhaps it's why I stood my ground with

Martha, refusing to be the only one always doing the compromising. The rift between us felt like an ever-widening chasm. And soon after, our living situation became tense, a palpable unease filling every shared space. I hadn't planned on looking for a new place, but it started to seem like the only feasible option. Just when I thought I had one more headache to deal with, in came Mickey with a timely solution.

"Since I'm staying in the city for my new job," he began, "why not share my flat? It's honestly more space than I need." Given the circumstances, the offer seemed almost serendipitous." And soon splitting rent bills with Michael quickly became my new routine. It's also about I delve a bit deeper into my past for my readers.

Chapter IV:
F&F (Friends & Family)

My mother, Amna, was a radiant young woman in Islamabad when she crossed paths with my father, Benjamin. As the story goes, my father was there on business. Their chance meetings turned into profound conversations, and soon, they found themselves entangled in the intricate dance of love. Benjamin's persuasion ability played a pivotal role in broadening Amna's horizon, urging her to consider different geographies for both love and life.

Within a couple of years, they exchanged vows, their lives oscillating between the U.S. and Pakistan. Yet, like any other family, we had our shadows too, but ours was among the darker ones. When Mom was twenty-five and expecting me, she was blindsided by a chilling revelation about my dad. He was arrested in Pakistan on drug charges. Amna's first instinct was to believe he might be a user. But the truth was far more daunting: Benjamin was establishing connections in Islamabad to channel drugs through multiple countries and target the Eastern European market.

Luckily, he was released swiftly. My mother, with her strong maternal instincts, intervened in every move he made. While part of her wanted to approach the authorities, the thought of jeopardizing my safety, the unborn child she was carrying, held her back and she kept her silence. Fearing retribution from those whose interests she'd disrupt, she chose separation and sought the sanctuary of a new homeland, the U.S. I thus took my first breath under the bright California sun a few months later.

Despite Amna's efforts to protect me from these chaotic happenings, I found myself learning about the truth. My father attempted to connect with me frequently, and I welcomed his attempts. But soon, his name was on the wanted list, and he vanished from my life, never to step on U.S. soil again. As for Amna, she danced with love twice more. By the time Michael became a part of my flat mate entourage, she was single, and ever the romantic, searching for her prince gain, and despite her chaotic private life, she still managed to excel in her professional life.

Shortly after, my mom implemented additional security measures for my safety and took me to an unfamiliar location. She cautioned me that if anything were to happen and we couldn't locate each other, this place should serve as a checkpoint or a hideout, all without anyone's knowledge. This secluded spot was situated near Amador City, to the north of Sacramento, perched on a hill with several cottages scattered nearby, witnessing minimal human activity. Her concerns stemmed from the possibility of criminals from my dad's circle finding us. If they ever did, this location, with its well-concealed, garage-style building, would be our refuge.

I remember she used to be really paranoid years ago, but recently, it seemed like she'd almost forgotten all about it. She even came up with a code name for the safe house—whenever she said we were going to "Stay Away," it meant we were heading to that hidden spot. And if she ever told me to "Stay Away" on my own, that was my cue to go there and stay put. It all felt like some kind of secret code, probably because she didn't want my dad to know about the place ahead of time.

In the end, her ambition never diminished despite her inner turmoil. Honestly, I owe a lot of my looks to both my parents. I've heard tales of my father's striking appearance. As for my mother? One glance at her and you'd see a quintessential Pakistani beauty. It's probably why I've often been nicknamed "Jasmine", even if it's a bit off the mark. After all, Jasmine was Arab, but then again, not everyone's adept at discerning precise racial nuances.

Many people don't truly appreciate the gravity of managing bills. Maybe it's because it is such an ordinary part of adult life that we forget how complicated/complex and demanding it can be, especially for those in college who have to deal with studying, working, and living separately, but yet all at the same time. I am certain that adolescents, well protected by their parents' security, are rarely aware of this burden. They may naively assume that life will carry on as seamlessly as it has once, they step out on their own. However, reality hits hard when they're suddenly confronted with a stern reminder. It's time to pay your own bills! It is then that the grumbling begins; countless soon moan about the meager amounts left over after settling their expenses that are due.

I wasn't exempt from this shock, either. Even splitting costs with Michael, I hadn't anticipated the hefty sums that bills could too soon total. Thankfully, my part-time job buffered some of the impact, leaving me with some modest savings and a bit of spending cash. Still, in my moments of direst need, I found myself knocking on my mother's door for assistance. The first two times, she turned me away, declaring, "You chose to leap from the nest prematurely, thinking independence was child's play. Now, deal with the reality of your choices." The third time, though, she relented and graciously extended help to her daughter.

Life began to find its ongoing rhythm. Between work, college, and occasional gym sessions with Abbigail, I felt anchored. Michael introduced me to Lilly, who I then, in turn, introduced to Abbigail. Just like that, we formed our little squad. If you've been observant here, you've noticed that my close circle predominantly consisted of women. Some might speculate that because I had trust issues with men–particularly the straight ones. But honestly, I was swamped with work and studies, with barely any time remaining for romantic escapades. I also firmly believe that a staggering 99.2% of men struggle to maintain a purely friendly relationship with their counterparts unless bound by strong moral or ethical ties. So, ladies, if you've managed to find those rare male friends who aren't trying to make a move every chance they get, hats off to you! You've struck gold in finding that rare 0.8%.

If the human body had its own dedicated enthusiast, it would undoubtedly be Abbigail. She wasn't just into fitness; she lived and breathed it. Abbigail grew up in a family where fitness was merely an afterthought. Then, a chance encounter with a yoga instructor during her teenage years ignited her passion. From then forward, she plunged into every fitness regime imaginable, from CrossFit to HIIT, making her a great go-to person for any health-related queries. Her Instagram profile was a whirlwind of motivational quotes, healthy recipes, and workout routines. Still, beneath the athletic exterior, was a girl who believed in balance–she loved her occasional pizza nights just as much as her morning green smoothies.

Lilly was a dreamer, a sylph in a world brimming with noise. While most of us grooved to the latest chartbusters, Lilly's soul danced to the symphonies of classical music. We first encountered each other (without introducing ourselves) at a college cultural gathering. While others were playing the latest pop tunes, Lilly stepped up on the stage and wowed us with her Kathak dance–a traditional Indian art form. Her costume spun gracefully as she moved, the bells on her anklets softly tinkling in the background, and her eyes blazing with raw emotion. It was completely captivating.

Hailing from a family of musicians, dance wasn't Lilly's first love. That was the cello. But a visit to India during her gap year exposed her to the world of classical dance, and there was no turning back. She trained rigorously, embracing its history, spirituality, and technique. But she didn't stop at Kathak. Over time, she ventured into ballet, flamenco, and even traditional Chinese dances. For Lilly, dance wasn't just an art; it was a bridge connecting her to diverse cultures and stories. Abbigail's exuberance and Lilly's elegance balanced each other perfectly in our quadro, making us feel totally complete. They both dedicated themselves to their individual interests, teaching us the importance of commitment.

Friendships, endless journeys, and whimsical adventures are all well and good, but when gritty reality taps on your shoulder, you've got to be ready to face that music and enter the world of, shall I say, brutal capitalism? Don't get me wrong; I have a love-hate relationship with capitalism. I support it, mostly, but it's also an eye-opener when you're thrown suddenly into its whirlwind.

Chapter V:

Extroverted Days

Securing a proper job is the most tangible manifestation of this reality. And let's not even start on the experience of job interviews. I used to roll my eyes at the very mention of them. Why all the formalities, I thought? It felt like an age-old tradition that had overstayed its welcome. However, I soon realized that the skills acquired for handling an interview could be extended to other realms, like entrepreneurship or even personal hobbies.

So, let's dish about Brad, Martha's boyfriend who's always stirring the pot. Despite the heaps of less-than-flattering things I've said about him, he did drop a truth bomb once. Picture this: right before I was gearing up for my first big job interview, with Martha being my personal cheerleader, Brad and I got tangled in one of our classic debates. I was all about singing hymns to the almighty university system, and there he was, playing devil's advocate, throwing me a curveball. He tossed out, "Hina, universities are more than just brainy boot camps. They're the ultimate networking fiestas, and it's those connections that'll be your golden ticket, not just the fancy diploma." I was just about to throw Bill Hobs and Nolan Fique in his face as my counterargument when he zinged in with, "But hey, didn't they first get their foot in those ivy-covered doors? Just shows. They knew where the real game was played." And there I was, mouth agape, without a comeback, as he smirked, probably thinking he'd won that round.

I won't lie. Those words stung a bit. Not just because they came from Brad, but because they carried a chunk of truth. While the idea of studying anywhere, even in a bathroom, if one was truly passionate, sounds laughable, the underlying message was clear: Universities are less about academics and more about networking. So maybe, just maybe, Brad had a real point here.

Indeed, there's something to be said about acing job interviews. Sure, on the surface, it seems like a rite of passage to land a decent job. But scratch a little further, and you'll realize an interview is a masterclass in negotiation and persuasion. Think about it: The more times you hear "yes" in life, the more doors will swing open. If you become adept at swaying people, persuading friends, or just generally getting nods of agreement, those reactions paint the picture of a successful journey. And here's another little secret I stumbled upon. Sales jobs are absolute goldmines for honing such skills.

I used to be quite skeptical about the whole CV and resume hoopla. To me, they were just flashy advertisements for one's life. But just like in marketing, if the product, i.e., YOU aren't up to the mark, no amount of jazzed-up advertising is going to save the day. That's the bare truth. Right? CVs and resumes might get your foot in the door, but it's your skills, wit, and negotiation tactics that will seal the deal.

I realized I was a bit behind the times when it came to honing my negotiation skills, so I decided to sharpen them by taking on job interviews as practice. After all, life is too short to leave important decisions up to luck only.

The days were rolling on, professors came and went, and while some classes made me scratch my head, others had me totally hooked. With all that going on, my brain was just running a marathon. Then, in the middle of the usual college whirlwind, a surprise popped up. On my bus ride home, my hand brushed against a slyly placed note in my bag. Smooth move, right? It was from Derrek; another sophomore like me. The note read: "Hey Hina, I couldn't help but notice the vibrant energy you bring to class. How about we channel some of that energy over coffee? If you're game, let's meet at the campus café this Friday at 5 p.m. Warmly, Derreck."

Naturally, I replied "no." Yet, for some reasons beyond me, both Michael and Abby seemed hell-bent on me giving this date a shot. Oddly enough, Derrek lived right next door to Martha, and since Martha and I were on a no-talk basis, the last thing I wanted was any added drama. So, no matter how much Abby and Michael campaigned, I held my ground and turned down the idea of a date.

One night, an invitation found its way into my hands—the senior class was hosting a get-together and Abby and I had been asked to attend. Michael, who would have qualified as an alumnus, received an invitation, but chose not to go. Hoping to sway to some great Chicago house beats, I was a bit bummed to find the music scene was not to my taste. But then, things took an interesting turn. The evening transitioned into an open-mic poetry session, and while a handful of guys managed to sway the crowd with their verses, it was Derrek who stole the show.

He took center stage, there diving into this intense piece about fiery passion, age-old romance, and the kind of undying love that inspired the gladiators to battle fiercely for their heart's desire. It was all very dramatic. and I'll have to admit, impressively delivered. But then came the cringe-worthy climax. He ended his recital with something along the lines of, "To the fiery spirit and the radiant beauty that is Hina," and pointed directly at me. Before I could fully process just what he had said, he strutted over, beckoning me to join him for a dance as the music kicked in. I was momentarily taken aback, but then just flashed him a wide grin, embraced him briefly, and stepped back. It was the gentlest way I could think of to decline without bruising his spirit in front of everyone. He wasn't a bad guy; he just wasn't my guy. As the night wore on, I overheard snippets of conversations—people who were playfully throwing around the term 'SIMP' when referring to Derrek. It was a trend then to label someone trying too hard to impress their crush. It irked me to see how just a term could be so misused to demean someone's sincere feelings.

Deciding to intervene, I did what Hina does best. I flipped through the script. After striking a deal with the DJ (offering him a bribe of three joints tomorrow), the pulsating beats of Chicago house music enveloped the room. My heart raced in tandem with the beats. Every eye was on me, but I was fully in my element, lost in the music. As my feet glided and twisted, my hands painted stories in the air. I had trained in house dance, so this was my playground. From the corner of my eye, I spotted Derrek, his gaze unwavering. I spun and twirled my way over to him, and in a bold move, extended my hand and invited him into my world. The surprise on his face was evident, but he didn't blink. He matched my energy step by step. His movements were fluid, fully complementing mine. We danced as if we'd been partners for years and effortlessly stole the show. It felt electric, and for a few minutes, we were the heartbeat of that party.

By the next day, the rumor mill was churning. The whispers suggested that Derrek and I were an item. However, the first thing

I did was to make sure he knew where I stood. I was open to being pals–genuine, platonic friends. Not because there was anything amiss with him, but because my current journey was all about self-growth and personal evolution, not romance.

Chapter VI:

Lilly's Cello

By that time, summer was peeking around the corner, and the close of our third year was right on the horizon. The upcoming 22nd of June wasn't just a marker of time; it was also Lilly's birthday. We'd been bantering back and forth about what we should do to celebrate from beach parties to city adventures. But then, in true Lilly fashion, she waltzed one day, a mischievous twinkle in her eye, and declared her heart's true desire.

"So, my lovelies, I've had this little fantasy tucked away for the longest time," she confessed, her tone dripping with drama. "Imagine me, my cello, all of you, and the spectacular backdrop of Yosemite National Park. A camp, some tunes, and our wild souls all together. Sounds epic, right?" She playfully arched an eyebrow, daring anyone to disagree. "I trust that none of you darlings will disappoint me with any last-minute dropouts. Right?"

As one always does when a dear friend makes such an enchanting proposition, we jumped on board without a second's hesitation. And the universe conspired in our favor, too. The day Lilly chose to fell on a Sunday–a blank slate of opportunity with no obligations. Michael, my ever-resourceful buddy, somehow managed to borrow an old SUV from Dan, his latest flame of oh maybe three weeks? What audacity to ask so soon! But that was Michael for you. They'd apparently met at a football match, and their romance was just budding.

Three hours on the road later, with Lilly's beloved cello nestled safely in the back, we were there. Can you believe that in all my 22-odd years living in California, I'd never set foot in Yosemite? Quite the oversight, considering its beauty, knocked the wind out of me. Michael, being the adventurer that he is, boasted about knowing the most prime spots. But Lilly? She was on a mission. She had her heart set on a specific location, and nothing was going to sway her from going there.

The universe had other ideas. The park was teeming with tourists; every scenic spot and stunning view was filled. Still, our girl Lilly didn't give up hope that her perfect spot was still there waiting only for us. She kept her fingers crossed and hoped against hope that her dream place was still quiet and waiting.

We finally arrived there, right beside a river and deep within the embrace of the forest. The ambience? It was pure magic. Seriously, if any writer stumbled on this place, they'd be cranking out novels like a machine! But there was a tiny hiccup–another group of people were already there. Not close enough to eavesdrop, but visible enough to slightly dampen our spirits. We thus gave Lilly a collective pep talk, urging her to own the moment and play her heart out, audience or no audience.

So, with a fire in our bellies and anticipation in our eyes, we quickly set up our temporary abode, and before the golden hues of the evening kissed the skies, Lilly's stage was set. She made us promise - and not just a regular promise, but a cross-your-heart-and-hope-to-die kind of promise–there'd be no recording, no videos, no sneaky snapshots. This was to be an experience, something only cherished in the confines of our minds, etched into our souls. We were all more than ready to let the music wash over us. You know, in life, there are those moments, those utterly raw, unplanned, and ethereal experiences that you just can't fabricate or plan. This was one of them. Lilly, with her cello cradled lovingly against her, looked like some otherworldly muse. And when the first notes of Debussy's "Clair de Lune" whispered through her strings, you'd think time itself was holding its breath.

This piece, though originally written for piano, had this haunting different beauty when played on the cello. Like a silken thread of memories, it twined through the air, caressing us with tales of love both lost and found. It spoke of silent glances, heartbeats shared, and the gentle sigh of lovers under a moonlit sky.

I caught a glimpse of Michael, and oh boy, for a guy who'd talk your ear off, he looked entirely lost in the world that Lilly was weaving. There was an intense vulnerability in his eyes, as if the music had unearthed old, buried stories in his heart.

Abby, ever the passionate one, was lying on the grass with her eyes closed, content and relaxed, as if she did now have a care in the world. Her fiery personality seemed to come alive with each note, her expressions conveying her intense delight. The atmosphere was filled with emotion, making it feel thick with that splendid tension.

Nature seemed to be in tune with us too, as the trees swayed gently, perhaps in rhythm to Lilly's music. Maybe they were conducting their own silent orchestra. It was as if Yosemite itself had become part of our little audience, totally appreciating the harmonious blend of human art and nature's majesty. That day, we weren't just in nature; we were a part of it.

Sometimes life's melodies are as unpredictable as the notes that were cascading that day from Lilly's cello. As she continued pouring her soul into her performance, a different kind of rhythm emerged a distance away. I spied the flicker of a flame. And one isn't supposed to light fires in Yosemite at night, but hey, rules are always meant for some of them to break. Right?

It seemed like a full-blown party was erupting amidst nature's sanctuary–laughter, the thump of music, the clink of bottles. As much as I wanted to ignore it and stay focused on Lilly's magical performance, I could sense the pull it was having on Mikey. It was in his DNA to be drawn to lively beats and the promise of a good time. That boy's extroverted spirit is like a moth drawn to a flame. With a slight tilt of his head and a questioning look, he took off, leaving behind the serene realm the rest of us were engrossed in and loving.

Abby quickly followed suit. I guess the allure of an unexpected adventure got the better of her, too. I looked on, aghast and somewhat disappointed. Really? Leaving Lilly in the middle of her heartfelt performance? But life's always throwing curve balls, and people? They're the most unpredictable of all those curve balls.

As for me, I chose to stay by Lilly's side. I might not be a hardcore classical aficionado, but the purity of that moment, the bond of friendship with her, meant more to me than a wild soirée in the woods.

The soft patter of wheels against the ground suddenly caught my attention. I turned to see an automated wheelchair approaching, navigated by a young lad with an air of innocence that juxtaposed beautifully with our natural surroundings.

He drew up close to where Lilly was playing and then looked in my direction. There was an unspoken understanding as our eyes met, both of us clearly connected by the ethereal music. Standing up, I was instantly pulled into the world of this stranger who had been so captivated by Lilly's playing.

"I hope I'm not interrupting," he began, his voice carrying a soft, foreign lilt. "The music was too mesmerizing to ignore, especially in this serene environment."

Returning his smile, I replied, "No interruption at all. Feel free to enjoy it."

As we continued to exchange pleasantries, curiosity got the better of me. "I'm Hina, by the way. You don't sound like you're from around here."

The boy chuckled, "Quite perceptive! I'm Nico. Nico Frauzs from Germany It's my first time here on this land, America!"

"Right, how nice!" I replied. He then started listening to Lilly, as if he had known her for a long time.

As time passed, Nico seemed completely immersed in the music, a picture of pure joy. The irony was clear. While our closest friends had been lured away by the allure of a modern party, a stranger from a distant land had been drawn to the classical beats of Lilly's soul. Life, as they say, always works in mysterious ways.

Raising an eyebrow playfully, I asked, "Are you flying solo here?"

Nico's eyes sparkled with a dash of mischief. "Oh, not quite. Me and my mom are touring around. She's somewhere nearby. I just got lured by the enchanting melody of that cello. Knowing her, she's probably on my trail right now as we speak."

That was a light bulb moment! Could his mom be partying with the same group that had lured away Mikey and Abby? I gestured toward the lively group. "Could your mom maybe be right over there?"

His chuckle was light, and there was a warmth in his eyes. "Nah, she's not the wild partying type. We were just debating about the right time to hang around here. She got sidetracked by some folks taking pictures of the landscape. So, I just snuck away."

The earnestness and depth in his voice made me wonder. Sometimes I feel like people who've faced challenges early in life have this innate kindness. They just get 'pain', enabling them to be kind to others, but then, what about those who let their traumas turn them dark and bitter? Ugh, diving into the depths of psychology felt like trying to read hieroglyphics without a Rosetta stone.

"She must be worried. No?" I remarked, a touch of jest now in my voice.

"We weren't too far apart, to be honest. And she caught a glimpse as I zoomed off in my..." He paused for a slight dramatic effect he wanted, then gestured toward his wheelchair, "... my Ferrari over here." That playful twinkle in his eyes was infectious.

Grinning, I shot back, "Looks like we might have another audience member joining us soon!" Then, before we could continue our banter, the melancholic strains of Lilly's cello transitioned into something more intense. It was like a storm building up, powerful yet delicately controlled. The finale of her performance was now upon us, and the atmosphere grew thick with emotional anticipation.

Nico, with a hint of playful teasing and curiosity in his voice then, stated, "You've been sneaking glances toward there a lot," nodding in the direction of the bonfire. "Worried about that fire they've lit?"

I chuckled, "Nah, it's not about the fire per se... I mean, sure, I hope they don't accidentally torch the place, but..." I sighed, the weight of the situation pressing down on me for a split second, "two of our posse decided they'd rather join that party than stick around for Lilly's gig."

His brows lifted in understanding. "Ah, you wanted the gang to stick together for her performance, huh?"

I shot him a mock-serious glare, "Look at you. You're just the Mr. Detective! But yeah, it's Lilly's birthday bash today."

That realization seemed to light up Nico's face. "That's... actually incredible. Celebrating with such a heartfelt performance in this setting? Kudos to..."

"Lilly," we both chimed in simultaneously, sharing a quick, amused glance.

Continuing, I added, "She's had this dream for a while, you know? Playing her cello, right here in the lap of nature, surrounded by friends, waiting for this moment." My gaze shifted towards Lilly, her silhouette radiating a serene passion.

Nico nodded thoughtfully, "It's disappointing when things don't pan out exactly as planned. But friendships aren't about picture-perfect moments, right? They're weird, unpredictable... kind of like a roller coaster. No thrill on a flat ride, is there?"

His perspective took me by surprise, and a chuckle escaped me, "Well, when you put it like that... Guess you're onto something."

He flashed a heartening smile, "Every moment has its beauty, well, well. Sometimes, it just takes a second look." His ears perked up slightly, catching the sound of someone approaching - the unmistakable footsteps of his mother, I presumed.

"You know," he began, it's interesting and fascinating."

"I know, right? " My response was prompt, but soon enough I understood he had something else on his mind.

Nico's face lit up with a warmth as he began, "You know, this 'Clair de Lune' that Lilly is playing, it translates to 'The Light of the Moon'. And, just like the moonlight, it has its own tale to tell." His eyes took on a distant look, momentarily wandering the paths of melodies floating around. "The music, it has a whimsy, almost as if it's playing hide and seek with its own story."

After a brief pause, as if he was collecting fragments of stories he'd once heard, he continued, "When Debussy poured his soul into this, he stood at a junction in music history. You can almost hear the delicate dance between the old and the new–between the Romantic era and Impressionism."

Drawing in a gentle breath, as if he was inhaling the music itself, Nico mused, "But what always catches my heart is Debussy's restraint. Imagine creating such a masterpiece and then keeping it hidden for over a decade before finally releasing it, waiting for the right time to release it into the world. Much like your friend, Lilly, choosing and waiting for this special evening for her music."

Feeling the depth in his words and the new dimension they brought to Lilly's performance, I murmured, "It is astonishing, isn't it? How a piece of music can hold so many emotions, stories, and moments within its simple notes."

But wait, who is this kid? He's like a decade younger than me and yet, he's dropping wisdom bombs like a seasoned philosopher meets world traveler and he radiates positive energy.

Nico met my gaze, his expression soft yet profound. "Exactly. Every melody, every note, they're like threads that connect us through time, binding hearts, sharing emotions, and echoing stories from ages past."

He paused for a moment, his gaze seemingly searching for the right words. "Does it really bother you, you know, being left alone here while your friends wandered off?"

I blinked, caught off guard. "I what? Hmm... It doesn't exactly hurt, but yeah, it does bother me."

"I see," he began, but I cut him off, curious about his own social circle.

"And you? What about your friends? Do you have many and do you share a lot in common?"

He shrugged lightly. "I have one close friend, that's it."

"Mm, sounds pretty sufficient to me!" I said, trying to sound upbeat.

"Kind of,"

"I guess for introverts, seeing friends leave might be more painful. Good thing I'm not too introverted, right?" I quipped with a wink.

He smiled half-heartedly. "Yeah, maybe. But sometimes, I think it could be comforting as well."

I raised an eyebrow. "Comforting? Really? Oh wait, introverts enjoy feeling lonely, don't they?"

He turned his gaze skyward, a thoughtful look crossing his face. After a brief pause, he answered with a warm, wise smile, "Not at all actually... we introverts like being alone but never lonely."

"So, there you are," another voice suddenly chimed in and broke the conversation.

I glanced up to see a woman approaching. Unmistakably, it was Nico's mother.

She offered a playful smirk to her son. "Diving deep into philosophy again, are you?"

She then turned to me and introduced herself with a warmth that mirrored her son's.

I responded with a smile, "It's really nice to meet you."

As if on cue, Lilly's performance drew to a poignant end.

"Oh, it seems I missed most of it," she said, taking in the ambiance.

"Still, the bit I did catch was magical."

Nico nodded with enthusiasm. "It was something special, Mom."

His Mom cocked her head slightly. "Remember, if we linger too long, we might miss out on tomorrow's plans."

He sighed, his gaze drifting momentarily before replying, "Yeah, you're right."

Lilly, now having wrapped up her soulful performance, glided over to our small group with impressive grace. A breeze ruffled her hair, her cheeks flushed with the mix of adrenaline and satisfaction at having poured her heart into her music.

"Hi," she began with her characteristic mix of humility and pride, extending her hand to Nico's mother, "I'm Lilly. Thank you for joining my performance, even if just for the end."

Nico's mother smiled very warmly, "The pleasure's mine. The piece you played... it evoked so much emotion in me. Nico tells me it's Debussy?"

Lilly nodded enthusiastically, "Yes, "Clair de Lune." One of my absolute favorites."

Nico chimed in, "My mother has an ear for the classics, although her heart beats faster for opera."

His mother raised an eyebrow, her smile unwavering, "I wasn't aware such combinations even existed. Sounds... well, intriguing."

A round of chuckles enveloped all of us, and while I felt the urge to check on the others, only Lilly seemed eager to venture away and do so. I just found myself in the midst of a spat between the newly acquainted family.

Nico's mom, with a sigh of resignation, now explained, "Our itinerary's taking us to Arizona, then Texas, before jetting back to Hamburg, well, via London, technically."

"Mom, you seriously think I'm leaving America without setting foot in Vermont?"

His mom responded, an exasperated edge to her voice, "It's completely out of the way, Nico. Going east when we're this far west? Rescheduling would be a logistical nightmare. And then there's the matter of our flight..."

"We can change our flights. It's doable," he insisted.

"Nico!"

He tightened his grip on his wheelchair's armrests. "I promised I'd bring back some original Vermont maple syrup. I'm keeping that promise."

I watched the back-and-forth, as awkwardness between mother and son creeped in. Their words painted a clear picture: Nico was clearly hell-bent on fetching some authentic Vermont maple syrup, perhaps for a close friend.

His mother, taking a moment to collect herself, finally said, "He'll understand, Nico."

Despite the tension, Nico gave me a departing nod, murmuring his admiration again for Lilly's performance, and asked me to convey his farewell to the others. As he began to wheel away, their debate continued. Through the dimming light, the last words I caught were, "You know how much he means to me."

Their figures dwindled in the distance, the scene leaving me pensive. The whole ordeal had a strange air to it, particularly Nico's last words. They tugged at my thoughts about love and friendship. I'd always leaned more towards the rationalistic, often overlooking the emotional. Yet moments like this were stark reminders of the value of genuine connections. After all, isn't life about finding a balance? Miss one aspect, and life starts to feel a tad bit hollow. "We really are social beings, aren't we?" I mused aloud.

Pushing the thoughts aside, I headed towards the other group, only to witness what can only be termed as an absolute debacle. Turns out, lighting a fire in the park was a big no-no, and the officials were none too pleased. The situation escalated quickly, but somehow, after much hullabaloo, we managed to slink away. But trust me, that's a story for another day.

Chapter VII:

Double Promise

In a world where I finally felt like I was leveling up, (indicate the meaning here) my job took off, and miracle of all miracles, my grades decided they loved the new altitude too. Then, as luck would have it, Martha and I found ourselves crossing paths. But who was Brad? Neither of us seemed inclined to bring him up, and in truth, I was avoiding the topic while I could see she was hoping to avoid having to restart the whole thing. Summer soon came waltzing in, offering its golden respite, and with it, my mother's perennial suggestion: "How about Pakistan this summer?" She had that always hopeful glint in her eyes.

"You've only seen Bhoot on the screen, haven't you? Don't you want to meet him in person?" she pressed on, a flicker of mischief in her eyes.

"I... Mom... maybe on New Year's Eve?"

And Bhoot? That was my grandfather, Iqbal. Mom had once told me the story of his nickname, a tale woven with threads of bravery and mystery. During the Soviet invasion of Afghanistan, he was one of the fearless souls from Pakistan who had stood with the Afghan defenders. They said he was a wraith on the battlefield, slipping through the shadows, always emerging unscathed from the fiercest of skirmishes. His comrades, awed by his uncanny survival, christened him 'Bhoot' — the Ghost. It was a name that carried the echoes of his silent, spectral presence in the heat of battle, a moniker that held stories of a man who was more phantom than flesh in the eyes of his foes.

But here I had my own plans, and obviously I did not do them, thus spent my summer mastering the art of... well, chilling out. A wholesome blend of binge-watching TV shows, researching my favorite intellectual topics, absorbing tales through audiobooks, hitting the gym (without Abby - she was off living the rockstar life), and having a personal revelation about trans fats and cholesterols. Yup, and one scary lipid test later, I was that person in the grocery store aisle who was squinting at nutrition labels. Occasionally, I'd even hit the console for a game or two. Social media? Not my circus, not my monkeys. Although, I will confess that Abby's faux account was my personal periscope in the digital realm. As August rolled around, Michael got into the whole 'adulting' phase by getting a job, leaving me flying solo. And then, in the twist you never see coming, my mother, after my travel rebuff, apparently found her newest Romeo, the fourth one. And by the way, he had charm written all over him.

Senior year (my graduating one), 2022-2023, started with a bang. While the first part was all rainbows and sunshine, the real drama I soon discovered was yet to unfold.

What is the point of having contacts, anyway? The whole idea of university had me pondering, thanks to a debate with Brad. He made a point, which, as I've already mentioned, that universities aren't so much about the quest for knowledge as they are about finding the right set of contacts to propel you forward in life. It's a notion that is both philosophical and practical in its essence. So, in my final year, I started observing my peers with fresh eyes. I wanted to discern how many were truly engrossed in the essence of learning and how many were playing the long game called low-key networking. I distinctly recall one class discussion where a student drew parallels between modern economics and the purchase patterns of avocado.

It was interesting, and yet felt more like a JobHut post than an academic insight. This view isn't to undermine institutions like Harvard. If your determination is right, you can get a top-tier education anywhere, even in your bathroom while taking a prolonged bubble bath. What Harvard really offers is the allure of its unique networking realm. heard in the conversations in hushed tones in grand libraries or animated debates over mocha lattes in hipster cafes. The intersections of backgrounds, legacies, and ambitions make these settings invaluable. Indeed, it's not just the curriculum; it's the coffee breaks that can change your destiny. Back at my alma mater, that experience was a blend. For many, the university was about finding themselves, forging genuine friendships, and yes, occasionally strategizing about the future. Brad's words obviously held some truth, but that truth was far from Brad himself. He got f-ed up, and he did it big time, and it cost me a lot of focus, effort, and anxiety while Martha was in an awful state.

It was mid -October, and Team Awesome reconvened, albeit with Mikey playing a bit of hide-and-seek due to his job and our class schedules doing the cha-cha. But hey, we managed to do our 'weekly world-saving meeting' consistently. Martha and me? Well, we sort of evolved into 'campus nod-buddies'. We'd exchange pleasantries when our paths crossed–all very civil, of course. One day, I realized Martha had pulled a Houdini. It only took me. about two weeks to realize she was MIA, and my internal alarm bells began to chime. As tempting as it was to reach out to Brad for intel, doing that just felt like opening a can of awkward worms Ah, but the universe always has a Plan B ready. In my case, it was Derrek. A quick text and voilà, we were doing the whole coffee and catch-up routine. He nonchalantly mentioned having spotted her around her place recently.

"Hold up. When was that?" I queried. Derek paused, probably searching his brain's archives, before narrowing the time down to a couple of days ago.

"About two days ago, I think. Yeah, it was Tuesday."

Relief washed over me. At least she hadn't taken off on a tropical escapade with Brad. Derek and I chatted a bit more about classes, the latest movies, and just the general ins and outs of life. And just as we were about to part ways, in a genuine show of concern, he offered,

"Look, if you're really worried, I could swing by her place, see if everything's all right.", I gave Derrek the green light and 48 hours later, he was spilling the beans.

"She seemed... usual. Well, maybe a smidgen more 'introverted'," he started out. "What's 'more introverted' for her? Did she start a collection of dust particles?" I quipped. He chuckled,

"Well, she spoke sparingly, and her eyes... I dunno, looked larger, I guess."

"Bigger eyes? Like puppy dog eyes, perhaps? Those usually scream that 'I'm on the brink of tears.'"

"Not quite." Derek hesitated, now searching for words. "Think... existential crisis vibes. On the upside, though, she did offer some of her own lasagna."

"Hmm," I pondered for a quick beat. "Any off-beat comments?"

"Nah, just a shift in demeanor. Nothing that she verbalized."

"And what about classes? Why is she playing truant?"

"She mentioned a recent cold and said she didn't want to risk catching another because of her anemia and also something about her weak immune system," Derrek tried to recall.

I burst out laughing, "Buuuuullllshit, is that her excuse? I've heard better ones from 5-year-olds avoiding kindergarten." Derrek chuckled and nodded in agreement. "It was a tad flimsy."

I arched a brow. "Wait... during your heartfelt tête-à-tête, Brad didn't pop up in the conversation at all?"

Derrek paused, thinking hard. "Actually, no. Not a peep."

I sat back, now incredulous. Martha was not name-dropping Brad? That was like fish, not swimming. There was something wrong. In all her previous encounters with anyone, Brad was always a constant topic of discussion. The fact that he didn't come up at all now was alarming. I felt a deep sense of unease. It had to be that their relationship was broken, but I just didn't realize then how significant that was.

Slipping into my best undercover detective mode, I tried to move stealthily. However, anyone who knows me would attest that 'stealth' is probably a word absent from my dictionary. My sneaky attempts were about as inconspicuous as an elephant in a china shop. It didn't take long for my team to catch on.

"It's probably just some Disney romance she dreamed up that didn't quite play out," Abby threw out casually, while twirling a strand of hair around her finger.

Michael, ever the wise owl of the group, looked contemplative. "Well, if it's a heart thing, maybe it's best to give her some space. You can't really paint a smile on a broken heart. They've got to patch it up themselves. Rush it, and it leaves a scar."

Lilly, with a melodious voice that could soothe a grizzly, pitched in. "But guys, if she's really down in the dumps, she might need a friendly ear. Even the heaviest burden feels a tad lighter when shared."

The room filled with the clink of coffee mugs, the hum of the ceiling fan, and a thick cloud of contemplation. After taking in the symphony of their well-intentioned advice, I decided on a course of action. I'd pay Martha a visit myself, armed with some herbal tea, open ears, and an insatiable curiosity. Maybe, just maybe, between sips and stories, I could piece together the puzzle.

Then, Martha looked around after glancing straight at me, then gave me a belated smile and said, "Come in." I stepped into her apartment, the familiar place we once had shared. I was engulfed by a wave of nostalgia–the potted plants we'd bought together, the aroma of her signature vanilla-scented candles, and the cozy corner where we'd spent countless (but only a few) nights chatting. It was all the same.

As I settled deep into the plush sofa, she handed me a cup of her signature brew, strong and aromatic.

" I've heard rumors of a certain someone skipping lectures. Anemia acting up again?" I began, trying to start the conversation on a lighter note.

Martha gave an unconvincing chuckle. "Yeah, just needed some rest, you know?"

I tilted my head, studying her face for a moment. "You know, the thing with anemia is that it doesn't prevent one from attending Becky's party last week or that trekking trip I saw on your Instagram."

A hint of surprise flashed in her eyes. "Okay. Maybe I just needed a break from everything... and everyone., and also, I thought you were not using any socials."

I rolled my eyes but dismissed the social network topic smoothly and decided to dig a little deeper. "Or maybe someone? Like Brad?"

She hesitated, then sighed deeply. "Can we not talk about him?"

I stood up, sipping my coffee, and began to walk around the room. "You've always been an open book to me, Martha. Your actions, your words, the slightest change in your tone—they all tell a story. And right now, they're screaming at me, telling me that something's wrong."

Martha's eyes started to glisten with tears, and I saw that she was battling to keep them at bay. "It's just... complicated."

I approached her gently, put a reassuring hand on her shoulder. "Talk to me. Please."

She shook her head.

Then I nodded my head.

Then she shook her head again.

And I also repeated my nod, signaling pressure.

And finally, her face changed, as if the river was about to come outta her eyes...

She inhaled sharply before speaking, her voice shaky. "Brad was always going on about his world-traveling friend, like he was some kind of hero. That night at Brad's place, when his friend showed up, we ended up drinking wine. Something felt off. It didn't sit right with me."

I clenched my fists, feeling a surge of protectiveness. "Oh Martha..."

Tears welled up in Martha's eyes, and she couldn't hold them back any longer. "I left as soon as I could, but the memory just won't fade." She paused, her voice breaking. I could see the turmoil in her eyes, a storm of hurt and betrayal.

In the aftermath, the truth became painfully clear. Brad had orchestrated a situation where his friend overstepped boundaries with Martha, suggesting a 'threesome' without her real consent. Despite her resistance, their persistence left her feeling powerless. The following day, instead of owning up to his wrongdoing, Brad twisted the narrative, making Martha feel at fault–cruel manipulation. Her heart wasn't just broken; it was shattered. And the ordeal didn't stop at emotional trauma; it escalated to a physical breach; a line crossed that could never be uncrossed...

I pressed Martha gently, asking why she hadn't taken the story to the police. I also cautioned her that if she mentioned still having feelings for Brad as a reason, it would be hard for me to remain calm. But that wasn't it. Brad and his so-called 'best friend', Dazzy Bee or whatever ridiculous name he went by, had coldly anticipated this night. They warned Martha that she was the only one intoxicated that night with alcohol, implying that her account would be deemed unreliable against that of their sober testimonies. Moreover, Brad had a neighbor who, by some twisted stroke of luck, claimed to have glanced into the house twice that evening and was willing to vouch for Brad if Martha pressed any charges. To add insult to injury, Brad threatened that those kinds of allegations would jeopardize her standing at the university and tarnish her future prospects with everyone and anyone, including professors and, later on, employers. Was justice really this skewed? Should anyone feel so terribly helpless after facing an assault? I wanted to believe in a system that protected victims, but Martha's anguish made me doubt it was there. Through her tears, she made me promise not to involve the police of my own accord, not to share a single word with anyone as well.

Swallowing the truth was like a pill that gets stuck in the throat and won't go down easily. I found myself caught in a storm of doubt and frustration. I wasn't well-versed in the legal intricacies–the whole charade of evidence, witnesses, and whose words would carry more weight. But the dark undercurrents of Brad and Dazzy Bee's histories were something I could delve into quietly. That investigation was eye-opening.

I stayed true to my word, keeping Martha's secret cloaked and hidden in the shadows. now and then, my squad would probe, seeking answers about her sudden change. With a heavy heart, I'd give them the rehearsed lines–the anemia or how she was taking the breakup with Brad and how he had cheated–harder and more. But what ate at me was the weight of the unsaid. We used to share every high and low, every giggle and tear. Yet here I was, guarding the most painful secret of all. They say friends share everything, but I guess life does have its exceptions.

Well, Martha made a return to campus, and to everyone's surprise, she was on par with the syllabus. Of course, her swift mind and her love for books had always been her best allies. On the surface, life seemed to have returned to its rhythm for her. The only visible change was the absence of her infectious smile. It was gone. Many attributed it to Brad's absence. But the haunting truth was that she was masking a pain that was far more profound, and I was the lone custodian of that dark secret. Seeing her daily facade was like a knife twisting in my heart, with each passing moment reminding me of my silent promise.

The weeks turned into a haze, and then came a close call. It was one of those ordinary evenings, cooking with Michael and Abby. The weight of the secret threatened to spill from my lips, but I clamped down on it firmly. What was it that was keeping me silent? That night, as the city lights blinked outside, a spark of clarity hit me. Derrek! If there was anyone who could offer counsel or help, it was him.

When we met at our regular cafe, the gravity of the situation rendered me unable to even look at the menu. I just began, "Derek, I'm about to betray a promise I made to Martha, but you're the only one I trust with this story."

His eyes widened in anticipation. "I knew it," he said, leaning in. "There had to be more to Martha's story than just Brad and anemia."

Nodding, I took a deep breath and said, "You have no idea." I narrated the entire harrowing ordeal to him, not missing a beat. When the weight of my words settled in, I looked him directly in the eyes.

"Derek, I can't do this alone. I need you."

Chapter VIII:

2023 Transition

The dawn of our new and final semester approached, and with it, 2023. You know that feeling when you walk into a five-star restaurant with high expectations, banking on rave reviews from your crew? You take a bite, and the dish is, well, meh. But you don't voice your mild disappointment because there's still a lot of evening left to turn things around. Yep, that was 2023 for you. We all harbored that shimmer of hope that the rest of the year would make up for its overly bland entrance.

I could almost hear the gears turning in your brain. "Isn't this supposed to be about a whirlwind of interviews and Hina's roller-coaster ride through them?" Ah, patience! There was method to my madness. You see, diving straight into any interview escapades without giving you a glimpse of the chaos that preceded them would be like skipping the appetizer and heading straight to the main course. Trust me, you'd be missing out on the seasoning. And as we've established, seasoning, or shall I say 'nourishment', is crucial.

The way Michael's career graph shot up was impressive, to say the least. Before anyone realized it, he had been promoted, sidestepping a level in the financial sector of his firm. Given his recent breakup with Dan (which, to their credit, was amicable and mature), one could be forgiven for speculating if he'd charmed his way to the top with some office romance. But nope, Michael was a dedicated worker and a maestro in his financial domain.

Meanwhile, Lilly greeted the new year with Canadian vibes. And me? My mom and I had a clear, but unspoken, pact. No matter what, we always ushered in the New Year together, just the two of us.

"Guess what? I performed a solo near Niagara Falls!"

Wait, did Lilly just say that? Lilly, with her cello, challenging the roaring waters of Niagara? But then again, that's Lilly for you - always subtly pursuing her grand dreams. Different strokes for different folks, I guess. Take Zach, for instance, a dear friend from Brooklyn. His annual New Year's ritual? Partying in an underground techno club in Berlin. Imagine the clock striking midnight in the midst of thumping bass and frenzied dancing - no fireworks, no sentimental movie moments on a couch. Just pure wild energy.

Me and Mom kept things chilled on New Year's Eve. We sipped some bubbly, laughed at our memories of the past twelve months, then called it a night. Every spring, my work that I had initially enjoyed became more monotonous. It wasn't unenjoyable, but I couldn't stand being on autopilot anymore. In search of something new and exciting, I started looking for a full-time job to make sure I was well-prepared after graduation. After meticulously crafting my CV, ensuring that every detail showcased the best of me, I began the somewhat daunting process of job applications. Each application was dispatched with a mix of hope and trepidation. I didn't bombard all the eleven firms at once, either. Instead, I spread out my applications, taking time to personalize each one based on that company's ethos and role requirements. By the time May's flowers started to bloom, I had hit the send button on the last application. And! Most importantly, my mom handed down her Ford Fiesta to me because she bought a new car. But identifying cars isn't my strong suit; they pretty much all look the same to me.

Chapter IX:

The silent vow

Lilly, who was always one to plan ahead, was already in full-blown birthday preparation mode, even though it now was only the tail-end of March. She had visions of a grand soirée, and every time we talked, she had a new idea or theme in mind.

The atmosphere on campus was electric. With the realization that this was our last semester, everyone seemed to have kicked into high gear. The space was brimming with determination and a hint of fond remembrance. Abby and I were lucky; we shared two classes. Those classes were a mix of academic rigor and light-hearted moments. Our shared notes, whispered jokes, and exchanged glances made the tough academic load bearable. Martha, on the other hand, had become something of a rare sight. Our schedules were diametrically opposite, making our casual run-ins less frequent. I missed our spontaneous coffee breaks and impromptu study sessions, but I understood–we were now both caught up in the whirlwind of wrapping up our college life.

The campus was buzzing with a different kind of energy that day. The student council had organized a university-wide scavenger hunt, aptly named "GSU Quest". The objective was simple but daunting: Solve a series of intellectual riddles and challenges that would lead you to various landmark locations around the campus. Each participant was handed a booklet containing the first riddle, and from there forward, they'd all embark on a journey of wits. Some riddles required knowledge of the campus history, some dipped into literature or science, and a few were pure logic puzzles. It was the perfect blend of intellectual challenge and physical activity.

I teamed up with Abby, and we dived headfirst into solving the first riddle. As we meandered about, it was quite a spectacle, seeing clusters of students huddling like penguins, furiously scribbling on notepads, and animatedly arguing over their next steps. At one juncture, we faced a quirky challenge: pinpointing a local plant in the university's botanical garden–like a botanical 'Where's Waldo?'

During a quick pit stop, I chatted up Raj, the computer science whiz. "Man, these puzzles are no walk in the park. Didn't see that coming," he remarked, his eyebrows knitting in bewilderment. "Totally. It's a refreshing twist from the snooze fest of regular classes," I quipped back. We exchanged riddle insights, tiptoeing around the answers like they were top-secret.

By the time Abby and I hit landmark number four, our brains felt like they'd run a marathon. Deciding to park ourselves on a bench for a breather, Derrek sauntered over. "Hey, how's the riddle wrestling match treating you?" he inquired. Abby, puffing out her cheeks, confessed, "It's a brain bender, but heck, it's a blast. We're tackling riddle number five now." Derrek, with a nod, shared, "I'm just a spectator today, but wow, these riddles could stump Einstein!"

He then dropped a little gossip bomb. "Hey Hina, I've got someone you should meet. My buddy from Utah is city-visiting next week. You two are like two peas in a green pod." My curiosity piqued, "Oh?" "Yep, Adrianna's her name, and she's a green warrior through and through. She's been turning lifeless rooftops into lush jungles and kickstarting community gardens," he elaborated. Intrigued, I responded, "That's pretty awesome!" Abby, with a playful nudge, teased, "Looks like Hina's found her agricultural soulmate."

Derrek laughed, "Exactly. I thought you two would hit it off. She'll be here next Wednesday. What do you say? A coffee catch-up perhaps at our usual spot?"

I considered it for a moment. "I'd love to meet her. It sounds like we have a lot in common."

"Great," Derrek said, clapping his hands together in delight. "I'll set it up."

Abby leaned in, whispering teasingly in my ear, "See, Hina? All your talk about soil and plants is finally paying off in the social department." I rolled my eyes but couldn't suppress my smile.

In the soft ambiance of our apartment, the rich aroma of basil, garlic, and tomatoes wafted through the air. I'd decided to cook my famous pasta *aglio e olio*, a simple dish, but when done right, a true symphony of flavors.

Michael eagerly twirled his fork into the pasta and remarked, "You know, if this whole agricultural thing doesn't pan out, you could always become a chef."

I chuckled. "Relax. It's just pasta, Michael. Not molecular gastronomy."

We took a few more bites, savoring the food together, before I ventured, "Have you ever wondered why some people love cilantro and others think it tastes like soap? It's a genetic thing, you know."

"Really? That's fascinating. It's like how some people love pineapple on their pizza and others think it's the eighth deadly sin."

I laughed. "Exactly! It's wild how our genes do dictate our taste preferences. I mean, can you imagine two people being deeply in love and then finding out one of them hates the other's favorite food? Talk about a love tragedy!"

He snorted. "That would be the Romeo and Juliet of the culinary world, wouldn't it? Death by disagreement over pizza toppings."

Then, as we were wiping away tears of mirth, Michael cleared his throat. "Speaking of clashing tastes," he began, "don't forget about tomorrow. I'm introducing you, Abby, and possibly Lilly, as well, to some of my friends from work."

I raised an eyebrow. "Should I be worried?"

He grinned cheekily. "Let's just say, be prepared for a debate about the best type of cheese."

"Oh, boy," I sighed dramatically. "Life's real philosophical questions. Right?"

Michael winked and replied, "Especially the ones that truly matter!"

The next day broke, wrapped in a golden glow that felt like it was out of a fairy tale. We were headed to Outer Sound, a place that always tickled my curiosity—was it the tunes or the treats that made it so special? Well, today was the day for revelations! Even the name Outer Sound sounded like a gateway to an enchanted land, echoing with stories of diners, secret exchanges between lovebirds, and the ever-present, life-enriching jazz. And guess what? It was jazz day! Time to wiggle those toes to some groovy beats!

We snuggled into our snug spot, and oh, there was a live band prepping, their instruments shining like treasure under the dim, inviting lights. I could sense it—this evening was going to be drenched in silky tunes and deep, heartwarming melodies.

Our table? Oh, it was a masterpiece! The dishes looked like they were crafted by artists, whispering promises of a taste bud-tickling journey. And the showstopper? A bottle of Château Margaux. Yep, that famous vino. I'd heard the legends, and now I was about to dive into a glass of it. Excitement was an understatement.

"Ooh, going all out, aren't we, Michael?" I ribbed him as he gave the wine a swirl, savoring the scent like a connoisseur.

He grinned. "Only the best for my favorite people."

We clinked our glasses to the tune of a lively jazz melody. The vibrancy of the wine and the animated conversations — from the foolish to the fascinating — made for an unforgettable evening. I can still remember discussing whether jazz was like a balm for broken hearts, all the while marveling at how this night was perfectly blending intoxication with entertainment.

"I often wonder," Michael said, a mischievous twinkle now in his eye, "about the first person who decided to squish grapes and let them ferment. Wine is essentially grape juice gone wild."

Abby chuckled. "And yet, it's considered a luxury. Similarly, why are truffles so pricey? They're just fungi!"

I couldn't resist responding, "That's rich coming from someone who adores truffle fries."

But before Abby could whip up one of her famous retorts, her face shifted to surprise. "Isn't that... Brad?" She murmured, almost to herself.

Michael and I followed her gaze. Sure enough, Brad was there, looking a bit more polished than when I last saw him. Beside him was a familiar figure with tattoos lining his arms. A jolt of recognition shot through me. Dazzy Bee. But I couldn't say anything, couldn't even hint that I knew more than I should know.

Wanting to divert attention, I suggested, "How about we try the seared scallops? They're said to be phenomenal here."

Abby caught on and nodded. "Sounds great! And maybe another bottle of wine, too?"

"How about a different kind? Let's explore our wine horizons."

As the evening progressed, Mikey's work friends, including his boss, made their way to our table. Without acknowledging Dazzy Bee, or rather Jesse, his true name, I recalled the pieces I had put together about their lives. Jesse was the heir to a massive transportation empire. His father, David, had ties to our Dr. Governor, being a significant supporter both personally and financially. On the other hand, Brad's lineage could be traced back to a renowned tennis player who, while not globally acclaimed, was still a sensation in a few states.

I often found myself contemplating the reach of their influence. If Martha had decided to take her case to the police without concrete evidence, would an investigation even have begun, let alone hold them accountable? I had my reservations, especially since I discovered that Brad's so-called eyewitness neighbor was a former employee of Jesse's father. Regardless of whether that neighbor had truly witnessed anything that night, I was certain he'd be biased toward those two.

Amidst all this light-hearted chatter, I could feel Brad's eyes on me. He was seated in a position that provided him with a direct view of me. We exchanged no gestures, no nods, or winks, just a mutual understanding to remain strangers. At some point during the evening, a toast was proposed. While everyone was engrossed in the camaraderie, raising their glasses, I found myself locked in a silent standoff with Brad. As the word "cheers" echoed around us, I barely mouthed the toast, my eyes unflinchingly fixed on him. My glass was the only one that stayed firmly fixed on the table.

Are we just going to walk by him,
Will he say hello?
He's so quiet, too quiet.
Maybe he knows I know something,
Something I shouldn't know.

Anyway...

The atmosphere felt thick with tension and unspoken words. Fortunately, the night concluded, and our exit path didn't lead us past Brad and Jesse, saving us from an uncomfortable encounter.

Everyone was tipsy and cheerful, I stayed alert.

Chapter X:

Friends without Foes

Just imagine sending your precious CVs to eleven, yes eleven, firms and then biting your nails, waiting for a reply. And when the notification bell does ring, it's almost like getting ready for weekly lottery output. So yes, I got three responses! Two were, let's say, a bit clingy. They wanted cover letters, references from college professors, the whole shebang. I mean, come on! But the third, oh the third! It was a golden ticket to a virtual tête-à-tête, a pre-interview via a video call.

I circled the date on my calendar, tried on six outfits, and eventually settled on the seventh. The call was such a breeze, with a lovely lady from HR who had the most delightful lavender backdrop. She navigated through the usual terrain of past work, campus life, and even had the cheek to ask what my most embarrassing moment at university was.

The interviews were quite a mixed bag. She was curious about the projects I had worked on and the roles I took on during group tasks. Was I the leader, the mediator, or the 'just-let-me-know-what-to-do' person? We then did a deep dive into my last internship. I had to elaborate on a challenge I had faced and how I overcame it, which, let me tell you, was the narrative equivalent of navigating a minefield in high heels.

She also threw in a few hypothetical situations, 'What would you do if...' type of questions. There was a hint of the usual 'Where do you see yourself in five years?', but that was more like, 'How do you envision your growth within our company?'.

Lastly, we laughed about university life, swapped some 'during the exam' anecdotes, and then, with her promise to get back to me soon, we wrapped up. Fingers crossed, toes crossed, everything was crossed!

Then, after a ten-day wait, I received an email from the second company that had requested my references and cover letter. Of course, I had promptly sent them over. They provided me with two potential dates. I had to pick one for an in-person interview. Naturally, I opted for the date closest to my graduation.

All right, sit tight, kiddos! Picture this scenario: Job interviews are like first dates. No, seriously! You're putting on your best self, trying to impress, hoping they'll see the 'real' you beneath all the razzmatazz. You're both asking questions, figuring out if you're right for each other. Some dates, er, I mean interviews, feel like a perfect soufflé–they rise beautifully, and you're on cloud nine. Others? More like a failed pancake flip–are messy and downright cringe-worthy.

Still remember the in the grand restaurant of life, it's okay if every dish doesn't turn out to be a gourmet masterpiece. After all, sometimes the most memorable meals are those quirky, unexpected ones. So, wear that pasta sauce stain like a badge of honor and march forth courageously. Job interviews, much like disastrous first dates, are just a rite of passage on the hilariously complicated journey of adulting!

Finals, those sneaky little critters that always show up, were encircling us like a pack of wild coyotes stalking their prey. With them on the prowl, leisure was a word that became far removed from our vocabularies. But, as the universe would have it, we managed to scrounge up an evening amidst the madness, a little respite before we dispersed into our individual academic battlefields. I found myself in our usual café haunt, a hot cuppa in hand and Derrek by my side, eagerly anticipating the carb-overload we were about to indulge in and enjoy. Abby's absence made for the perfect excuse to slightly steer off the diet trail. We were just about to drift away into our own little world when the shrill ringing of the entrance bell and the sound of three familiar voices shattered our happy peace.

"Found you!" Lilly's chirpy voice sang out.

"Caught you red-handed," Abby chimed in, eyes twinkling. Okay, so the greeting was a tad awkward. Not because rendezvousing with Derrek was some top-secret affair. (Or maybe it was) But because friends, being the adorably nosy beings, they are and when friends have overactive imaginations, things can go hilariously south. They love playing up innocent situations. And this situation was prime fodder for them. They nudged, winked, and we all laughed off the supposed "date".

Before the fun could escalate further, Derrek, ever the gentleman, cleared his throat. "Oh, by the way, my friend Adrianna will be joining us soon. You remember Hina, the introduction I was talking about?"

"Aha! The plot thickens. Sneaky rendezvous, Hina?"

I rolled my eyes, chuckling, "This is not an Agatha Christie novel, Mikey! Abby, you remember, right? Derek had arranged this meeting ages ago." Abby responded with an enthusiastic nod, confirming my alibi and the positivity went up.

Right after Mikey's cheerful announcement, the café's door chimed its signature tune, and in walked a woman who looked like she had been created from of all the most beautiful trends in modern art. Her cropped hair was framed around her face with absolute perfection, and it glowed like burnished gold in the afternoon light. She wore a black shirt with short sleeves that revealed her breathtaking tattoos; each one was vibrant and unique, telling stories that made onlookers smile. She looked elegant and yet carefree, an embodiment of joyous sophistication.

Derek stood up, a proud smile now adorning his face. "Everyone, meet Adrianna," he announced, gesturing toward her.

Adrianna, with a confident stride, approached our table, her eyes bright with curiosity and warmth. "Hello everyone," she greeted, her voice melodic, with an undercurrent of excitement. "Derek has told me so much about all of you."

Lilly, always the outspoken one, leaned in, squinting slightly. "Those tattoos! Are they tales of your adventures or just a dash of artistry?"

Adrianna chuckled. "A bit of both, actually. Some memories, some just whimsy."

Mikey, never one to miss an opportunity to joke, quipped, "Well, you've got our attention now! With ink like that, you've surely got tales worth a listen."

Adrianna bubbled up with excitement. "He told me that you, Hina, are a whiz at all the green thumb stuff I adore. Agronomy, right? And wasn't there a dash of archaeology in your mix? I'm practically buzzing to gab with someone who's into eco-friendly farming and the DNA dance of crops."

I blinked, a bit gobsmacked, not just by the topic but Adrianna's turbo-charged zest. "Oh! Yup, that's me," I replied with a giggle. "It's a rare treat to bump into someone in the wild who's jazzed about the secret life of plants and earth-friendly growing."

Abby gave a theatrical eye roll. "And there it is. Just when we thought inky art was today's flavor!"

Lilly nudged Abby playfully. "Hey, let them bond. We all have our different things."

As we all settled into our seats, Adrianna's eyes never left mine. There was something about the way she looked at me, as if she were trying to read every thought that crossed my mind. It was both exhilarating and nerve-wracking. We began talking about our shared interests, and before I knew it, the hours had flown by. The conversation was easy, natural, and I found myself opening up to her in a way I hadn't with anyone in a long time. It felt like we were the only two people in the world and completely lost in our own little bubble.

Suddenly, the sound of Abby's phone ringing broke the spell. She apologized and stepped away to answer it, leaving the rest of us alone.

While Adrianna shared insights about the diverse soils of California and some avant-garde theories on her phone screen, my eyes caught a unique tattoo on her upper arm. It had been in plain sight all along, but up close, it was downright captivating.

"Is that... inspired by Eastern mythology or something?" I inquired, curious.

"This one?" she replied, glancing at her arm. "Oh, not exactly. It's a mix of several tattoos. I fell for one design and then, instead of getting rid of it, I decided to evolve it by blending in others."

"Wow, that's genuinely remarkable," I admired.

"Thanks!" she beamed.

The tattoo was a stunning display of artistry—a fusion of a circle and lines stretching in every direction, symbolizing the cardinal points as if casting beams. Intricate letters were nestled within these lines, adding a layer of mystery. And encircling this entire design were two hands, adding a finishing touch, fine touch.

Derek took the opportunity to order another round of drinks, and I realized I had been so engrossed in our conversation that I hadn't even touched the one I had. As I took a sip, Michael shot me a glance and subtly gestured that he wanted a private word, away from the boisterous chatter of the café. Stepping outside into the gentle night, the faint hum of all the conversations followed us.

"This Adrianna is a curious one," he began, eyes narrowing thoughtfully. "She's undeniably passionate, but it feels like she's mining information more than sharing. Have you noticed she often makes you talk more?"

I quirked an eyebrow, my lips curving into a sly smile. "Why, Mikey, are you planning on switching teams? How's Dan, by the way?"

"Dan? Oh, we're the same. But on a recent trip, there was this stunning blonde German geek I met in France."

I blinked, "Wait, wasn't that the work trip? The one where you said you were going to Brussels?"

Michael rolled his eyes. "I said we started out in Brussels. But Paris was our last stop before flying back."

"Oh! I met someone from Germany too! Remember when you and Abby betrayed Lilly and—"

"Shut up," he interjected, his eyes widening in mock horror.

I giggled, "Yes, when you two jumped ship to join the other team? Anyway, there was this young lad in a wheelchair from Germany. He and his mom stopped by, taken in by Lilly's music."

Michael chuckled, "Let me guess, you've got yourself a new beau from Germany, too?"

I playfully swatted his arm. "You're absurd. That kid was what? 14? 15 max!"

The evening buzzed with chuckles and the warm fuzzies of budding friendships, spiced up with the news that Adrianna was going to be our Sacramento sidekick for a spell, maybe till the leaves start to tango with the fall breeze.

Now, let's chinwag about the curious tango of some friendships. Like, peek at Laura and her squad. They've got this ping-pong banter that's almost like a dance. They dish out sneaky side-comments about each other when the coast is clear, yet face-to-face, it's all sunshine and rainbows. Beats me. Ever since my knee-high-to-a-grasshopper days, I've been all about the good vibes club. Clinging to any tie-up that's more drama than delight? Nah, that's not how I roll.

I learned this: Stay away from anything and anyone that brings negativity.

We've got this one ticket to the ride called Life. Sure, there's chatter about reincarnation, living life after life, but if our noggin doesn't keep the memories, if our viewpoints and recollections get a reboot each time, isn't this the one life we truly get? There's just one version of me, Hina, with these particular memories in this specific universe. So, why let stressful friendships rain on our parade? Unless, of course, we're tangled up in some emotional spaghetti that's got us feeling like we're buddies with our burdens.

This ride we're on, with its one-of-a-kind memories and adventures, is our treasure. Why let it slip through our fingers over nonsense? I'm not in the business of handing out life maps to folks, but sometimes, I can't help but ponder where the line is between throwing someone a lifeline and just plain old judging. It's a fine line, really easy to trip over.

Sometimes I think about Michael, living under the same roof as me, sharing countless meals and memories. You'd think I'd have him all figured out. But no. Most times, he's this ball of energy, filling every room with his contagious laughter and endless chatter. Yet, there are those rare moments, those abrupt pauses in his demeanor. Suddenly, he becomes this introspective person, his analytical side surfacing, making decisions with an uncharacteristic cold precision. It's like watching a familiar movie, villain like, only to discover a new scene you never noticed before. It's intriguing, but also a tad unsettling. No offense meant Mikey.

Next week marked the final curtain call for our finals, and my room turned into a battle-station, littered with textbooks and notes. Every so often, Mikey would saunter in, loudly proclaiming,

"Need help with any of this? Remember who's the genius here!" I'd roll my eyes and pretend I hadn't heard a word.

Finally, when it was all over, I figured I owed it to my abs and the few extra cookies I'd devoured during the study marathons to hit the gym. Abby's sessions always did the trick. Yet, the moment I hopped onto the treadmill, Abby shot me a look, waving her hands dramatically, "Hina, get off the treadmill and come here!"

"What's the emergency?" I grumbled, hopping off. She pulled me aside, her eyes wide. "So, get this. Martha's ex and Adrianna–yes, Derek's pal–they're a thing now!"

I blinked, totally taken aback. "You're pulling my leg."

"Nope. Matt spotted them cozying up at the Esquire Movie Theater. Brad was treating her to popcorn like it was some kind of romantic gesture!"

"Wait, which Matt is that?"

"Lilly's ex, Matt Solomonca," she clarified.

I huffed, "Boys are the new gossip mills. Seriously, all they do now is dish out who's seeing who."

Abby rolled her eyes. "It's not like that."

I raised an eyebrow. "Oh really? Did he drop hints or spill it like hot tea? And, by the way, the last thing Martha needs right now is this kind of news."

She sighed, "I know." Looking more frustrated now, she got on a treadmill and motioned for me to join her on the next one. As I climbed on, she glanced over. "So, what's our next move?"

I responded with a shrug, "For now? Nothing. But Adrianna needs to know what she's getting into with Brad."

She nodded, "Yeah, she really does."

Whenever I sit down to spill my life's stories onto paper, the memories don't always line up, ready for the parade. Instead, they meander back, piecing together the colorful mosaic of my past. Like this one time, a few days post the Adrianna bombshell, when our crew got tangled up in a classic conundrum. The burning question was whether Adrianna was the type to swoop in on someone's old flame, or if the universe was just playing its quirky games. You know the drill, that girl rumored to be a magnet for others' exes. Was it her plan, or just cosmic irony? In such dramas, the newbie—Adrianna, in this case—often gets skeptical glares and hush-hush talks, particularly from the ex's buddies.

Meanwhile, as my friends mulled over their love life puzzles, my brain was juggling academic and career plates. The academic world was a suspense thriller too, with professors holding our final grades and, basically, our future prospects close to their chests. And right in that whirlwind, Lilly decided to quiz me about my side gig and the looming job interviews. "The first interview's tomorrow, at the printing and publishing firm, right? And the other, let's see... in about six days," I replied, trying to keep my calendar straight in my head.

She began, "Good luck, and don't forget--"

"Ugh, Lilly," But Mikey cut her off.

"You don't even know what I was about to say," she retorted.

"I bet it was one of your motivational pep talks."

Lilly shot him a glare. "You're insufferable."

"Okay, break it up," I intervened, looking at Abby. "Can you ask Matt-the-not-spy to see what's brewing between Brad and Adrianna?"

"Hina, for the last time, he's no spy! And he wasn't gossiping," Abby sighed.

"Sure, whatever you say," I replied nonchalantly. "Just make sure you get me some info before I see Adrianna and Derrek on their bowling evening." With that, I left them to their bickering, focusing on getting some real rest for my first in-person, full-time job interview. Life sure wasn't slowing down.

Chapter XI:

First Nonstudent Job Interview

The morning air was nippy, the sort that nudges you toward an extra cup of coffee and a bit more gusto. This wasn't just any regular day in Sacramento; it was the day of my debut in the real professional world with an unaided, full-on job interview. No university chaperones or mom's pep rallies to back me up—just me stepping into the ring with the corporate giants.

The outfit dilemma? Oh boy, it was a whirlwind of thoughts. The suit felt too stuffy, the jeans too laid-back. After a bit of a fashion show and swapping outfits thrice, I settled on a sharp, navy-blue pencil skirt and a crisp white blouse—a nod to the classics with a sprinkle of my own style. The shoes? Matching pumps with just the right heel height for that extra oomph of confidence. I kept the jewelry understated—a delicate gold pendant and petite hoop earrings. As for the hair saga, let's just say my curls, and I had a moment before agreeing on a sleek, low bun. A dab of mascara and a stroke of nude lipstick, and there I was, all set to conquer, or at least impress, the interview panel.

The battleground? VSP GLOBAL, a giant in the eye care insurance arena nestled right in Sacramento. Maybe not the flashiest sector, but renowned for its stellar work environment and open doors for eager grads like me.

Crossing the threshold of VSP felt like stepping into a new chapter. The place was alive with a modern vibe, brimming with activity. I spotted a few anxious faces, likely in the same interview boat. With a deep breath, I marched up to the reception, marking my presence.

The wait felt like forever, though it was just a brief ten minutes before I was guided into a bright conference room. There, two figures awaited—a formidable woman in her forties with an authoritative aura, clad in a sleek charcoal suit, and a younger, approachable man in a crisp white shirt and black pants.

"Good morning, Hina. I'm Diane, the HR manager here," the woman introduced with a handshake, pointing to her companion, "And this is Alex, one of our team leaders." Post the warm-up chit-chat, the real deal began.

Diane kicked off, "Can you walk us through your CV, highlighting experiences you think align with this role?"

Inhaling deeply, I embarked on my tale, weaving through my academic and practical journeys, spotlighting leadership stints and my industry zeal.

Alex jotted down notes, sparking a flicker of nerves in me. Was he impressed, puzzled, or just doodling?

He chimed in, "What steered you to VSP Global specifically?"

Channeling my homework on the company, I responded, "VSP's reputation for excellence and it's nurturing approach toward employees caught my eye. It resonates with my career aspirations." Inwardly, I cheered. *You're doing great, Hina! Keep the ball rolling!*

The conversation flowed from there, with more questions about my aspirations, team experiences, and what I'd bring to VSP. With each answer, I could feel my initial nervousness wane a bit, replaced by a growing sense of confidence. This was just the beginning of my professional journey, and I was here to make an impression.

Diane, looking mildly impressed (or was it my wishful thinking?), inquired, "How do you handle criticism or feedback?"

I paused, thinking about the countless group projects and that one time when Jessica totally trashed my proposal. But this wasn't about Jessica, so focus!

"I believe feedback, whether positive or negative, is essential for personal and professional growth. I take it constructively, assess its merits, and then work on improving. It's a continuous learning process." *I hope they don't ask for specifics. Jessica's face is popping into my mind.*

Alex chuckled a bit. "Last one for now. If you were an office supply item, what would you be?"

I blinked, taken aback by the oddity of the question. But then, it was one of those quirky personality questions. *All right, game on.*

"I'd be a highlighter," I quipped. "Bold, hard to ignore, and always bringing attention to the essential things."

Diane and Alex exchanged glances, a hint of a smile playing on their lips. I sat back, silently congratulating myself for not making a complete fool out of myself.

Good job, Hina.

You've got this!

Diane raised an eyebrow, leaning forward slightly, her fingers steepled together. "Well, Hina, perhaps that wasn't the last question." There was a playfulness in her tone, but her eyes were sharp and attentive.

All right. Take some deep breaths. More hurdles to jump over.

"Can you describe a situation where you had to deal with a difficult team member and how you approached it?" Diane asked, her gaze unwavering.

With a nod, I remembered one instance very clearly. "During my university project, there was a team member who consistently missed deadlines. Initially, I tried to cover up for him, thinking he might be having a bad week. However, when the pattern persisted, I sat down with him to try to understand what was causing these delays. It turned out he was struggling with some personal issues. We reallocated some tasks, and I suggested he seek counseling services provided by our university. The project was completed successfully, and he thanked me later for understanding and helping him through a rough patch."

Diane seemed satisfied with the answer. *Phew, one down.*

Then, without missing a beat, she inquired, "Can you walk us through a time when you had to work with limited resources and still managed to achieve the desired outcome?"

This one took me a bit off guard. I fumbled mentally, trying to recall a specific event. "Uh, during one of my internships, we were supposed to present a marketing strategy. However, the software we usually relied on crashed the day before. With the deadline looming, I... um... improvised by using basic tools and free online resources. I had to simplify the presentation, focusing on core ideas rather than flashy graphics."

Diane noticed my hesitation, her lips curving into a small, understanding smile. "It's always about adapting, isn't it?"

Was that a trick question or a save? My inner voice mused, "Absolutely. It's the challenges that push us to innovate and think outside the box."

Alex nodded, scribbling something once again. *Here we go with the scribbles. A doodle? A note? A shopping lists? Who knows?*

Diane leaned back in her chair and exchanged a brief glance with Alex, who seemed to have finished his mysterious scribbling session. "Well, Hina," Diane began, her voice carrying that calm, practiced air of finality, "Thank you for coming in today. It's been truly insightful getting to know more about you and your experiences. We'll be in touch once we've completed our interview process."

I stood up, trying to suppress the mixture of relief and anxiety bubbling together inside me. "Thank you for considering me," I replied, attempting to sound as professional as I felt. Alex extended his hand, and I shook it firmly, followed by Diane's. As I exited the room, the cool air of the hallway gave me a momentary reprieve. The corporate artwork on the walls, which initially felt intimidating, now seemed less daunting. *Okay, Hina, that went pretty well*, I mused, allowing myself a silent congratulatory pat on the back.

Walking through the maze-like corridors of the building, I couldn't help but overhear snippets of chatter, phones ringing, and the distant sounds of a printer churning out sheets. These mundane office sounds made the place feel alive, reminding me of the world I was eager to step into now.

Upon reaching the glass-fronted exit, the sunlight streamed in, painting its warm hue on the marbled floor. I pushed open the door, taking a deep breath as the fresh air of Sacramento filled my lungs. There was a slight breeze, and it ruffled my hair, feeling like nature's own part of encouragement. *All right, universe. Let's see where all this leads*, I thought to myself.

As I walked down the pathway leading to the parking lot, the weight on my shoulders felt lighter than when I'd arrived. The interview was done, the ball was no longer in my court, and there was an odd comfort in knowing that. There's something incredibly liberating about having done one's best and knowing that the next steps, whatever they might be, are part of the grand adventure still ahead.

I reached my car, I mean my mom's car, glanced back at the towering edifice of the company. *Well, VS {Global, it's been real. Maybe I'll see you soon. Or maybe not.* Either way, I quickly drove off, and the city sprawled out before me.

The buzz from the interview was still zipping through me, like I was floating on cloud nine. Ever get that vibe after nailing a big challenge, where all you crave is to sink into your sofa, dive into a mountain of ice cream, and lose yourself in the absurdity of reality TV? That was me, right at that moment. Because, honestly, the whole build-up and showdown of a job interview is an emotional whirlwind. It's exhausting, no joke. Emotions, they're sneaky like that—silent energy zappers.

Just as I was getting ready to settle in for a lazy day spent listening to my favorite songs, it dawned on me. The typical "oh no" moment. I remembered that something important had come up and I couldn't put it off or cancel. It was a big deal. Glancing at my watch, I noticed I now had under two hours left to change direction, freshen up, and reign in my racing thoughts. All the plans I'd made to relax after the interview had vanished. But such is life — always surprising when you least expect it. *All right, Hina*, I thought to myself. *Time to shape up!* I hurried to the bathroom.

The weight of the day still hung heavy on my shoulders. The feeling of those high heels, not usually my go-to-choice, oddly gave me strength, some sort of power. Maybe it's the sound they make— a confirmation of presence. The rhythmic echo of my steps filled Stonecutter Way, leading me to an old building to find Derrek standing nearby.

Chapter XII:

Legal Task

"We're cutting it close, you know," Derrek commented, a touch of worry lacing his voice.

I let out a quick breath. "Sorry about that. It's been... a day. Is he expecting us already?

Derrek glanced at his watch. "He moved the meeting to today, remember?"

"That's probably why I spaced. My job interview earlier threw me off. Sorry."

His eyebrows knitted in concern. "How'd that go?"

"Let's put all that aside for the time being," I suggested, steering the dialogue back on track. "Let's focus on this first." Navigating up to the second floor, a heavy door stood before us. Its presence was magnified by a metallic plate that had words engraved on it:

"Brandon M. Anderson
Attorney at Law
Specializing in Criminal Law & Victim's Rights"

Taking a deep breath, we knocked, the sound echoing a touch louder than expected. Almost immediately, a stylishly dressed secretary ushered us inside. We took our seats, the weight of anticipation settling heavily, as we awaited the attorney's entrance.

The door opened, and a man in his fifties now stood before us, a stark contrast to the youthful photos that littered his online presence. His grey suit was tailored to perfection, and a bold purple tie added a touch of character to the ensemble. While the age difference between his internet presence and reality could have been jarring, the glowing reviews on his proficiency as a lawyer immediately put me at ease.

"Thought you two might stand me up," he commented with a lightness in his tone while extending a hand toward us in greeting. The handshake was firm, yet brief. With a swift motion, he then directed us to the plush seats in front of his desk.

While he shuffled some papers, clearly intending to tidy up his workspace, he raised his voice slightly, directing his words to another room, "Nancy, they strike me as coffee aficionados. What do you think?"

Both Derrek and I interjected, "No, thank you," almost in perfect unison. However, moments later, the same Nancy glided into the room with a tray bearing two steaming cups. Her efficiency was admirable. "Thank you," we mumbled, slightly embarrassed for turning down the gesture, only to accept it moments later.

We took a moment to adjust in our seats, and I couldn't help but notice the abundance of rings adorning the lawyer's fingers. Each one was unique, indeed ostentatiously large, making them all hard to ignore.

Brushing his adorned hands together, he leaned forward slightly, eyes fully piercing as they shifted from Derek to me. "All right let's get down to brass tacks. What can I do for two lovely folks like you?"

Derrek began, his voice slightly shaky. I then quickly cut in, driven by urgency and the need to lay out our situation specifically.

"Thank you for finding time to see us today," I began, my voice unwavering. He acknowledged my gratitude with a subtle nod, then indicated for me to proceed. "We're here because we believe your experience and expertise might be crucial for our delicate matter."

He motioned for me to continue with a clear casual, "Go on."

Taking a deep breath, I ventured, "I'll paint a hypothetical picture. If a young man were to attempt... to violate a girl, and she believes there's insufficient evidence to press charges, what might be her best recourse?"

For a moment, the room was engulfed in silence. His intense gaze bore into both of us, making every second feel like an eternity. Then, with an edge of keen observation, he responded,

"When people present 'Hypotheticals,' it's often more personal than they let on. So, let me be direct. This isn't just a random query about the law, is it? You need guidance through an intimate ordeal."

Derek shifted uncomfortably beside me, but I was able to maintain full eye contact with Mr. Anderson, our selected attorney.

"We're treading on delicate ground here," I began, each word chosen with precise care. "The individual in question, the girl, believes that coming forward might cause more harm than good. The repercussions, the potential slander, the scrutiny - she's terrified of them. As for the evidence, as she claims, it's primarily her word against his. There are no physical marks, no witnesses. It occurred in a setting where it was just the two of them."

Mr. Anderson rubbed his temple pensively. "It's not uncommon for victims to feel this way," he started, "The fear of not being believed, the potential backlash, the trauma of having to recount the incident repeatedly. It's very daunting. However, silence seldom serves justice." He smiled.

Then he leaned forward, his gaze unwavering. "I can't make promises without a full understanding of the situation. But know this. Even in the absence of physical evidence, there are ways to build a case. Testimonies, behavioral patterns, corroborative evidence, any past history... every detail matters."

He paused, giving me a moment to absorb his words before continuing. "But you need to understand something. This journey, if embarked upon, will be a tough one. It demands strength and resilience. If your friend decides to move forward, she needs unwavering support. Are you prepared to give her that support?"

The weight of his question bore down on me, but the resolve in my heart felt firmer. "Yes," I responded, "Whatever it takes."

"Did you check marks on her body yourself?" he asked, stealing a glance at me.

I replied with a hint of confusion, "No, I didn't. She was confident there weren't any."

"Was this individual someone unfamiliar to her?"

I hesitated, then admitted, "No, absolutely not. They had been dating for a while."

There was a longer pause, making the atmosphere in the room even tenser. Finally, he sighed, "It's a tragedy when relationships devolve to such levels."

I felt a pang of guilt, realizing I had failed to mention another critical detail. Now rushing my words, I said, "I apologize for the confusion. I'm quite nervous talking about it, and it slipped my mind. There was another individual involved, another male, his friend. They tried... together."

The look on Mr. Anderson's face shifted significantly. His eyebrows furrowed in concern. "You're indicating this was a group effort?"

Feeling cornered, I responded, "I'm uncertain about the meaning of 'group,' but there were two of them. They were best friends. The boyfriend subtly tried convincing her that it was in her best interest to 'enjoy' a time together with both of them. When she declined, they persisted and then they both..."

"Attempted?" Mr. Anderson finished, the tone of his voice betraying a hint of anger.

I nodded, "Yes."

He leaned back, taking a deep breath. "These circumstances are graver than I initially assumed and yes, two people already count as a group, in the eyes of law, and that scenario is considered much more severe."

In my head, I was thinking, *'Why does it matter how many were involved? The main point is the victim and how she feels.'* Then I refocused back on Mr. Anderson, eager to hear his expertise.

He leaned forward slightly, his face serious. "So, tell me again, how did you determine that there wasn't enough to build a case?"

I then recounted the entire situation, from the intimidation about ruining careers to the challenges posed by her intoxication. "And about the witnesses, which seem to work against her. The only witness, their neighbor, seems more likely to support the boys rather than her if it comes right down to it."

He nodded thoughtfully. "The aspect of her being intoxicated does add complexity. It can make it more challenging to prove non-consensual activities, especially in the eyes of the law. But it's not an insurmountable obstacle. And as for the witness, remember, just because that person might testify in favor of the accused doesn't mean the testimony will be accepted without scrutiny." I felt a glimmer of hope. Maybe, just maybe, there was something we could do to help her. I felt a pressing question forming on the tip of my tongue. Derrek caught my eye and placed a cautioning hand on mine. He could almost read my thoughts, worried I'd accidentally drop too obvious a hint about the identities of those involved. With a slight nod, I altered my approach to frame the question more discreetly.

"And what if these individuals," I began cautiously, "happen to have ties with influential families? You know, the kind that are deeply entrenched in politics and big businesses, especially in this city?" Mr. Anderson's composed demeanor faltered for a split second. Clearly, he hadn't anticipated this curveball. His eyes darted between Derrek and me, trying to gauge if we were hinting at specific names.

"Exactly who are you referring to?" he inquired, a hint of trepidation in his voice. I held firm, ensuring I didn't betray any more than I intended. We had a promise to keep, after all.

Even without the weight of the promise, the entire situation felt like we were drowning in a pool of despair. If I genuinely believed that breaking my word would inch us closer to justice, I would've shattered that promise without a second thought. But that wasn't the reality of the matter. Today's consultation was more of a grim confirmation of... disappointment.

Mr. Anderson leaned back in his chair, steepling his fingers, his demeanor contemplative. "Given what you've presented," he started cautiously, "the first challenge would be gathering concrete evidence. Even under regular circumstances, these cases are complex. With the potential involvement of high-profile individuals, it... complicates matters further."

Derrek shifted nervously, his patience thinning. "Complicates it? How so?"

The lawyer took a moment, seeming to choose his words with care. "When there are influential entities possibly involved, they can, unfortunately, sway perceptions. - And with your friend not willing to approach the authorities, our stance becomes weaker." Mr. Anderson took another moment, letting the weight of his words settle in before continuing. "But obviously, even high-profile individuals and their families aren't immune to the law. If they're caught, they'll face justice. However, with your friend's reluctance to speak out or bring the case forward, it becomes nearly impossible. They could easily turn the tables, accusing her of deliberately trying to tarnish their family's political reputation or seeking financial gain through fabricated charges."

I swallowed, my throat now dry, "But isn't there some loophole? Some legal avenues we haven't explored?"

Mr. Anderson looked at me, his eyes sympathetic, yet guarded. "We can look into every possible path. Sometimes, however, it becomes more about the practicality of pursuing a case than its formal legal feasibility."

As the minutes ticked on, the conversation began to hint at an unpleasant truth. It appeared that odds were not in our favor. Derrek and I felt the weight of the situation, a sobering realization that justice might remain elusive. After a bit more discussion, the subtle indicators became clearer, and the path forward seemed less hopeful. With final handshakes, we left Mr. Anderson's office.

As the building's door closed behind us, the sound of the bustling city streets filled the void of silence that our tense meeting had left. The heels of my shoes clicked more aggressively against the pavement, a clear sign of my own frustration. Taking a moment to breathe in the fresh air, my fingers curled around the purse strap, my hand squeezing it with increasing pressure until my knuckles shone a stark white.

Turning to Derrek with a stormy expression, I blurted out, "I told you this would be pointless. See? It was just as I told you."

He paused, looking deep into my eyes, as if searching for a way to alleviate the weight I now felt. "We still had to try, Hina. Trying was the right thing to do." I locked eyes with him, searching for the reassurance I so desperately needed. His conviction momentarily pacified my frustration. Nodding twice, my simmering anger subsided. Without another word, we walked toward where we'd parked mom's car.

Chapter XIII:

Plan C

There I was, waiting for my final results. While doing so, some of us had already started planning how graduation would look, a beautiful sunny day, a gentle breeze playfully messing up our meticulously styled graduation caps. It's that kind of weather where the sun warms your skin but doesn't quite make you sweat. Perfect, right?

The campus grounds would be transformed, resembling less the daily hustle and a grander celebration space. Chairs would be arranged in neat rows, all facing the grand wooden podium adorned with garlands of white and blue–the university's colors. Fluttering overhead, a sea of balloons and confetti would be ready to be released the moment that the final name was called out. An orchestra might be a bit too much for the setting, but I envisioned the soft chords of a guitar in the background, setting the tone for this amazing and long-sought momentous occasion.

My friends and I would be seated in the middle rows. Abby would be fidgeting, adjusting her gown for the hundredth time, probably thinking of the gym session she was missing. Mikey, that ever-dramatic soul, would already be tearing up on our mobiles while chatting, while Lilly would be scanning the crowd, looking for her family and secretly hoping her ex wouldn't show up. As for me? I'd take a deep breath, soaking in the palpable mix of anxiety and excitement. I'd clutch the edges of my gown, reminding myself that after all the sleepless nights, caffeine overdoses, and existential meltdowns, this was it. This moment, frozen in time, would be a testament to our journey, our growth, and the myriad stories that found their life within GSU' walls.

But hey, I'm getting ahead of myself here, aren't I? Back to reality - On the immediate horizon, two big dates were circled in red on my calendar. First, a bowling extravaganza with Derrek and Adrianna. Two days later, I had a job interview with a local printing company. Now, after confidently surviving that first nerve-racking interview and receiving some genuinely encouraging smiles from the panel, you'd think I was ready for the big leagues. I really thought I could handle any of them. So, imagine my surprise when they didn't call back. Not a word. It was like they'd vanished into the Bermuda Triangle of Human Resources. Back then, I had no clue why, but I guess that's a mystery for another day.

Now, I cut to the bowling alley. I was lacing up my rather fashionable bowling shoes when Adrianna slid into the seat next to me, curiosity lighting up her eyes. "This is my first-time bowling, but Derrek says you're a bit of a pro. Right?"

I laughed. "Oh, you could say that. I'm the self-proclaimed champion of Golden State's unofficial bowling league."

"Unofficial?"

"Yeah, we don't have the bureaucratic credentials to make it official, but trust me, in our social circle, I'm pretty much undefeated."

Adrianna looked impressed. "Wow, that's amazing. I hope I can pick up some good tips from you."

"Absolutely. Think of me as your unofficial mentor for the day," I replied, winking. And just like that, it was game on.

Shuffling my feet on the glossy bowling alley floor, I found myself hoping that Martha wouldn't make one of her surprise appearances. The last thing I needed was a mini drama to unfold right now. Given that I wasn't entirely sure about what Martha knew regarding Adrianna and Brad, it was like playing emotional Russian roulette. Then, in a stolen moment, while Adrianna freshened up, I quickly yanked Derrek aside, my voice hushed, "You think Martha knows about Adrianna and Brad?"

He raised an eyebrow. "Do I look like a mind reader to you? Or Matt?"

A subtle smile escaped my lips. "Do you think it's going to become an issue?"

His sigh was laced with a hint of annoyance. "Predicting human behavior? That's an advanced level of guessing, even for me. But for now, we're here to bowl, right?"

"All right, Mr. Philosophy," I teased back.

Our brief exchange was interrupted when Adrianna returned. I could see the slight hesitation in her eyes as she approached. Something more than just bowling was on her mind. Reaching out, I took her hand, guiding it to show her the ropes of the game. It was a light moment, but then she asked, "Hina, can I ask you something?"

"As long as it's not outside the game" I gave a sly grin and raised my arm, my fingers gripping a bowling ball.

Her expression grew serious, yet still smiling. "Not a single worry, agronomy is our thing, isn't it?" Then a small pause emerged before she continued," I've heard things... about some of your friends being a bit... well, unhappy about me and Brad."

"You mean you're talking about their 'friendly concern'?" I responded, air-quoting it for emphasis. "Look, it's like an unwritten rule of friendship–everyone's entitled to an opinion on exes. Past relationships are the favorite fodder for jokes and judgments, ex-relationships are always the subject of criticism."

"I just don't want it to become a big thing, you know? Especially between you, me, and... Martha," Adrianna said, the weight of the situation clearly evident in her eyes.

Trying to inject a bit of levity into the conversation, I quipped, "Honestly? If you wanted to, you could elope to Vegas with Brad. I'd just ask you to send me postcards."

Derrek, clearly caught off-guard, then exclaimed, "Hina!" His protest was eclipsed by the satisfying sound of crashing pins, as I rolled a near-perfect ball. "But we have our own game, don't we?" I quickly hurled the bowling ball toward the pins and achieved the highest score - 10.

Later, when the match was coming to an end, the sound of the machines blending with the cheers and groans from the other people there bowling. The tune from my phone, specially designated for Lilly's calls, started ringing. She didn't usually call us. We normally invited her to hang out or to join a planned activity. I swiped the phone to answer. "Lilly? What's up?"

She was quick and to the point. "I have something for you, Hina. Something I want to show you."

Slightly taken aback, I asked, "What about Abby? She's usually your partner-in-crime for these kinds of things."

A faint chuckle came from her end. "She won't appreciate it, but I know you will." My mind raced, juggling my schedule, and I was just about to decline, remembering my job interview in two days. However, the intrigue in Lilly's voice got the better of me.

"Are you free to come to a ballroom dance event?" she asked.

"Honestly, Lilly, in two days I have—"

She cut me off. "I'll get you a Victorian dress if you don't have one."

That was so like Lilly, always a step ahead, always with an answer ready. I smiled, letting the weight of the pending job interview lighten a bit. "All right, all right. Victorian dress and all I'm in." The agreement sealed; I felt the warm tingle of excitement about the upcoming dance event. Sometimes, unplanned adventures were the best kind.

In the bizarre way that life's little moments often align, I found myself lurking just around the corner. The others were behind me, close enough to eavesdrop, but far enough to remain hidden, and Adrianna's voice floated toward me, "Look, it's a long, long shot, but you know how I support you, but there's still..."

Derrek quickly cut her off. "It's too early to worry, really early. I don't think it's troll good going in the wrong direction." Just as they all were about to round the corner, I propelled myself forward, continuing towards the exit, as if I had not even been standing there.

Chapter XIV:
'That' Interview

When I woke up the next morning, Michael's side of the house was oddly quiet. I later found out he and Dan had decided to reunite for one of their spontaneous adventures. Who knows where they went? But I wasn't too concerned; I felt invigorated after having achieved that so-often elusive full 8-hour sleep for the first time in months. My morning routine began in earnest. Taking some advice that I'd recently gleaned from a wellness article; I made sure not to eat or drink anything — not even my beloved coffee — before heading out for a morning jog. The article claimed that a pre-breakfast run could ramp up my energy, focus, and confidence, especially if I was prepping for an event demanding those attributes. So, with that objective in mind, I hit the streets for a solid 25-minute run.

Upon returning home, that post-run euphoria was palpable. My energy was soaring, and I felt good about kickstarting the day that way. I rewarded myself with a slice of my favorite blueberry pie (blessedly made with stevia and devoid of that pesky refined sugar) and a cup of aromatic coffee. Then came the task I both loved and dreaded — selecting the perfect outfit. I was scheduled to visit the printing company, and I wanted to make an impression. After what felt like a personal home-fashion-week, I finally settled on a chic ensemble: a sophisticated purple dress with a contemporary inner corset, parts of which were tastefully visible, and a classic overlay. The finishing touches? A pair of killer high heels that screamed confidence.

Heading to work, I had this gut feeling that my days at the farmer's marketplace were numbered. Confidence coursed through me. I was almost certain that after the interview, job offers would come flooding in. My attire for the day was quite a departure from the norm, easily radiating an air of sophistication. As expected, my appearance raised some eyebrows, eliciting a mix of compliments and playful jibes. But none of it phased me. I just shared a friendly rapport with everyone there, as always.

Once my shift ended, I glanced at the clock, realizing I had just under an hour before my interview. With no time to dally and the bus running late, I hailed a taxi to ensure I reached it on time. As we navigated the bustling streets, a familiar flutter of anxiety began to rise. By the time the cab pulled up outside the imposing facade of PeakPapers, I had to take a deep breath to steady myself.

You might maybe wonder, "Why was I interviewing at a place that wasn't directly related to my major?" It's a fair question. The answer lays in two parts. First, our graduation wasn't complete, meaning I hadn't officially received my bachelor's degree yet. Secondly, once I had that degree in hand, I could cast a wide net. I started applying everywhere, from positions like an archaeology assistant (which was an unpaid role, solely for experience) to more expected roles in agronomy. In today's world, being versatile is the key. At least, that's what I used to think.

Stepping into PeakPapers, I was met with an open-concept workspace. Bright natural light filtered through the large windows, illuminating rows of modern desks with sleek computers and ergonomic chairs. There was a gentle buzz of productivity in the air–the soft click-clack of keyboards, hushed conversations, and occasional laughter. I approached the reception desk, where a young woman with a pixie haircut and a vibrant smile greeted me. "Hi, I'm Hina Strubel. Here for the job interview at 6 pm."

She glanced down at her schedule book. "Ah, yes, Miss Strubel! We've been expecting you. Take a seat in the waiting area, and someone will be with you shortly." Thankful for the warm welcome, I took a moment to observe my surroundings. On one side, there was a casual lounge area with comfortable couches and a coffee station. On the other side was a glass-walled conference room where a team was actively engaged in what seemed to be a brainstorming session. The dynamic atmosphere was both energizing and nerve-wracking.

Only a few minutes passed later, a tall man with a friendly demeanor approached me. "Miss Strubel?" he called out. I nodded, and he motioned for me to follow. We navigated a series of corridors until we arrived at a nondescript room. Inside, a woman sat engrossed in a stack of documents, her sharp eyes scanning the pages before her. There was an air of confidence, even arrogance, about her, evident in her posture and the set of her jaw. The man took a seat beside her, and almost instantly, they were locked in a hushed, seemingly intense conversation. Their body language was exclusive, shutting me out completely as though I was not there. A growing discomfort settled over me as the minutes ticked by. Were they assessing me without even looking in my direction? Or had they forgotten my presence entirely? I was used to being the center of attention in interviews, not sidelined. As I tried to remain composed, a thousand thoughts raced through my mind. Should I interject? Wait patiently? Or maybe take out my resume as a subtle reminder of why I was there? The woman peered at me through her glasses, her eyes void of emotion.

"Miss Strubel, it's nice to finally meet you," she uttered in a detached tone. A long pause followed, and the air hung heavy between us. I was starting to get anxious when she broke the silence.

"Well," she began. "I think we can begin with why someone with your skill set would be interested in joining PeakPapers? What makes you unique and qualified for this role?"

I drew a deep breath to steady my nerves, inhaling courage as I exhaled anxiety. "Every sector has its own distinct story," I began. "Agriculture, printing–each industry has its own narrative of progress, evolution, and making ideas vivid realities. From what I've seen of PeakPapers, there's far more than just a company here–it's an organization that brings tales to life. With the varied experiences I can bring to the table, I'm confident I can devise fresh perspectives on any challenge, contributing innovative solutions for success."

The woman leaned back, her gaze never leaving mine. "Miss Strubel," she began with a patronizing tone, "considering you come from a diverse background and not directly from the printing or publishing industry, how can you assure us you won't be overwhelmed with the technicalities? Printing is not just about 'storytelling,' as you put it. It's a lot more intricate than that."

At that moment, I quickly created a name for this woman: Ms. Sharpnose.

Before I could reply, the man jumped in, his eyes gleaming with a hint of mischief. "Yes, and how do you plan on adapting to an industry that's constantly evolving? From digital transformation to sustainable practices, there's more to it than meets the eye. How will your..." he paused, glancing at my resume, "background in archaeology help here?"

I could sense their underlying intent. It was a classic move to corner an applicant, making them second-guess their own decisions and qualifications. But I was prepared.

"Every field, whether it's archaeology or agronomy, gives us skills that can be applied elsewhere. From archaeology, I've learned to pay attention to details and value history. In terms of the evolving printing industry, change is something I've always embraced. My diverse experiences can offer a unique perspective, especially for problem-solving. I see challenges in printing as chances to learn and grow even more."

The woman arched an eyebrow, clearly not expecting such a response. But I could also detect a begrudging respect in her eyes. She exchanged another glance with the man before continuing, "Well, let's discuss the technicalities then. Can you explain the difference between offset and digital printing and in which scenarios you would recommend one over the other?"

Caught off guard by the unexpected technical question, my mind raced, trying to pull together any strands of knowledge I might have on the topic. While I had done some basic research on the printing industry, this specific question had eluded my prep. Instead of admitting ignorance, I opted to lean into logic and common sense. Taking a deep breath, I began, "Well, offset printing, as the name suggests, involves transferring ink from a plate to a rubber blanket, and then to the printing surface. This method might be more suitable for large volume printing due to its efficiency and consistent quality."

Right?

I paused briefly, trying to recall anything specific about digital printing. "On the other hand, digital printing doesn't use plates. Instead, it directly transfers the image onto the material. It might be more suited for shorter runs or when personalization is needed, given its remarkable flexibility."

I hoped my answer made sense, but the subtle change in the woman's expression indicated otherwise. She leaned forward, her face showing a mix of skepticism and amusement. "That's an interesting take," she remarked, "although I must say your understanding of the two methods is really a bit... superficial."

The man, attempting to mask a smile, added, "Your logic isn't entirely off, but there are nuances to these methods that require a deeper understanding." My cheeks flushed with embarrassment, realizing that I had indeed just mis-stepped. But still, I appreciated the chance to answer, even if I hadn't hit the mark. It was a stark reminder that no matter how much we prepare; life always will throw a curveball or two throw our way. The man cleared his throat, straightening his tie as he did.

"Miss Strubel," he began, with an air of feigned politeness, "Let's dive a bit deeper, shall we? What's your understanding of the color gamut in printing? And how about the implications of color profiles in different printing technologies?"

I could feel the heavy weight of his gaze, the challenge behind his words. It was evident he wasn't just testing my technical knowledge; he was looking to fluster me, see if he could rattle my confidence. His tone was layered with thinly veiled sarcasm. It was a deliberate attempt to highlight any potential ignorance on my part.

Taking a moment to compose myself, I replied, "While my in-depth knowledge of the color gamut and its intricacies is limited, I do understand its importance in ensuring print quality and consistency. Color profiles, on the other hand, are essential for maintaining color accuracy across different devices and printing techniques."

He now leaned back, interlocking his fingers. "Interesting. It's crucial to ensure that the colors you see on your screen match what gets printed. But there's more to it than just that. For instance," he said, pausing for dramatic effect, "how do you think Pantone colors come into play?"

I hesitated, grappling with the sudden depth of the discussion. But I wasn't going to let his tactic deter me. "Pantone colors," I began cautiously, "are standardized colors that ensure consistency across different platforms. Still, I must admit that the intricate details of how they intertwine with other elements of printing elude me a bit."

His smirk was all the confirmation I needed of the amusement and the condescension he now felt. "Well, it is essential to know these nuances in this industry," he remarked, emphasizing the word 'essential.' As he spoke with such confidence and almost delight in pointing out my gaps in knowledge, the nickname 'Mr. Knowitall' formed in my mind. Yet, as clear as his attempt to belittle me was, there was a lesson hidden within this exchange. It wasn't just about possessing knowledge, but also about acknowledging one's limitations. This journey was far from over.

He leaned forward, his fingers steepled, eyes gleaming with a new line of questioning. "You mentioned adapting to new industries, Miss Strubel. Tell me, "He began slowly, drawing out the suspense, "how would you handle a disgruntled customer who claims the color on their large banner isn't matching the business cards we printed for them earlier? Especially when they're adamant that the error is on our end."

I felt a prickle of unease. It was a situational question, one that didn't just test knowledge, but also experience and temperament. "First, I would apologize for any inconvenience caused," I began, "then I'd inspect the products to check for any discrepancies and cross-reference them with the original designs."

He interrupted, a sly smile now playing on his lips. "But let's assume you find no fault on our end. The products are as they should be. Yet, the customer is irate and threatens to tarnish our reputation. What then?"

I hesitated for a split second; the weight of his gaze was very heavy. "In that case," I ventured, "I'd try to find a middle ground. Maybe offer a discount on their next order or suggest a re-print at a reduced rate."

His laugh, though subdued, echoed with superiority. "Ah, Miss Strubel, you see, appeasing isn't always the solution. Sometimes customers need to be educated. And sometimes," he paused, leaning in closer, "They need to be shown the door. After all, not all business is good business."

At this point, my confidence began to waver, giving way to a rising tide of insecurity. The self-assuredness I had clung to, fueled by the success of my last interview, was disintegrating swiftly, crumbling like a fragile sandcastle that was facing the unrelenting waves of the sea and a rising tide. Doubt coursed through me, and I felt my heart race, the familiar throb of anxiety echoing in my ears. I now questioned my every move, wondering if my responses were just making me look more and more like a deer caught in the headlights.

These two people, it seemed, weren't merely seeking a new hire. They were on a hunt, seeking out weaknesses, eager to pounce on any hint of uncertainty in the applicant. Their intent appeared to be more malicious–almost as if they reveled in the opportunity to trample over the aspirations of unsuspecting candidates like me. My once steady foundation of self-worth had shattered, reduced to jagged fragments.

The professional, poised persona I had meticulously crafted for myself for this interview seemed to dissolve suddenly, replaced by a much younger, much more vulnerable version of me. I felt like 'baby Hina,' way out of her depth, struggling to keep her head above water in a storm she hadn't ever seen coming.

"You are so very fresh from academia's embrace. What makes you think the corporate world is ready for you?" He began, a sly twinkle shining in his eyes.

The interview wrapped up about five to seven minutes after that question, and I hurriedly left the building. When I stepped outside, it felt like the whole world had shifted during just the brief time I had just spent inside.

You know that sensation when you're on the brink of feeling ashamed, but you don't want to succumb to that truth? You sense its creeping approach, but you can't exactly pinpoint its origin.

Moments like this underscore the truth that our emotions are shaped by perceptions, and everyone perceives the world in a unique way, molded by their own experiences and genetic blueprint. Just because I might find certain things unsettling or embarrassing doesn't mean everyone else will... What we think and feel is the result of a complex combination of experiences, feelings, and responses that we have collected and are interconnected deep inside us to how we interpret and react to various situations, Yet, on the flip side, there's a common ground where most of us can find consensus. Internally, we will acknowledge certain norms or values that seem universally accepted across societies, leading to shared reactions or perspectives on specific issues. It's as if there's an unspoken understanding, a communal code of conduct. Hello, Hobbes!

As I made my way home, my mind remained in turmoil. I wrestled with the notion of embarrassment and shame, trying to gauge if others felt the same intensity of emotion I did, and how much I should allow those feelings to consume me. These many reflections occupied my mind up until the moment I stepped through the front door. Mikey was quick to pick up on my mood, as the aura of victory I usually radiated after an interview was notably absent. It was always reflected in my interaction, or the lack thereof, with him. I was today reserved, encapsulated in a bubble about my personal reflections, and barely responsive to the world around me.

The fallout from the interview had another casualty too: my commitment to Lilly. I'd promised to join her for the ballroom dancing event. In the state I was now in, dancing, an epitome of expressive freedom and joy, was the last thing on my mind. I backed out of the event, and though Lilly was visibly upset, she restrained herself from voicing her disappointment. Yet a silent tension lingered, one more reminder of that day's failures.

That night was also marked by my minimal interaction with Mikey. Every attempt at conversation was met with only monosyllabic responses. I was present in body, but my mind was still captive of that day's events. Sleep was a sanctuary, an escape into a world where the failures of the day could be momentarily forgotten. But as dawn broke and a new day beckoned, the same familiar feeling of unease still clung to me. It was that unsettling realization that you're trying to convince yourself that you've moved on, and yet deep within the self, fragments of disappointment and regret longer, unshaken. It's the same feeling as when you are lying to yourself and saying that you've moved on, but the subconscious part of your mind does not agree.

In an effort to lift the dark cloud over me, I entered the world of the Internet. It was a place where answers were supposed to be found and new experiences could be shared. "What does a successful job interview look like?" I typed on my computer. Page after page of tips, anecdotes, and expert advice immediately filled the screen. Yet with every word I read, the reality of my perceived failure was only magnified. It was a spiral taking me further downward, and I knew I needed to pull away and fast.

Skipping Abby's gym session was a much-needed escape. However, Mikey and Abby noticed my desolation and conspired to drag me out for the evening, a decision I'd soon be grateful for making. That night became a turning point, leading me down a path where I discovered a passion that I didn't know I ever had. The passage of time has a way of healing wounds, and in my case, it was no different. Within a short span, Lilly and I reconnected, our bond stronger than before. The minor hiccups of the past were quickly forgotten as we shared laughs, stories, and our dreams for the future. Only now, there was something different in me–an ember that had been kindled and was now growing into a shining flame.

The experience of that disastrous job interview lingered in my thoughts. It wasn't just the humiliation or the disappointment; it was the realization that I had placed my self-worth in the hands of strangers. I never wanted to put myself in such a vulnerable position again, feel that kind of embarrassment. This decision pushed me to more introspection. The more I thought about it, the more appealing the idea of charting my own course became ideal. The allure of creating something from scratch, of having my own destiny in only my hands, now began to consume me.

I started envisioning a world where I wouldn't be judged by panelists or confined to the parameters of specific descriptions. I wanted a world where I'd be my own boss, making the calls, and bearing the fruits of my labor. The entrepreneurial flame in me had been ignited. I dreamed of starting a venture, maybe in retail or perhaps via exploring the vast potential of the online marketplace. This decision wasn't just about financial independence; it was about carving out a space where I felt truly valued and always in control.

So, in line with my newfound direction, I made a bold move. I canceled all pending job interviews. It felt liberating, like breaking free from chains. The practical side of me understood the need for a steady income, so I held onto my part-time job. It gave me a safety net, allowing me to strategize and brainstorm about my future business without the immediate pressure of paying. That was bills piling up.

As all this change was unfolding, another big thing appeared on the horizon — graduation. It felt wild thinking about closing out my school days, after all the exams, late-night study sessions, and unforgettable moments I had with friends. I felt a mix of excitement and nostalgia already. Graduation wasn't just about ending one chapter. It was also about the new adventures for me waiting around the corner. With everything going on and graduation coming up so soon, it hit me. I was on the edge of diving into a whole new world and one I was shaping for myself.

The next few days just kind of smushed together, filled with waiting, a bit of excitement, and lots of jittery nerves. Graduation was getting closer, exciting and a bit scary for all of us. It felt like we were right on the edge, about to jump into something totally new after leaving the cozy corners of our college. Every spot around campus seemed extra special, holding all the good times, tough spots, and wins we had here, all about to turn into memories. Soon.

PART II

Chapter XV:

The Graduation

That special morning, I woke up to sunshine doodling on my walls, feeling an odd peace. Today was no ordinary day—it was Graduation Day, our big leap from the cozy nest of GSU into the big, wide world. Outside, everything looked extra sparkly, like the trees and the breeze were in our big secret, celebrating with us.

Usually, I'd be lost in plans for my future business, but today, that had to wait. It was all about soaking up the now, feeling the buzz of excitement as we all geared up to cross this magical line together.

Sure, history's full of graduation ceremonies, but ours felt like it was our own epic story, each of us a chapter, every glance a story. Slipping into my gown, reality hit: this was the big moment, the end of one adventure and the start of another.

The ceremony was a blast, more than we'd ever imagined. Hearing our names called out was like music, a nod to our journey filled with ups and downs. Walking that stage, with cheers and claps all around, was a moment frozen in time, a moment to just breathe in and relish.

The campus was buzzing, alive with graduates in a mix of joy and wistful nostalgia. Leaning against our iconic statue, I fixed my cap and gown. Then came Sarah, the one who'd forget her head if it wasn't screwed on, missing her tassel today of all days. We laughed, recalling her shoeless mishap for a major presentation—she was our ray of sunshine, always.

Then Alex joined, his cap blinking "Alumnus Alert!"—always the joker, keeping our spirits up during those late-night cramming sessions. His flair for funny had us chuckling again.

As the familiar graduation march started, Sarah, Alex, and I linked arms, stepping in sync, wrapped in our shared memories of jokes, secret codes, and stargazing promises. Then Jake, my freshman buddy, popped up, his grin as mischievous as ever, asking if I ever thought we'd get here.

Post-ceremony, the vibe shifted from formal to party mode, everyone in high spirits. Abby and Lilly, my ride-or-dies, went wild when it was my turn on stage. After, amidst the festive chaos, Clara, always quiet, handed me a poem, capturing our shared journey. Then came Abby and Lilly, juggling plates of food, gowns billowing, faces beaming. Together, we had dived into memories and dreamed up future escapades, celebrating not just our academic achievements, but the laughter, tears, and bonds forged at GSU.

At the lively gathering, everyone's focus shifted to a makeshift stage at the lawn's end. Graduates and guests huddled around, their chatter turning into whispers of excitement. Golden State University Sacramento had this cool tradition, "Graduates' Remarks," where any student could hop up, grab the mic, and spill their guts—stories, memories, or even belt out a tune. Some had prepared heartfelt speeches, others shared funny college tales, sparking a wave of giggles.

One moment really stuck with me. Samuel, usually Mr. Serious in class, surprised us all by whipping out a ukulele. Just as he got ready, a screech from the speakers made him jump, sending the ukulele flying. But quick as a wink, he caught it with his knees, turning a near-disaster into a comedy show. We all cracked up, even Samuel, who joked about making an unforgettable exit.

The laughter lightened the mood. Then, Derrek, always brimming with confidence, sauntered over with his soccer buddies, all donned in team scarves over their gowns.

"Enjoying the show?" he teased. Abby couldn't resist a jab about soccer players and comedy, sparking a hearty laugh from Derrek. He reminisced about our campus debates and pranks, like convincing folks the physics building was haunted—a stunt Abby claimed as her brainchild, much to Derrek's playful protest.

Our banter was interrupted when one of Derrek's friends, clearly hungry, nudged him to wrap it up. Derrek, with all sincerity now, shared a heartfelt goodbye, praising the shared memories and fun. Abby's response was a cheeky wish for him not to stumble in the "real world."

The campus green had transformed into a party zone, with tents and snack stands everywhere. Lilly, ever the firecracker, dragged me over to Professor Callaghan, our mentor who lived in tweed jackets come rain or shine. His passion for his field was contagious. "Professor Callaghan!" Lilly practically shouted, engulfing him in a hug. "Remember our almost epic lab fire trying to redo that old-timey experiment?"

He chortled, his glasses nearly taking a dive.

"Forget it? It's a miracle the lab's still standing! That's one for the 'what not to do' in science history books." He gave us a knowing look. "But you two always cooking up something bold, weren't you?"

Not far off, Professor Li was holding court with some classmates, her philosophical musings interspersed with travel tales and the odd joke, keeping everyone on their toes.

Then Martha strolled up, her presence as commanding as ever. "Graduates, huh?" she said, a mix of pride and seriousness in her voice. Lilly and I shared a look, knowing Martha's journey had been no cakewalk.

"It's a wrap on one chapter, and the ink's just warming up for the next," she mused, attracting a crowd hungry for a piece of her sage advice, her calm demeanor anchoring the excited chatter around her.

Professor Martins, the campus's Indiana Jones, wove into the mix, spinning his yarn about the time he mistook a relic for a rock. His flair turned the tale into a mini epic, drawing laughs and wide-eyed looks.

Professor Martins, with a twinkle in his eye, began to share one of his "field misadventures" with the gathered students and faculty. "So, there I was, knee-deep in mud, convinced I had found a significant archaeological artifact," he started, his voice laced with a hint of self-mockery that immediately piqued everyone's interest.

The students leaned in, knowing Martins' stories usually had an unexpected twist. "It was cylindrical, ancient-looking, and I was already dreaming of the headlines," he continued, building up the suspense.

The crowd was hooked, hanging on to his every word. Professor Li, who knew Martins' penchant for dramatics, smirked from the sidelines. "Was it the lost scepter of King Arthur?" she interjected, earning a round of laughter.

Martins chuckled, playing along. "Close, Li, close. But no, after carefully extracting it and cleaning it off, I discovered it wasn't a relic of old but... a very old, very rusty spark plug."

The revelation drew a burst of laughter from the audience. "Yes, ladies and gentlemen, I had discovered the ancient remains of what must have been a truly majestic... lawnmower,"

Moments.
All these moments to remember.

As the day wore on, the mood turned reflective, the sun setting the perfect backdrop for reminiscing and dreaming. By the photo booth, Abby was holding court, recounting our infamous freshman camping misadventure.

"Imagine us, supposed to enjoy a chill camping trip, and there we were, playing lost in the woods thanks to my 'excellent' navigation and Hina's map that might as well have been a treasure hunt clue," she exaggerated, sending everyone, even a couple of professors, into a laughing fit.

In the background, Samuel, undaunted by his earlier ukulele fiasco, was strumming away, sparking an impromptu musical gathering. The setting was like something out of a feel-good movie—soft music, a gentle breeze, and a sense of togetherness, wrapping up our university days in a perfect, melodious finale.

The campus was buzzing with on-the-fly fun. A Frisbee game kicked off, roping in students and professors alike, showing that you're never too old to toss a disc around. Then, there was the tug-of-war showdown, with graduation cords as the rope—professors vs. students, arts vs. sciences, all in a good-natured tussle.

While the games unfolded, Martha found a quiet spot on a bench, diving into deep talks with a circle of students. Earlier laughs had given way to intense discussions, her words sparking debates and inspiring the younger crowd with her wisdom.

Meanwhile, Lilly and I hit the food stands, lured by the scent of grilled goodies and zesty drinks. Mid-sip, Lilly whispered, "Did you see Professor Reynolds by the sweets? He's still holding court with his stories, just like in class!" Sure enough, there he was, captivating a group with his tales, probably mixing in with some love-life sagas from his younger days.

Our laughter paused when someone yelled for a speech. Everyone gathered around Derrek, who, with his usual flair, hopped onto a table, raising his glass. "Here's to our adventures, the friendships forged through all the deadlines and exams, and to our future—like a blank page waiting for us. Cheers to our GSU spirit!" The crowd cheered, glasses clinked, and the energy was infectious, capturing the essence of our journey—filled with fun, learning, and spontaneous wit.

Diving into the job hunt and corporate ladder climbing kinda soured my taste a bit. Yet, it also opened my eyes to new possibilities. A messy interview sparked something inside me—a drive to be my own boss, to shape my own path. Now, at this graduation bash, my mind started wandering, picturing all the incredible paths everyone here could take if they dared to stray off the beaten path like I was planning to.

My attention got snagged by a lively pair in graduation gowns. The girl was all decked out in badges from clubs and societies, while the guy was passionately sharing a travel story. In my daydream, they teamed up to create 'Pins & Tales,' a travel agency crafting trips inspired by your college clubs and adventures.

Then there was this guy, lost in a chunky book, while his buddy tried to coax him into the party. They struck me as the perfect duo to start a 'Read & Roam' café, a place where books meet interactive theatre, offering a feast for both the mind and the palate.

My eyes then drifted to a family—mom in a deep chat with her daughter, dad soothing a hyperactive kid high on sugary treats. I imagined them running 'Family Frenzy,' an event planning biz that could handle any kind of party pandemonium, especially the sugar-induced kind.

Over there was Professor Reynold, still the center of attention with his stories. I pictured him launching 'Past Pages,' a platform where seniors share their life stories, turning history lessons into personal narratives.

A pair of girls from my class, always locked in environmental debates, were at it again. In my head, they started 'Eco-Edits,' a consultancy turning businesses green and sustainable, blending profit with planet care.

Then there was the tech-obsessed crowd, always with the latest gadgets. They'd be perfect for 'Tech-Tinker,' a startup transforming old electronics into cool, functional art.

As I let my imagination dance, I wasn't just daydreaming. I saw a world brimming with potential, where everyone's unique traits could lead to exciting ventures beyond the usual 9-to-5.

Martha's voice yanked me back to reality. She'd caught my distant gaze and inquisitive smile. "Cooking up new worlds?" she asked with a playful look.

I laughed. "Sort of. Just picturing all the unique businesses everyone here could start playing to their own strengths."

Martha's eyes sparkled with a mix of wisdom and mischief. "Ah, the power of imagination," she said with a twinkle in her eye. My daydreams weren't just for fun—they came from a storm of feelings and big questions stirring inside me, especially after that job interview. I kept pondering what it really means to succeed and what we have to give up on getting there. Even as we all chatted and laughed, my brain was busy picturing what the future might hold for each of us.

Now, on this graduation day, I was deep in thought about the new reality we were all diving into—leaving the structured world of school for the wild, wide-open world of work. It felt like I was trying to knit together all sorts of life stories—triumphs, setbacks, big leaps, and even the quiet moments that don't make headlines but are still part of our journey.

For every venture that I imagined, I was subconsciously seeking answers. If that bubbly duo started 'Pins & Tales', would the colorful vibrancy of their passion endure, or would the harsh, unyielding reality of running a business alter its hues over time? Would the perceived success of the family and 'Family Frenzy' hide silent dinners and unspoken stress, and would business plans soon take precedence over bedtime stories? These mental machinations weren't born from cynicism, but from a silent awakening within me. I was coming to terms with the realization that success wasn't a linear journey, and neither was it uniformly defined. Every graduate had a universe of potentialities, and with each imagined venture here this day, I was exploring all multifaceted realms of achievement and failure, victory, and loss. The reason behind these musings was deeply rooted in my journey - a transformative experience that had begun at the bitter junction of a disastrous interview. I'd touched the cold, unyielding floor of failure then and found, in that singular chilling touch, the warmth of true self-realization.

I now stood at the precipice where the structured narratives of educational achievement met the chaotic, unscripted, and often unforgiving world of professional life. Every imagined venture, every calculated success, or concealed struggle was a mirror reflecting my own uncertainties, aspirations, and the unending question: what comes next?

Choices.
Paths.
Is this what we're taught to follow?
I chose my path, yet... it's all a plan, no action.

The sky turned dark as the graduation progressed to its end. I stood there, admiring the surrounding joy. Every hug and every cheer were promises of more to come; Today and other days like it, we were hopefully going to be able to still overlook the darker sides of ourselves, our neighbors, and even our closest friends. When there is laughter and joy in the air, it is easy for us to become naïve. Such moments are still remarkably beautiful, however, despite their extraordinary innocence.

Chapter XVI:

Little Too Early

In a classic post-graduation twist that could only have been scripted by the universe—or perhaps a sitcom writer—I discovered a peculiar trend. Barely ten days had passed since we tossed our graduation caps into the Californian sun, and yet, there was an odd stillness in the air now. Most summers after a term ended, there was a mad dash—a flurry of holiday plans and travel itineraries. This time? Crickets. Even the relentless wander lusters, Lilly and Abby, were suspiciously silent about any jet-setting plans. As for Michael, well, he's always been a steadfast worker bee, so his groundedness, both figuratively and literally, was expected. But there's where the plot thickens. Just as I was about to diagnose my friends with a severe case of post-grad inertia, they sprang a surprise on me. Europe, they exclaimed! A grand tour, no less. And the cherry on top? They wanted me to join them with a departure set for several months in the future. Somewhere in late fall! It was as though they'd all been secretly bitten by the *'carpe diem'* bug.

A whirlwind of thoughts about this Europe trip kept swirling in my head, so I decided to unwind with Michael at our favorite downtown fish spot after our work. As we chatted, waiting for our salmon, who walked in? None other than Derrek and Joshua. We shared a quick look, and without missing a beat, they headed over and grabbed a seat with us, turning our quiet evening into an unexpected reunion. Derrek and Joshua settled into their chairs, giving a sudden burst of energy to the space around our table. The mellow ambiance brightened immediately, reminiscent of the countless animated lunch breaks we'd had on campus.

Joshua, with his always familiar glint in his eyes, leaned forward. "Hina, the buzz is that you, Lilly, and Abby are planning to paint Europe red. True?"

"Oh, you know how it is," I replied with a playful smirk. "A whisper here, a rumor there, and suddenly everyone's talking about it. But yes, Europe's the plan." Derrek chuckled. "Trust the GSU network to keep everyone in the loop."

The conversation then began in earnest, as I enjoyed the salmon that had been cooked to perfection and washed it down with a glass of crisp white wine. Derrek entertained us with stories from his final year in college, while Joshua brought up the time that we almost missed a submission deadline. As we all chatted, I couldn't help but marvel at the paths our lives were taking. Here was Michael, ever the entertainer, telling stories that seemed straight out of an evening comedy show. Joshua, with his ever-knowledgeable analytical brain, was always ready with a comment that made us think. Then there was Derrek. Mikey, now almost two years into the post-college world, seemed to wear his experiences like a badge of honor.

"Mike," Derrek began, genuine curiosity coloring his tone, "It's been a while since you stepped into the 'real world'. How's it all shaping up?"

Michael smiled. "It's a different kind of challenge, that's for sure. Uni prepared us well, but there's nothing quite like navigating the real -world work dynamics.

Joshua kicked back, flashing a grin. "Yo, Hina, you still digging around in dirt and old relics, or has the fancy euro history and farming vibes caught your fancy?"

I couldn't resist an eye roll; that's him for you, always dragging up our past, especially those midnight cram fests surrounded by my piles of soil samples and ancient pottery.

"Pssh, I've leveled up from decoding dirt and tripping over old treasures in my dreams, thanks,"

"But c'mon, those were the days, right? Your dirt-digging detective work was top-notch when the rest of us were just snacking away."

"Let me clue you in, I've upped my game," I clapped back, not about to let him snag the glory. "Now I'm wondering if Tuscany's vineyards need a sprinkle of Hina's agronomy magic or if Rome's ruins are itching for a new kind of hunt."

"Ah, so you're thinking of sprinkling a little 'Hina magic' on the old world, huh?" he ribbed, with a twinkle of mischief. "Just don't get too wild, or you might kick-start a whole new renaissance."

"Isn't stirring the pot the whole point of what we do?"

Joshua raised an eyebrow, his smirk spreading. "For sure, just make sure your 'stirring' doesn't end up as a 'what the heck was Hina thinking?' moment."

I paused, "You ever think your obsession with my dirt tales and artifact adventures is just you dodging your own academic drama?" I threw back, my tone sharper, flipping our banter on its head with a gaze that cut through the chuckles.

"Dodging? Hina, really?"

"Oh, for real," I pressed on. "It's chill to eye someone else's grind, right? Pop off a snarky one-liner here, drop a sarcastic zinger there. But what about your own treasure hunts, Josh? You're like the dude chilling on the sidelines, quick to comment but not diving into the dirt or planting seeds."

The vibe around the table shifted. Derrek's chuckles tapered off, and Michael's eyes bounced between Joshua and me, tuning into the electric tension. His laid-back mask slipped. No smiles now. He peered over, eyes mixed with a dash of shock and maybe a slice of respect. "So, we're stripping off the gloves now, huh?"

"Nah, Josh," I responded, level and firm. "This ain't about dropping the niceties. It's about peeling off the banter mask and getting real with what we're up to, what we're crafting, who we're morphing into."

Joshua locked eyes with me, absorbing the weight of my words. Yet, there was no backing down in his stance—a silent, steadfast vibe I secretly respected.

"So, we're doing this, then?" He fixed me with a look that cut right to the core, suggesting there was more to him than the casual facade we were used to.

"I've been busy, Hina," he said, his voice lower. "My works in the realm of ideas and strategies, not something you can see or touch."

The arrival of our drinks provided a brief interlude, the clink of ice in Joshua's glass marking a momentary pause in our conversation.

"I'm a thinker, not a maker. My progress isn't always visible, but it's there."

His statement hung in the air. *Was I too focused on tangible achievements to value the quieter, less visible forms of progress? Hmmmm.*

"I don't parade my efforts, Hina," Joshua continued, a slightly different voice. The table fell silent.

"Sorry, Josh, guess I jumped the gun there."

Our gazes met. No hard feelings, but things felt different. Like we were just peeling back the layers, getting a real glimpse past our go-to labels.

Feeling the need to lighten the mood, Derrek nudged Michael. "Yo, Mike, that ancient ride of yours ever makes it to 'classic' status, or is it still a museum piece?"

But wait.
Look at Josh's face.
He is still smiling. But differently.
Is he okay?

Michael let out a louder voice, shaking his head. "That old clunker? Yeah, she's up and running. Not quite the 'classic' I bragged about, more like a relic. But hey, she does the job."

"Only Michael could turn a rusty sedan into a dream ride." Now was my time to join in.

"What's the word, Mike? Gonna strut that beauty in a vintage show anytime soon?"

"Nah, D," Michael shot back with a smile. "Give it another couple of decades, though, and we might have something."

Joshua, now caught up in the jest, chimed in. "Sure, and by then, we'll be zipping around in hover cars, leaving your 'classic' eating cosmic dust."

Now he is back!

The laughter that followed was a welcome shift, a collective exhale, as we all found solace in the easy, playful chatter.

That night was shaping up to be way more interesting than I'd bargained for. Just as the restaurant started winding down, guess who strolled in? Yep, in the middle of my chit-chat, I spotted him. Mr. All-Too-Familiar himself, Ben. He waltzed in like he owned the place, picking a spot where I couldn't miss him if I tried. With a cool flick of his hand, he got the waiter's attention, ordered something, and then bam! He's giving me that 'hey, long time no see' wave, as if we were buddies catching up, not exes with a four-year silent movie between us.

Chapter XVII:

We all got that one "Ex"

My relationship timeline wasn't crowded at all, to say the least. Only two significant names marked its short expanse. The first was a whimsical childhood entanglement with my neighbor, peppered with naïve promises of everlasting love and laughable wedding plans. But adolescence has a funny way of evolving one's emotions. Two years in our paths, predictably, diverged.

Then there was Ben. We'd met a year before university, instantly clicking like two puzzle pieces that never knew they were missing their counterparts. However, as is often the way of young love, the winds of change swept through, and we parted ways a couple of months before I began my academic journey. It wasn't a turbulent end, just a soft, mutual acceptance of evolving trajectories. Still, obviously there were some arguments during our time together. I find it hard to believe that any relationship in existence is without its hardships and disputes. If such a bond does exist, I suspect it is only a facade.

Ben was at it again, giving me the 'come hither' signal with more oomph this time. Michael, perched like an eagle, caught the silent movie unfolding, while Derrek and Joshua, clueless to the mini-drama, kept yapping away.

Taking a big gulp of courage, I slid my chair back, tossing out a quick "Be right back," and strutted over to Ben's table, feeling all eyes on me. Those few steps felt like a walk on a tightrope, teetering between a casual peck on the cheek or a straightforward hug. Before I could decide, Ben was up and at it, pulling me into a hug that was just right, not too close but not just-for-show either.

Settling into my seat, I met Ben's intense stare, that all-too-familiar half-smirk playing on his lips.

"Hina," he started, all smooth and composed, "looks like time's been your BFF."

"Yeah, time's the ultimate glow-up artist, isn't it?"

He gave me a once-over, a spark of mischief in his eyes. "Gotta say college life's done wonders. You've stepped up, more grown-up, more... damn, I'd say irresistible."

A blush crept up my cheeks, and I fired back, "Flattery won't get you far, Ben. I'm wise to your tricks now."

His laughter filled the space. "You're still sharp, still got that spark. I've missed that."

A brief silence fell, the background buzz of other diners and the distant clatter of dishes filling it. "So, what's up with the royal summoning?" I couldn't help but ask. My curiosity piqued.

Leaning closer, Ben's voice dropped a notch. "Can't a guy catch up with an old buddy? Especially one who's dazzling as ever?"

Meanwhile, back at the ranch, Derrek, trying to play it cool, nudged Michael and muttered, "Who's the dude?"

Michael, keeping it low-key, murmured back, "That's her ex."

Ben, still oozing that familiar charm mixed with a dash of seasoned weariness, leaned back, his eyes crinkling with a smile.

"So, how's life been kicking, pumpkin?" he teased, a playful lilt in his voice, bringing back a flood of memories.

I looked at him, a smile tugging at my lips. "Pumpkin? You're still into that? Some habits die hard, I see."

He smiled, a sound deep and resonant. "Some things are worth holding onto. You know, I've often wondered about us, where we went off course."

Caught now a bit off-guard, I replied, "Life happened, Ben. We grew, changed, wanted different things."

Ben gave his drink a thoughtful twirl. "Yeah, I get it. But you know, sometimes I miss how simple things were back then. Before we had all these big dreams and tough realities to deal with."

"Those were good times, for sure. But hey, we're on different tracks now, living our own stories, aren't we?"

"Yeah, that doesn't mean we can't take a little stroll down memory lane, right? Swap a few stories from the journeys we've been on?"

"Still the smooth talker, huh? But let's not wander too far off into nostalgia land."

He lifted his glass in a quiet cheer–a nod to the old days, our past selves, and this random meet-up. Leaning forward, elbow on the table, he looked genuinely curious. "So, Pumpkin, what's the big game plan post-grad? Still chasing the architecture or archeologist dream?"

'He does not even remember properly.'

I gave him a playful eye roll. "Well, for now, I'm rocking this part-time gig at the Sacramento Farmers Market. It's a bit of a whirlwind but super eye-opening." I hesitated, thinking about whether to spill the beans on my budding business idea.

Ben noticed my pause and gave me that 'I'm all ears' tilt of the head. "C'mon, out with it. I can see those wheels turning."

With a deep breath, ready to let the cat out of the bag, I said, "Okay, so I've been toying with this whole entrepreneurship thing."

"Really? That's gutsy. What's the game plan? What field are you diving into?"

"Well, given my current gig at the farmers' market, I'm thinking... a tech start-up focused on, let's say, gourmet - digital lettuce?"

'Golden rule number 4: Never share your business idea with your ex.'

"Digital lettuce? Of course. It's the next big thing. It should pair well with virtual tomatoes."

Matching his grin, I quipped, "You bet! Every leaf of lettuce comes with a dash of virtual reality flavor." We paused, our easy back-and-forth making the gap in our history feel like a tiny blip.

Ben's eyes took a little tour of the restaurant. "Pretty swanky compared to the market scene, huh? So, what's the scoop over there? How are the stalls and the daily grind?"

I welcomed the shift in our chat. "Oh, it's buzzing non-stop. The market's like its own little universe. Each day's a fresh episode in the saga."

Ben's gaze lingered on my friends, and his eyebrows arched rather inquisitively. "New crew?" he asked, nodding toward Michael, Derrek, and Joshua.

I caught his curious glance at my crew and flashed a sly grin. "Yep, those are my squad members from GSU. We're like the-team of academia," I added, a twinkle of mischief in my eye. Ben's gaze hung a bit on Michael, trying to crack the code of our interaction. That classic Ben move–the eyebrow quirk, the head tilt–he was silently stitching together tales, no direct questions needed.

Switching gears, Ben leaned closer, his voice dipping, "So, post-grad life, market hustle, startup dreams... what's the 411 on the love life front?" He tried to sound nonchalant, but I could hear the real query underneath. I chuckled lightly, knowing he was dancing around the subject.

"Life's a carnival, Ben. Full of things to explore and devour. As for the romance angle? Let's just say my hearts on its own little expedition." I kept it vague, savoring the enigma. Then, out of the blue, his hand reached out, fingers aiming for my cheek–a throwback gesture from our past. My first impulse was to dodge, but his expression made me hesitate. It was a soft, reminiscent touch. "That spark's still there, pumpkin," he whispered, his thumb gently grazing my skin.

I felt a catch in my throat. "Guess s..so"

"Come with me," he said, suddenly standing up. "There's something I want to show you."

Though really surprised, curiosity got the better of me, and I followed him outside, the hot night air a stark contrast to the cool of the restaurant. He led me to a spot that was dimly lit by a nearby streetlamp. From his pocket, he produced a small, intricately designed key chain. It was our old promise token—a trinket we had bought on our first trip together.

"Do you remember this?" he asked, holding it out.

I nodded, a rush of memories flooding in. "How could I forget?"

He chuckled, "I carry it around, a reminder of those good times." His sentimentality caught me off guard. In my memories, Ben was always the assertive, take-charge guy—someone who led with confidence and rarely showed vulnerability. This tender moment felt out of character, and a small voice inside my head questioned if this person was truly Ben or some facsimile, molded by time and circumstances.

He seemed to sense my internal deliberation. "Life changes us, Pumpkin," he said softly, his gaze holding mine firmly.

"Apparently so," I replied.

After a few more exchanged words, ones that blurred and felt inconsequential in the face of the emotions that dominated the night, I immediately felt the need to retreat back to more familiar territory. "I should get back," I murmured.

He nodded, a touch of sadness crossing his features. "It was good to see you," he said very sincerely. Returning to my table, the atmosphere had shifted palpably. Michael, Derrek, and Joshua all looked up, their expressions now different. I could feel a blend of curiosity and concern in the air as I slid back into my seat. The clatter of utensils and quiet conversations around the restaurant blended into the background, further highlighting the silence at our table.

Michael broke the silence first. "So, that was... Ben?" he asked, tone suggesting a mix of curiosity and surprise.

I nodded, still processing the brief, but intense, exchange I had just had with Ben. "Yes, that's him," I said, my voice laced with a mix of emotions.

Michael leaned back, his eyes studying me with both curiosity and concern. He had heard enough about Ben from my tales to sense the complexity of our past. Derrek, however, was relatively new to that saga and so was still piecing together the puzzle.

"Everything cool?" Derrek asked, his gaze alternating between me and Ben, who was now seated a distance away.

I let out a deep breath, my fingers tracing the rim of my wine glass. "Old chapters, they sometimes reopen and try to replay when you least expect them."

Derrek nodded, the corners of his mouth tilting downwards, a subtle hint of his sensitive nature. "I can only imagine," he said quietly.

"I appreciate that thought," I responded, the warmth in his tone offering a level of comfort.

"So, spill the beans. What's up with Ben popping up after all this time?" Michael dove in.

I paused, mulling over how much to share. "Maybe he's after some closure, or, you never know with Ben, anyway. ,"

I caught Derrek giving me the 'I'm here if you wanna talk' look, but he kept his curiosity in check, respecting my space.

Wanting to shake off the heaviness, I switched gears. "You know, I've heard legends about the desserts here. Who's ready to dive into some calorie chaos?"

Derrek's face lit up; all previous tension was forgotten. "Now you're talking my language! Bring the dessert!"

Chapter XVIII:

Brainstorming My Brainchild

That night had wrapped up on a positive note, and Ben had exited the scene, seemingly disappearing from the city, or at least from the circles I moved in. In the following days, I tried to maintain a rhythm between work and my typical routines. But that flicker of curiosity, the itch for something more, was incessant. ClipClock was a bust, but that wasn't going to deter me. I needed a fresh plan.

A few friends tossed the idea of drop shipping my way. I was no e-commerce whiz, but the way they laid the idea out for me was pretty straightforward. "Think of it as having a store online," they'd say. "You've got all these cool products on display, but here's the kicker—you don't actually keep them stocked. Nah, when an order pops in, you buy the item from someone else and have it sent straight to the customer's doorstep. You're the curator, not the keeper." A neat concept, I thought. No clutter, no stockpiling, just me as the savvy connector between buyer and seller.

Yet Abby, with her insatiable appetite for authenticity, popped that bubble. She told me her younger brother had been grinding away at this drop shipping gig for a while.

"The golden times for drop shipping have already flown by. That's his verdict," she shared. The ease of starting up was a siren song, but the actual sailing, according to him, was against big tides of saturation and fierce competition.

Her comment left me wondering where I could find shelter from the stormy sea of technology. Where was the place for my 'more'? Although my everyday routine kept calling, the spark of curiosity deep within me refused to be snuffed out. Still, I took the plunge, dipping into my savings. The first sizable dent I made was a whopping $700 and then more on purchasing analytical data. I bought me new insights into the past two years of several states online shopping habits. The most bought items, the least touched, and everything in between. Did I wholeheartedly trust these numbers? Not really. There always was a sneaky thought that maybe they were just numbers cooked up in some data factory. Still, I chose to believe the stats were close to the truth—mostly to keep my sanity intact.

After nearly a week of sifting, sorting, and (let's be real) squinting at those stats, I managed to trim them down to three potential goldmines: makeup, electronics, and (would you believe?) women's lingerie. Now, by the usual logic, makeup or electronics should've been the go-to. Their sales were soaring way beyond everything else. But here's where things got really intriguing. Lingerie, while not the big shot in the room, had started picking up its pace. In just the last five months, its sales trajectory has gone from a lazy stroll to a confident jog.

That change is what caught my eye. Instead of going with the obvious giants, this underdog was showing some promise. It whispered growth and hinted at untapped potential. With a mixture of intuition and a dash of daring, I decided, "Why not? Let's give this lingerie game a whirl."

Starting something new can always feel a lot like diving into a book that has no cover—full of potential stories, yet uncertain where they'll all lead. The early chapters? Always the most challenging, but also equally defining. You know, with just this dream growing in my head, there wasn't exactly a successful blueprint around me to emulate, especially not in the lingerie game I was diving into now. At first, it was just me, myself, and my endless doubts. But soon enough, Mikey swooped in, becoming my unofficial co-pilot, guiding me through every hiccup and hurdle. What was square one? Lingerie. Yeah, those delicate, mood-reflecting pieces we often take for granted. There's always a certain dance between the practical 'wear and tear' brigade and those who live for the luxe, the lace, the ooh-la-la. I was caught in that tango, trying to cater to both worlds. But in the end? Style took the crown.

I didn't just want to play the buy-and-sell game. Simply importing cheap goodies and jacking up their prices. That wasn't me. It might work for many, buying low from places like China and selling high here, but I wanted my personal stamp, my essence on whatever I sold. It wasn't about just reselling; it was about reshaping, adding my own touch. Making every piece a little more... Hina. While the allure of creating something entirely from scratch tempted me, the practicalities of sewing and crafting a whole lingerie line were financially daunting. The price of starting fresh would drain my savings and funds, which wasn't an option. There was no way I was going to approach my mom for a loan either. That would be like admitting defeat, a white flag that said that I couldn't carve my own path. I was resolute. Whatever I did would be within my own means—combining my earnings, my modest savings, and sheer willpower.

The most viable solution? Well, Mikey (the ever-pragmatic brain) pitched the idea of vintage revamping. Instead of starting anew, why not breathe life into a few pre-loved pieces? The plan was to hunt down vintage lingerie, give them a thorough cleaning, and then infuse them with my signature touch. This could mean adding logos, restructuring, or even dismantling and re-sewing some pieces to create an entirely new look.

With determination now in tow, I scoured various websites and found two prime spots in California to source from. As time passed, my network expanded, and I began importing from other states too. At that point, my finances had to be meticulously mapped out. About 35% of my savings were earmarked for essentials, like bills and rent, covering the next half a year. Another 20% was for my personal expenses—think food, transportation, and the occasional treat. The remaining 45% was my business pot, divided between procuring items and marketing them. Any salary I'd receive in the coming months, I'd put straight back into this budding venture.

I vividly recall my very first purchase—a cool $890. A mix of camisoles, bralettes, and bustiers. It was the beginning of what I hoped would be a successful endeavor. My vision for my fashion line was apparent from the very beginning. I'm a big fan of the show 'Downton Abbey' and gravitated towards its gracious charm, the conversations, the manners, but most of all, the fabulous outfits. A bit of investigation revealed that the series was heavily influenced by the Edwardian era—a time celebrated for its superior style.

Making something that combined the traditional Edwardian grandeur with a modern flair was a tricky task. My job was made even harder due to time constraints, but when I finally achieved the perfect balance between classic and contemporary, it was worth all my effort. The end product spoke for itself.

Presenting everything to Mikey and Dan got reactions that were, well, mixed. "It looks like something women in their 30s or 40s would be all over!" they exclaimed. While the praise was heartening, my dream was a broader appeal. True, making Edwardian elegance palatable to a younger, more modern audience wasn't a walk in the park. But then again, when was fashion ever easy?

In a world where most shy away from revealing the true figures behind their finances, I'm choosing to lay my cards on the table. While many keep their savings history close to their chest, in this capitalist era where transparency meets personal privacy, I'm taking the road less traveled, and revealing my income here. So, let's break from the norm: I'll share exactly how much I had and what I started with. When I scooped up my first collection of camisoles, my savings account boasted a decent $11,200. After setting aside 55% for the essentials and my miscellaneous expenses, a tidy sum of $5,040 remained, not including my part-time earnings from the farmers' market.

Web creation was a gray area for me. I'd initially feared that establishing a website would be a pricey affair. To my relief, I stumbled upon these pre-built e-commerce platforms that were budget friendly. I mean, who fusses over a tailor-made site when the products speak volumes, right? So, without further ado, I connected with this dynamic duo from India via an online freelance forum. They whipped up a fantastic, ready-to-use e-commerce site for a mere $550. How's that for a bargain? seemed okay. Navigating the marketing world was like trekking through uncharted territory for me. I had a flair for sales, a knack for winning a customer over with words. But devising a grand plan to sell products? That was uncharted territory. This is where Mikey stepped up to the plate.

He swiftly pointed out, "In today's digital age, sometimes the old-school methods make a bigger splash because they stand out." He suggested a mix of tangible marketing—think posters and flyers scattered across Sacramento—with a dash of digital outreach. His reasoning? Reviving the 'forgotten' grabs the attention motif. I decided to up my stock, purchasing four more bras, which set me back $240. The remaining funds? Poured straight into this blended marketing plan. So, there I was, darting through J Street, Capitol Avenue, N Street, 15th Street, and even the Garden Highway, arms full of flyers and posters showcasing my revamped bras and all other, all boldly marked with: 'Belle Epoch Envy - Pre-order Now!'. And before you bombard me with questions about the name, save it. I have no plans of dishing out its backstory. Let's just say it's up to the customers to vibe with it or not. And so, just like that, Belle Epoch Envy took its first breath.

Now, I could dive deep into every tiny detail, but let's fast forward a bit. The initial two weeks? Radio silence. But just when I thought maybe Sacramento wasn't ready for my vintage-meets-modern blend, the emails started trickling in. Yep, good ol' emails. I guess the charm of physical flyers hasn't faded just yet. My first two orders? Mailed out with a mix of excitement and anxiety. And by the time the last piece of that collection found a new home, which was in just under twenty days, we were rolling in enough profit to stock up and gear up for round two.

Mikey, being the strategist he always was, piped in with some golden advice: "Stay in touch with those who've already bought from you, Hina. Maybe give them a little extra off on their next purchase or throw in a thank-you note. Makes them feel special, ya'know? Ups our chances of them coming back." And just like that, the plan for retaining our budding clientele was set.

Racing against time on Belle Epoch Envy, I barely noticed Mikey's shift from his binge watching the marathon until his offhand comment caught my ear. "Kinda out there, isn't it? You dodging the whole dating game like it's a sport?" he pondered.

"Mikey?" I raised an eyebrow, a mix of amusement and surprise flickering in my gaze.

"Just saying," he quickly added, meeting my eyes. "Everyone's balancing their love lives with their hustle, but you? You're all in on this biz like it's your one true love."

I couldn't help but laugh. "Oh, knock it off," I retorted, brushing off the hint of truth in his words. "Been there, done that with the whole romance gig, weirdo."

He leaned back, an arm casually slung over the back of the sofa as he continued, "You see Lilly? One could assume she's not into relationships or doesn't care about that sort of thing, but she's got quite the radar for it. Did you hear? Someone sent her a massive bouquet just the other day."

I raised an eyebrow, a grin playing on my lips. "Big deal. Flowers don't mean a thing."

"Speaking of the heart stuff, what's the scoop with Derrek?"

My fingers stalled mid-air; my attention now fully snagged. "Derrek? What about him?"

"Don't play coy. That poem declaration of his was hmmm, ya know... Stories like that don't just vanish. You think a guy spills his guts and then just shrugs off a 'let's be pals'?"

With a sigh that carried a mix of annoyance and resignation, I responded, "Look, Mikey, Derrek and I have been just friends for ages now. It's been chill, no drama."

"Speaking of blasts from the past... Ben ever crosses your mind?"

I almost snapped a quick 'nope' but decided to take a beat. "Sure, some memories pop up now and then. Doesn't mean I'm hung up on the guy."

Mikey just laughed, clearly enjoying the banter before smoothly changing the topic. The day went on and the other days followed. The same tone. The same mood. The same spirit.

Sacramento's end-of-summer vibe was bustling, not quiet at all. Even with the students gone, the tourists were out in force, making the city buzz with energy. Juggling new stock and flyer handouts, I was busier than any final week back at college.

Then, one afternoon, while deep in my flyer-distributing zone, I spotted Brad and Adrianna strolling by, all cozy and hand-holdy. Given our past, my gut reaction was to bolt, to avoid any chance of awkward encounters. But as they got closer, I figured, why not embrace the moment? I straightened up, slipped back into my marketeer mode, and greeted them with a pitch. "Hey there! Check out the latest trend in lingerie. Might catch your fancy!" I said, waving a flyer at Adrianna, diving back into the hustle with a newfound sense of daring.

Brad greeted me with a mix of surprise and warmth. "Hina? Wow, didn't expect to see you hustling flyers. What's this about?"

I flashed a grin back. "Life's full of surprises, Brad. Yep, I'm out here repping my own brand now."

Adrianna, curiosity piqued, snagged a flyer. "These designs are pretty cool. I'm gonna check this out." Brad, clueless about our history, started, "Adrianna, meet Hina—"

We shot each other a look, a silent pact to keep it smooth. "Pleasure to meet you," we chimed in unison, putting on a show for Brad.

"I'm dropping a fresh collection soon. Keep an eye out. And Brad, catch you around," I said, diving back into my promo groove.

Brad shot me a playful look. "Hit me up when you start doing men's lines, yeah? I might want in." With a friendly nod, they strolled off, leaving me to my bustling afternoon.

These two...
You will be the last person to hear my success, Brad.

The day was still bright when I found myself frantically hitting Derrek's digits. It took a solid three days and a bunch of missed calls before I finally got through. "Dude, where've you been? I've been on your tail trying to catch you!" I fired off, my words tinged with a hint of worry.

Derrek sounded like he was caught off guard. "Oh, uh, just some family stuff," he answered, sounding a bit off-key. Family stuff?

Derrek's not the type to bring up home life. "Everything is cool on your end?" I pressed; curiosity piqued.

He hesitated, then let out a long sigh. "Yeah, sort of... nothing to write home about." There was a heavy pause, the air thick with unspoken thoughts.

"You're sounding off, dude. But hey, no pressure. Wanna hit up our old haunt tonight, clear the air?"

His response threw me for a loop. "Can't swing it tonight," he said, totally unlike him. We were those 'drop everything and meet' kind of friends. This shift had my mind racing—was something up?

On my second go, he agreed to meet me the next day at our usual spot. This change in pattern had me all kinds of curious. What was going on with Derrek?

Chapter XIX:

Derrek Samfield

So, there we were, ensconced in our usual café nook, with Derrek looking like he was about to share the secret recipe for his grandmother's famous lasagna—but it was no recipe he then shared. "It's my dad," he started, the words trickling out like molasses. "This farm saga isn't about just turning dirt over. It's about him, his dreams, and this old-world grip he has on reality. It's all slipping away."

He took a breath. One of those deep ones that you know is preparing for producing impact. "That farm was less 'Green Acres' and more 'Alcatraz' for me. My Dad sees it as this shrine to tradition, where sweat equals success. But me? I felt like a square peg that was being rammed into a round hole every time I stepped into those fields."

A chuckle escaped him, but it was the kind laced with more sadness than humor. "Leaving? Well, it was not that easy. It was like declaring independence from a kingdom where I never asked to be royalty. But you know what was really weird? With each step away, I felt like I was leaving bits of myself behind, so of like breadcrumbs, except the birds were snatching them up before I could turn back."

'He's learned to talk like me, hmmm,' I thought to myself.

His eyes met mine, carrying a storm of emotions, a testament to the inner turmoil swirling in him. "It's a real pickle, Hina. There I was, caught between wanting to plant my feet in new soil and feeling this tug, this relentless yank on my heartstrings that were pulling me back to a place that is as familiar as it is stifling."

As he unfolded his tale, layer by layer, I saw Derrek in a new light. He was not just the jovial guy who could spin a yarn or crack a joke, but someone grappling with the real stuff of life — identity, family, and the messy, tangled web of belonging and seeking change.

He looked up, his eyes meeting mine, filled with a raw intensity.

"The farm's been struggling, bad weather, failed crops, mounting debts. It's like everything that could go wrong has gone wrong. Dad's not getting any younger, and Jake got a family of his own now. Matt was stuck in the middle, just like he always was. I want to help, I really do. But going back there makes me feel like I'm betraying myself, reopening wounds that never fully healed. It's complicated, especially now that I'm going to start working full time this fall. Going back there would mean quitting my job even before I started it."

Now there is the real Derrek.

"That podcast thingy?" I spoke.

"That right"

"Oh well," and I pressed a finger on my chin.

Farm.
Family.
Brothers.
Conflict.

Indeed, there it was. Derrek's family drama unfolding like a farm soap opera right in front of me, the kind where brothers grumble and dads dictate with an iron fist—or in this case, an iron tractor. It was like watching a macho standoff, only with more cows and less gunfire. Derrek's tale made it clear to me. His Dad was the farm's unofficial emperor, his word was law, and his brothers just pawns in the great ongoing agricultural chess game.

The youngest brother, Matt? He was in Switzerland, neutral territory in the family feud. But the eldest? Oh boy, he was the family's version of Mount Vesuvius, ready and eager to erupt at the slightest provocation. When Derrek packed his bags, big bro didn't just wave goodbye. He practically branded him a deserter, hurling the term 'traitor' like it was going out of style and telling him not to let the barn door hit him on the way out.

Then there was Derrek, right here, stuck between a rock and a hard place—or more accurately, a plow and a desk job. The guy was a mess. He was wrestling with guilt, and what I had to guess was a hefty dose of existential dread.

So, what's a friend to do? Derrel needed advice, something to buoy his spirits or at least distract him from the familial typhoon he'd just sidestepped. I had to come up with something and quickly, a nugget of wisdom or a slapstick joke, anything to ease that furrowed brow and give him a sliver of hope that told him that "Yes, you can run from the farm, but hey, the farm doesn't have to run after you."

Back at the café, the plot thickened further over carrot pie, which I ordered in a moment of culinary optimism. Derrek, on the other hand, was too wrapped up in his dilemma to entertain any idea of dessert.

"So, you've got this epic job on the horizon, student loans shadowing your every move, and now a family farm saga, too? (I was already getting badly beaten up by student's loans)" I summed at all up, trying to keep the mood light and as optimistic as I could, "You're sure a magnet for life's little ironies."

He chuckled weakly. "Something like that. Choosing between the job and the farm feels like I'm deciding between getting a root canal or having a wisdom tooth pulled."

Nodding, I forked a piece of the pie, its carroty essence wafting up strongly. "Tough call. But hey, life's not just about choosing between two unappealing options. It's about finding a third one, one hidden behind the carrot... or in this case, in the pie."

Derrek raised an eyebrow. "So, you're saying that my life's a pie now?"

"Exactly," I said with a grin. "And every pie has layers. Your job and the farm, they're just ingredients in the bigger picture. What if there's a way you can mix them up, maybe create a new recipe for success?"

He leaned in, his curiosity clearly piqued despite his skepticism. "I'm listening, but I'm not promising. I'll taste test your metaphorical pie."

"Fair enough. Let's say this café sources its carrots from a farm. Your family's farm deals in dairy and potatoes. Right? What if you could find a local business that needs exactly what your farm produces? You can then cut out the middleman and streamline the process."

Derrek twirled a spoon absentmindedly. "So, my grand career plan then is to become a potato peddler?"

"Not just any peddler," I countered. "A strategic one. Think of the task as direct farm-to-table marketing. You'd be surprised how many businesses value that kind of authenticity these days."

We decided it was time for a change of scenery, so we kicked off the process. We swiftly exited and made a beeline for the nearest grocery store, aiming to pick up some healthier choices and do a bit of quick shopping. Now we were chatting and browsing in the grocery store.

He smirked, shaking his head. "By the way, you have a way of simplifying things that makes me wonder why I'm not a millionaire yet."

"Well, not everyone's a carrot pie expert," I joked, nibbling on the pie still in my hand after we left the cafe. "But hey, maybe your farming smarts and fresh job skills could mix as well as... carrots in a pie."

"We've been out of that cafe for a while, and you're still hung up on that carrot pie, huh? Alright, I'll mull it over. But just so you know, if I end up peddling potatoes on the street, you're the one I'm pointing fingers at."

"Deal," I said, raising my fork in a salute. "Just remember, every great idea starts somewhere. And sometimes, it's hiding in the most unexpected places–like a conversation over carrot pie."

He stopped, a packet of pasta in his hand, and looked at me. "But Hina, it's not just about selling a few extra crates of potatoes.

It's about the sustainability of the whole farm. The legacy. It's... complex."

The grocery store was almost full of consumers, and I wanted to escape the place quickly.

I nodded, placed a jar of pickles into my basket, then turned to him with a reassuring smile. "Understood, Captain Farmville. But hey, even the most successful empires had to pivot sometimes. Rome wasn't built in a day, and it certainly didn't thrive by sticking to the same old gladiator games."

"Pivoting, eh? Maybe I should introduce Dad to that concept. Probably go over as well as a tractor dancing in a ballet."

"As long as you don't start pirouetting in the fields, you'll be fine."

The conversation shifted as we neared the checkout, a casual segues into personal territory. "So, any word from her?" I probed, a hint of mischief now in my tone.

He sighed. The can of beans in his hand was now more a prop than a grocery item. "Silence. Radio silence. Either they've bonded over their shared love of silent treatments, or they're plotting my intervention."

"Let's hope it's the former," I replied, trying to keep the mood light, as we unloaded our eclectic selection of items onto the conveyor belt.

That's when the familiar, inescapable voice of my mother cut through the air. It made me freeze mid-motion. "Hina? What a coincidence!" There she was, the matriarch herself, with Linda in tow, right behind us in the checkout line.

Chapter XX: Random Encounter #14

My mom's here,
Oh no.
No.

My brain did a quick calculation of my possibilities — escape routes (none), potential excuses (plenty but flimsy), and the likelihood of a prolonged conversation (extremely high). I plastered on my best 'surprised but delighted' face:

"*Mom! Linda! Fancy seeing you here among the aisles of destiny.*" I thought about saying it out loud.

But then I decided against that route. So, here is what I did.

"Mom? What... are you doing here...?"

Linda, always the cheerful one, smiled even bigger and brighter, but by now I had no idea who she really was.

"Just embracing the local charm, Bunny," Mom replied, her eyes glinting with that special blend of mischief and maternal pride as she glanced at Derrek, who suddenly seemed extremely interested in the nutrition label of a cereal box.

Sacramento wasn't exactly her usual haunt. "Since when are you the roaming project type, Mom?" I probed; my curiosity now piqued.

She laughed, the sound light and airy, like a melody that somehow fit perfectly in the grocery store's symphony of beeps and chatter. "Life's a project, Sweety. And I'm just here, adding a bit of Mom-flair to Sacramento."

Introductions were made, and Linda's handshake was warm, her enthusiasm genuine. "I've heard so much about you, Hina!" she exclaimed." I couldn't help but wonder what version of my life had been serialized for her entertainment.

Mom's interjection pulled me back. "Linda's the one who's been making all the noise at Radio Silence. Quite the change from her reporting days. Right?"

Radio Silence... the name sparked a vague memory, but that memory was lost in the sea of surprise at finding my mother here, of all places.

Her next comment, though, was pure Mom. "So, this European escapade of yours—is it on pause? These groceries scream 'homebody,' not 'world traveler.'"

Now caught off guard, I fumbled for words. "It's not like that, Mom. Just... exploring local delights!" I said, throwing a lifeline glance at Derrek, who was now intently inspecting a box of tea as if it held the secrets of the universe.

"Oh, the sagas of young love!" she exclaimed, winking at Derrek, who only offered a sheepish grin in return. My cheeks flamed with embarrassment. How could she put me on the spot like this in front of... everyone?

"Mom, it's just grocery shopping."

She just chuckled. "Hina, dear, every good story has a bit of mystery and misunderstanding, just like this one does." Then she winked at me. She switched gears and told a light-hearted tale of getting lost with Linda in Bogotá, turning their confusion into a mini adventure. Linda's laughter confirmed it had been a trip to remember.

"But let's get back to us," Mom said, returning to her favorite subject—me and Derrek. "Sometimes, a little detour does lead to the best surprises," she hinted with a playful sly nudge.

I felt my face go warm. "Mom, we're just friends," I insisted, hoping she'd drop the matchmaking act.

But she wasn't convinced. "Oh, I know, I know. Just friends," she said.

"Really, Mrs. Strubel," Derrek added, "There's nothing to tell."

But Mom was having none of it. "I'm just saying, sometimes friends turn into something more. It's all part of life's fun. Right?"

Trying to turn the tables, I quipped, "How's your love life, Mom? Any new chapters?"

She laughed, not missing a beat.

"Love is like a painting, darling. Sometimes you need a few drafts before you get it right."

"And as for you two," she said, giving us a sly knowing look, "Maybe you two are still sketching out your story."

Even in the middle of a grocery store, Mom could make any conversation feel like a scene from a sitcom. It was embarrassing, but also kind of sweet in its own, Strubel-family way.

I rolled my eyes. "That's a stretch, even for you, Mom."

"Oh, but life is the grandest canvas of all, Hina," Amna continued, her voice laced with a lot of life experience. "And it's filled with more shades and colors than you might think. Including those you're not so eager to paint with right away or ever."

Derrek, who had been quietly observing our exchange, now wore an amused smile, clearly entertained by our ongoing banter.

"Life's too short for monochrome, Mom," I shot back.

"Variety, my dear, is the spice of life. And sometimes, the most surprising blends do create the most beautiful pictures. Right Linda?"

She robotically nodded in agreement.

Her gaze flitted to Derrek again, then back to me, her message clear, but unspoken. Amna had a way of making her point without ever saying it directly. Her knack was both frustrating and fascinating.

"Okay, Picasso, let's just stick to the grocery list for now," I said, attempting to bring the conversation back to much safer territory.

I finished our conversation without adding more embarrassment than I already had felt, and Derrek could not help but laugh, even if he did not appear to be laughing on the outside. I could tell he found it all hilarious. My mother was my friendly nemesis, especially when it came to our exchanges of wit and sarcasm. No matter how hard I tried, however, I never quite matched her sharpness. She was always a step or two ahead. Despite this advantage, we still shared a close bond, marked by special days at home and family celebrations. Yet in public, it was always still a playful battle of words between us. Even now, I'm puzzled about why she was in that particular Mart in Sacramento that day. She lived in a different city and usually traveled to other states for work. However, I rarely pried into her job details. Working in the media sector is exhausting, so I figured she needed a break from talking shop whenever she was with family.

****

Skipping all the boring bits, let's now dive further into Derrek's little adventure. Post our chat, he turned into a sort of detective, probing into the farm's mysteries over the phone with Matt as his trusty sidekick. They were like the dynamic duo of agriculture, minus the capes.

With newfound knowledge about their less-than-popular goat milk, Derrek hit the local scene. Picture him, post-work, marching from one cheesemaker to another, pitching his heart out. And there I was too, in my own little world, spreading the word about my business with the same zeal, although with flyers, not cheese.

Despite his hustle, however, Derrek's campaign hit a wall. No bites, no buyers—just a whole lot of "thanks, but no thanks." Frustration was an understatement, but then an unexpected twist happened. Matt, the youngest of the Samfield brothers, watched Derrek's attempts and got inspired. Taking the baton, he ran with it, and lo-and-behold, he struck gold, breathing new life into the farm's sales. Matt became the family hero, but Derrek found comfort in being the unsung inspiration. A quiet victory, but still a victory, nonetheless. As for me? Life was a whirlwind of work, plans, and a looming European trip. Lilly's romantic escapades, however, nearly slipped by me. She snagged a guy from Arizona who had a flair for grand gestures—flowers, a stunning Furisode dress from Japan, the works. Before we knew it, they were the talk of the town, leaving me wondering.

"When did all this happen?"

****

Just four days before my European escapade, I found myself meeting Derrek again near our old campus haunt. In my hands was a bundle of documents, neatly packaged with a note on top that read, "Federal Wiretap Act (18 U.S.C. § 2511)." Handing them over to him, I offered a piece of advice. "Check out the highlighted sections. They might pique up some interesting motivation."

Derrek scanned the note, his expression a mix of curiosity and apprehension. "It's not just about the law, Hina. It's... it's been a long time, hasn't it? There's no case here!"

Checking my watch, I felt the tick-tock pressing on me, with Europe just around the corner. "Patience is key in the hunt for... well, anything worthwhile," I shouted back at Derrek, now quickly making my way to my mom's car. In my haste, my foot found a rogue boulder. A near-tumble ensued, a little dance of almost-falling that I'm sure looked as graceful as a giraffe on ice. But, hey, I recovered with a quick hop and a skip, and landed in the safety of the car. No time for stumbles when adventure awaited me. I could just barely make out his voice in the distance.

"You've never even hunted in your life!!" I left, and my mind started to swirl with the many things I still had to do. I was filled with anticipation about the path ahead of me and the new sights that lay in wait for me to see and love.

Chapter XXI:

Friends in Europe

My friends are the real MVPs, not just for the Europe plane tickets, but for their endless empathy and sharing spirit. I was buzzing with excitement about our Munich to Bremen express—think fairy tales, Glühwein, and cobblestone charm, all packed into a quick two-day adventure.

Then there was Lilly's love life subplot. Suddenly, she was pondering if jetting off to Europe is wise without her new beau. We had to nudge her back to reality: "Girl, it's a BFF extravaganza, not a couple's retreat!" Our motto? Boyfriends can sit home and wait.

Amsterdam surprised me; it's not just a party hub; it has a chill vibe too. Except for Michael, who decided to explore the city's psychedelic offerings, leaving me to navigate his shroom-induced giggle fits. It was a wild ride, but it ended up being more amusing than alarming.

Next stop: Brussels. Playing pretend politician amidst that city's grandeur was a quirky highlight for me. Then, Bruges—with its enchanting, old-world vibe—completely stole my heart. I totally saw myself embracing the café life there, sipping coffee, and soaking in the quaintness everywhere.

Room arrangements? I went solo while the rest of us split up. Bruges' café culture actually had me daydreaming about a permanent move until reality chimed in—my business back home needed me.

Speaking of business, I tried to dodge any Belle Epoch Envy hiccups by prepping my customers for my absence. I thought I'd outsmarted any potential issues, but nope—some unexpected orders and impatient customers proved me wrong. Lesson learned: entrepreneurship doesn't pause in European getaways. It was time to plan my 'Fix Everything' operation once I was stateside.

So, that's the gist of my Euro trip—a mix of friend shenanigans, unexpected business lessons, and a whole lot of daydreaming about café life in Bruges.

****

Our last day in Bruges? We were in total adventure mode–we rented a kayak and did the whole canal tour thing. Seriously, the canals in Bruges are something else. Every twist and turn had me wondering if I could stay there forever. Paddling through those storybook waterways was like seeing the city through a wonderful magical lens.

Our grand itinerary was all thanks to Abby and Michael's planning. They decided to skip France (a bit of a bummer, I know), and the next thing we knew, we were on a train to Switzerland. Hello Zurich! We hung out there for a couple of days, soaking up all the great Swiss vibes.

Then, it was Italy's turn for five days–yep, another train ride. Milan was up first, and let me tell you, that city is as fabulous as they say. We even made a side trip to Lake Maggiore and Bergamo. Lake Maggiore? That came with its own drama.

First things first, though. We landed in Milan and got settled. Then, in true tourist style, Abby had us hitting every shopping street in sight. But when supper time rolled around, it was just me, Abby, and Lilly. Michael was MIA. We were low-key freaking out. I mean, two hours of radio silence in a foreign city. Not cool. Then he showed up, out of the blue, with this random blonde guy in tow. They sat with us and talked as if nothing had occurred.

They plopped down at our table and acted like Michael's vanishing act was no big deal. Lilly? Oh, she wasn't having any of it. Not at all. You might look at her and think 'delicate flower,' with her gentle voice and angelic vibe, but trust me, she has a spine of steel.

"Guess who I ran into?" Michael beamed, practically radiating with excitement.

"Michael, this isn't a game. We're in a new city, and you just go off and disappear?"

His smile wobbled a bit. "It was all spontaneous, you know? We got caught up and... well, time slipped away."

She softened, but stayed firm. "Send a text, Michael. It's not rocket science. We were worried sick."

The stranger with Michael looked like he just wished he could vanish. Lilly wasn't loud, but her message was crystal clear.

He attempted a charm offensive. "Totally my bad. I'll ping you next time, cross my heart."

Lilly wasn't quite ready to drop the curtain on this act. Not yet. "Promises are good, Michael, but let's aim for a bit more... awareness perhaps? It's just a quick text."

"What can I say? Bumping into old pals is kind of my thing. Though, I do admit, it doesn't always work out for the best."

Lilly wasn't buying it. "It's less 'superpower' and more 'super hassle.' You better remember that we're a team here."

After a long pause, Michael got the message. "Understood, Captain. I'll keep the lines open next time."

The tension had eased, and the mysterious stranger now piped up, his accent adding a new flavor to the mix. "Really sorry for the mix-up. Didn't mean to stir the pot in your group." So, just like that, with a sprinkle of humor and a dash of humility, the conversation found its way back to lighter territory.

Abby, with her usual quick wit, declared, "I think the mix-up is all Michael's handiwork." Then, looking at Michael, she teased, "Aren't you going to introduce your friend?"

Although slightly defensive, he responded, "I was just about to before the interrogation squad jumped in. Everyone, this is Mattias."

We all chimed in with a nicely synchronized "Hi Mattias." It seemed to catch him off guard. He nodded, a shy smile flickering across his face, as he glanced at Michael.

Lilly, always the inquisitive one, asked, "Are you from Italy?"

Mattias shook his head. "No, I am from California."

"What?"

I couldn't help but burst out laughing. Poor Lilly completely missed the mark with her guess.

"What? I am so sorry," she stammered.

"Nah, it's cool," "I get that a lot—people say I've got an overseas accent."

"But there's more to him than just—" Mikey started to chip in but got cut off by Abby and Lilly yelling in unison, "Shut up!"

"So, you live around here or just studying?" I tried to steer the conversation.

"No, no, I'm just touring with my brother," he explained.

"I think we might stay a bit longer," Abby added.

As we talked about heading to Lake Maggiore and the rest of our trip plans, Mattias seemed a bit bashful, clearly flirting with Mikey, though it was pretty mutual. Before we could pick out a good wine from the menu, a loud, almost screaming voice caught us off guard:

"Aha, so that's where you are!"

I jumped; the sudden shout was unexpected. But the real surprise was seeing who it was.

"JOSHUA?" Abby yelled.

I was checking out the menu when Joshua strutted in, and I just froze, the menu in hand.

"Thought I was just frying under the Californian sun? Ha-ha, Hina, couldn't miss the chance to see your mishaps here in Italy."

"It's more like Michael's mishaps," Abby chimed in.

"Hey, I don't—okay, wait a sec," I interrupted, then asked, "So, you're traveling too, Josh?"

"Yep, me and my brother," he confirmed with a nod.

"Your brother?" Abby and I exclaimed at the same time.

And, sure enough, Joshua gestured towards Mattias. We knew Joshua had a brother, but we'd never met him, and we definitely didn't know Mattias was his brother. Seriously? They don't even look alike. Plus, Mattias is a total math whiz—a genius, really—and Joshua couldn't be further from anything science-related.

It turned out Michael had been in touch with Joshua, and they'd planned for him to meet up with us here in Italy, along with his brother. And as a bonus, it seemed Michael had set himself up to flirt with Mattias, which I wasn't too happy about. I mean, I believe in honesty....

After swapping stories and sharing some laughs, I was ready to head back to the hotel, but the group insisted on dragging me to a karaoke bar. On the way, I managed to pull Michael aside for a quick, quiet conversation away from the others.

"So, what's up with Dan?"

He just flashed that grin of his. "Dan? Oh, we're still a thing. Why do you ask?"

"So, you guys are still together?"

"Absolutely. He's expecting a souvenir from here."

His answer left me a bit unsettled. 'Cheating isn't a joke,' I said, confronting him. "Are you seriously hitting on Mattias, Joshua's brother? I mean, not that it matters but, something else does. " As soon as I said it, I second-guessed myself.

'Maybe they're in an open relationship, and I'm overreacting.'

Michael just shrugged off my question with a laugh and a cheeky comment before heading back to our friends in front. He seemed to shake off any possible unease with a bit of liquid courage, but his response had got me thinking.

'Even relationships that look solid have their hidden troubles.' With friends like Mikey, we tend to overlook things that we wouldn't tolerate elsewhere with others.

Imagine if we were the ones cheated on, or if it was a movie plot—we'd be outraged at such characters, I thought. It struck me as a curious double standard, but I didn't let it cloud my mood.

We sang, danced, and drank until the night was ours. Abby nearly got kicked out of the karaoke bar after a spat with the security guard; as she stormed out, I caught him muttering, "That American and her stupid ego." But tensions eased, and before we knew it, he was back with us, singing along.

The next day, we dragged our headaches to the train station and waited for our train. As I settled into my seat, I let my thoughts drift back to the previous day's events—the conversations, the little dramas. Life, much like our trip, was peppered with unexpected twists. Yet, each twist only seemed to heighten the thrill of the journey.

Cheating,
Love story,
Laughter,

Travel,
Joy, what else?
No, not cheating!
I closed my eyes and stretched. I had a long train ride ahead of me!

Chapter XXII:

Lake Maggiore

Imagine yourself at Lake Maggiore. Guys, it's. not your average lake, but a nature-crafted masterpiece, nestled between the Italian and Swiss Alps. It's like Mother Nature got extra creative, blessing the lake with blues so vibrant they'd give the sky a run for its money.

There, I stumbled upon this quirky story about Maggiore. Locals say the lake's got moods - it's chilly in the morning, playful by noon, and gets all mysterious by evening. Like it's showing off or something.

There are towns around the lake, and each one's got its own charm. Stresa's like a page from a vintage novel, while Ascona's the artsy kid, all colorful and full of stories.

But wait, the Borromean Islands steal the show. They're like little paradise chunks floating on the lake. Isola Bella? It's so stunning you half expect a Disney princess to pop out and start singing.

One evening, this old fisherman tells me, if you're lucky, the lake whispers at night. Not with words, but echoes from the past - secret lovers, poets getting inspired, travelers finding peace and more.

So, there I was, sitting by the lake one such night, watching the water gently lap against the shore, and I couldn't help but feel there's more to Maggiore than meet the eye. It's like the lake knows all the secrets of the ages, and if you're quiet enough, patient enough, it just might share a whisper about it all with you.

This lake's got stories, the kind that make you want to lean closely and listen intently.

Way back, centuries ago, Lake Maggiore was the summer hotspot for the rich and royal. Imagine lavish parties on private boats, with dukes and duchesses sipping fancy wine under the stars. But that's where it gets interesting — there were rumors, whispers really, of a hidden treasure sunk deep in the lake.

Legend has it that a wealthy duke, let's call him Duke Enrico, had a thing for shiny stuff. Gold jewels, you name it. But then, there was also drama! A rival family, jealous of Enrico's bling, planned to raid his castle. So, what does our duke do? He loads all his treasure onto his fanciest boat and sails into the night.

But here's the twist — a storm hits. A massive one. The boat goes down, taking all of Enrico's treasure with it. And guess what? It was never found. Fast forward to now, and there's still talk about the lost treasure of Lake Maggiore. Scuba divers, treasure hunters, even random tourists with snorkels, all hope to find Enrico's sunken bling.

So, there I was too, chilling by this historic lake, half expecting to see a glint of gold from the corner of my eye. But instead, I got something else — a local telling me about a secret underwater city. Yeah, you heard that right. A city beneath the waves, all Roman ruins and forgotten history. Some say it was Enrico's secret escape, a sort of underwater palace. Sounds like something out of a movie, right?

As the sun set over Lake Maggiore, turning the water all shades of orange and pink, I couldn't help but wonder about the secrets it held. Was there really treasure down there? An ancient underwater city? Or was it all just tall tales and tourist bait? Either way, it was fun to hear and all.

I was soaking up the sun the next morning and this local, let's call him Marco, dives into this tale about the underwater city. It's all like, "Not many know about it, but it's there, hidden beneath the lake." My imagination's now doing somersaults. An underwater city? Seriously?

Marco goes on, talking about how this city was a marvel of Roman engineering, a place where Duke Enrico could escape from his royal duties and maybe stash more treasures. I mean, who needs a bank vault when you've got an underwater city? Right?

Now, I'm no history buff, but this story had me hooked. Marco even mentioned secret passages connecting the lake to the old castle ruins on the shore. *'Imagine sneaking through those tunnels, swimming right into history,'* I thought.

Then, out of the blue, Marco offers to take me and my friends on a boat tour around the lake. 'You might not see the city,' he says with a wink, 'but the lake's got plenty of secrets to share, too.'

So, there we were, gliding over the glassy water, all eyes peeled for any signs of submerged ruins or, you know, Duke Enrico's lost treasure. Every shadow in the water had us leaning over the side, half-joking and saying, 'Is that it?'

On the boat, as Marco was weaving tales about Lake Maggiore, I noticed that Mattias, the quiet math whiz we'd recently met, was deep in thought, gazing at the lake with a curious intensity. He wasn't much for swimming or selfies like Mikey; instead, he had this unique way of getting lost in his own world, lost in the equations and numbers probably dancing in his head.

'You know,' Mattias piped up suddenly, 'The depth and expanse of this lake could be analyzed mathematically to hypothesize the most probable locations of any sunken objects.' His eyes were bright with the excitement of having a puzzle to solve.

Lilly, always intrigued by a bit of intellect, nudged him. 'So, you think you could figure out where Duke Enrico's treasure might be?'

Mattias chuckled, 'Well, it's not quite that simple, but it's an interesting problem.' He started explaining the mathematics of sonar and underwater topography, but then lost most of us after the first few sentences. The guy was on a whole different level when it came to numbers.

While Abby and Mikey goofed off in the water, Mattias was off in his own world, talking stats and algorithms to anyone who'd listen—or not. Joshua tried chatting up Lilly about her new guy, but Lilly was too caught up in Mattias's math buzz, completely zoning out on Josh. I just chilled in the sun, entertained by how our chilly day turned into a full-on math lesson.

As we headed back, the sky a blaze of colors, I caught Mattias scribbling formulas in a small notebook. 'You really think you can find the treasure?' I asked him, half-teasing.

Mattias flashed a timid yet mischievous grin. "Perhaps one day I'll solve Lake Maggiore's mysteries with math."

I smiled.

Chapter XXIII:

Motivation Comes from Rivalry

That evening, as we dined by the lake, our chatter blended into Marco's stories, Mattias's math musings, Joshuas's attempts to take all the attention to himself, and our shared chuckles. It felt like a mix of old-world myths and our modern-day antics.

The wine flowed freely, and Mikey and Mattias seemed to be caught in a silent contest of who could drink more. They wouldn't admit it, of course, but it was pretty obvious.

After a few drinks, Mattias turned from a math nerd into quite a talker. Suddenly, it was all about life stories and quirky queries instead of numbers.

He suddenly asked, "Ya all know Julia, right?"

"My cousin," he finally blurts out after an awkward ten-second silence.

We all nod.

"I don't know, man. I think she might be seeing Professor K..."

"Matt!" Joshua cuts him off sharply and makes a cutting gesture with his hand, signaling him to stop talking.

"I mean, that's what people say, but nothing's confirmed. It's just a rumor. Plus, I don't even go to the same university as you guys," Matt tries to backtrack.

"Matt, rumors are everywhere, and that's a serious accusation, especially these days—it usually starts with guys," I chime in, trying to diffuse the situation a bit.

"Yeah, I'm just worried, you know?"

"And you think I'm not? But you need to learn to shut the fuck up if you're not sure about what you're saying and where you are saying." Josh snaps back, frustration clear in his voice.

Mattias scratched his head, clearly confused, but it was obvious the alcohol was talking more than he was. He rambled on a bit and then switched gears to rave about how cool Julia was—like how she aced her very first job interview. Aced her first interview? Okay, let's rewind here.

"She's about your age, just finished university. Speaks four languages—French, English, Spanish," he listed almost proudly.

"Someone's forgetting that we actually study together," Lilly interjected, stopping him in his tracks.

Yeah, the alcohol was definitely talking.

He blushed a deep red and shrugged. "Oh yeah, right. Whatever, anyway."

But he continued regardless - "We're always ribbing each other. She teases me about my obsession with numbers, and I make fun of her endless scribbling, her 'ink on paper' fantasies. But it always ends up in a draw. She had her first job interview recently. We all teased her, said there was no way she'd get it—it's a major company, and they usually don't want greenhorns. But guess what?"

I had been half-listening, my mind wandering to my own business ideas, but something about the job interview snagged my attention, pulling me back.

Mattias couldn't hide his excitement. "She nailed it. The company's an exciting new start-up under a larger tech firm, all into health gadgets and stuff. They normally want experienced folks, but there she was, Julia, no big experience, just charisma and confidence. Walked right in and rocked it. They called her back almost right away. It's proof that it's not all about your resume. Sometimes, it's your attitude that makes the difference."

Everyone applauded verbally.

Mikey glanced at me.

It piqued something in me.

His story struck a chord with me. I listened, silent but inwardly buzzing with thoughts. For the rest of the evening, I was quieter than usual, lost in contemplation. The next day, it was obvious to everyone that something had changed; I was wrapped up in my thoughts, distant.

'Job interviews,' the phrase echoed in my head, taking me back to that one interview that had shattered my confidence, Mr. Knowitall, and the other woman. But on the other hand, this one pushed me toward my hidden desire.

'If Mattias's cousin could break through those barriers with sheer confidence, why can't I?

Once we settled into our hotel, I fired up my laptop to tackle the pile of assignments and orders waiting for Belle Epoch Envy. I crunched the numbers, weighing potential losses against potential gains, before snapping the laptop shut. But then, like a shadow creeping into my thoughts, that one raw nerve–the interview, yes, that particular interview–started gnawing at me again.

'Why am I fixating on that humiliating experience now? I've got my own thing going, so why does it bother me?' I wondered.

That evening sparked something in me. I've always believed in confronting my fears head-on–no running, no hiding. So, I made a bold decision. I would prep for that interview like a boss again. I'd learn everything there was to know about the industry, nail the interview for the same job, same place, same people I was once rejected from, and then–here's the kicker–I'd turn it down. It was my way of closing that chapter in my life and on my terms.

Also, let me tell you, having your own gig changes the game. When you're desperate for a job, nerves can get the best of you. But now? I had Belle Epoch Envy as my safety net. That alone boosted my confidence. It wasn't just about landing the job anymore; it was about proving to myself that I could land it. It was a strange mix of revenge and self-validation, but hey, we all have our ways of dealing with our ghosts, don't we?

Our days by Lake Maggiore, then Bergamo flew by, and before we knew it, it was time to bid farewell to new local friends and head back to Munich. Our flight back to the States was looming, and I was left grappling with a strange mix of emotions and some newfound resolve.

Chapter XXIV:
Let's Enter The World of Interviews

Flying has never been a big part of my life–I've just taken a couple of domestic trips, a jaunt to Mexico, and that onetime flight to Islamabad. At first, the whole airport-flying thing freaked me out, but eventually, I got into the rhythm of it, except for one thing— people clapping when the plane lands. Seriously, why do they do that? It's a total cringe.

So, there I was, nestled in my window seat on the Boeing plane, leaving Munich behind and heading for JFK. My mind was like a TV that is stuck between channels–should I focus on prepping for the interview or fixing up Belle Epoch Envy? Then it hit me. If I messed up my business, that would torpedo my confidence for the interview. They were connected, like pieces of a puzzle. Belle Epoch Envy needed to be rock solid if I was going to ace that interview.

The plane touched down at JFK, and to my relief, no one clapped–thank goodness for small mercies. Next up, we had a domestic connection to SMF, but had a brutal five-hour layover. And yes, hopping continents does take it out of you. It's no small deal.

Abby and Lilly were total snapshot queens. They' always capture every moment with a flurry of photos and share them online. It was like they were curating a digital scrapbook of our adventures. Me and Michael? We were at the total opposite end of that spectrum. You'd hardly ever catch us snapping pics. I firmly believe that obsessing over photos kind of zaps the magic out of being in the moment. It shifts the focus to crafting a perfect digital image, and suddenly, you're not really there in person anymore.

Michael got that too. We were on the same page when it came to living in the moment, not through a lens. So, guess what? We ended up with just two photos from the entire trip, and both were group shots. We were more about storing great memories in our heads than on a cloud or a feed. There's just something about holding onto experiences in your mind, letting them live there, unfiltered and raw, that feels more real to us.

****

So, just like that, we were back home. The next day, Mikey vanished off the radar. He didn't have work, so I figured it had something to do with Dan. Part of me wondered if he'd fess up about Mattias or keep it under wraps. If they weren't in an open relationship, keeping it a secret felt like committing all kinds of wrong to Dan.

Left to my own devices, I dove into tackling the backlog at Belle Epoch Envy. Checking our online shop, my heart sank a bit–four negative reviews had popped up. Customers had been grumbling about delayed orders and a lack of responses for over a week. 'Get into damage control mode,' I thought. I hustled to prioritize these orders, combed through my collection, and got the expedited shipments rolling, even though it meant extra costs. To me, customer satisfaction was the key–every positive review is a new building block for your business's reputation, and it's a long- term investment!

After all that hustle, I hoped these customers might reconsider their negative feedback. But no dice–the reviews stayed put. I told myself, 'Don't let it get to you,' but that is always easier said than done, right?

With the pending orders finally under control, I shifted gears to get ahead of the future ones. It was a three-day marathon of planning and organizing, but I managed to get Belle Epoch Envy back on track. With that job out of the way, it was time to tackle the next item on my agenda— the job interview.

The company I had in mind was in the printing business, yes, that one. I hopped online to see if they were still hiring for the position I had initially applied for, and yes, that job interview had left me in ruins. After some serious scrolling and searching, it hit me–they didn't have any openings listed. It looked like they'd already filled the spot.

Still, I wasn't about to let that small detail stop me. I put on my detective hat and, after a bit of sleuthing, managed to dig up the HR department's number. I called them up, all guns blazing, asking if the position was still open. The answer was a flat-out 'No.' Never one to give up easily. I pushed further, asking if there were any vacancies at all. All I got was a curt "No, we don't," followed by a swift goodbye.

"What now?"

Left in a bit of a daze by this unexpected turn of events, I found myself mulling over what to do next. I had conjured up all sorts of scenarios in my head, but this one I hadn't anticipated.

You know when I do my best thinking? I used to believe my brain kicked into high gear when I was out walking, music playing in my ears, or during those long, contemplative showers. But lately, I'd discovered my creative sparks often fly best when I'm sprawled on the couch, half-watching TV shows. It's like my mind drifts into its own little world, piecing together lots of ideas into good solutions.

That's exactly what happened that evening. I was lounging on my couch, flicking through channels in search of something binge-worthy, when an idea zapped through my brain.

'What if I just pivot and apply to different companies in the same industry? Or try for the same role elsewhere?' It was a simple and yet very effective plan, and I felt like a weight had just lifted off my shoulders. This idea could be my way of getting the closure I needed, a chance to rewrite that one chapter that still bugged me badly.

I dashed to my bedroom, my mind set on one thing–opening my laptop and diving into a deep research session, undistracted and focused. My mission? To scope out printing companies in and around Sacramento. The truth? There weren't many options. I found only three companies, and just two were hiring for the position I wanted. And, as luck would have it, only one had an open vacancy.

With a mix of excitement and determination, I started clacking away at my keyboard. First up was my resume and CV. I'd set aside an entire day just for that task, scouring the internet for the best, most creative tips and tricks–anything to make my application stand out. Beginning with the basics, 'Hina Strubel' and my birthdate, I spent a solid seven hours meticulously crafting what I considered a masterpiece. Every detail, every word, was chosen with care. It turned my CV into a true work of art, and trust me, with today's technologies and online reach, you can do just that.

But the real fun? That was the motivational letter. It needed to be something special, something unique., I've learned that a motivational letter isn't just about showing how badly you want the job or how much you will be contributing. No, it's a test of your creativity. They're not just looking for well-crafted words or a passionately written plea. They want to see your originality, your ability to think outside the box. And that, my friends, is where I really shine. This was my personal playing field, my best game.

Still, I wasn't really in the mood to write; my period was looming, and PMS was hitting me hard. During times like these, I usually need to keep busy, and tackling creative tasks feels nearly impossible. My go-to escape is either zoning out to ambient music or mindlessly watching TV, not really absorbing anything, just staying superficially occupied.

However, this time, I pushed myself hard to break that pattern.

'Who really cares about Hina's life story?' I thought, as I sat in front of my laptop. It's a common misconception that spilling your life experiences into a motivational letter scores big points. But let's be real–it doesn't. Trust me, no recruiter wants to wade through your autobiography. They've got a pile of applications in front of them and zero time to read personal sagas.

The trick? Blend a bit of the abstract with reality, and sprinkle in some humor. It's a delicate balance–the humor should be there, but it's got to be subtle, just a hint to keep things interesting.

So, what did I do? I decided to give the printing industry a playful roast. Picture this: the industry's struggling in 2023, desperately in need of a lifeline. Then comes an almost divine sign, hinting that salvation might just lie in the hands of, well, women. The narrative I spun was about these special heroines ready to pull the industry successfully into a new era.

And what about the grand finale of my letter? I positioned myself as one of these special saviors. Not just for the company, but for the whole darn industry. It was cheeky, a bit bold, and totally me.

Turning my attention back to Belle Epoch Envy, I dove into developing new concepts and spent hours sketching designs for bras and corsets,

That was the toughest task yet. Thanks to PMS once again, each line on the paper was helping to solidify my ideas. I won't lie; my drawings looked like they were done by a five-year-old. Still, they served their purpose, helping me piece together my creative vision.

However, one aspect of my business strategy clearly needed a revamp — the physical marketing approach. Running around town, distributing flyers, and putting up posters was eating in my time. It was effective once, but now? Physically, there was no time, especially when digital advertising promised a broader reach with less legwork. Thus, I started planning a shift to more online-centric promotion strategies. Maybe I'd keep the flyer routine to once a week, just to maintain a necessary physical presence in the community.

The days had rolled by since I submitted my first application, and with the peaking of my period, an anxious energy gripped me. *Why limit myself?*' I thought. The idea of exploring opportunities outside my current scope was exhilarating. I had already crafted a slightly embellished resume for the printing industry; still in pain, I escaped into thinking: *what if I applied the same creative approach to other sectors?*

With a newfound sense of daring, I researched various industries in Sacramento, from the latest tech startups to small, niche firms. I scrutinized every job listing I could find, regardless of whether they were hiring or not.

Amidst the ongoing flurry of tweaking resumes and crafting cover letters, I was also grappling with the peak throes of my period. There I was, a chameleon of CVs, injecting a dash of flair here and a snippet of embellished experience there, while all the while also navigating the tumultuous waves of cramps and mood swings. Each application saw me down new hu and, skillfully adapting to the demands of various industries, powered by an arsenal of coffee and pain relievers to combat the relentless period pain that timed their peak to match my job application marathon.

Then, just as I was basking in the glow of my multitasking prowess—balancing period woes with job application acrobatics—my phone buzzed with an unexpected jolt. It was an interview invitation! I almost fumbled with my phone, a mix of hormonal flux and genuine surprise gripping me. Excitement fluttered within, intertwined with the nagging pangs that were erupting from my abdomen.

"The interview's tomorrow?" I echoed in disbelief, my mind racing, not just with prep strategies, but also with how to manage period discomfort on such a crucial day. As I dove into preparation, a gentle reminder echoed in the back of my mind. My goal was to snag the offer, triumph in the challenge, not necessarily to embark on a new vocational journey.

When Lilly later learned about my period-timed job- hunting escapade, her expression was a cocktail of awe and concern, likely marveling at how I had managed to juggle the intensity of period pain with the stress of securing job interviews.

"Isn't it kind of unethical? You're just leading these companies on," she queried.

But here's my take–I'm not out here trying to be some champion of universal justice. I'm just doing what I feel is right for me. And this whole 'interview for fun' thing? I never saw it as bad or a waste of anyone's time. HR departments are there to sift through applicants. It's their job to hire and fire, right?"

"But what about the companies that think they've found their perfect candidate in you? Isn't it a bit unfair to lead them on?" Lilly pressed; her eyes were now wide with concern.

"Look, if companies can pick and choose who they hire, turning down people for whatever reason including discriminative ones, then I figure I've got the right to say 'thanks, but no thanks' too," I shot back, my tone firm, but buzzing with strong energy. "I'm not trying to get revenge or anything like that. It's just how the game's played." And with that thought, I closed the book on her argument.

So, let's get back to the matter at hand–this interview. It was time to put my plan into action.

Chapter XXV:
Guiding through Interviews

Driving to Inkspire Graphics, I strongly focused on the task ahead. 'First impressions matter,' I told myself as I walked into the building, projecting a blend of professionalism and approachability. The reception area was typically corporate–efficient and unassuming. I checked in with a practiced and friendly nod.

In the waiting area, I reminded myself, '*Sit confidently, but stay approachable.*' Body language was crucial. I was soon called into the interview room and found myself facing Ms. Anderson, Mr. Barnes, and Ms. Richardson. Each panelist demanded a different approach, but I was ready.

Ms. Anderson was all business. "Can you describe your experience in the printing industry?" she asked. I leaned forward to engage. '*Show them you're interested and knowledgeable, but not an industry insider,*' I thought. "While my background is in e-commerce, it nicely intersects with printing in marketing materials," I answered, connecting my experience to their field.

Next, Mr. Barnes, with his laid-back attitude, asked about digital printing. Mirroring his relaxed posture, I replied, "Digital offers agility and customization, while traditional printing provides a unique quality." '*Balance your answer to show flexibility,*' I reminded myself.

Ms. Richardson's creative flair was evident. "How would you approach a project needing creativity?" she inquired. I leaned back, fully relaxed. *'Let your creative side show.'* "I'd start with the client's vision, adding a creative twist for a unique impact," I shared.

The interview continued with a question about my future goals with Ms. Anderson. I spoke of evolving and adapting, whether in e-commerce or another sector. *'End on a note of growth and adaptability,'* I thought.

I also took a moment to compose myself. *'Every answer is a performance,'* I reminded myself.

Ms. Anderson then asked, "How do you think your e-commerce experience will benefit our printing company?"

I leaned in slightly, showing eagerness. *'Link your answer to their needs.'* "E-commerce has taught me the importance of quality and timely delivery–crucial for printing. I understand the client's perspective, which can be a valuable asset," I explained.

Mr. Barnes, with his easy-going demeanor, then asked, "How do you handle tight deadlines and stressful situations?"

Mirroring his relaxed posture, I smiled lightly. *'Show that you're unflappable.'* "Stress is part of the game. I prioritize, stay organized, and always keep communication open. It's about staying cool under pressure," I replied.

Ms. Richardson chimed in, "What would you say is your most creative solution to a problem you've encountered?"

I leaned back, projecting a mix of thoughtfulness and creativity. *'Time to shine with your problem-solving skills.'* "Once, I had to redesign a product layout at the last minute. I used the opportunity to introduce a more user-friendly design, which actually improved the overall product," I recounted.

Ms. Anderson interjected with a more technical question, "What's your experience with the latest printing technologies?"

I paused, giving the idea a thoughtful nod. *'Admit your limits but show willingness to learn.'* "While I haven't used the latest tech, I'm very quick to learn and adapt. I'm always updating myself with the industry advancements," I answered honestly.

As the interview drew to a close, Mr. Barnes asked, "What motivates you in your work?"

I smiled. This was my pitch. *'Connect it back to your passion.'* "The drive to create and improve. Whether it's my own business or contributing to a team, I thrive on seeing ideas come to life and evolve," I shared.

Concluding the interview, I stood up and offered a firm handshake to each panelist. *'Balance confidence with gratitude,'* I thought. Each handshake was tailored–professional with Ms. Anderson, a bit warmer with Ms. Richardson, and very friendly with Mr. Barnes.

Stepping out of the building, I felt a sense of achievement. *'You played it just right, Hina,'* I congratulated myself. The experience has been empowering, a testament to my growth and confidence.

Stepping back into my house, a bubble of excitement fizzled inside me. It was that kind of buzz you get when you've just aced something and you're itching to share it. Without a second thought, I whipped out my phone and hit up Mikey. "Hey, let's not let this night go to waste. How about we round up Lilly and Abby and make an evening of it?"

Abby was game, but Lilly was off on a romantic date with her boyfriend. So, it ended up being just Abby, Mikey, and me.

We hit a string of bars, each with its own quirky charm. The streets of Sacramento were humming with life–the perfect backdrop for a girls' night out (well, minus Lilly). We were like a trio of night owls, flitting from one lively spot to another, the air rich with our laughter and chatter about the trip and, of course, my recent interview escapade as well.

I missed having Lilly around. Her absence was noticeable in our little group. But hey, when love calls, you gotta answer, right? I imagined her having her own kind of lovely evening, and the image brought a smile to my face.

****

Before autumn wrapped up, a bunch of stuff went down–some big, some not so much. I'm not about to bore you with every tiny detail of my life, so let's just hit the highlights. By November, Belle Epoch Envy was on a roll, sales ticking up nicely. Thing is, I hit a snag–it felt like I was running in place. My sales were steady, but I wasn't seeing any growth. It was like I was stuck on repeat, and that got me thinking. If I didn't expand my operations, I'd max out at this level. Expansion was the next big step, but I should hold that thought because my interview saga wasn't over yet.

I kept firing off applications to all sorts of companies in various industries. My collection of resumes and motivational letters was growing–a whole wardrobe of professional personas, you might say. The only thing I didn't change? My name. I mean, I wasn't about to go incognito. Still, part of me wondered how long it'd be before these companies started talking to each other and realized I was popping up in interviews all over town.

By the end of November, I'd chalked up 13 interviews. Yeah, you heard that right–thirteen. Here's the rundown on where and how they all went down.

From the start of autumn to the end of November, my days were a blur of interviews–a solid two months of stepping into different roles. Each interview was a new scene in this peculiar drama I'd set myself in.

I kicked off with Green Tech Innovations. I tweaked my resume to highlight my eco-friendly initiatives in my business, adding a pinch of my agronomy background. *'Let them see you're about more than just profit,'* I thought. It worked–they called me in, curious about this business-savvy environmentalist.

Vista Marketing Solutions was next. I spun my e-commerce experience into a digital marketing saga. *'Make your online success stories shine,'* I mused while crafting my resume. They were intrigued by my self-made digital footprint.

The interview at Sacramento Brew Works was a shot in the dark. I emphasized my creative marketing campaigns, hoping to catch their eye. *'Show them you can think outside the bottle,'* I chuckled to myself. And sure enough, they were interested in hearing more.

Creative Minds Media was a match. I played up my content creation skills, painting myself as a multimedia storyteller. *'Let your creativity be your headline,'* I thought. They were hooked, inviting me to discuss my ideas further.

With Aurora Apparel, I leaned heavily into my passion for sustainable fashion, making my resume a testament to eco-conscious business practices. *'Dress up your achievements in green,'* I planned. They called, eager to meet the mind behind the eco-friendly concepts.

Infinite Logistics was a tougher nut to crack. I focused on efficiency and sustainability in my own business, positioning myself as a green logistics enthusiast. *'Talk about turning Green into gold,'* I encouraged myself. They were intrigued enough to invite me for a chat.

By the end of November, after a whirlwind of 13 interviews, I was amazed at how far my chameleon skills had taken me. Some companies responded, others didn't, but each application was carefully tailored, each resume a new story to tell. It was more than just a game. It was a journey through the corporate world, a test of my ability to adapt and transform. And in the process, I discovered more about myself than I could have ever imagined. I discovered Hina, the entrepreneur, the storyteller, the ever-adapting dreamer.

At Green Tech Innovations, their 'Behavioral Interview' question aimed to uncover how I handle real-world situations. "Tell us about your approach to sustainability," the interviewer probed. Companies use these questions to predict future behavior based on past actions. As I detailed my experience, it felt like I was explaining the ' cause and effect ' process in business decisions, illustrating how past actions inform future strategies.

In Vista Marketing Solutions, the 'Situational Question' was their tool to gauge problem-solving and critical thinking. "Describe a digital campaign you spearheaded," asked the interviewer, eyes keenly focused on me. This type of question helps employers understand how a candidate might navigate future challenges. My response was a walkthrough of my decision-making process, like teaching a class and offering the steps of strategic planning.

At Sacramento Brew Works, their 'Competency-Based' question aimed to assess specific skills–in my case, creativity. "How do you innovate in branding?" they asked rather casually. Such questions let companies measure a candidate's skills against job requirements. I turned my answer into a showcase of creativity in action, almost like a case study presentation in a marketing workshop.

Creative Minds Media asked about 'Creative Thinking' to test originality and adaptiveness. "How do you keep content engaging?" This type of question is common in dynamic fields, where thinking outside the box is key. My answer was akin to sharing tips and tricks on a creative writing course, highlighting the importance of innovation.

For Aurora Apparel, the 'Targeted' question focused on aligning my skills with their mission. "What's your strategy for marketing sustainable fashion?" Here, they were looking for alignment between my abilities and their brand ethos. My response was like giving a targeted lecture on mission-driven marketing strategies, emphasizing the fit between personal skills and company goals.

Infinite Logistics used a 'Problem-Solving' question to assess practical, actionable skills. "Your plan for sustainable logistics?" They wanted to see if I could translate challenges into solutions. My explanation was like a step-by-step guide in a logistics course, demonstrating how to turn theoretical problems into real-world solutions and precisely so.

The moment I walked into Cascade Data Analytics; I could tell this interview wasn't going to your run-of-the-mill interchange. The office was a hub of quiet intensity, and Ms. Abaribe, my interviewer, had a sharp, inquisitive air about her.

Her first question was a curveball. "If given a dataset on consumer behavior without a specific objective, how would you extract actionable business insights?" Instantly, I recognized the question as a test of not just my analytical skills, but also my creativity and initiative. '*Think like a detective, Hina,*' I coached myself. I outlined a plan to segment the data, identify trends, and draw correlations to market behavior. I was also very careful to keep my explanation grounded, showing a realistic grasp of data analysis complexities.

Ms. Abaribe, seemingly impressed, followed up with, "Can you tell us about a time when you had to make a decision with incomplete information?" This was classic 'behavioral interviewing'–trying to unearth my decision-making process. I shared an experience from my business, where I had to trust my gut and make a call with limited data. '*Show them you're not just about numbers, but also about instincts,*' I decided.

Then came a question that delved into team dynamics. "How would you communicate complex data findings to a non-technical team?" This question was about my ability to simplify and teach. I explained by using visuals and everyday analogies, admitting that while I wasn't always perfect at this task, I believed in clarity and understanding. '*It's okay to show you're human,*' I reminded myself.

As the interview drew to a close, Ms. Taylor posed a thought-provoking question: "Where do you see the role of data in the future of business strategy?" This query was more philosophical, a chance to showcase my broader thinking. I talked about data as a storytelling tool, a way to predict and shape business narratives. '*Be visionary, yet relatable*,' I aimed.

Walking out of Cascade Data Analytics, my mind was buzzing. Each question had peeled back a layer, revealing more about my capabilities and areas for growth. I wasn't just there to impress; I was there to learn and reflect. This interview had not been just an exercise; it was a journey into the heart of data, a field both daunting and fascinating. And in taking that journey, I found new respect for the power of information and the art of interpretation.

After endless effort and an unquenchable desire for wisdom, I finally saw the results of my hard work. My skills in crafting compelling cover letters and preparing for interviews were honed to perfection. The key? It's simple. Do thorough research into the current trends and traditional methods utilized by each specific industry. Being well-versed in the latest buzz within the field can make one sound like a seasoned insider during interviews.

I spent hours scouring the Internet, devouring articles, and listening to podcasts. It was crucial for me to stay up to date on the latest trends and timeless topics in their industry. I had to integrate this knowledge into my conversations, giving off an air of experience and expertise, even if I was just starting out in their world. The key was to demonstrate not only solid preparation but also genuine interest and engagement with their work and the desire to grow.

Every interview was like stepping into a new character's shoes, absorbing my lines, and nailing my role. It was like the world of interviews had become my stage, and I was getting pretty good at that acting gig. Basically, even if your resume is a bit on the "light" side, you can still ace an interview by being a quick study on industry buzzwords and trends. Sure, watching videos helped, but diving into articles and memorizing a few key terms was my secret sauce.

After gracefully bowing out from the array of job offers that I'd snagged (collecting and attending them), I decided a celebration was in order. Lilly's boyfriend was throwing a massive party–not a Sacramento shindig, but a full-blown bash in a rented house. Just as I was prepping for a night off from my interview persona, a message from Derrek popped up. *"One hour late is fashionably acceptable,"* I mused quickly and joined him for a walk down J Street.

"You're glowing, girl. How did a European adventure transform you?" Derrek joked, his laugh echoing down the street.

I threw him a mock-serious glance. "And you? What's the latest with the podcast gang?"

"All smooth sailing," and he shrugged.

"And the farm?"

"Tough times, but my little bro's diving in headfirst. He's got big plans."

That answer made me grin. "Heard anything from them lately?"

"Nada, radio silence," he responded, and then his tone shifted. "But hey, that's not what I wanted to chat about."

"Oh? Spill it, then. What's up?"

He got this real serious look.

"You got the letter, didn't you?"

"A letter?" I blinked, thrown off. "What letter?"

He paused, a cloud of realization passing over his face.

"You haven't? Then why?"

'*Not that drama again please,*' I internally groaned. We walked in silence, the city lights twinkling around us, until Derrek broke the quiet.

"Come on, share some Euro trip tales. Was it as epic as your Instagram made it look?" he prodded.

"Ah, you know! Despite Michael turning into Mr. Bean for a bit, and Joshua jumping out of nowhere, it was a blast. The guy's fine now and, lesson learned, I mean Mikey."

He glanced at my outfit. "Off to another midnight interview?"

"Ha! No, heading to Lilly's party. And before you ask, it's a solo mission tonight. Abby and Mikey are already there."

"Didn't mean to hold you up," he said, a note of apology in his voice.

I just offered a light smirk, wanting to keep the surrounding air breezy and uncomplicated.

We approached a line of taxi cabs that were bathing in the soft glow of streetlights, signaling our casual stroll was ending. Derrek paused. His hand grazed the cab's door handle, a silent harbinger of our parting.

"Hey, before you jump into that taxi," he began, his voice dipping into a softer, more introspective register, "I've got to tell you... this was really nice. We should catch up like this more often, don't you think?"

I felt a tiny, uneasy flutter in my belly, a subtle dance of emotions I wasn't quite prepared to dissect.

"Yeah, it's been good," I replied, my tone trying to mirror the lightness of the evening. "Life's full of these unexpected little detours. Right?"

He looked at me, eyes wide, like he was trying to read my mind or maybe just find the last piece of pizza. "Chatting with you is a breeze," he said with a grin. "It's like we're replaying our greatest hits, but somehow, the tune's catchier now."

I managed to pull together a smile, although I felt like I was lifting weights with my face. His words hung in the air, heavy and mysterious. "Cheers, Derrek. You've got the listening skills of a pro," I tossed back, steering clear of the deep end of the conversation pool.

His demeanor shifted, a layer of seriousness enveloping his words. "Forget the letter," he muttered, almost to himself, and then, locking his gaze with mine, he ventured, "Hina, I need to be honest about something..."

My heart tightened, anticipation knotting my stomach. '*Not now, please,*' I silently pleaded in my head.

He pressed on, "I've been doing some thinking... and I feel like there's something more here between us."

I cut in, my voice laced with a mix of kindness and resolve. "Derrek, our friendship means the world to me. Let's not blur those lines. We're great as friends. Isn't that enough?"

A flicker of frustration, maybe even a dash of hurt, crossed his face. "I get that we're friends. But what if there's more? I can't just shut off these feelings."

My response was a soft exhale, a bid to ease the growing strain. "I don't want to give you false hope. Our friendship is something I cherish. Mixing other feelings into it... that just doesn't sit right with me."

He pushed back, his tone tinged with a blend of insistence and vulnerability. "You're viewing this conversional all wrong. It's not about complications; it's about possibilities. Why shut the door on what could be?"

A spark of irritation ignited within me. "It's not about fear or avoidance. It's about being honest with where I am right now, with what I can give. And also, Derrek, what you're seeking... It's just not the right time!"

He shook his head, his face a canvas of disbelief. "So, that's it? You're just going to close the door on this without even thinking it through?"

"I know myself," I replied, trying to steady my voice. "And I know this," I motioned at the space between us, "isn't what I want." Even as the words left my mouth, a part of me questioned if the words were too harsh, too final. But the die was cast; the words hung irreversible in the cool night air.

The conversation with Derrek had reached its crescendo, leaving a palpable tension between us. After a few more agonizing minutes, his voice dwindled to a whisper, heavy with resignation.

"I get it... I thought maybe... but I guess I was wrong." His face was a blend of disappointment and a kind of weary acceptance.

I ached to soften the blow, so murmured, "I'm sorry, Derrek. Let's not let this change us." But the words got lost somewhere on the way to my lips, leaving me mute, trapped in the awkward silence that now enveloped us.

I slumped into the taxi's backseat, and a wave of sadness washed over me. "We both need some space to figure things out," I whispered to no one, acknowledging the silent surrender to our predicament.

I caught a last glimpse of Derrek through the window, his figure receding into the night, every step heavy with the weight of our conversation. It dawned on me then, how fragile our connections with others always are, how easily they can fray and come undone with only a few missteps.

As the taxi pulled away, I felt the distance growing, not just in miles, but in our connection, too. The night that was supposed to be fun had turned into a reflection of what had just unraveled. The party no longer seemed important; my mind was caught up in deep thoughts about our now uncertain friendship.

When the taxi driver asked again where I was headed, my frustration bubbled up: "Why did this have to happen now? Time like this...what about them, how the news will reach me!?" I let out a sigh, feeling overwhelmed by it all.

The driver looked puzzled initially, thinking I was chatting him up. But after a beat, he caught on to the fact that he just needed to hit the road and get moving.

Chapter XXVI:

Au Revoir, 2023

Christmas was filled with excitement as I strolled through and shopped in the festive market. And before I knew it, New Year's Day had arrived, catching me off guard and knee-deep in what should have been a break from work. My plan to ditch the business hustle, ignore the siren call of pending orders, and definitely not peek at any more job applications had gone spectacularly awry. By 10 PM on Christmas Eve, I'd powered through all of it, sort of like a holiday superhero with a to-do list instead of a cape.

I was just about to switch gears in social mode, curious about my friends' festive antics, when the doorbell chimed. Enter Mom, unexpected as a snowstorm is in California. Oops, I'd totally forgotten to tell her about our New Year's Eve plans!

She scanned my room, a chaotic blend of business and interview prep. "You don't need these jobs, you say?" she quipped, eyeing the papers strewn about.

"It's a hobby, Mom. Kind of like extreme sports, but with less adrenaline and more paperwork," I tried to explain, but she just shook her head, half-amused, half-baffled.

Before she could dive into a motherly lecture, I steered the conversation toward something productive. "Actually, you could help me with something. I'm on the hunt for office space for Belle Epoch Envy."

"Already assembling a team?" she inquired, brewing her tea with a detective's precision.

"Not yet, but I'm planning ahead. It's smart to do that."

We bantered back and forth, our little debate a festive sparring match until the clock nudged closer to midnight. We welcomed Christmas with a clink of champagne glasses, the holiday magic enveloping us. Lying there, my head in Mom's lap, I let the rhythm of her gentle breaths sync with the ticking of the clock. In that tranquil cocoon, I found myself drifting in a sea of nostalgia. These moments, so fleeting and yet so profound, were rare gems. They reminded me of childhood innocence, the warmth of shared laughter, and the unspoken bond that only a mother and a daughter understand. It was more than just comfort; it was a reminder of life's ephemeral beauty, a poetic embrace of time itself.

Still, my friends were scattered like stars in the holiday sky. Mikey with Dan, navigating family dynamics; Lilly in snowy Canada; Abby in Carmichael's family haven. Each in their own little world of holiday cheer.

Back in my world, Belle Epoch Envy was on a roll. That wasn't just the fruit of my labor; it was like catching a lucky break in a game of cosmic bingo. The novelty of my lingerie line was hitting the right note in the Golden State.

Mark, aka Tyrese from Detroit, the guy that Mikey had introduced me recently, was the unexpected ace up my sleeve. He was the Robin to my entrepreneurial Batman, handling the behind-the-scenes action, mailing, inquiries and replies with a flair that was turning my chaos into a symphony. Tyrese, better known as Mark's story, was a slice of high school legend. Back in Detroit, in a quirky act of rebellion, he'd taken to calling every teacher 'Mark,' regardless of their actual name. It was his unique way of thumbing his nose at authority, a harmless prank that soon caught on. Before he knew it, his friends flipped the script, and he became 'Mark' to everyone. It was a nickname that stuck, a badge of his playful defiance. Now, as my right-hand man in this lingerie empire, Mark was channeling that same spirit further, turning our daily grind into something unexpectedly a lot of fun.

As December waned, my interview tally hit an eye-popping forty-five. Sounds like a marathon, right? Well, it felt like one, but I was nailing everything, juggling interviews like a circus act. Each one was its own little adventure, stories I'll have to share another time–they're too good to gloss over here.

Before the clock struck midnight, ushering in 2024, December was a whirlwind. It felt like I had lived a year in just a month, from drifting apart with Derrek to my Belle Epoch Envy business taking off like a rocket. And smack in the middle was Lilly's boyfriend's party–an evening sprinkled with a mix of anxiety and laughter. Let me take you through that night.

****

I rocked up to the party an hour and fifteen minutes late. My phone, which I'd ignored during the taxi ride, was buzzing with missed calls from Abby. As soon as I stepped into the party zone, Abby pounced on me like a cat on a laser pointer.

"I've been looking everywhere for you! You've made me miss my chance with the Bretz twins. They were both flirting with me, and there I was, playing detective for you," she half-scolded, half-laughed.

Caught off guard, I fumbled for a response. "I... uh, was with Derrek," I said, my voice tinged with sadness.

"Oh, so that's what's up with our little Hina bird? Look at the two birds building the nest!"

I shook my head, not really in the mood to dive into the details and was not really what she thought them to be, but Abby, sensing my reluctance, didn't press further. She knew better than to dig into emotional landmines during a party. She promised we'd dissect the whole Derrek situation later, over coffee and possibly some hangover food.

The rest of the night was a blur of music, laughter, and Abby trying to balance her twin flirtations. Despite the earlier drama, the party seemed to be a much-needed distraction. It was one of those nights where you laugh a little louder and forget the world outside amidst the bubble of music and twinkling lights and meeting new people.

The party was hosted at a grand two-story house in Rocklin, boasting a sprawling yard with a shimmering pool–a setting straight out of an upscale magazine. As I sauntered through the yard, my eyes caught glimpses of familiar faces, but I didn't stop to mingle just yet. That's when Abby caught up with me. Together, we ventured inside.

The interior was a blend of old-world charm and modern party vibes. I guessed the house dated back to the 1920s, judging by the black-and-white photos adorning the walls, interspersed with artistic paintings that added a touch of real elegance. The color scheme of greyish brown was offset by the soft glow of party lights, creating a cozy, yet sophisticated atmosphere.

This event wasn't your typical wild dance party. It was more refined–what we like to call an 'Adult Party.' The music was a low hum in the background, more for ambiance than for dancing. Conversations were the main event here, with guests clustered in various nooks of the house talking.

As is typical at such gatherings, people naturally formed into groups. Some lounged-on chairs and sofas, deeply engrossed in discussions about mundane and yet amusing topics, like someone's husband receiving a medal for an odd talent. In another corner, a 'boys' club' animatedly chatted about MMA and other guy stuff.

Abby and I strolled down the hall, finally catching sight of Michael, the life of the party, clearly deep in chatter with a duo of damsels. One was an old school chum, and the other a mystery guest. The scene was like a page ripped out of the "Holiday Gatherings for Dummies" book–old pals reuniting, new faces mingling, all marinated in the festive spirit.

Michael, the ever-gracious host, waved us over. "Ah, here come my favorite people! Hina, meet Mia–we go way back, practically since we were just tots. Mia, this is Hina and Abby. And this charmer is Natalie." His introductions were like a maestro conducting an orchestra.

Natalie flashed a grin that could melt snow, which we mirrored, exchanging pleasantries. Driven by a pinch of curiosity, I nudged Michael, "So, where's the belle of the ball?" hinting at Lilly.

He gave a shrug that could rival Atlas. "Oh, she's probably with Logan, or orbiting some other party constellation. You haven't bumped into Logan yet. Right?"

I shook my head. "Nope, the stars haven't aligned with us."

"I have," Abby interjected, her smirk loaded with an entire saga left untold.

Our quest to find Lilly (or her mysterious beau) continued. We were lured upstairs by the symphony of poker chips and suppressed chuckles. Not that Lilly seemed the poker type, but who knows? Stranger things have happened at holiday parties.

Halfway up, Martha, like a ghost from a christmas past, materialized and headed straight for us. Her sudden entry was more startling than finding out your Secret Santa is actually Santa. What her tie was to Logan or why she was here was as clear as eggnog. Her invitation to this festive jigsaw was something we hadn't anticipated.

"Hey, Martha, I did not expect to see you here," I said, my curiosity now spiking and offering a greeting with my hands.

As Martha approached, her greeting was casual, almost distant. There was a coolness in her tone, like she was addressing someone she barely remembered. A few words were exchanged, but the atmosphere was slightly tense.

Abby, sensing my growing discomfort and increasingly sour mood, stepped in to keep the conversation flowing. "So, Martha, how's life post-university? What are you up to these days?" she asked, her voice bright and engaging.

Martha responded with a nonchalant shrug, "Same old, really, just minus the college part. And you two?"

Her gaze seemed to deliberately be avoiding me, focusing solely on Abby. It was becoming increasingly apparent that Martha might have caught wind of my past interactions with Adrianna, and possibly even knew about Brad and Adrianna's dating situation. Her coolness toward me was a subtle and yet unmistakable sign of disapproval.

I won't lie. It stung a bit. But then again, life is never a straight line. It's a complex web of relationships, each with its own set of dynamics. People have their own perceptions of right and wrong, and sometimes, one connection can lead to having friction in another. It's just the way things go in life–unpredictable and often a little messy.

Martha's focus remained on Abby, but I felt compelled to engage, despite the chill in the air. "Martha, good to see you're doing well," I offered, trying to bridge the gap her coldness had created.

She glanced at me briefly, and her response was curt and devoid of warmth. "Yes, it's... interesting to see you here." Her words hung in the air, clearly heavy with unspoken sentiments, before she swiftly turned her attention back to Abby.

"So, Martha, any exciting plans for the New Year?" she asked, her voice attempting a bridge over troubled waters.

Martha's reply was polite, but distant, "Just the usual, nothing too grand." She glanced at her watch, a subtle signal of wanting to move on. "Well, I should mingle. Enjoy the party, Abby, Hina."

She was halfway down the stairs when I called out to her, hoping to get a lead on Lilly's whereabouts. "Hey, by any chance, have you seen Lilly? You know, my 'fake fragile friend,' our party princess?"

She paused, turned back with a puzzled look. "I don't think she's even here tonight."

Confused, I pressed on. "What? Isn't she supposed to be with Logan?"

Martha's expression shifted to realization. "Oh, you mean Lilly!" She gracefully descended the stairs, her voice trailing behind her like a melodic echo. "I was under the impression you were referring to Adrianna."

In that moment, standing on the staircase, a wave of emotions washed over me, and I felt frozen. Abby's giggle, usually a sound I welcomed, now grated on my already frayed nerves. It wasn't just the mix-up with Martha that bothered me. It was the accumulation of the evening's events–the strained conversation with Derrek, the unexpected coldness from Martha, and now this response. I felt a small knot of frustration forming in my chest.

The laughter, which was supposed to lighten the mood, only underscored my unease and confusion. I was teetering on the edge of snapping, ready to unleash the frustration bubbling inside me, when Lilly's call sliced through my brewing storm.

"Girls, over here!"

We followed Martha, navigating the lobby's twists and turns until we stumbled upon a quaint room off the balcony—a place that had eluded our initial sweep of the area. The thought of finally meeting Logan, Lilly's latest catch, didn't exactly thrill me. Typically, I'd be the one in the corner, brewing a batch of critical remarks and snide observations. Yet, surprisingly, the atmosphere this time was oddly disarming.

The room buzzed with chatter from a small crowd of about six, all strangers to me. Lilly, radiating excitement, hastened to make introductions. It turned out these were Logan's acquaintances. Watching Lilly's eager gaze, I mustered a smile, totally determined not to rain on her parade.

Abby, ever the social swimmer, dived into the conversation pool without hesitation. In no time, she was deep in a chat about diet and fitness with a tall fellow from the group.

So, there I was, adrift in nods and half-hearted smiles, feeling somewhat alien. It's one thing to be the party's pulse; it's quite another to feel like a puzzle piece from a different box. Yet, for Lilly's sake, I donned the mask of enthusiasm, curious about this Logan who had captured her affections.

Logan, a transplant from Arizona, visited Sacramento occasionally. He stood out with a stature that wasn't athletic, but undeniably still had presence. His features were conventionally attractive, complemented by a hairstyle that nodded to the 70s and yet adapted for today. His style was on point, effortlessly blending classic and contemporary for the evening's ensemble.

The age gap between him and Lilly was about nine or ten years, or so he claimed. With folks like Logan, you learn to take things with a grain of salt—there's always an air of enigma. Yet Logan's real draw was his magnetic charm. He possessed the kind of conversational gravitas that naturally commands a room, the sort who finds their element in the spotlight.

As he engaged with the group, I couldn't help but dissect his character, peering beyond his words to grasp the essence of his persona.

So, there I was, caught in the crossfire of Logan's charm offensive. He tossed a couple of questions my way, trying to reel me into their chat. I bobbed and weaved through the conversation with a few lights, non-committal remarks. Just when I thought I was off the hook, the topic turned to banks' love affair with debt.

What a lame topic.
All these people are in suits.
Talk about banks.
Finances.
BORING!

A guy from Logan's circle started ranting about how banks are practically pickpocketing people these days. Heads were nodding, and the air was thick with bank-bashing, until Logan, Mr. Smooth, jumped in with a different tune. There he was, playing the knight in shining armor for the banking system. I couldn't help but raise an eyebrow.

Given his posh background, it wasn't a shocker that he'd lean toward defending the moneyed elite. I leaned back against the wall, watching the verbal tennis match. It's funny how where you come from can color your view of the world. For Logan, given his silver spoon upbringing, it was like he was on a different planet.

These guys are great at ruining any party mood.

I stayed on the sidelines, a silent spectator in this dance of differing viewpoints. It was like watching a live documentary — taking a peek into how the other half thinks and argues. It's moments like these that remind me of the intricate patchwork of opinions and backgrounds that we all come from.

Watching the conversation unfold, I noticed Logan skillfully steering everyone toward his viewpoint. It was mesmerizing how he managed to sway the crowd, with Lilly looking on, her eyes gleaming with admiration, nodding along to his every word like a besotted schoolgirl. That's when I felt the urge to jump into the fray.

Oh Jesus, I can't be a spectator for too long.
Hina, equip up.
Ready,

I leaned in, catching his eye, and asked calmly, "I'm curious," my voice calm but firm. "If banks truly have the customers' best interests at heart, why do they often increase interest rates on loans during economic hardships, further burdening those already struggling? Doesn't that seem more like capitalizing on people's misfortunes than supporting their clients?"

The question lingered, slicing through Logan's smooth spiel. A hint of astonishment flickered in his eyes, while Lilly's gaze darted, now keen on his reply. It was simple, yet potent, probing the depths of the banks' supposed goodwill. Logan paused, perhaps carefully crafting his response. Then, with a nod, he dove in. "Spot on, Hina, the rising interest rates are a head-scratcher, especially when times are tough. But think about it: if banks don't tweak their rates in tune with the economy, they might wobble financially. And if a bank topples, it's a domino effect–everyone feels the pinch, not just the big shots. It's all about keeping the ship steady, making sure the bank can weather any economic storm." Lilly's eyes shone with a mixture of pride and understanding as she listened to Logan. The room seemed to absorb his words, clearly reflecting on the delicate balance between financial stability and social responsibility.

As the chat with Logan meandered on, it was more like a friendly tennis match of ideas than a boxing match over bank policies. We smoothly shifted gears from the nitty-gritty of banking to the grand tapestry of capitalism and its brushstrokes on art, masterpieces, and the financial sector's role in the cultural landscape.

I tossed in my two cents, further kindling the discussion with a notion that might have sounded more at home in a Bohemian café than a finance seminar. The deeper we dive into the sea of financial entanglements, the less we swim in the oceans of authentic creativity. I suggested there's a certain dilution of value, a fraying of the moral fabric, when the world is colored solely in shades of profit and expenditure. It's as though our feverish chase for financial success simply casts a long shadow over our quest for meaningful, enduring cultural legacies.

Leaning in, I made my point clearer. "Here's the thing. The more we're caught up in money matters, the less freedom we have to create truly impactful art. Banks are at the top of the money world and have a lot of power and often prioritize profit over more meaningful endeavors."

The room paused, mulling over the idea. Logan, with a contemplative look, absorbed the critique.

Then, one of his buddies piped up, "But don't you think that's oversimplifying, Hina? Banks do bankroll artistic projects, fund galleries, and back cultural festivals, right?"

I nodded, acknowledging his point. "That's true, and it's a valuable contribution. But often, these sponsorships come with strings attached, shaping the art to fit a certain narrative or commercial interest. It's rare to find art that's purely about expression and not influenced by the need for it to be financially viable." I took a small pause before I continued with an emotional tone. "The essence of art is to convey emotions, challenge norms, and provoke thought. But when artists are burdened with financial constraints, their creativity is funneled into what sells, not necessarily what matters. And banks, as major financial players, inadvertently contribute to this issue by reinforcing the idea that financial success is paramount."

Logan, with a thoughtful look, broke the brief silence. "I see your point about the balance between financial support and artistic freedom. But, let me ask you this - when was the pinnacle of artistic expression throughout history?"

His unexpected inquiry took me by surprise, but I quickly composed myself. I refused to reveal my confusion, so I replied with the first thing that came to mind. "The Renaissance," I answered confidently. "It was a period marked by some of the most incredible artworks, all created within a relatively short timeframe."

"*This answer should surprise him,*" I thought.

For a moment, an odd silence hung between us, thick enough that you could almost see it. I half-expected Logan to press on with more questions, maybe challenge my views with a 'why' or 'how.' But he didn't. Instead, he just nodded, absorbing my point rather agreeably, and steered the conversation in a different direction.

He dove into a passionate spiel about the Renaissance, painting a picture of an era exploding with artistic genius. He described Europe's stunning monuments, lifelike statues, sky-grazing churches, and storytelling paintings.

"So, artists were pretty much living the dream of creative freedom back then? Tough to imagine churning out those masterpieces if someone's breathing down your neck," he said, eyeing me and almost daring me to disagree.

I leaned forward, ready to volley back. "True, those Renaissance folks had their patrons, like lords and royalty, but it's not quite the bank scenario we have now. Back in that day, it was more like a supportive handshake–'I'll fund your painting, you make our chapel look heavenly.' Nowadays, it's like banks have their hands on the steering wheel, driving creativity down Profit Lane, which might not always be the best route for pure, untamed artistry."

Abioye, one of his buddies, was now tuning into my frequency, nodding along and confessing that he shared my enthusiasm for the topic. That bit of camaraderie? A real boost was pushing me to delve further into the debate. And then there was Lilly, casting those adoring looks at Logan–talk about love being blind! She seemed oblivious to the crux of our discussion and not seeing where my points were landing pretty solid punches.

As the evening meandered on, with champagne glasses clinking and bubbles performing their merry dance, everyone seemed enveloped in their own personal bubbles. Then Logan, on the brink of setting down his glass, turned to me with a new theory: Banks, according to him, were like the shadowy benefactors of the arts, not intruders, but instead silent supporters, lifting the art world from behind the scenes. My eyebrows couldn't help but leap towards the ceiling. Was he serious?

Then there was Logan, giving his champagne glass a final twirl before turning to me, eyes alight with the promise of a grand revelation. "Regarding the Renaissance–the zenith of our art history," he began, his tone a cocktail of wistfulness and veneration. "It's more than a mere era; it's a saga about how those shadowy entities you're wary of, like banks, played a pivotal role in art's splendid unfolding. It's one tale nestled within another tale. Understand?"

I gave a slow nod, inviting him to unravel his narrative. My interest was now piqued, and he dove in fully.

Logan's eyes momentarily wandered, as if sifting through history's rich mosaic. "Consider this," he ventured, his voice now laced with reflection. "The Medici family were the Renaissance's trailblazers, akin to today's tech moguls, but their domain was art, not gadgets."

Leaning in, his excitement almost palpable, he painted a vivid scene. "Imagine Florence, alive and pulsating, a crucible of creativity. There, amidst the fervor, were the artists, the future icons. Think Botticelli, conjuring vistas no one had even dared to dream. Michelangelo, transforming inert marble into raw, palpable feeling. Then there was Leonardo, the era's visionary, paralleling the innovativeness of someone like Bill Hobs today."

With a reflective chuckle, Logan continued, "But here's the clincher. These virtuosos, they required a leg up, a benefactor. Enter the Medici, who were financiers, indeed, but also special visionaries who recognized and nurtured groundbreaking talent. They weren't mere coin hoarders; they were architects of opportunity for these creative maestros."

He punctuated his point with a tap on the table. "Consider 'The Birth of Venus.' It's not just art; it's a bold manifesto. And its financier? The Medici. Michelangelo's 'David'—it transcended the mere display of craft; it was a paradigm shift in artistic expression. And its patron? Again, the Medici."

His eyes sparkled with enthusiasm. "You see, the Medici understood that art was more than just pretty pictures; it was a dialogue across time. Their banking was the spark that ignited the creative explosion we now call the Renaissance. But really, it was like the Big Bang of artistic expression."

Logan, now brimming with curiosity, dove ever deeper. "Let's talk turkey for a moment. The Medici weren't just dabbling in art; they were serious players. They invested something like 600,000 florins in the arts. Convert that to today's cash, and you're looking at around $460 million. Yep, that's million with an 'M.'"

He paused, allowing the sheer scale of that investment to resonate. "Imagine that—without the Medici's deep pockets, many Renaissance masterpieces might have just remained figments of the imagination. Their financial backing was crucial. No Medici money, no 'Birth of Venus,' no 'Primavera' by Botticelli."

Logan leaned back, a contemplative hand now running through his hair. "Ponder this–without their support,

Michelangelo's 'David' could have remained an uncarved block. And Leonardo? We might never have known the 'Mona Lisa' or his groundbreaking inventions. It's staggering to think that the Medici's financial influence was a linchpin of the Renaissance."

His expression grew more intense. "But here's the real takeaway. It wasn't just about splashing cash. The Medici had vision. They realized that by funding artists, they were nurturing the seeds of a cultural revolution, one that would resonate for ages going forward."

He leaned closer, his tone hushed, as if sharing a secret. "So, when we admire Renaissance art, we're also seeing the impact of finance on history. The bankers, The Medici's banking, wasn't just about growing wealth; it was about cultivating a lasting legacy, one that painted our world in richer hues and broader strokes."

Listening to Logan's historical deep-dive, I was itching to jump in. My fingers were fidgety, itching to fact check him on my phone. So, surreptitiously searched under the table, ready to call him out on any misstep. But annoyingly, his facts were on point. It was like looking for a flaw in a flawless wall—everything he mentioned about the Medici was pretty much accurate.

Admitting that truth even to myself was tough — I was out of my depth here. Renaissance and banking? Not exactly my everyday reading material. So, I kept my realizations tucked away, hidden behind a mask of polite nods and the occasional 'Hmm.'

As Logan wrapped up his comments, however, I saw my opening. "But what about now? Are banks still the art world's backstage heroes, or has the scene changed?" I asked, trying to steer us back to the here and now.

Logan's answer was swift and precise. "Everything's fast-paced now. Banks have spread their wings, interests have diversified. It's not that they've stepped back from the arts; it's just that the arts are today just one piece of a much bigger puzzle."

As he spoke, I could see his mind was already half on the next event. He glanced at Lilly, a silent cue that it was time to move on. "We should head to the speeches," he said, a subtle shift in his tone. Lilly and Logan moved toward the main hall; their steps clearly synchronized. I trailed a few steps behind, my mind still wading through the sea of information that Logan had just poured out to us.

As Logan had mentioned, the speeches were an integral part of the evening's festivities. He had set up a quaint stage in the entrance hall, complete with microphones. The idea was simple yet engaging invited members would step up and share something—maybe a slice of motivation, a quirky New Year's resolution, or just a spontaneous thought.

Before the speeches kicked off, Michael and I took a leisurely stroll through the yard, the cool air brushing against our faces and refreshing us. Our conversation naturally drifted to Logan. "He seems all right, decent even," Michael said, yet with a hint of skepticism in his tone. "But don't you think there's something too polished about him? Like he's playing the part of a good boyfriend a bit too well." I nodded in agreement, though a tiny voice inside me wondered if jealousy wasn't coloring my judgment at least a little.

Never before had I felt such defeat in an argument, especially not from men.

But was it truly a defeat? Or something else?

Maybe not. You see, even the tiniest detail, a fact from history that you are not aware of, can shift your perspectives significantly.

Our stroll took us near Martha, who was perched on a chair outside, deep in conversation with another girl. I gestured for Michael to talk to her, while I hung back, not feeling up for any chit-chat. I noticed Martha glanced my way a couple of times. I ducked the gazes, pretending to be absorbed in the distant hum of the party.

By the time Michael returned, the speech event was in full swing. Party members were already on stage, their words weaving a tapestry of motivation and aspirations. In the midst of it all, Michael slipped in a question about Derrek. " I heard from Abby that there's some drama brewing there? Is there?" he asked, his curiosity barely contained. "It's a mess," I replied tersely, "but I'll fill you in on the details later."

Standing smack in the middle of this swanky crowd with everyone clutching their drinks like lifelines—champagne, pina coladas, you name it—I couldn't help but tune out Mr. Bald-and-Beautiful on stage, waxing poetic about love and all that jazz. Seriously, if I wanted a sermon on love, I'd watch a Rom-com.

But hey, when you're stuck in a sea of people who are all pretending to be touched by generic speech #5, what do you do? People-watch, of course. It's like a game: guess the career. Take Mr. Slick on my left, for instance. All sharp suits and sharper gaze. Hedge fund guy? Startup whiz? Or how about Ms. Power-Heels in front of me? CEO of something fancy, or maybe a lawyer who could sue you before you even said 'hello'?

It's funny how in a not-so-funny way, these shindigs turned into an unofficial 'who's more successful' contest. There I was, sizing up everyone, stacking their imagined achievements against mine—and my little venture, Belle Envy Epoch. Isn't it weird that playing this mental career chess game made me feel a bit better? Maybe. But hey, a girl's gotta find her entertainment somewhere in a huge cocktail of motivational speeches and alcohol, right?

Lilly sidled up to me, a mischievous chuckle escaping her lips. "Guess what? Logan's gearing up for his grand speech," she said, her eyes twinkling with a mix of amusement and anticipation.

"Oh, really? And how's that making you feel?" I asked, tilting my head slightly, curious about how she was taking on the whole spectacle.

She beamed. "I'm actually pretty stoked. This is exactly the kind of party I've always dreamed about. Fancy speeches and all."

I nudged her playfully. "What about the cello? Wouldn't this shindig be ten times better with your music? Like that time in Yosemite?"

Her face lit up for a second, then she brushed off the compliment with a brisk wave of her hand. "Oh, stop it, you're making me blush," she laughed, trying to hide a flattered smile.

Just then, her attention was hijacked by Logan, who had started his spiel on stage. She was all in, of course, soaking up his words as if they were the last drops of a secret potion. I was amused as I observed her getting lost in his oratory.

Logan, seizing the spotlight, was like the conductor of a symphony of ideas, zigzagging through topics with the ease of a pro. He jumped from the holiday's cheer to the anticipatory buzz of New Year's, spinning his words like a DJ crafting a seamless track. It seemed he was on a clear mission to rev up the crowd and teleport them straight to the jubilant moment of New Year's countdown.

Just as you thought he'd found his rhythm, BAM! He hit a sharp turn. Out of the blue, he tossed a question into the crowd, "Who's already scribbled down their New Year's resolutions?" The audience responded with a mixed bag of nods and indifferent shrugs.

Then, as if pulling a surprise from his sleeve, he dove into a spiel about the essence of making wishes. It wasn't just about the wishes themselves, he pontificated, but the gumption behind them. He spun a yarn about how our hopes and dreams are powered by our grit. It felt like he was trying to stitch together a grand narrative, tying the simple act of wishing to the robust engine of human will.

With the crowd now wrapped around his finger, Logan pressed on. "Think about it," he urged, mixing zest with a touch of philosophy. "Each wish we cast into the future aren't they just sprouts of our determination? It's not merely about hoping; it's about igniting our will, steering it toward our aspirations, whether consciously or subconsciously."

He strutted across the stage, gesturing passionately, locking eyes with his audience. "Be it a yearning for success, love, a dash of adventure, or a slice of tranquility, it's our will that's the real MVP. It's the engine always chugging behind our aspirations, the invisible "oomph" nudging us always ahead."

After a dramatic pause and letting his words marinate, he added a twist. "But," he said, his grin hinting at a playful challenge, "Here's the brain teaser: Are we really the captains of our fate? Do we truly have free will?"

The room was wrapped in a heavy silence, as if Logan's probing question had put everyone's thoughts on pause. Each person was now lost in a sea of contemplation, mulling over his words that lingered in the air, inviting deeper reflection.

Just as a couple of attendees seemed poised to step up and join the conversation, possibly to toss in their viewpoints or challenge Logan, he grabbed the microphone again with the ease of a seasoned performer, not ready to let go of the narrative reins just yet. With a knowing glance toward Lilly, who seemed to be in on some private joke, he continued.

"Do we?" Logan echoed his own question, this time fixing his gaze on a tall fellow, the kind whose nose you notice, who was caught up in showing something on his phone. Surprised to be suddenly spotlighted, the guy looked up, a tad flustered, "Well, on a day-to-day basis, sure," he ventured, "but if we're diving deep, it's still up for debate, isn't it?"

Logan's laughter was light, and yet it resonated with a deeper undertone of wisdom. "Exactly," he affirmed, turning the conversation into a casual chat. "It's when we apply philosophy to the everyday grind that it truly earns its keep. That's where theories finally meet reality."

The guy with the notable nose, now fully engaged, cleared his throat, ready to share his thoughts. "Look, every day we make choices, from picking our breakfast to deciding our daily tasks.

These may seem trivial, but they're our will in action, our personal stamp that we put on the day."

He paused, wanting his words to resonate. "And on a larger scale, think about the major life decisions we make–careers, relationships, where to live. These are monumental, always shaping our journey. They're influenced by various factors, yes, but ultimately, it's us at the decision wheel."

Now, Logan, with a twinkle of mischief, leaned on the podium, captivating the room. "But let's go deeper," he proposed, "We fancy ourselves as the authors of our destinies, but what if our so-called 'free will' is more of an elaborate act, directed by unseen forces like biology and circumstance?"

He strolled across the stage, relaxed, yet somehow compelling. "Take your morning coffee, laced with sugar. Seems like a simple choice, a kickstart for the day. But here's the twist: that sugar is hijacking your brain chemistry. Suddenly, you're more upbeat, and decisions come with a zing. Is it you in the driver's seat, or is it the caffeine-sugar combo?"

Logan's smile broadened, but his gaze was penetrating. "And it's not just about your diet. Think about the stress that kneads your thoughts, the cultural scripts you follow, the echoes of past emotions. We're like puppets, dancing to a tune we hardly recognize, oblivious to the strings directing us."

He paused, letting the idea simmer. "We cherish the notion of control, of our choices being purely ours. But the reality? It's like trying to catch fog. Our so-called control is swayed by a myriad of internal and external forces that come from the societal pressures to the whispers of our subconscious."

Leaning in, Logan's voice softened to a near whisper. "Every choice, every 'free' decision, is influenced by a cocktail of factors. The sugar in your coffee, societal norms, the murmurs of your inner voice–they're the puppeteers in our grand performance."

He straightened up and added thoughtfully, "Next time you're proud of your willpower, just think — we're all influenced by a bunch of different things, some as simple as your morning coffee."

He took a pause, then wrapped up his speech with a powerful idea. "In life, we think we're writing our own story, but often, we're just following a script written by something much more complex."

His words trailed off, and a buzz of conversation started up in the room. People looked a bit shaken, their faces showing a mix of confusion and deep thought. Logan's words had hit home, making everyone reconsider how much control they really had over their choices, stirring a sense of wonder and a bit of discomfort.

Logan, now sensing the shift in the room, stepped back to the microphone. There was a gentle smile on his face, a knowing look in his eyes. He waited for a moment of silence before adding his final thought: a twist.

"But by the end of the day," he said, his voice softer now, yet carrying a weight that drew everyone's attention back to him, "that's the main reason why I find humans, people, so fascinating. Because even though we might grapple with the idea that we don't have absolute free will, every day, we wake up holding onto hope. And isn't hope itself a form of free will? The hope that we can change, that we can make a difference, think of that! That tomorrow might be different from today–it's that hope which keeps us moving, keeps us dreaming. In our personal hope, we find our freedom, our power to influence the script of our lives, however subtly. Happy Christmas and a new and more hopeful New Year, my friends!" His speech had ended, and Michael and I, both impressed, were still looking toward the stage. I half-expected Michael to fall in love with him, but instead, he just smirked and muttered,

"That hypocrite bastard," before casually walking off with a tap on my shoulder. The evening was clearly dragging its feet until Logan, playing the part of a magician, vanished and then poof! He reappeared with Ben,

YES, WITH BEN,

I mean, gosh!

My ex, as if he were Logan's new assistant. Cue the dramatic gasps!

Internally, I was all alarms and sirens.

First Martha here, Now Ben?
How do they know each other?
Why was I so clueless?
What kind of party is this?

But externally? Ice cool, I tossed Ben a casual, "Okay, what's up? Since when are you and Logan the besties?" Ben, Mr. Smooth, claimed they'd been pals for ages. News to me!

Mikey's face was priceless–he looked like he'd just walked into a surprise party... for someone else. He grabbed Lilly quicker than a cat on a hot tin roof, and off they went, probably to whisper or hyperventilate in peace.

So, there I was, stuck in chit-chat land with Ben, reminiscing about college like we were two old friends, not exes. Logan, gearing up for another monologue, kept it short this time, maybe because of the unexpected guest.

But then came the twist! Amidst the small talk about stocks and cars, Logan and Ben turned the spotlight on Belle Epoch Envy, my baby. They were throwing around numbers like they were on a game show, studying my statistics and sales, nearly hitting the mark.

Here's the kicker though. Ben, suddenly in tycoon mode, proposed they buy a big chunk of my business. "How about 80% of Belle Epoch Envy with you as the boss lady?" he asked, dropping a cool million-dollar offer like it was just another Friday night deal.

It was just another evening, right? From casual catchups to "Let's buy your company" in one smooth transition. Welcome to my life sitcom!

I mean, that was some serious cash for my fledgling venture. They must've seen something sparkly in Belle Epoch Envy. Half-tempted, dollar signs were practically dancing in my eyes. But as the conversation wrapped up, I lay it down straight - "Thanks, but no thanks." I'm not selling, not even a sliver.

The whole situation didn't sit well with me.

Remember, Hina, you've got that rule: when TWO random things align too neatly, it's a red flag. Hold off on any big moves—that's the golden rule.

Their faces? Picture the total surprise, like they'd just seen a ghost.

They hit me with a barrage of questions, all but telling me to redo my math and reconsider. But my mind was made up. Externally, I kept the tone sweet as honey, but inside, it was a firm 'no way, José'. The chapter closed with me telling them, "Hey, maybe next year. By then, investors might be throwing around 3 million. Who knows, maybe you guys will be in that mix then." I flashed a smile and nudged them toward the last dance of the party.

Ben, bless his heart, tried to return to the business topic for the rest of the night. But I was having none of it. I dodged him like a pro. He got the hint eventually.

Then there was Lilly. She was all 'why the no-go on the offer?' But I flipped the script, asking her if she knew about Ben's grand entrance and the buyout plan. She was in the dark about the whole Ben-ex-factor, only clued in a bit on Logan's offer.

Abby was MIA, nowhere to be seen, and stayed that way until the next day. And Michael? He was in a full-on 'Are you sure?' mode on the way home. He thought I should've mulled over it more. But then he ended with, "I'm proud of you. Showing those guys that they can't control everything? Priceless."

We wrapped up the night dissecting the whole Derrek situation. Michael, for some reason, was Team Derrek. He kept nudging me for weeks, saying I should reach out, talk things over. At the end he said "We can't afford to lose people that easily. Remember, eventually we realize that people are our greatest assets." The next remaining weeks–I was navigating a flurry of interviews — four in-person and three online — and Christmas Day finally rolled around. It's always been my favorite time, especially wandering through the festive Christmas market in Sacramento. The vibrant lights, the cheerful buzz, it's all magical.

And then on December 31, as the clock inched closer to midnight, my mom and I prepared to welcome the New Year. With just a minute to go, we raised our glasses in a toast, a silent blessing exchanged in our eyes. The clock struck 12, and we chorused "Happy New Year," embracing each other tightly. Then, in a soft, heartfelt whisper, she added, "Naya Saal Mubarak Ho." That moment, so simple and yet so profound, was the perfect start to the New Year.

I sometimes forget,
that simple thing,
do matter the most.

Chapter XXVII:

The Minus One Rule

The next two months in the New Year were a blur of feelings and changes for me. It had barely begun when a series of complications started to cloud my horizon. The unexpected appearance of Ben at the party kept replaying in my mind. What did he and Logan truly want from my Belle Epoch Envy? Their intentions were as opaque as a foggy morning.

Navigating through the Derrek dilemma was like trying to untangle a pair of earphones left in your pocket for too long. On the one side, there were all the knotted feelings and unfinished symphonies of 'what-ifs.' How to stride ahead? My heart was scripting its own drama while my brain was all about logic, leaving me solidly stuck in the middle, probably looking as perplexed as a cat confronted by a mirror.

Amidst this emotional tug-of-war, there was Belle Epoch Envy–my brainchild, not to be confused with an actual child because, let's be honest, it was way less messy and cried less. However, it was picking up steam, craving the kind of attention a *diva* demands before hitting the stage.

And then, there were the job interviews–my very own comedy show. The practical me viewed them as about as productive as a hamster wheel, a loop of hopeful hellos and polite goodbyes. But deep down, a rebellious streak whispered to me that they were my ticket to some elusive fulfillment, a quest for a sliver of sanity in my whirlwind of thoughts. It seemed like I was hunting for a needle in a haystack, but hey, at least they kept things interesting.

This turmoil resulted in a natural withdrawal from most of my social circles. The only exception was Michael, my constant in this storm, mainly because we shared a living space. One evening, he invited Dan over for supper. It was a surprisingly relaxed and pleasant evening, given Dan's elusive nature. I'd barely really seen him before, almost as if he was a ghost in our circle. But that night, he was very much present, and his company was a welcome reprieve from the relentless tide of thoughts and decisions that had become my daily companions. Dan might have been sports fanatic, but he wasn't completely clueless about the business world. Even as Michael playfully poked fun at him, Dan held his own, especially when the conversation swiveled to my Belle Epoch Envy. He was as skeptical as I was about Logan and Ben's sudden interest in buying my startup. "People don't just waltz in and make offers like that," he said, echoing my own doubts.

No, they don't.

But wait, maybe they really like my idea.

As we huddled together, picking apart every conceivable scenario, I blurted out, "What if Ben's still hung up on me, and this is all just some grandiose plot?" Dan and Mikey were quick to dismiss the thought. The idea of Logan orchestrating a massive business venture just to play matchmaker seemed too far-fetched for them.

Dragging Lilly into our whirlwind of theories was a no-go. She's got the kind of heart that could shatter at the slightest tremor, and I couldn't bear to tarnish her bliss with my whirling business paranoia. We tossed around ideas, but each one fizzled out in a cul-de-sac.

However, something sticky and needy then happened. Fast forward three weeks, and the story took a twist. Abby, our go-to for all things current, burst in with a piece of gossip that caught us off guard. She flaunted an advertisement for women's lingerie, marrying Edwardian grandeur with a dash of modern flair. It wasn't my handiwork, yet it echoed my style, my signature designs. The ad was cloaked in anonymity, no designer was credited, only a date that teased there would be a grand unveiling.

The revelation hit us like a ton of bricks. This wasn't just happenstance; it had the stench of foul play, and not even Abby's quips could lighten the gravity of the moment. Michael's expression was a cocktail of both astonishment and worry. This saga transcended mere market rivalry; it felt like an intimate attack on my artistic essence. The atmosphere thickened with tension, everyone sensing that we were now entangled in a game with skewed rules.

As the countdown to the lingerie showcase ticked away, the enigma of who was behind the pilfering of my designs (actually stealing my designs) only grew denser and more intense. Tyrese, or Mark as some know him, stood by my side, adeptly fielding a barrage of emails and customer inquiries with the poise of an experienced virtuoso. While he held down the fort, I was caught in a whirlwind of conjuring up new creations and overseeing the logistical ballet of shipments, a relentless tug-of-war between innovation and operations.

During all this chaos, I had somehow overbooked myself with job interviews. The math was ludicrous—over forty interviews in a single month. That meant that on some days, I was hopping from one interview to the next with barely a moment to breathe. Strangely enough, these interviews had become my escape, my version of 'chill time' that used to be TV shows and lazy couch evenings. Now, it was the ritual of prepping for interviews, a bizarre respite from my daily grind and usually a welcome one.

But here's the kicker–with my mind constantly split between Belle Epoch Envy and these interviews, my performance started to slip. Rejections started piling up, a growing stack of 'nos chipped away at my confidence. It was disheartening, watching my once solid interview game falter so badly.

Added to my already overflowing plate now was the task of polishing my interview skills and sprucing up my motivational letter. It felt like standing at the foot of an ever-growing mountain. I'll get into how I tackled that hurdle successfully later. For now, let's just say it involved a hefty dose of self-reflection and a renewed dedication to mastering the art of the interview.

The streets suddenly burst to life with new posters and flyers, all emblazoned with 'Belle Epoch Envy.' But the designs–the bras and corsets — belonged to a collection I'd never seen and were starkly different from mine. We were collectively stunned. It felt like a surreal twist in a movie, except this movie was all too real.

What?
How?
When?
Why?

In a frenzy, we roped Lilly into the mix, desperate for any shred of useful insight. Her response was a blend of surprise and confusion–she was as clueless as us. Michael, ever the detective, dug deeper and unearthed the address of this mysterious company using my business name. But the real shocker came when he uncovered the registration papers: 49% was owned by Ben Erkenzel and 51% was owned by Logan Missfield. They had hijacked my Belle Epoch Envy as their trademark.

That bastard.

I mean those bastards.

I am going to set them on fire.

I was a whirlwind of emotions–confused, angry, ready to storm their castle. It seemed blatantly illegal, a clear-cut case of intellectual theft. But why? What was their endgame? As I ranted about trademarks and legalities and how I was going to sue them, Michael hit me with a question that stopped me full in my tracks: "Hina, did you register your trademark?"

Trademark.... trademark

Is that a logo?

Oh no, I know what that is.

I was dumbfounded.

"Isn't that automatic when you register the company?" I asked, naively hoping for a yes.

Michael's face said it all. The realization hit me like a ton of bricks.

Shit!!!

I had secured my business but left my brand's identity unprotected in the legal wilderness. I had been blindsided, like walking through a glass door you didn't see coming. Here I was, thinking I'd done everything right with Belle Epoch Envy, only to discover I'd missed a crucial step. Michael, armed with his laptop and a furrowed brow, laid it all out for me. Registering a business and trademarking a name? Thet were two different beasts. I felt naïve, like a kid who thinks closing their eyes makes them invisible.

In my world, where creativity reigned supreme, the dry intricacies of legalities seemed like background noise. But here I was now, paying the price for tuning them all out. The law, as Michael made painfully clear, doesn't care about your passion or how hard you've worked. It's black and white and yet complex–a maze of ifs and buts.

My brand, my precious creation, was a local flame that hadn't yet set the national stage afire. Without that widespread recognition, my assumed 'ownership' of the name was as fragile as a house of cards. The real kicker? Registering with the USPTO. That would have given me the legal armor I'd unknowingly knew I was without.

My initial fire, that gut reaction to go after Ben and Logan, simmered down to a flicker, as the reality of my situation set in. Still, not all hope was lost. If I could prove Belle Epoch Envy had enough of a footprint, enough of a whisper in the marketplace, maybe, just maybe, I could swing the legal pendulum in my favor.

Why would anyone need to register anything else?

Come on, like really?

Amidst all this confusing legal jargon and overwhelming emotion, I reached out to Ben. A meeting. A confrontation, perhaps. It was a desperate grasp of understanding, or maybe a futile attempt to reclaim what I felt was mine. It was a long shot, but in the face of losing part of your soul, you take every shot you can get or find, Men have grown what too accustomed to taking things that do not belong to them from others.

That evening, Ben chose the same café for our meeting, the place where it all began, with my friends and the tangled web of Belle Epoch Envy. But fate, it seemed, had other plans. I had an interview lined up at the same time, with some of the top real estate moguls in Sacramento. It was a pivotal moment, a crossroads–do I meet Ben, or do I chase another opportunity to validate myself, even though these interviews weren't directly benefiting my business anymore?

I chose the latter, the interview, and asked Ben to reschedule and that turned into its own mini- saga. Initially, he played hard to get, claiming his schedule was packed. But two days later, there he was, calling me up, casually mentioning he was at the Central Library, enjoying stalking books, and inviting me to join him. The irony wasn't lost on me.

The interview with the real estate tycoons turned out to be quite different. It was a big fish, a chance to test my newly polished skills. I had revamped everything–my resume, my cover letters, and most importantly, my interview techniques–tailored specifically for this kind of high-stakes meeting. It was more than just practice now; it was about proving to myself that I could swim with the sharks, that I could hold my own in any arena, not just the familiar waters of Belle Epoch Envy.

Mulling over the Sterling & Grant Associates interview, a lightbulb went off in my head regarding the peculiar dance of real estate job interviews. I uncovered a pattern that had previously eluded me. These interviews dive deep into real-world scenarios, a far cry from the abstract hypotheticals of other industries. That is especially true for roles drenched in sales. Consider the typical icebreaker, "Tell us about yourself." What seemed like casual chit-chat was actually more akin to showing your hand in a poker game. They weren't just perusing my resume; they were digging for stories about my sales sagas and client negotiations.

"You see, if I'm to be utterly transparent, my authentic sales experience originated by my hustling at Sacramento's farmers market. The rest of my resume? Well, let's just say it's been seasoned with a pinch of creative flair. I've been on a bit of a quest, testing the elasticity of truth in my resume and interviews. It's an art form really, blending reality with a dash of fantasy, to see how this different concoction fares."

Then we veered into resilience territory. Merely stating I could weather a storm wasn't going to cut it. They yearned for tales of my captaining my vessel through turbulent seas, embodying poise, and tactical genius—the bread and butter for real estate warriors.

The interview's main course? Technical grilling. When Ms. Grant inquired about rejuvenating lackluster properties, they weren't fishing for cookie-cutter responses. They craved actionable strategies, a dash of market savvy, and yes, how a simple makeover or a strategic reshuffle could transform a property's narrative. Here's where you had to demonstrate you were not just a real estate enthusiast, but a true connoisseur of the trade.

Woven throughout the interview was this subtle thread of ethics and legal adherence—reminding me that in the real estate realm, integrity walks hand-in-hand with acumen. As I strode toward the interview room, my brain was abuzz with the mantra I'd adopted from yesterday's prep: "Don't just parrot facts; stitch them into your narrative. Immerse yourself in the market, beyond the transaction. In this slick world, let your candor shine. It's as much a trust game, as it is about the transactions."

So, for those braving the real estate interview battlefield, here's a nugget of wisdom: Embed yourself in the local property scene. Become the go-to guru for what's trending and what's tanking in your own domain.

Then, dive into the numbers. Get a grip on financing, from the ABCs of mortgages to the intricate dance of investment schemes. It's not merely about selling spaces; it's about unraveling their financial essence. And guess what? I didn't just stumble upon this insight; it took some online sleuthing and splurging $11 on an e-book. Who says you can't buy wisdom?

But let me toss in a little golden nugget of advice that comes straight from my playbook: Arm yourself with a couple of anecdotes about navigating tricky waters–think along the lines of a nail-biting negotiation or a client who's more twisty than a pretzel. Your approach to these little dramas can speak volumes about your character. Almost every interviewer threw this curveball at me although of course they each had their own unique spin on the question.

Meeting Ben at the library was a different playing field altogether. He knew me, knew the real me, well enough to see right through any embellished stories I might spin. The usual narratives and creative liberties I took in job interviews wouldn't work here. With Ben, I had to be straightforward, especially since he and Logan were holding upper legal cards.

I found him in the library, absorbed in the rows of books. It was a side of Ben I hadn't seen or known–a book lover, perhaps it was a recent interest he hadn't mentioned before.

But no, I'd wager this bastard is just playing at being the "Intelligent" type guy.

He didn't dwell on it, though. He started with the usual small talk, asking how I was. But frankly, I wasn't there to dance around pleasantries. I barely contained my anger and needed some answers.

Cutting through the niceties, I went straight for the jugular.

"Just tell me, Ben. Why? Why did you do this?" My voice was a cocktail of frustration and the desperate need for clarity.

He took a moment, perhaps weighing his words, and then he finally faced me. His explanation was about perspectives, suggesting I was misunderstanding the whole situation, that it was really beneficial for everyone. That only fueled my anger more. I shot back, calling his actions cowardly.

"You could've chosen any name for your brand. Why mine? Using Belle Epoch Envy–that's a targeted strike, Ben. Is this some personal vendetta? I need the truth, now."

How can he be serious?

Ben's calmness, coupled with that smile–not one of those sinister grins, but off nonetheless–threw me. It was as if he believed nothing wrong was happening, and I was just missing the point. "You've exploited my mistake of not trademarking. How can you spin that as something positive?" I challenged him.

"Hina, look, we gave you a generous offer. Investing over a million in a startup? That's rare. You could've accepted, but you let your ego lead. What did you expect would happen?" he countered.

"So, you're admitting this is some kind of punishment?" I shot back, incredulous. "Sounds like an expensive way to get back at me, Ben!"

He chuckled, a mix of amusement and disbelief, shaking his head gently.

"No, no, Hina, this isn't about punishment. You're missing the bigger picture here. You've got a business that's brimming with potential, but it's like a plant trying to grow in the shade. It needs more than just a little sun. It needs a whole new environment to thrive. And that's what we're offering."

I opened my mouth to protest, but he continued, his tone taking on a more persuasive edge. "We're still on the table with a deal. Think about it–shut down your current operations and merge them with ours. We're talking about giving you a 20% stake in a much bigger, well-funded venture. And you won't just be a name on the door; you'll be actively in charge for a whole year."

He leaned in slightly, trying to gauge my reaction.

"It's essentially the same deal we proposed earlier, but now with even better financial backing. Together, we can scale Belle Epoch Envy to heights you've only dreamed of. So, what do you say, Pumpkin?".

Pausing for a moment, I tried to process what Ben had just laid out before me? For someone who usually prided herself on quick thinking and fast reactions, I found myself unusually slow, mulling over his words. A strange cocktail of emotions was brewing inside me–anger laced with an incredulous chuckle.

So here he was, a man straight out of medieval times, who believed he was entitled to:

Take properties,
Take lands,
Take people,
Take women,

"So, this is it? This is how you think it works? You believe everything is just there for the taking? That's not a generous offer, Ben. It's manipulation, plain and simple. And not just any manipulation–we're talking about a high-level, narcissistic business ploy. People get upset about being manipulated in personal relationships, but this one? This is something else entirely."

I struggled to find the right words, my usual eloquence faltering under the weight of my disbelief. "It's disrespectful on an entirely different scale. You're not just ignoring my decision; you're steamrolling it. Wow, Ben. Just... Wow." The words tumbled out, a mix of shock and disdain, as I tried to wrap my head around the sheer audacity of his proposition.

In that moment, the shift in Ben's demeanor was stark–from calm and almost jovial to dead serious. He must have realized that his 'generous offer' was not being received as intended, but rather as a deeply flawed move. His tone became more earnest, delving into business logistics, spouting numbers and percentages, and marketing expenses. But I was only half-listening. It all felt like a smokescreen, a feeble attempt at justification.

"How long have you known Logan, anyway? And whose brainchild was this whole scheme? I want the truth," I pressed him.

"I've always been honest with you. Logan and I go way back, but why does it matter, Pumpkin?" he responded, still using that nickname that I was now starting to loathe.

"Stop calling me that. Why have I never seen him around you or heard about him?"

"We were in different states, kept it casual, you know.

"And just who came up with this idea?"

"You'd probably think it was me," Ben said, defiantly and evading a direct response.

"I'm asking for a straightforward answer, Ben."

"I am being straightforward, Hina. You're the one dramatizing this situation," he retorted.

I recalled our earlier meeting in the café and the way he inquired about my business. Now, it all seemed that it had been too calculated, as if he had been plotting or keeping tabs on me. Yet, every time I pondered this idea, the thought of a million-dollar investment muddied the waters. It seemed improbable for someone to spend that much just for a personal saga.

We moved around the library, and he occasionally glanced at the books while we talked. My attempts to learn more about Logan were met with either non-specific answers or more ambiguity.

"So, the papers show Logan owning 51% and you 49%. Does that make him the mastermind, the boss of this plan?"

Now, I'm tossing him a bit of bait, the kind that men dislike, the kind that pricks their pride and status.

"No, it just means he invested a bit more in the LLP than I did," he explained.

I raised an eyebrow, now ready to delve deeper, but Ben cut in first.

"You've always been like this, Hina. Always overlooking something crucial. Missing the trademark–it's not an accident. It's just you. Who you are. You get everything else right but always miss a key detail, just like you did in our relationship."

I stared at him, baffled and now furious. "What are you even talking about?"

"Do you trust all your friends?" he suddenly asked.

"What does that have to do with any of this?" I shot back, my eyes narrowing in suspicion.

"I guess you do, like most people do," he said nonchalantly, then smiled and turned back to the bookshelf. His evasiveness was infuriating, every answer leaving still more questions in its wake.

My anger was teetering on the edge, a volcano about to erupt. I was at a crossroads–I could unleash my fury, maybe throw a punch or two his way, or just walk away. I chose the latter, my pride nudging me toward the quieter exit. I turned, adjusted my bag, and started to walk away, but Ben wasn't done. His voice, louder now, chased after me with his parting words.

And those words sparked me suspicion, Jealousy, Anger.

"Here's a little wisdom from my journey, Pumpkin, something that might shed some light for you. You know, folks often wear rose-colored glasses when it comes to friends. Most of us have a handful of pals, around 3-5, with whom we share our deepest secrets. But have you ever pondered where betrayal originates? It's not the strangers or the obvious foes we need to watch—it's those within our inner circle. Betrayal is a common tale, hinting that the threat often lurks among those we trust most. Since my teenage years, I've adopted what I call the 'MINUS one' rule. Imagine you have a group of friends; always consider that one among that group may turn on you, maybe they're even scheming as we speak. This approach isn't about feeding fear; it's about fortifying your defenses. Expecting a possible betrayer keeps you on your toes, preserves your well-being. It's not the cheeriest outlook, but it's kept me vigilant and, in its own way, kept me secure."

Now frozen in my tracks, I stopped. but I didn't turn around. Ben's voice continued, his words weaving through the air like that of a serpent.

Minus one?

"Hey, what if you only have one or two friends?"

"Even then, you need to entertain the possibility that this one might betray you."

This bastard's thinking seems pretty dense, almost bordering on sociopathic behavior.

Yet, despite that, his words managed to trigger my suspicions.

"Think of it this way–statistics don't lie. People often blind themselves with the idea of having unique, special bonds. But at the core, humans are driven by survival and self-interest. These instincts often eclipse friendships. Sure, there are strong, unbreakable friendships, but they're rarer than people like to believe. Everyone thinks they're the exception because of the memories shared with their friends, but it only takes one moment, one action, to shatter it all."

I don't want to add more details here. He just kept blurting these ideas, his theories.

It was almost like he had copied Logan's behavior and pasted it into himself.

I couldn't stand it, so I ended the meeting quickly.

We parted ways, and I hurried out.

My mind was a massive whirlwind of thoughts, as I drove my mom's car. I was so rattled, I barely managed to keep my focus on the road. Was Ben just being manipulative again, or was there a grain of truth in his cynicism?

But wait, there was this part that had almost fucked my brain. One particular part.

Could one of my close friends, directly knowing my business, have so easily betrayed me?

Even though I tried to avoid directing my thoughts in this direction, it still hit me like a bolt out of the blue,–Lilly. She was the only one who connected me, Belle Epoch Envy, Logan, and Ben. That thought was like acid in my mouth. Could Lilly, of all people, be involved in this situation? But why would Ben drop such a hint if he and Logan were actually working together?

GOSH ALMIGHTY!

FUCK IT!

The more I thought about it, the more the pieces seemed to fit, and yet it felt so wrong. Lilly, my friend, caught up in this web of business and betrayal? It was a possibility I couldn't ignore, even as every part of me rebelled against the thought. The drive home was a blur, my mind racing faster than the car. Even so, what could she tell me, anyway? and most of all, why would Ben hint at such a thing, such distrust if he was really allied with Logan?

PART III

Chapter XXVIII:

Fedora Guy

The meeting with Ben left me feeling like I'd hit a dead end. Sure, there was a lot of talk, but did I really gain anything substantial? It seemed not. There were words, yes, but did they give me any new insights? Not really. Instead, they had just laid down the obvious gauntlet, so now it was my turn. I braced myself for what felt like a business showdown - a race to see whose Belle Epoch Envy would flourish first and best - theirs or mine.

My slight advantage? I had an established clientele. They boasted deeper pockets and the trademark. Yet, in the complex dance of business, especially in a capitalist setting, tiny details can indeed make a big difference. My existing customer base could be my trump card. If I could demonstrate nationwide brand recognition, their trademark claim might weaken. After all, they were newbies, their business was barely off the ground. It was a matter of who could cement their brand's presence faster and better.

In the midst of all the planning, Michael had interjected his own ideas. He suggested I focus more on expanding and infusing fresh creativity into my Belle Epoch Envy. A direct face-off between Ben and Logan wasn't the best strategy. Then he dared to propose that I stop attending interviews. No way was I giving that up–those interviews were a lifeline, a crucial part of my routine, energizing me for all the other battles I now had to face.

So, I continued,

Juggling everything.
Managing interviews, favoring the online,
To ease the schedule.
But still zipping around,
For in-person meetings.

My plate was overflowing,
Dreaming about Belle Epoch Envy,
Unraveling Logan and Ben's scheme,
Accepting the harrowing idea,
Of betrayal among friends,
And keeping my finances in check.
Each aspect,
Demanding its own important
Share my attention.

BOOM - Brain

Then Mikey reminded me, "Derrek, you totally forgot about him." Right, Derrek. Yet there was another piece in my ever-growing puzzle. How much could one girl handle? It felt like standing in the eye of a storm. Oh Boy! What next?

The following two weeks were a whirlwind, each day heavier than the last. I powered through a marathon of job interviews, feeling exhausted and convinced I'd botched every single one. Surprisingly, though, I landed three major projects, one even linked to the Internet industry. Meanwhile, Ben and Logan couldn't touch me legally–their LLP was too new, giving me a precious window of time to roll out a new marketing blitz for Belle Epoch Envy.

Gathering the troops, Abby and I huddled over strategies. I hesitated before involving Lilly, but eventually, I called her in. We laid everything out–the whole saga, minus the unsettling last bit Ben had said to me. Lilly's reaction was one of shock, followed by a flurry of creative ideas and different perspectives. She also prodded me, "Are you sure you're not missing something here?"

At first, it felt like a typical brainstorming session. But as the hours ticked by, Lilly seemingly bending over backward to rationalize Ben and Logan's actions, and something in me snapped. My patience had left the building, and I couldn't hold back any longer.

"Lilly, you're wearing love goggles! You can't see the red flags when you're busy painting them pink because of Logan," I exclaimed and threw up my hands up in exasperation.

Lilly, ever the diplomat, replied with a hint of a smile, "Oh, Hina, it's not about being Team Logan or Team Hina. I'm trying to be the referee here and see the game from all angles."

The atmosphere was so charged, you'd think we were slicing tension, not cake. I leaned in closer, my emotions on my sleeve, voice quivering just a tad. "Okay, let's frame it like this: Character A craft her dream brand, only to have her ex and his buddy clone it, even stealing the name, totally stealing her thunder. If this were a script in a Rom-com, minus romance and with a pinch of corporate espionage, who would be the villain?"

Michael's stealthy handhold under the table was my silent cheering squad. But my gaze? Totaling on Lilly, waiting for that lightbulb moment.

Lilly mulled it over, the silence thickening between us before she finally chimed in, "Put in those terms, it screams foul play against Character A. Yet, knowing you and Logan, it feels like we're not seeing the full picture."

I had literally tried to show her what was happening from the neutral side, so of like without love-blinding it all, but she had decided to stay blind, I guess.

"That sounds like bias, not objectivity," I snapped back, my frustration now spilling over. "How well do you really know Logan, Lilly? His past, his teenage years, anything before you met? You didn't even know he was close to Ben. Are you sure you're not missing the big picture?"

Abby interjected, but I was well past the point of calm discussion. Michael's grip tightened, a silent plea to me to calm down, but I was spiraling.

"Have you known his past life, what he was doing in his teenage years or before, or a little after? You did not even know he was close friends with Ben, my ex, so what do you call knowing him well? Maybe you don't know him at all. Does that give you any idea about putting feelings first than being non- biased?" I finished and my gaze locked with Lilly's.

Michael tried to gently pull me away, as Abby voiced her concern about my sudden outburst. But I couldn't stay there a moment longer. I abruptly stood up and made my way to the balcony, needing to escape the suffocating atmosphere of the room and gather my thoughts in a cooler solitude.

After the heated exchange, Lilly did offer an apology, although it was somewhat half-hearted. She promised to dig deeper, ask

Logan some tough questions. I almost dismissed the idea, but I accepted her apology, although not fully convinced. Abby suggested I should apologize too, but I didn't. In my mind, I was in the right.

But then, everything escalated. Ben and Logan actually opened a physical shop named Belle Epoch Envy, right near J Street. It was a bold move and one I hadn't anticipated. They had the funds, so they were making a big play. It felt like I was losing the visibility battle, their physical presence better able to draw in the clientele that I was vying for. My window of opportunity was narrowing and very fast.

Desperate, I turned to my mom for help. We met in Davis, where she was working on a media story. Initially, she braced herself for a financial plea, ready to launch into her usual lecture before ultimately saying" no". But when I laid out the whole situation in detail, she was genuinely taken aback. "Let me see what I can do," she said.

I needed her to unearth any link between Logan and Ben. The mystery surrounding them was thick, and I needed clarity, a way to strategize effectively. Time, however, was not on my side.

By early February, the results were mixed. I managed to gain 34 new customers and made sales to 13 regulars. The numbers weren't terrible, but in this race, I was in now, they felt insufficient. I didn't have the exact figures for the copycat Belle Epoch Envy, but from what I could tell–their bustling store, the foot traffic–they seemed to be outpacing me. Their dual approach of using online and brick-and-mortar retail was working. Each time I passed their shop and saw the crowd, it chipped away at my morale. The situation was becoming increasingly grim.

By then, I'd also racked up nearly 180 job interviews, a mix of online and in-person. Initially, I'd been doing pretty well, but then things hit a standstill, I had faced numerous rejections in recent times. Maybe word had gotten out about me, or more likely, my life had turned into such a chaotic mess that I couldn't give my all to prepping for these interviews. Yet, through it all, I had learned a ton–probably more about acing job interviews than anyone else in my state.

I also had this crazy goal in mind–hit 1000 interviews. Why? Because I wanted to make a mark, do something extraordinary, and then write a book about it. When you're not tied down to a 9-5 job, answering a boss, you've got the freedom to chase such wild dreams. But as free as I was to pursue this secondary passion, reaching that 1000 mark by the end of summer was now looking increasingly unlikely.

I was at a crossroads. I could either drop everything–my business, the whole Ben and Logan situation, and my unfinished business with Derrek–and just focus on the interviews, or I could try to juggle it all, with the very real risk of failing at everything. So, in typical Hina fashion, I chose the latter. I decided to balance it all, a daring move that meant keeping all the plates spinning without letting a single one crash. It was a bold, maybe even a foolish choice, but it was mine and mine alone.

President's Day fell on the third Monday in February, and Abby and I decided to unwind at a concert at the Crocker Art Museum. Michael was out with Dan, and Lilly had hinted she might drop by with updates on what she'd unearthed so far. At the concert, I spotted Derrek walking with someone who looked like a younger version of him–probably his brother. My instinct was to avoid him, not out of any reluctance to see him but to dodge any possible awkwardness.

He's near that camp.

No, near that beer shop.

Okay, he is moving toward Cam. A Direction.

Shit, I'll be spotted.

Okay, he is gone now.

Abby nudged me to go talk to him, but I hesitated. Then, as fate would have it, Derrek approached us, all alone, out of nowhere. Our greeting was the epitome of casual, the kind of exchange you have with an acquaintance you bump into unexpectedly. There were so many things I wanted to ask–about his brother, about the unresolved issue or business between us–but the words just wouldn't come out. Instead, we stuck to safe, superficial conversation.

"Say Hi to Michael for me, will you? We might have him on our podcast," Derrek said casually, breaking the brief silence.

Abby, ever the joker, chimed in, "A podcast with Michael? Ha! Make him famous, please!" And just like that, our brief encounter ended.

The next day, Michael was all over me with questions about bumping into Derrek. His curiosity was palpable, and I could tell he was both surprised and intrigued by the mention of a podcast or perhaps just by Derrek actually approaching me.

The battle for the name was a bit of a joke, really. My e-commerce site wasn't exactly professional-grade–I'd hired an amateur to set it up–but at least the name was mine. Their site, however, went for an abbreviation, something like B.E. E followed by a string of characters. It was clever in a way.

It didn't take long for my friends to notice that their website traffic was skyrocketing past mine. It was a harsh reminder that, in the start-up world, money talks. They had the financial muscle to push their site forward, and it was obviously working.

I kept plugging away with flyers and posters, and I even started handing out questionnaires to customers. It was my way of keeping Belle Epoch Envy in their minds, building recognition for the day when it would hopefully really matter.

March rolled in like a whirlwind, bringing the spring storms with it. In the first two weeks alone, I had thirteen job interviews lined up. Then, something odd happened, and I stumbled across an online article about a girl changing her appearance and name for job interviews. It wasn't exactly my story, but it was eerily similar. They didn't have all the details right, but it felt like my secret was out. As a result, I started scaling back on interviews, channeling more of my energy into Belle Epoch Envy.

The new season meant a new collection, which also meant a new budget. My finances were stretched thin, as I poured more into marketing, cutting back on my own expenses. My stress levels soared, and my interest in job interviews waned. My once-beloved hobby was slipping down my list of priorities as financial concerns now took center stage.

Discussions with my friends about the situation also often ended in frustration. Their copycat version of Belle Epoch Envy won, and it stung. The idea of taking legal action as my last resort loomed over me. That was a high-stakes gamble–I could either win back my brand or lose everything I'd worked for. That thought alone was enough to keep me up at night.

When I finally looked into getting a lawyer, I found that the costs were eye-watering.

"What did you expect, Hina? Lawyers don't come cheap," Michael said when I mentioned it. I argued that the fees seemed too much for the average person, but he did have a point. "Look, it's not much compared to what they can win for you in a case," he reminded me. He was right, lawyers often fought against big companies and won settlements that dwarfed their fees. So, I managed to scrape together enough for the initial consultation, where I was advised to gather every bit of documentation and client testimonials related to my company. It was a monumental task, but totally necessary for the case.

Then, something unexpected happened. In February, I had received a few emails asking for job interview tips, which I hadn't paid much attention to at first. I sent out a couple of responses, but that was it. Come March, I was surprised by follow-up emails that were full of praise for my advice. A girl from Iowa, along with her friends, were particularly struck by the way I'd written my interview tips.

And, by the way, that girl? She morphed into this almost mythical supporter, akin to a fairy godmother. Bless her heart.

Sometimes, small support carries with a bigger ability -

To change.

They even asked if I'd ever considered writing fiction or non-fiction. I had dabbled in short stories in my teens, but nothing serious.

These kids were not just thankful for the interview advice. They actually saw potential in my writing. They suggested that if I continued going to so many interviews, I should consider writing a book about it. To be honest, I had always toyed with the idea of writing a book, not about interviews, but about my overall achievements to inspire other girls who were facing tough choices in this cutthroat capitalist world. But this was a new angle.

Discussing it with Abby, she saw the potential too. "If you can find the time, why not try it?" she encouraged. "Write about your job interviews, but spin them like fiction, sort of like short novels."

When I mentioned this idea to Michael, he looked at me with that usual straightforward gaze of his and said, "Why not make some capital out of it?" Maybe this was indeed an opportunity, a chance to channel my experiences into something creative, something uniquely mine.

Juggling another new project, however, seemed like an impossible feat. My plate was already overflowing, and the thought of adding something else right now was overwhelming. Writing every story based on interviews? It was a tantalizing idea, but realistically, how could I manage that task along with everything else?

Lilly, meanwhile, wasn't much help with the Logan and Ben situation. She regaled us with what felt like a rehearsed narrative of Logan's past–his Stanford days, a master's degree, family business ventures, and then the friendship with Ben in L.A. (That's where it all had started) It all sounded so scripted, and I had no way to verify the stories. Doubting Lilly didn't sit right with me, but I couldn't shake off a nagging sense of skepticism either. I had to take her word at face value.

Regarding the creation of B.E. E, Lilly confessed to having a heated argument with Logan. He had insisted that what they were doing was somehow for my benefit, for everyone's benefit. But even if that were true–and that was a big 'if'–it reeked of poor judgment. It felt manipulative, disrespectful. It was as if they thought all the decisions were theirs to make, with no consideration for me, or perhaps even women in general. This time, though, I didn't push Lilly for more. The whole situation was just too convoluted, and I was too drained to dive any deeper into it.

Each revelation, each piece of the puzzle, just added to the complexity of the situation. I felt caught in a web of half-truths and corporate machinations, with no clear way out. The idea of adding a book-writing project to this mix seemed ludicrous. I had to prioritize, focus on the battles I could win, and maybe, just maybe, find some space for myself amidst all the chaos.

My Mom's sudden re-entry into the mix threw me a bit off balance. "Come down to Davis, and I can fill you in on what I've found. Or maybe bring that boyfriend of yours," she said, with a hint of teasing about Derrek–clearly unaware of the latest developments. She had just got back from a dreamy trip to the Virgin Islands with her fiancé and was buzzing with stories. But those had to wait. I was zeroed in on the task at hand.

I needed a ride, and Michael was my go-to. We waited for the weekend, and when Sunday finally rolled around, we set off for Davis.

Initially, what my mom shared seemed unspectacular, almost trivial. But then she pointed out something odd–there were no photos, no mutual friends, or neighbors who could vouch for Logan and Ben's history together. It was like they had no shared past that anyone could confirm. That was suspicious.

"Mom, I'm dying to hear all about your amazing trip to V islands and get the scoop on husband number four, but that's got to wait. First things first, okay?"

Then she showed me a photo. At first glance, it looked like an ordinary–Logan with a party buddy, meeting two guys I didn't recognize. The dude on the right was dressed all classic in a grey fedora and suit, standing by another guy who was sporting glasses. It appeared as though Fedora Guy was introducing Glasses Guy to Logan and his friend, captured mid-handshake, all smiles and formalities.

"Okay, Mom, and?" I asked, not seeing where this was leading. She shrugged it off as just a 'reminder photo' for future reference. I was perplexed, but I let it slide, pivoting to ask about Arizona instead.

Mom confirmed Logan had grown up in Phoenix. She had even talked to his old neighbors. But when it came to Ben, the trail was cold. No one in Logan's supposed neighborhoods, at Stanford or the high school Logan attended, remembered him. "You've done quite the digging," I remarked, very impressed.

She smiled, then added, "There's been no overlap between Logan and Ben for years, except this year."

"This year?" I echoed, clearly puzzled.

"Sorry Honeybee, last year, 2023," she corrected. My curiosity piqued.

"So, what's their connection?" I asked, glancing at Michael, who now also seemed equally intrigued.

"Ben, he's from Sacramento and L. A, right? Well, a friend helped me check on him. Did you know he was arrested the year that you two were dating?" she revealed.

"Arrested?" I was taken aback.

"Yes, but there were no convictions. It's not public, but he was involved in a bar fight in L. A that left several people injured." Her words left me stunned, my mind racing with the new information about Ben. He had never told me anything about it, but then again, I was too young to understand back then when I reflect back on it now.

"Do you know the specifics? Why exactly was he was arrested? What happened?" I asked, my curiosity piqued.

"No, Sugar, no solid details. He was arrested temporarily and released the next day. It's not public knowledge whether the arrest was even related to the bar incident; it's just what witnesses reported at the time."

She then pulled out her phone, showing me a photo. It wasn't a physical copy like the first, but a digital snapshot of another photo. She zoomed it for a better view. "Do you see them?" she asked.

I squinted at the screen. "Wait, that's Logan and the Fedora guy again," I tried to make sense of it.

Then, it hit me, and my jaw dropped in disbelief. The man standing next to the Fedora guy wasn't the same person in the earlier photo. It was Ben. Michael peered over, confirming my suspicion. The same scene, the same characters, but with Ben replacing the unknown guy.

"What's going on here? Why is the same scene repeated with everyone except Ben who is replacing the other guy?" I asked, and my brain tried to connect the dots.

"It's not just Ben. The locations are different too," my mom pointed out. She held the first photo next to the phone. "See, the first one's in front of the Jiggle Bar in Phoenix, and this one with Ben is in L. A, outside Merchant's Fish Restaurant. Look at the backgrounds. They're different."

I stared at the two images, now side by side, each a piece of a puzzle that seemed to grow more complex with every new discovery. The same people, different locations, and Ben was somehow intertwined in it all.

Now it was Michael's turn to speak, trying to piece together the clues. "So, there's evidence here they knew each other before the party, right?"

"Seems so," my mom confirmed.

"And do we have any idea when this photo was taken? Before or after Lilly got involved with Logan?" he asked. His question sent a ripple of realization through us.

We exchanged glances, the implication of his question now dawning on us. "Oh boy, it's hard to pinpoint the exact timing of the photo, especially since the original is on paper and I only took the digital version recently. But it looks like it was taken in early spring, my little darlings," Mom replied.

"Early spring... And Lilly met Logan in late summer. Hmm," Michael mused.

"But that doesn't really clear anything up. It just adds more unanswered questions," I pointed out, now feeling a mix of frustration and intrigue.

Mom then leaned in, her tone more assured. "Here's the deal. The guy in the Fedora, he's not just a friend of Logan or Ben's. He's a solo businessman. Not officially, but he does broker connections between interested parties."

"What?" Michael and I both exclaimed, surprised.

"He facilitates introductions between potential business partners. Say you need someone to ship your items cheaply to New Zealand. Instead of scouring the market yourself, you pay him, and he finds the right person for you. He's been working with Logan for years, and these photos suggest..."

"He was introducing people to Logan, those people whom Logan found interesting or useful," I said, finishing her thought.

In that moment of silence, a thousand thoughts raced through my head. This Fedora Guy, setting up connections for Logan, and

Ben was a recent addition–it all pointed to one thing. Logan and Ben had been spinning lies, and not just little white lies, but big, elaborate ones. Why? It had to go back to Belle Epoch Envy and to me. There was no other reason that could make sense.

My thoughts drifted to Lilly. "Lilly... has Logan been lying to her as well?" I murmured more to myself than to anyone else. Michael just shook his head, his expression clearly mirroring the turmoil I felt.

As Mom started to get up, I couldn't let the discussion go. "Mom, is there anything else? Anything at all?" She just shrugged. "Nope, that's it." That was Mom–always straight to the point. She left, saying she would call me soon.

Michael looked at me, clearly impressed. "Your Mom's done some serious digging. How did she even find all this? And those photos–they're not just anyone's game."

I couldn't help but feel a surge of pride. "Moms in the media, Michael. Journalists have their ways, you know. Digging up information, uncovering the hidden–it's what they do best."

Chapter XXIX: Into The Wild

"Letters after stealing my dreamchild business,"

I put a pause on gathering stories and interviews for my "maybe someday book," and that's where I left off. But then, life threw some bigger stuff my way, giving me a positive nudge to pick up where I left off. So, here I am, back at it, trading the pen for the keyboard to keep the story going.

This spring was a turning point in my life's story. When I first began to recount my tale, it might have sounded whimsical, even light-hearted. But the reality was a stark contrast–these past four years were a maelstrom of drama and tragedies, each more intense than the last. Every twist and intense turn in my life always seemed to happen in spring, leaving me to deal with the aftermath in the hotter summer.

There was Belle Epoch Envy, for instance. Tyrese and I sat together, poring over our recent orders, our calculations painting a picture of the potential profits for the upcoming month.

Arizona - yes

Colorado - Yes and no

Texas but there - Yes Yes Yes, Tyrese was shouting! ...

Debit card went to minus, so are you renewing? - Yes Yes.

Eventually, there came a moment, heavy with unspoken truth, when we glanced at each other, and a mutual understanding dawned without a word being uttered. We were losing–it was a hard, gut-wrenching realization, but it was a precise and accurate one.

On the 4th of April, our counterparts at B.E. E, the copycat version of Belle Epoch Envy, hosted an event. They unveiled their new collection amidst an entertainment spectacle–a lingerie giveaway that drew a considerable crowd, predominantly women. It was a clear signal that they were gaining the upper hand.

Michael and I were both worried as we went over our documents. We showed them all to our lawyer and explained everything, including how Ben and Logan's B.E. E was becoming more popular. The lawyer said our chances in court were slim since B.E. E was more famous now. She'd fight for us, but she didn't expect to win.

Sure. that's what every lawyer says. Losers or not.

It would take a long time and cost a lot, with no sure outcome. For days, I wrestled with the decision about the lawsuit. Finally, with a heavy heart, I chose to postpone legal action against Ben and Logan. Instead, I focused on bolstering my brand's recognition and making Belle Epoch Envy unassailably more credible.

But was I making the right decision?

Is giving up really that easy?

Hina...

I said Hina! ...

Yes, it is easy when you have a backup plan already in motion!

That night, swept away by Joshua, Michael, and an unexpected Lilly, we hit the bowling alley, a welcome detour from all the chaos. Amid the clatter of pins, Lilly and I bridged the gap that stress had widened between us, affirming our bond beneath the din of rolling balls and falling pins. "We're still tight," I assured her, her embrace a silent echo of our mended ties.

I skirted around Logan and Ben's betrayals but also dropped hints for Lilly to stay guarded. "Watch out for men's silver tongues," I quipped, masking my advice as jest. She understood, though, her second hug laden with her silent acknowledgment.

Our laughter veiled a shared solitude, mine being steeped in a silent skirmish against unseen adversaries. Yet, amidst this camaraderie, a sliver of solace flickered. We ended the evening with a toast, joking about Abby's health obsession. I decided to walk home, using that quiet time to think.

On that walk, an idea hit me. I remembered the positive feedback on my interview stories. "What if each lingerie piece I sell comes with a story, mixing fiction with job interview tips?" The thought of blending these two worlds excited me.

By the time I got home, I was full of ideas.

Bras

Corsets

Underwear,

Each would offer unique tutoring stories.

But not their own stories,

The real ones,

My experiences,

Me, sitting in the offices.

Me, responding to the Hrs.'

The Job interviews!

EMPOWERING!

I envisioned a collection where every lingerie piece tells a story, offering something more than just style, instead of a connection, a shared experience. This new direction felt right to me, like a fresh start, merging fashion with stories to create something truly unique.

I spent the entire night lost in this brainstorm, with Mikey asleep beside me, oblivious to the storm of creativity traveling in my head. Frantically, I scoured the Internet, searching for anything remotely similar to my idea. I found nothing. After two days of intense thought and planning, I decided to take the plunge. It was time for a rebranding, a fresh start, and yet even with the modest finances at my disposal, I knew I'd need a loan.

First, I pitched the idea to Michael. We brainstormed and concluded that not only should we change the name but also the trademark and do it immediately. By 'change', I meant tweaking it, adding a word or letter here and there. The plan was audacious, even maybe a little crazy, but it felt right.

Applying for loans turned out to be a tougher ordeal than I anticipated. Every business loan I applied for slammed the door in my face. I finally managed to secure a personal loan of $8,500. Not a fortune, but enough to breathe new life into my cherished Belle Epoch Envy. My rebranding strategy was simple, yet intriguing. We transformed Belle Epoch Envy into "Based on Stories of Belle & Envy." It had a nice ring on it. Right? Each lingerie piece would carry the tagline "Based on: Stories of Belle & Envy," promising customers a monthly dose of interview stories with tips and guidance, a useful blend of real-life experiences and a dash of fiction.

We threw ourselves into marketing this revamped brand. The website underwent a transformation, our emails got a fresh facelift, and we announced the changes to our entire customer base. It was a whirlwind of activity, and I was constantly buzzing with excitement.

Then, there was the Iowa girl–the one who'd sparked this whole idea. I sent her the results of our rebranding efforts, and to my delight, we started talking regularly. She was incredibly supportive, cheering me on from the sidelines. It felt good, knowing there was someone out there who believed in this crazy venture of mine.

As spring continued, I plunged deeper into my rebranding project. The Iowa girl and I exchanged numerous emails, discussing the finer points of the storytelling concept and sharing our recent triumphs and tribulations. Our correspondence was uplifting and motivational. We sometimes discussed our personal lives, and she occasionally offered valuable insights into both marketing and customer engagement. I also attempted to entice her with a promising position if my latest project was successful, but she hesitated, claiming she was still studying, but kept that option open.

I decided to take a leap of faith and started an online community for my brand. I set up forums, blog posts, and even began posting videos of myself discussing different lingerie styles and their accompanying stories. I received surprisingly positive feedback, and my subscribers grew steadily. Let me break it all down for you. What really went down? With this new twist in the tale, Ben and Logan were pretty much out of taking legal moves. They couldn't sue me anymore because I wasn't using the Belle Epoch Envy name. Instead, I had this unique, quirky combo — a mash-up of two different worlds under a fresh, distinct banner. And who was the star of the show? It turned out there was a whole crowd of people just itching to dive into my treasure trove of interview stories.

This new venture sucked up my time like a vacuum. Attending physical job interviews soon became a mission impossible, so I did what any self-respecting, slightly desperate entrepreneur would do–I started concocting fictional interviews. If my brand was all about spinning tales, blending fiction with dashes of real-life women's empowerment, then why not stretch my creative muscles? So, I started dedicating three to four hours almost daily to crafting these stories.

You know what? It worked like a charm. My collection of interviews, both real and imagined, ballooned in no time. Before I knew it, I had crossed over 500. It felt like running a marathon in the world of storytelling and job interviews, each step a new adventure, each story a new conquest. One evening, as I was immersed in crafting a fictional interview, my phone began to ring. Initially, I ignored it, thinking it was just a distraction. Then I glanced at the screen and saw it was Derrek calling. I hesitated. At first, I thought maybe it was a misdial,

But the ringing did not stop.

It did not.

My eyes started sliding.

It's no misdial, huh?

... and the persistent ringing told me otherwise. Curiosity piqued, I put my writing aside, cleared my throat, and answered with a casual, "Hi there."

We exchanged the usual pleasantries, the "how are you's and "how's life treating you all, but then Derrek dropped a bombshell that perked me up in an instant.

"You won't believe what happened! Brad and his friend–Oh, I forget his nickname–they've been arrested and are waiting for their trial!"

"What? What?" I stammered, my mind racing.

"Yes, yes, it's crazy! Adrianna called the cops. Brad and his friend tried to force her into... well, you know. The police were quick to respond, but now their lawyers were scrambling to get them out on bail. It's going to be a hefty sum. Listen, Hina, there's more, but I can't say it all over the phone.

"You know, though. Right?"

"Right! The hearing is in four days. Meet me near the Sacramento Superior Court, before or after the hearing. Okay?"

As Derrek finished speaking, I found myself nodding in agreement without even thinking. My heart was racing, a jumble of emotions swirling insanely inside me.

Holy fuck.

Holy fuck.

Is it really happening?

Please let it be happening.

Nervousness, excitement, and a surreal sense of disbelief all hit me at once. I couldn't focus on the unfinished interview story in my notebook, as my hands were trembling. I just closed it.

I stood in front of the mirror for probably fifteen minutes, unable to move, as my mind raced with thoughts. I was trying to process the unexpected news I had just received. Time seemed to stand still as I stared at my own reflection, searching for some kind of clarity. Any kind. Eventually, feeling overwhelmed by it all, I stepped outside into the cool night air and aimlessly wandered under the glittering stars. Each step felt like an attempt to unravel the implications of what I had just been told. The idea of sleep seemed impossible, but eventually exhaustion caught up with me, and I made my way back home. Sleep was now my top priority.

Chapter XXX:

Plan C works

If you'd met me five years back, you'd probably not recognize the person I am today. Life's been a whirlwind, morphing me in ways I'm still trying to figure out. Before, I was just another girl, doing the usual–at least trying (and often failing) to catch the eye of any good-looking guy, getting caught up in who was texting or asking me out, fretting over the perfect lipstick for Jessica's birthday, or hunting down a potential Mr. Right while binge-watching a bunch of makeup tutorials.

But then, my time at GSU sparked a change. I was stuck on constant repeat, caught up in the same old cycles of social drama, beauty obsessions, and the pursuit of romance. This party, that party blah blah. blah Then something clicked. I realized I was chasing after a script that wasn't mine, letting trivial things dictate my happiness and worth. It was like I was on a merry-go-round of superficial concerns, not really living, just existing in a bubble of expectations and media eyeliner tips. That realization was my wake-up call. It steered me away from the endless loop of seeking validation through others and into a journey of self-discovery and genuine interest. Then came the morning that was just like any other when I awoke to a knot of anxiety in my stomach. It struck me that by following society's scripted path, I was, perhaps without even fully realizing it, conceding power to men, relegating myself to playing a mere support role in the grand narrative of relationships and life. It felt fundamentally wrong, like I was perpetuating a cycle that persistently continues to undermine women's real worth.

Let me lay it out here real straight–not everyone will agree with me, and that's okay. But based on what I've seen and lived, most men, if you really press them, would say they value women equally. Still, let's face it. Society kind of strong-arms men into taking that stance. Underneath, I suspect, a whopping majority of men don't genuinely see women as equals or take them as seriously as they do their fellow men. Bring up the topic, and they'll likely dive into a defensive tirade filled with statistics and convoluted arguments. On paper at last, proving their bias is a tall order, but if you're even slightly intuitive, you'll pick up on the vibe that comes from most guys, even though education and exposure to different cultures can tweak this mindset a bit.

However, when cultural and evolutionary influences reinforce these biases, changing them becomes an immense undertaking. Still, I hold on to the belief that the issue is not insurmountable. And if I ever let go of that conviction, you might as well consider me gone. Maybe surrendering?

The greatest criticism women face isn't when they're unseen. It's not when they're followers, nor when men brag about their body count stories, it's when they stand firm in their autonomy, proclaiming they don't need men for success. That's when the commentary by men transcends mere criticism and ventures into realms that are less justified and more emotional (?).

Do I hate men? No, not at all. Do I see the world as an unfair place? Nope. Do I view myself and other women as victims? Definitely not. Michael once said something that stuck with me, namely, that there's no cosmic rule mandating fairness in our lives. Honestly, I have to agree with him. Nature isn't about justice; it's about being what it is. And we, as part of nature, have the choice to either adapt and survive or strive to change and reshape things around us. Perceptions can and do evolve over time, and as I've come to realize at last, all beliefs are time-bound. Today's truth and its ideas may not hold true at a different age.

Back in those days, Ben and Logan's Belle Epoch Envy, buoyed by a significant budget, flourished on social media, their posts amplified and their brand visibility skyrocketing. They had carved out alliances with modeling agencies, propelling their enterprise to a vantage point I once dreamed of having for my own. Witnessing them usurp my brainchild was bitter, and yet during this turmoil, I stumbled upon a wonderful sanctuary in my writing. It became my solace, fully intertwining with the fabric of my lingerie business and offering a fresh narrative thread.

Within weeks, the tide began to shift. Sales inched upward, not yet eclipsing their own limelight, but still marking my independent ascent. Then, serendipity struck—a couple, introduced to me by Abby, saw potential in my venture. They weren't just investors; they were believers in my vision, offering support on far more equitable terms than any I'd ever encountered. Armed with their backing, I secured a modest workspace and gathered around me a team as invested in this journey as I was.

We ventured into publishing our stories, weaving through the printed word, testing the waters with Sacramento Interview Stories. It wasn't just a project; it was a harbinger of possibilities, a prelude to something far grander.

Encouraged by friends, I persevered with the job interviews, aiming for that thousandth milestone—a tapestry of real and imagined narratives that could be poised to captivate a diverse audience. It wasn't merely about reaching a number; it was about crafting a symphony of stories that resonated with seekers of guidance, aficionados of fiction, and lovers of lingerie, each thread a clear testament to resilience and reinvention in a world that's always constantly evolving.

After completing/ refining my latest fictional job interview narrative, I closed my notebook and decided on a hot shower to refresh myself–even though I had taken one just three hours earlier. The warm water cascading over me was soothing, but my mind was far from relaxed. As the shower hummed in the background, I find I was consumed by thoughts about the ongoing court hearing. Right at that very moment, a judge was probably deciding whether to grant bail to Brad and Dazzy Bee.

Or not. Should I think about it?

Or not?

These questions would keep drilling my brain until that moment came.

In the warm and protected confines of the shower, various courtroom scenarios played out in my head. The uncertainty and anxiety were all inside me, refusing to be washed away. Brad and Dazzy, with their family wealth and connections, were likely to have a formidable legal team. The principle of 'innocent until proven guilty' could tilt the scales in their favor, making bail a real possibility. Still, I also knew that the opposing team, i.e., the prosecution, might have a few aces up their sleeves too.

So Hina, where do you stand?

Where will you be standing in a few years?

Dressed and after a quick touch of makeup, I texted Derrek, who confirmed he was waiting near the Sacramento Superior Court. I hailed a taxi, but as it neared the courthouse, time seemed to stretch, each second feeling like an eternity. I needed a moment to collect my thoughts, so I asked the driver to let me out early, and I walked the remaining distance, about twenty to twenty-five minutes, letting the anticipation build with each step. The courthouse soon loomed in the distance. It was a symbol of justice, so I braced myself for whatever news awaited me.

There I was, lingering near the courthouse, watching a stream of faces, none of them familiar, floating in and out of the building. I wandered around for an extra fifteen to twenty minutes, wondering if the hearing had wrapped up and searching for Derrek. And then there he was. I quickened my pace toward him, and when he finally noticed me, we were close enough for a casual greeting.

We hadn't really spoken in months, and under normal circumstances, striking up a conversation might have felt a bit odd. But there was a more pressing issue at hand than our personal dynamics, and we both knew it. So, we dove right in, talking like old teammates, offering each other silent support from the get-go. Derrek even threw in a compliment or two about how I seemed to have changed for the better. I shrugged it off, joking that it was probably just my new makeup and dress.

His expression was practically radiating positivity. I couldn't help but think that something good must have happened; his smile was too big to contain. He was practically bursting with it.

"Has the hearing wrapped up?" I inquired, my eyes probably looking as wide as saucers.

With a grin, he signaled for us to move. However, I needed clarity.

"All done," he confirmed. "You're quite the eager one, aren't you?"

"They," he added, "are off to Sacramento County Jail. They'll be guests there for a handful of time until the Court calls them again."

My pace slowed, the news sinking in. I was tempted to plant my feet right there and demand every tidbit - about Adrianna, the case, the whole shebang, even if Martha was in the loop. But Derrek was relentless and nudged me forward with a hint of urgency. "She's just up ahead," he informed me, and I trailed behind him.

Not long into our stroll, Derrek halted, pointing towards a nook in the building that was dotted with benches.

"There, your treasure trove of info," he declared, nodding at Adrianna, who was perched on a bench there, awaiting us. Try as I might, words fall short of capturing the tornado of emotions I now felt - a cocktail of excitement, curiosity, relief, and a heart-pounding rush. Relief that justice was actually on the trail and awe at Adrianna's bravery.

As we drew closer, Adrianna rose to welcome us, her handshake firm. "How are you holding up?" she inquired. Yet my gut quickly steered the concern back to her.

"Hina Strubel!" she exclaimed as she stood up. In response, I offered a grin that I hoped mirrored the storm of feelings raging inside me.

It was a moment tinged with a bit of awkwardness, but that soon gave way to more natural conversation, punctuated by big, genuine smiles. There was a sense of camaraderie and shared understanding between us, a recognition of the gravity of the situation and the strength it took to confront it strongly.

Adrianna was the spitting image of her old self when she first hit Sacramento. Same face, though now framed by shorter hair, still in its familiar hue, accented with bold eyebrows and a fresh nose piercing. Her ensemble was on point — a light purple top, timeless trousers, and black, shiny high heels. Her fashion sense was spot on, and I couldn't resist admiring it.

"I caught wind of the scoop from Derrek. Those jerks got their just desserts, eh? The judge didn't hesitate to throw them behind bars. Right?" I probed, itching for her affirmation.

"Yep, the judge nailed it," she confirmed. "But let's be real. There wasn't much wiggle room. This isn't the curtain call, Hina. They're just stuck without bail for now. The main showdown for the final judgment is still on the horizon. But yeah, for the moment, we've snagged a tiny triumph we can cheer about. And by the way, you're looking stellar!"

Her words carried a mix of relief and cautious optimism.

"You're rocking it too. Seriously, that style is a total win on you. Now spill the beans — how's the ride been for you, and what's the scoop with the Court session? Any heat and pressure from their families?" I quizzed her, hungry for the nitty-gritty.

"Pressure? Pfft," she laughed it off. "When you're in the biz of unveiling skeletons in closets, getting flak comes with the territory. That's your media and the First Amendment. It's all part of the dance."

She then shifted gears. "About that day, it seems Derrek hasn't filled you in completely," she said, glancing toward Derrek, who immediately interjected, "We didn't get the chance to cover everything over the phone."

"Yeah, yeah," Adrianna responded, brushing it off and began her story. "I'm a bit pressed for time right now; the district attorney's waiting for me to discuss some case details. But I'll give you the quick version. That night, almost a week ago, I was at my apartment. Juan, my colleague, was working with me on a plant-related project and a podcast—you know, the one. However, he remained initially unnoticed by Brad well, as per plan. Everything was normal until Brad showed up with his ugly friend. He didn't even warn me he was bringing someone. When I opened the door, that's when he introduced us and started his charm offensive."

"Ah, the same old story," I said, half to myself.

Adrianna nodded and continued, "It's fascinating, really, how some guys hold on to those predatory traits, waiting for a vulnerable moment. Brad had been okay until then, with the usual ups and downs of any relationship. If I hadn't heard the story from you, I'd never have believed he was capable of something like this.

That evening, we were having a glass of wine–I made sure they drank first, of course. Jazz music was playing in the background. Dazzy Bee kept complaining, wanting something with a faster beat."

She paused for a moment before going on. "At some point, Brad started talking about his friends' relationships. They went on and on, story after story. I guess they thought that would warm me up for some 'intimate interaction.' Then Brad left for the bathroom, and his ugly friend took the chance to sit next to me. Tried to kiss me 'n stuff, and when I dodged, he tried again, managing a quick peck. I acted surprised, like 'what if Brad sees?' Then Brad came back, and they both subtly started hinting at a threesome. That was my breaking point. About half an hour later, Brad kissed me, but then it turned forceful, trying to push me toward his friend. I resisted, and things got physical. I started screaming at the top of my lungs. Suddenly, there was this loud banging at the door. They must have thought someone was entering or leaving my apartment, and they both took off after them. The minute they were out, I locked the door, called the cops, and wouldn't let them back in, even though they were pounding on the door."

She paused.

"Do..." She slowed down. "You know what that means?" and looked me in the eye.

Derrek was blinking his eyes, and then he caught up. I mean, he got the whole story, but he was missing a crucial detail, not that important for the whole case, but still an important detail, anyway.

I smirked.

Then I replied.

"Was dealing with the legal stuff tough? You know, working with your lawyer and all?"

"Oh, Jesus, not at all. I've had a long-standing relationship with my lawyer. He's assigned to our radio and newspaper, and I was pretty clued up on everything that could go wrong."

Now she hesitated again.

"But do you know what this really does mean, Hina? "Then she looked at Derrek, He glances back at her. his face saying he's had no idea what she was talking about. Then she continued, "Oh Jesus. "

I knew what she was talking about, and I knew what she was about to say or warn me about. But I did not have time for this, so I chose to feel admiration instead.

Hearing her, I couldn't help but feel a swell of pride. "How empowering and incredible! You've really made a difference in this world, Adrianna, not just generally, but especially for so many girls out there," I said, my voice thick with emotion and my eyes welling up slightly.

Now her smile vanished. No trace of a smirk. Her expression went blank, void of emotion. She cast a glance at Derrek.

"There were countless moments when I nearly convinced myself that it was all futile, that we were... I was just spinning my wheels, all for nothing, and maybe hurting the innocent, not just once, but over and over again."

"But look at you now—it all came together. Hats off to you, Miss Journalist. You turned the tide, this is success!" Derrek exclaimed with a mixture of awe and excitement.

"This success? Really, Derrek, you're still piecing it together? It seems you are still missing something. Hina, seems like you might need to fill him in on the whole picture," she added with a hint of irony and a smile.

I still understood her. I grasped every nuance of what she was conveying or attempting to do, and there was no urgency for elucidation.

All of these.

I didn't require it.

The world did.

They merely needed me to ignite a spark.

"It's alright, truly, Adrianna. You're phenomenal. Do keep us posted, okay? From what I gather, it's far from over, and the legal proceedings are ongoing," I hastened now to conclude the conversation, eager to depart with Derrek, well buoyed by a sense of joy, confidence, and pride.

Yet, we couldn't just leave.

As we concluded our discussion, Derrek merely nodded, offering Adrianna a comforting hug before trailing behind me.

But then we halted in our tracks.

"So, is this how you go? Will you be okay?" she inquired. She slowed down, yet her words trailed us as we began to distance ourselves. "With Hina stepping into danger?"

Hidden Chapter:

Broken Promise

There, my original chapter (to publish) was concluded, the plan was set, and I had no intention of altering it until an event of inexplicable shock and magnitude occurred, suddenly catapulting me into an entirely different realm. It was an event that shook my very core and reshaped my being, revolving around my mother, my sole family, the only blood relation I knew. Suddenly, the world as I understood it had transformed.

Perceptions do change, and thus,

So does my book.

The sentence that Adrianna suddenly threw hung in the air, unmistakably aimed at Derrek, causing him to pause, arrested by her words.

It took us a moment to exchange glances, seeking confirmation in each other's eyes. Well, Derrek seemed more to be seeking assurance that what he'd just heard was accurate. Then, with a sudden burst of movement, he spun around, taking three quick steps back toward Adrianna.

"Hina... in danger? What are you talking about?" he inquired.

Adrianna shifted her gaze from me to Derrek.

"Jesus Christ, you..."

"Look, I'm pressed for time, but I need to lay this thing out... Don't you recall how we kicked this off?"

Flashes of memory flickered through Derrek's mind.

"I remember, but how does that tie to Hina being in danger?"

"She's not currently, but that could change in a heartbeat. Maybe, maybe not. Dude, she orchestrated this entire ...scheme or operation or whatever you want to call it. I was just executing the plan, admittedly without full sight, but I had faith in it, and it materialized. But the brains of the operation? The architect of our success? Take a good look behind you!"

So, there I stood, a few paces back, my face unreadable, not advancing or betraying any emotion. Derrek glanced back at me and then turned his gaze forward again.

"I'm aware she was instrumental. It was our joint venture but..."

"But the nitty-gritty, the execution, the planning, the script, the timing. Who pieced that together? I'm not aiming to alarm you or seek pity. On the contrary, I'm grateful, profoundly so. We pulled it off together, but my worry is, what if those who got locked up, their kin, catch wind of it? You're not planning to spill the whole story in your book, are you, Hina?"

"The book?" Derrek echoed, puzzled.

I inch closer, trying to offer a bit of comfort.

"Look, I get your concerns, but relax. I won't share the story until everything's settled in court."

"Even after, things might shift," she interjects, then swiftly changes the topic, probably not wanting to dwell on the obvious tension.

"Anyway, this is all down to you. Those girls, they owe you big time. In an ideal world, everyone would be singing your praises. It's a shame how the justice system doesn't always lean our way, with the well-off and powerful often finding loopholes. But what you diddo? That's about filling those cracks the system leaves. All of you. I was skeptical at first, but you shone a different light on it all, driving me onward. It was a long haul, but it paid off," she says, pausing to take a breath.

She continued, "When Derrek called and asked me to come from five states away, I was surprised and excited. He never asks me to do that, but something about it felt right. The day you asked for my help, Hina, I saw something in your eyes–this mixture of emotion and a sort of helplessness. Your expression subtly revealed your disappointment with the world and its justice. You felt hopeless, and when I listened to you, I instantly believed Martha's story was true. I usually don't take sides without knowing both stories, so I got close to Brad to see if he was capable of such things. For months, I wondered if Martha's story was exaggerated, even until this day. But what's more important is the way you thought everything through, every possible move that would lead us to a successful legal hearing and invalidate their defense."

At that moment, I preferred remaining standing there in silence, not uttering a word. I could feel Derrek's glance shift toward me as Adrianna continued speaking.

He feels incomplete.

He missed something.

I bet he's thinking about that Wiretap ACT I passed to him.

Perhaps not.

"Hold up, hold up," he muttered. "...Every possible move that would lead us to a successful legal hearing and invalidate their defense...," he mumbles, turning his attention toward Adrianna. Then, like he's just pieced it together, he almost yelled, "We needed your help for the investigation, and you did it, and it was a hit. What's this about planning and running the whole show? What on earth are you both getting at?"

"Okay, let's go, she's got to be elsewhere," I say to Derrek.

"No, no, no. We're not going anywhere until you two explain what the fuck is happening here," he insists.

"Hina?" she prompts.

I nod and pull out my phone, signaling to Derrek that I need to make a call, and suggest he continue chatting with Adrianna in the meantime.

"She's got the instincts of a detective journalist," Adrianna remarks.

Now Derrek silently stares at Adrianna, prompting her to begin speaking. We didn't need any more tension at this particular moment.

"The trial isn't finished, and bail doesn't equate to a verdict or a final decision. They're just denied bail," she explains.

"I'm aware of that."

"It means things could shift, especially now."

"I understand that too," he responded.

"Your friend... she's aiming to... well, she's already working on a book. From what I gather, she's compiling stories about herself, her friends, and everything that's unfolding. What do you suppose will happen when it's public knowledge that the incident with Brad and his stupid buddy was orchestrated? It might lead the Court to dismiss our arguments and lean toward theirs. It's not straightforward, but it's certainly a concern."

"She won't publish, that's first," he interjects. "And secondly, what do you mean by 'orchestrated,' and how could Hina be in danger?"

"The danger is hypothetical, laden with 'ifs,' so I'd rather not dwell on it too much," she clarified.

"No, but now you have to."

"How much do you know about Brad Braxler and Dazzy Bee's families?"

"Not a lot, just that they're wealthy and such."

"Wealthy and such, huh? Ever consider there are always tales behind wealth and money?"

"Clearly."

"There's the kind that's known to the public, what we might call clean or legitimate money, and then there's the kind that isn't for public disclosure. It's not about the money itself, but its origins, where it comes from, and how it's circulated."

Now, Derrek was completely focused.

"This Dazzy Bee, or ..."

"Jesse" He finished her sentence by uttering Dazzy Bee's real name.

"Right, his father owns a shipping and logistics empire. Basically, he's got the Western U.S. ports under his belt, not to mention international routes–Central Asia, South Asia, South America... loads of money flowing in. But that's not the main point. The Feds have had their eyes on him numerous times, but always came up empty. Rumor has it he's involved in helping criminals transport illegal goods globally, and he's skilled at it. Arms, restricted items, sanctioned goods in and out of Russia, and so on."

"Criminal activities? Wow, are you serious?"

"Hold off on that. Wow, for now. This David Garcia, Jesse's dad, is a major supporter of the Governor. We're talking about campaign donations, Super PACs, in-kind contributions, and Dark Money Groups. They've been pals for a while."

"The Governor of California?"

"Yes, Dr. Martinez."

"Holy shit,"

"Exactly. Since Garcia's front appears clean, there's no need to hide their friendship. Now, let's move on to the Braxler family. Brad is into tennis, like his dad, who was quite a name in several states. Brad's dad is also married to Michelle Kim. Does that name ring a bell?"

"Nope."

"I didn't think so. Why bother with who's crafting your healthcare policies?" she replied sarcastically, then continued,

"Michelle is the Chief Deputy Director at DHCS California and oversees Medi-Cal, a significant entity."

Derrek glanced at me briefly, then turned back, "What's DHCS?"

"For heaven's sake, it's the Department of Health Care Services. Medi-Cal provides health coverage to Californians with low incomes or certain conditions. It's a cornerstone of California's healthcare system. Do you see where all this is going?" He paused, then continued,

"Just in case it's not clear, we're talking about two influential families. One allegedly involved in dark money politics and the other a key player in California's healthcare. These families are interconnected, and here's Hina, your friend, the interview collector, who's played a major role in putting their next generation behind bars, with our collective efforts, of course. If this story gets out, they might target Hina, legally or otherwise. That's the concern!"

Skipping over the next few minutes of Derrek's obvious and palpable shock, I should note that he repeatedly slapped his large hand against his forehead and chin and paced around nervously while exclaiming, "Holy crap," until a new thought struck him, prompting him to inquire further.

"So, these details you mentioned, the plan Hina crafted—what exactly did she strategize that we need to keep under wraps?"

Adrianna glanced at her watch, noting the time, and began to expound without delay.

I had wrapped up my phone call, but continued the charade, now with a fake call, the phone still pressed to my ear, feigning ongoing conversation. I chose to keep my distance, not wanting to join their exchange.

"Hina's blueprint was sophisticated," Adrianna elaborated. "She didn't just collect evidence. She built a story so solid that the Court had to listen."

Derrek's brow furrowed, signaling his intrigue. He had always viewed me as a teammate, not a central strategist or something.

"Your friend had the foresight to utilize my journalistic access not just as a cover, but as a strategic tool that eventually led me to pitching my boss to put up a live stream project with our co-worker there, so we started podcast project about plants, and local issues. That made every piece of evidence we gathered bulletproof; I mean the recording itself."

He finally got it. - "The video of Brad flipping out... that was planned?"

"The footage you are talking about, of Brad's and Jesses sexual assault attempt, — it wasn't a lucky shot. It was deliberately captured during a live stream that was part of a legitimate project we were running. This wasn't just any project, though. Hina proposed a live broadcast that focused on community issues and plants in Sacramento, solo broadcast style, which provided the perfect backdrop for our recording."

Derrek now interjected, "So the Court accepted the video because..."

"Because it was part of an official journalistic endeavor," Adrianna cut in. "When Brad's defense claimed the recording was a violation of privacy, they hit a wall. Our footage was obtained during a scheduled live broadcast, which viewers could tune into at any time. Our guy 'naturally' reacted to my screaming and 'naturally' directed the camera to the room where we were gathered. It was public, transparent, and most importantly, very legal."

"Damn... So, that's why she asked me if you had published a video recently?"

"Correct, also an idea of hers. She knew that speed was of the essence. By broadcasting the incident promptly, we maintained narrative control, forestalling any potential interference or distortion. It was a play for transparency, anchoring the truth firmly in the public domain, "She paused. "You know of course once that becomes public knowledge, even the most influential powers will find it difficult to interfere and use their influence to avoid reaction or punishment. That's the essential component that Martha's case lacked."

Derrek stepped back, absorbing it all and then muttered like an old man.

"She has really put herself on the line with this," His words showed concern, but that concern was mixed with admiration.

"Exactly," Adrianna responded. "And that's why we all have to be careful and especially you guys,"

He finally began to nod in understanding as our conversation neared its end. It was then that Adrianna stepped closer to me, a hint of urgency in her approach, as if a crucial piece of advice lingered on her lips. I had to take off my fake phone, call out my ears.

"Listen," she began, her voice low, underscored by the gravity of her words, "Theoretically, they could be released at the next bail hearing, or perhaps after an appeal. And even if they remain behind bars, the narrative could still tilt in their favor. The legal landscape is never cut and dry—it's layered, filled with shades of gray. Do you understand?" I remained silent, soaking in her words, but Derrek chimed in.

"The fuck? That quickly? How could that happen?"

Adrianna exhaled deeply, a sign of the weight she was carrying. "At one stage, their defense challenged my presence in Sacramento, probing the real purpose behind the project Juan and I were so deeply engrossed in. It's common knowledge that my studies were in agriculture, not journalism. Our cover story was it was for 'friends.' Still, the live broadcasting from my apartment wasn't a guise—it was genuine. Yet, this alignment didn't fully compute for them, sparking doubts that perhaps we had ensnared the suspects in a well-woven web. Should they convince the Court at the next session that our actions were premeditated, they might depict the entire operation as an elaborate act, a narrative that we spun. Such a twist could undermine our entire case."

Derrek stroked his chin, lost in thought, Adrianna turned her attention to me, her eyes locking onto mine with an intensity that bridged our silent understanding.

"It's imperative, Hina," she stated firmly, "That this story remains between us. No word of it should find its way into your book, not a single line. Can I trust you with that?" Her words weren't just a request; they were a plea, underlined by a shared commitment to the truth and the delicate dance of justice we all were a part of now.

We silently agreed.

Just the three of us.

Or maybe it was just me thinking.

We hugged and waved goodbye.

Then Adrianna was gone.

Now it was just us two, standing there, looking at each other, wondering what to do next.

No plans, no next moves. We just stood still. He stepped closer, patted my head, and pulled me into a comforting embrace.

"It's okay" he said...

He didn't question me about how Adrianna and I had exchanged messages without his knowledge, nor did I bring it up. It was somewhat comforting that he wasn't angry, but whether he was disappointed, I couldn't tell.

Eventually, we decided it was time to stretch our legs and take a walk. Though we didn't say much, as we moved forward side by side, there was a sense of shared accomplishment between us. We knew that what we had achieved was only a temporary victory in a much larger battle. But for that brief moment, walking together under the open sky, we allowed ourselves to give in to the sensation of being winners, even if just for a fleeting second.

"You know..." Derrek began, his voice trailing off as we walked. "For a while, I was actually scared that Adrianna had fallen for Brad. It was like she was in denial about it and didn't want to face the truth with you."

"Oh, shut up!" I replied quickly, giving him a side glance.

"But now, I realize I shouldn't have doubted her,"

"It's only natural, what do you mean. Come on." I asked.

"You know, she... she was subjected to abuse in her early teens, as a child..." Derrek said, his voice trailing off slightly.

I slowed my pace, my reply coming with a sudden quiet strength, "Yes, I'm aware."

He glanced at me, a hint of surprise in his gaze and then shook his head. "Ah, Hina, did you discover this before she decided to join our cause or after?"

I shrugged. "What does it matter, anyway?

He chuckled, shaking his head more and in that moment, I felt a compelling need to shift our talk away from the immediate events to something brighter, but then I changed my mind again and answered him -

"When I learned about her past, it didn't change how much I respected her bravery and her important role in our mission. Her tough past just shows how strong and determined she really is."

"It does not" he said, continuing walking.

"Didn't know you were okay just casually strolling with me," I remarked with a playful edge.

"The heck? What's that supposed to mean?" He replied.

"Don't be stupid. You practically vanished into thin air after what I thought was our last encounter," I pointed out, a teasing tone now in my voice.

"That wasn't our last meeting," he corrected me.

"Sure, whatever you say,"

"Wait! What did you really expect, Hina? That I'd keep pursuing you relentlessly?" he asked, his shoulders rising and falling in a shrug.

"That's such a lame response,"

"Was I supposed to interpret some kind of hidden message from you?"

"I never said you had to cut off all communication, did I? Plus, we were in the thick of this whole situation with Brad and Adrianna, and then suddenly, you were gone,"

"Maybe because I thought you didn't want me to contact you. Isn't that usually the case? Right?"

"Hey, sometimes straight-up asking beats guessing, especially if you're in the dark. Look, I wanted you to get why I'm flying solo and plan to keep it that way, and this is where I am, as you just saw. There's just too much on my plate for any plus-one drama," I said, with a slight shrug. He paused, taking in my words with a thoughtful look, before smoothly shifting gears.

"Yo, no need to explain. On the other hand, I saw your shop in the center. I was going to congratulate you," he mentioned casually.

"That's not mine," I responded tersely.

"What?"

"It's a copycat. Ben, my ex, and Lilly's boyfriend stole my concept."

"What? I don't understand. What does Ben have to do with Belle Epoch?" he asked, clearly confused.

"That's exactly the point. He has nothing to do with it!"

"Whoa, hold on. I thought you were thinking of getting back with Ben," he said, perhaps teasing me now. I shot him a stern and furious look, unable to hide my anger.

Without planning it, I found myself opening up to Derrek about everything related to Ben and Logan's scheme. He grew increasingly frustrated as I spoke, muttering "Those bastards" under his breath and trying to offer words of encouragement. I also shared my new venture with him about blending interviews with lingerie sales, my new project, and my new brainchild. Our conversation flowed naturally until it was interrupted by my phone ringing again. I glanced at the screen–it was Mom.

"Mom?"

"Hi, Peanut, darling. How are you doing?" she asked.

"Fine, Mom. What's up? You almost never call me before the evening," I noted.

"Look at you, Miss Analytical. I'm on my way to Islamabad. Your Grandpa is ill, and I need to see him. But I have something to tell you–if you ever come across the names Verbas or Miss Weisser, stay away from anything related to them. Okay?"

I paused, confused by this unusual request. "What? Who is Miss Weisser, Mom?"

"I'll explain when I get back. Just remember what I said, all right? Love you, sweetie. Kisses, bye!" And with that, she hung up.

Her call had shifted my mood, and a sense of unease settled in. Derrek watched me with concern, but didn't press for details, only asking if everything was okay. "Of course," I assured him, though my mind was clearly elsewhere.

"So, I'm left with just decoded messages and have to try to decipher them. Right?" he joked.

"You shouldn't have to decipher anything," I replied.

"Yeah, sure, like you're the poster child for being straightforward,"

As we were about to go our separate ways, I threw him a line, aiming to offer a mix of pep talk and light-hearted jest. "Don't give up on me just yet" I said with a wink, and then I spun on my heel to leave. We both hesitated, caught in a rather clumsy ballet of looks and blinks. Derrek hung back a tad longer, as if his feet were glued to the spot before we both f made our awkward exit and vanished into our own corners of the world.

Chapter XXXI:

Venezuela

"What a dolt you are," Mikey's voice, both witty and patronizing, echoed from his room all the way into the kitchen, where I was scrambling eggs.

"Don't give up on me just yet? What's that stuff? What on earth made you say that? I'm all for you dating him, but come on, who even says that?" he continued, his voice carrying through to me as I cooked. At one point, I shouted back, accusing him of flirting and using low-level tactics and trying to cheat on Dan in Italy. He slowed down then, narrowing his eyes, and accused me of becoming increasingly stupid if I kept yelling.

"Anyway, what did he actually say? Did he kiss you afterward?" he asked.

"Stop it," I protested.

"What?" he just shrugged, feigning innocence.

"You're making it all sound super weird. What would a normal person have done, then?" I pressed, looking for and needed a more sensible response.

He stroked his chin, took a deep breath, and began his lecture.

"Anything but 'don't give up on me just yet.' The line sounds like something out of a 2000s princess quest cartoon. I didn't realize you were so into poetry."

"What poetry, bro, all cool?"

"It's super poetic, silly!" he chuckled, now making his way into the kitchen, and starting on his smoothie, while still continuing his playful ribbing. "Seriously, if he didn't say anything back, he was probably just as shocked as me. Not because you gave him hope or something, but because it was just so odd. Hina, just too odd ha ha. Anyway, you mentioned Brad's arrest. Tell me everything you know, like right now!" He was already seated at the table.

Details.

Details.

Yes, I know what to say and what not. For now, I'm sorry, Mikey.

I hesitated for a moment, feeling my hands tremble slightly as I stirred the eggs, but quickly regained my composure. Then, I shared with him the details of how the case unfolded and Adrianna's role as an undercover journalist who made everything public. I carefully omitted any mention of mine and Derrek's involvement in the whole scenario, as well as mentioning its pre-setup. I had my reasons for the secrecy. Yes, friends typically share almost everything, especially close friends, but there are times when exceptions must be made, like my promise to Martha, the commitment I made to Adrianna about keeping the plan confidential and not jeopardizing the case. I thought to myself, *when my writings become public, I hope you'll understand Mikey- and you too, Lilly and Abby. Let this book serve as my apology to all of you.*

Well, Mikey couldn't resist teasing me for days on end, playfully texting about Derrek and poetry–a combo I still couldn't quite grasp. Derrek was absent for several days, and I was completely absorbed in my work. There was no room for distractions, especially as the tally of my interviews–both real and fictional–was climbing past 700. I meticulously fine-tuned my motivational letters and dispatched them. A wave of energy coursed through me, igniting a fresh, exhilarating drive. Writing had become my new zeal, and my fingers danced across the keyboard each night, transforming a mere physical task into an unexpected therapeutic voyage.

While Ben and Logan's story was no longer front and center in my thoughts, seeing their social media triumph still stung. Belle Epoch Envy was slowly being equated with their brand. I strove to remain unaffected, and I couldn't overlook Lilly's predicament. Mikey supported me in addressing it all in my own way, often prompting me to prepare for a candid talk with Lilly about the reality of her boyfriend.

Boyfriends.

Boyfriends. Boy friends do lie.

I had to keep reminding myself of this to the truth.

Then I recalled something important and called Tyrese. I told him about a printing company that had had money troubles before and asked him to learn how they were doing now. He said "okay" and started checking on them now and then for me.

Life, however, always has its own plans. I was at the gym, anticipating Abby's arrival, when Logan unexpectedly materialized. My greeting was a cold 'Hello,' my stare a piercing one, body fully tense. This wasn't the reunion I had anticipated.

The dialogue that unfolded was peculiar. Logan maintained a regular tone, which somehow unsettled me. He inquired if I was open to discussion. Initially, I was puzzled, assuming he was revisiting a previously declined proposition. My thoughts swirled with strong disdain for him–did he genuinely believe I'd capitulate and align with them? That choice was off the table. Yet, his reference was to something entirely different, indeed a revelation that caught me off guard.

That Saturday, when I met him, it became clear I was missing a crucial piece of the puzzle. Before I could unleash my version of negativity on him, he backed off and left, but not before mentioning a temporary office space near Belle Epoch Envy where he had rented a small room.

And would wait there to talk. I almost shouted after him, asking if Ben would be there too, but he didn't respond. I couldn't even focus on my gym session after that, and I left the building before Abby even arrived. I felt bad about ditching her, knowing I'd have to face her questions later and her 'hawk-style' interrogation about why I had left her hanging.

When I reached the location, a man in his mid-40s greeted me and guided me through a series of small public offices, each rented by different individuals. He deftly navigated me to a room where Logan waited. As I entered, I noticed another man in the room, already engaged in conversation with Logan and making coffee, likely for both of them and possibly for me, too. They welcomed me as I sat down, however, choosing to remain silent, determined not to speak until they finished their part.

The situation then grew increasingly peculiar. Logan talked about my university days and the early stages of my startup, even complimenting Michael's impressive skills in mathematics. I maintained my silence, occasionally glancing at the man in the brown suit who sat beside Logan. He was interjecting brief comments into their conversation and sharing a chuckle with Logan.

It wasn't until Logan mentioned Lilly that I felt a twitch in my eyebrow,

This asshole

This oratorical ground worm,

He's there, right here in front of me.

It was a sign that he had finally caught my full attention. Realizing it, Logan seemed to understand he had hit a nerve and that he now had me completely engaged in the conversation.

"How dare you," I blurted out, the words escaping me before I could even think what to say. Logan and Mr. Brown Suit fell silent, taken aback by my sudden loud outburst.

"I'm sorry if I offended you by taking your brand's name. That was not my intention at all," Logan responded, his tone confident and yet also cautious.

"Cut the crap," I snapped, cutting him off mid-sentence. "That's not what I meant. How dare you bring up Lilly when you've lied to her about almost everything–your business, Ben, and him being introduced by some darknet broker to..." My voice trailed off as I tried to correct myself. I wanted to say, 'Mr. Fedora guy', when another image began to form in my mind.

In surreal,

slow motion,

my gaze, slowly

Shifted to the man in the brown suit. I looked at his face, and a wave of recognition hit me.

But beforehand, I started saying, *"Holy shit, holy shit to myself and there you go!"*

He bore a striking resemblance to the Fedora guy, only this time without the hat. The realization hit me like a bolt of lightning.

Logan seemed to catch on and glanced sideways at the man beside him. The Fedora guy, now fully revealed, cleared his throat awkwardly and addressed Logan directly. "Your coffee is getting cold. Didn't I add enough sugar?"

"No, it's fine without sugar," Logan replied, his gaze now locked with mine. Finally, he started smiling and continued talking.

"What a shame we're on opposite sides, given the brilliant and sharp mind you have," Logan remarked with a tinge of regret. "We could've built something extraordinary. Absolutely,"

"You'll still build, I'm sure," chimed in the Fedora guy, and I internally dubbed him 'Brownie.'

"Are we done with the flattery?" I asked.

"I bet Lilly would be jealous of all this praise," he retorted with a sly smirk.

I slammed my hand down on the table, my patience wearing thin. "Enough! If you don't have anything substantial to tell me, I'm leaving."

"But we've only just begun. A bit of small talk and introductions are necessary for any conversation," Logan insisted, persuading me to stay a few minutes longer.

Are these guys for real? That was the sole thought bombarding my mind at that moment.

"There are people interested in meeting you, wanting to work with you," he revealed.

"What are you talking about?" I asked, narrowing and then widening my eyes.

"Don't think of it as anything related to Belle Epoch Envy. It's on a whole different level, far more significant. We're talking about involvement with multi-million net worth industries and interactions with individuals who are highly connected in various sectors," he continued to elaborate, his tone hinting at the vast network and opportunities that lay right beyond the horizon. "This isn't just another business venture. It's an entry into circles where the stakes are high and the players are influential." he carefully emphasized the grandeur and potential impact of what was being proposed.

"It sounds incredibly shady. Why would anyone want to meet or work with me? Unless you're implying that I work for them. Is that the case?" I questioned.

M question might have been a clever trap well designed to extract more information than he was prepared to reveal.

A Logan only smiled, glancing at the Fedora guy before turning back to me. "Sometimes partnerships are misunderstood. People think they're working for someone, when they are actually in a partnership."

"Okay, that's enough!" I nearly shouted, now ready to stand up and walk out.

"I told you this wouldn't be easy," Logan muttered. Its t wasn't clear if he was addressing me or this Fedora guy. As I turned to leave, Logan was still looking in my direction with that profound smile.

"What the heck is this all about?" I demanded.

"Hina, you're an idealist, clearly someone who can bring about significant change, on a scale beyond your imagination. Join us on a flight to Venezuela in three days. There, a different future awaits you, and you'll meet someone who finds you very interesting," Logan explained.

I hesitated, sat back down, now puzzled. Venezuela? A flight? A different future?

"So, some rich person likes my work and want to collaborate. Why don't they come here themselves and see me?" I challenged.

"They're not interested in your business or how you started it. It's not about the lingerie empire," Logan clarified.

Now internally fuming, I thought, "*That fucker.*" Out loud, I just said, "I've had my fill of negativity lately. I don't need it anymore. I don't meet shady, faceless people. It seems you're working for someone else now. How amusing. Thanks, but no thanks." I stood up, moved toward the door, and opened it. Then, just as I was about to leave, Logan said something that made me pause and close the door.

I didn't just close the door, I stood there frozen, unable to move. Despite my efforts to remain unaffected, Logan's words hit me hard.

"How brilliant of you to set up such an elaborate scheme, using a journalist to trap someone with influence. For an ordinary girl, you sure went to extraordinary lengths. You must be exceptionally talented," Logan teased, and his words sent a cold chill down my spine.

"Don't worry, no one knows." Then he added, "Well, obviously no one except those in this room and the person waiting for you in Venezuela."

I was speechless, unsure how to respond to this overwhelming situation. With stress washing over me, I managed to ask, "How do I know you're not in league with those predators?"

Logan laughed heartily for the first time, and even Fedora guy cracked a smile. "With them? This must be a joke. They're not the type of people I associate with. Look, this isn't a threat. Even if you refuse to go to Venezuela, no one will speak of this idea. I certainly don't want to jeopardize things with Lilly. But think about it—meeting someone there could open up new opportunities for you," Logan explained and waited for my reaction.

I just stared at them, a mix of sadness and anger in my eyes. "Who are they?" I asked.

"You'll see when you meet them," he responded.

"I've decided... I'm leaving, and let whatever happens, happen," I declared, now ready to leave the room.

"You're giving her too much credit," The Fedora guy muttered. "Maybe so does Elen..."

Ellen? The name echoed in my head.

Why would she give me any credit and for what? Wait, this Ellen is the one they were speaking about?

A woman in Venezuela wants to meet me?

WHAT?

"Before you go, think," Logan pressed earnestly. "I know you're aware of the risks you've taken with your plan. "Consider this idea. - if Garcia's people find out about your involvement, are you ready to confront them? Are you prepared to step into a world you've never experienced before? There are several worlds out there, hidden from everyday sight, operating simultaneously, but unseen by most. You need allies, Hina. And right here and right now, you can make a big one," Logan pressed with an intensity that clearly hinted at the gravity of the situation.

I paused for a few seconds, weighing his words, but my decision was solid. I opened the door, letting it slam shut behind me. I rushed out of the building, nearly jogging to my mom's car. For the first time in a long while, I let the tears flow freely and stream down my face. The overwhelming mix of emotions made it impossible to drive right away, so I waited, taking deep breaths to try to calm myself.

I called Derrek, desperate for his support, but he was out on the farm and couldn't come right away. I drove home, wrestling with my emotions, trying to shove them down and appear normal. But the moment I stepped through the front door, the facade I'd been holding on to crumbled.

Mikey immediately sensed something was way off. He gently steered me to the lobby, where we sat down. I could feel the turmoil inside me rising like a tide, threatening to overflow. I struggled to keep my voice steady as I spoke with Mikey and tried to brush off his concerned looks and probing questions. But I was nearing my breaking point, and my words were becoming more strained, my breaths shorter.

Just as I felt like I was about to burst, the doorbell rang, slicing loudly through the tense atmosphere. Mikey, clearly puzzled, got up and checked the video screen. His eyes widened in surprise, and he blurted, "Holy shit." He swung the door open and there stood Derrek. He had sensed the urgency and rushed back to Sacramento just in time.

Chapter XXXII:

Amna Strubel

That evening unfolded with Derrek and me trying to alleviate the tension, assuring Mikey that my emotional moment was just a reaction to Ben and Logan's success with their brand usurpation. Derrek suggested I stay over at his place for a change of scenery, but I declined. However, I did spend some good time with him, feeling the need to share everything.

But do I tell him all...?

Do I...? Or not...?

"Venezuela? That sounds risky. I'm relieved you didn't get swayed by their offer," Derrek declared. Together, we mulled over the situation, agreeing that getting involved with Logan's mysterious connections wasn't worth the risk. Derrek pointed out that in today's world, where everything can be recorded and publicized, Adrianna's journalistic skills could be a powerful tool. If anyone tried to harm us, we could expose them with the media's help. I also planned to involve my mom and her newspaper for an additional layer of protection upon her return.

We walked through the park that evening, and I have to admit, being with Derrek was the biggest relief I'd experienced since my college days. After that night, it took a couple of days to clear my head. I found myself reading success stories of random people, seeking new inspiration. One morning, during my stretches, a strong thought crystallized in my mind: *No backing down now. I've come too far to give up. If I stop, I'll never forgive myself.* With that renewed resolve, I decided to focus solely on my job interviews and writing, staying committed to growing my rebranded business. Whatever the future held, I reasoned, it was better to face it as someone successful and recognized than otherwise.

Transitioning from June to July, then into the early days of August, I felt like I was on a psychedelic trip. I've never experienced one, but if Joshua and my other friends' descriptions were anything to go by, this was it–except my trip was playing out in real life, not just in my head. The events unfolded so rapidly and unexpectedly that it was like being in a movie. Yet, slowly, I realized that this wasn't a dream or a hallucination; it was my reality, both unyielding and extremely persistent.

My writing had now turned into a relentless pursuit. I churned out story after story, intricately weaving together fictional interviews with practical tips and life hacks. The narrative threads were detailed, interconnected, and resonated with readers.

Mikey often popped into my room to tease me, "Genius is here, need anything?". Admittedly, the financial rewards weren't immediate. Then, just before I attended my last real job interview, we hit a milestone: selling 112 pieces in July. My stories were gaining traction, invitations to podcasts were coming in, and my name had started making rounds in circles where I never imagined it would.

Yet not everything around me was a success story. There were darker, uglier happenings going on that I only began to grasp later. One stark realization did hit me hard. The usurped Belle Epoch Envy was a permanent closed chapter in my life, irretrievable and beyond any more competition.

Gone

But not for good.

Gone

But not for the world. For me.

In its place, I was carving a different path, one where I wasn't alone. I had my friends, the wonderful investor couple, and my mom. Speaking of her, that's a chapter in and of itself–a tough lesson and a burden I'd have to bear. But let's not get ahead of ourselves; there's more to tell before we get to that story.

Having only about two hours of free time each day, I was deep diving into my work. The number of job interviews I attended had started to dwindle, but I more than made up for that change by writing fictional interviews and handling the increasing demands of shipping lingerie. The combination of lingerie sales and the accompanying stories was really taking off. In June, Lilly's birthday approached, and I found myself reflecting on our early friendship days. I remembered how she used to play her cello, sitting in nature, sharing her pure soul through music. Now, I wondered, what kind of birthday would she prefer?

A casino party, perhaps?

Or how about inviting entrepreneurs from every state to talk shop and investments?

Or jetting off to see the pyramids with his prince, leaving us all in the dust?

The day of her birthday revealed a significant change. I was, of course, invited, but I hadn't paid much attention to the details of the venue. It turned out to be a sophisticated kind of party, not the wild musical bash you might expect, instead more of a networking event with an elegant standing buffet, expensive wines, and a mix of local influencers and Logan's acquaintances. Mikey and I weren't exactly shocked, but a part of me did feel a pang of sadness. The party seemed to reflect more of Logan's influence than Lilly's true spirit. The girl who once dreamed of playing her cello in seclusion was now hosting an extravaganza for extroverts. It felt like a bold irony to me, but I kept those thoughts to myself. If Lilly was happy, then I was content for her sake. I greeted her with a smile, showering her with compliments and good wishes, but I consciously avoided Logan, ignoring his attempts to talk. The whole experience left a sour taste in my mouth, and Lilly and I never discussed it. Perhaps it was better left unspoken.

Or perhaps I should have.

How do people often make quick decisions in such scenarios?

But

I am not a "person."

I am Hina.

The birthday bash felt laid back on the surface, but underneath, I was still wrestling with anxiety. Every glimpse of Logan sent shivers down my spine and made me question the murky world he alluded to. Was it the criminal underworld, corrupt politics, or something else entirely? And why was I being pulled into it? To manage my anxiety, I resorted to deep breathing exercises that helped stabilize my racing heart. As the end of June approached, another intriguing event took place. My friends and I had often discussed Brad's karmic downfall, but they were oblivious to the deeper implications tied to Martha's case and were unaware of them. Then, on one of those evenings, after having dinner with the couple who had invested in my project, I experienced an unexpected sight. Leaving the restaurant, I caught Ben's gaze from across the street. He was observing me, and to my surprise, I did not even hesitate for a second to cross the street toward him.

When we met, I didn't settle for a simple handshake. I firmly grasped his hand, pulling him closer with one hand while simultaneously clutching his shoulder with my other hand. "Walk with me," I commanded, setting the pace.

"Whoa, easy there. Hey!" he protested.

He then protested again.

But it was futile.

My grip only tightened.

My breath grew heavier.

His eyes widened.

"Just walk," I insisted, not loosening my grip even a bit.

Despite his protests, I didn't let go. We had moved about fifty to sixty meters before I finally stopped in front of a police station and faced him.

"This is your one and only chance, not just in this life but beyond," I said, my tone leaving him no room for argument. "Your next words need to be the absolute truth. How do you know Logan, and what exactly do you want with him?"

He appeared taken aback for a moment, then just as he began to speak, I cut him off with a sharp reminder: "Just remember, fucker, your next words better be the whole truth."

In my mind, I was prepped for some weird theatrical antics and was ready to shout for police help. It was a realization that quickly dawned on him.

"I... I was introduced to him," he began tentatively.

"No shit, but why and what for?"

"Is this an interrogation or what the fuck?"

"Call it what you want, but these all are straightforward questions. If you had been honest from the start, we wouldn't be here, would we? So, what was the real reason? Why?" My insistence was unwavering.

"Hold on, hold on Hina. Listen... It might sound complicated, but it's quite simple from my end. I am genuinely an entrepreneur, albeit a small-time one, and my interest in you was strictly business. It's just that there are others who want to work with you too, though not necessarily in a business capacity, and they thought I'd be a good fit, like a bridge," he explained, attempting to placate me.

Before I responded, I noticed he seemed very diminished.

Smaller.

Even more insignificant.

The man I once saw as straightforward and confident had shrunk into a mere shadow of himself.

"Who are these people, and what kind of work are we talking about? I need details, and I need them now." I refused to break eye contact.

"You're asking about Logan?" He was clearly trying to buy some time.

I simply raised an eyebrow and kept waiting.

"Okay, Logan and... some others. He's involved with a group I don't really know much about. They're well-connected though,"

"Let me get this straight, Ben." I started.

"You don't know these people, and yet you thought it was a smart move to connect me with them, when you're not sure if they're saints or sinners? And you're here still claiming you care about me?"

"It sounds worse when you put it like that. They're into some big-time business stuff. I didn't think they'd be a danger to you," he tried to reassure me.

"Stop. What exactly did Logan ask you about me?"

"He didn't ask much, just general stuff and all, what and what not, business and university related," he replied, but a bit too vaguely for my liking.

"Try harder, be more specific."

"He was curious if you had any experience running small businesses. That's all,"

"Yeah right" I snapped.

"Look, I'm sorry. I thought... Oh, I forgot. He did ask one more thing—whether you'd ever been in jail or had someone sent to jail," he added after a long pause.

That remark stopped me in my tracks. "He asked if I've sent someone to jail?"

"Yeah, that seems strange to me too, pretty much,"

BOOM

Me...

Alright, Hina. Pull yourself together.

Stay cool.

Breathe. Scratch that, deep breaths aren't my thing.

Shut your eyes, then snap them open. When you do, Hina, better decide fast on your next move!

I turned on my heel, barely containing my frustration. "Thanks for nothing, Ben,"

I walked away fast, his words still in my head, as I called Mikey to find out if he was home before I made up my mind about going straight there.

I approached my place and noticed Linda, a friend of my mom's. I'd met her once while out shopping with Derrek. She was just getting into her car, clearly having just left our house. Surprised, I hurried over to greet her.

"Hey, Hina! How's it going?" she asked, slightly taken aback, but not making any move to exit her vehicle.

"Hi! I thought you were coming to see me?"

"I was, but I'm in a bit of a hurry. I left a message with your roommate."

"Left a message? With Mikey?" I whispered to myself, puzzled by the brief encounter. Without further ado, Linda offered a quick goodbye and drove off.

The conversation left me feeling uneasy. Inside, I found Michael lounging on the sofa, a look of deep boredom, or maybe sadness, etched across his face.

"Hey, butterfly, what's going on?" I asked.

He just looked up, said nothing.

"Linda stopped by. Mom's blonde friend?"

"Yeah, she did,"

"So let me guess. She's started some rumor about us being a couple? She doesn't know Mom's already in on that joke,"

"That's not it,"

"What do you mean?" I felt the anxiety creeping into my face.

"Sit next to me."

"What's going on, Mikey?" My frustration was growing.

Reluctantly, I sat down beside him, waiting for him to explain.

"Well, it's your mom... she's been arrested,"

Chapter XXXIII:

Transition

I first started wondering about my dad when I went to school and noticed other kids talking about their families. It made me realize something was missing at home — a dad. My family felt incomplete, like a puzzle with a missing piece.

Mom had always been quiet about my dad, suggesting he worked far away. She even let me get letters from him, filled with promises of seeing me again, painting a picture that he was just on some extended overseas job. But the truth was darker; he was involved in illegal drug trading. I only saw him a couple of times when he picked me up from school. The first visit shocked Mom; by the second, she seemed resigned, perhaps forewarned. My Dad's reality was far different from the adventurous captain of a magical ship that he made himself out to be in his stories.

The day he left to buy me tacos and didn't come back was the last straw. He had vanished to avoid arrest for international drug trafficking, choosing that life over us.

Following that, Mom became brutally honest with me about drugs, their impact on society, and the fact that my father was a criminal who had made his choice very clear. While I didn't grow to hate him, I learned to let go of any expectations of his coming back.

Mom then pursued a career in the media, where she's worked in various capacities over the years, always striving to make a difference in her own way. My Mom had her fair share of successes and challenges, navigating life in a society where our family background was notably different. She often shared how tough it was to assert her place in a world that didn't always accept her. At 16, curiosity led me to search for my dad online, only to find a few obscure articles about an American involved in international drug trafficking in Central Asia. This revelation hit me much harder than his disappearance had, altering my childhood narrative of him drastically.

When Michael broke the news of my mom's arrest, my thoughts immediately raced to my dad. Was it possible he had reemerged, pulling her into his criminal world? Or could the authorities have wrongly implicated her as his accomplice? However, the reason for her arrest was shockingly unrelated to my dad's past crimes. It was something very unexpected and far removed from anything I could have imagined, and left me reeling from the revelation.

"A spy swaps. What in the world is that? Can you, for fuck's sake, slow down and explain?" I implored, my frustration reaching its peak.

Michael took a deep breath, as if he were bracing himself for a tough moment.

"Okay, okay," he muttered, almost to himself, as he searched for the right words. "So, this woman, a friend of your mom's, told me that your mom has been detained in Iran, accused of espionage, like a spy."

My eyes flashed up and down and finally settled on Mikeys face.

"A spy? You've got to be kidding! This is madness!" My voice cracked with disbelief and panic intertwining my responses. I paced restlessly, the room suddenly feeling too small. Alone, with no one to turn to—my mother and I had always been in each other's world without family or close friends nearby. I thought of reaching out to her most recent fiancé, but he was nowhere to be found.

Nowhere to be found at this time!

No one else.

Why at this time?

Why now!

Why is this happening?

"How is it even possible? Tell me I am dreaming now. Tell me, Michael!" "But wait. She was heading to Islamabad because of Grandpa's illness and got arrested in Iran? How does any of this make sense?"

"It simply doesn't," Michael agreed, his voice now heavy and shaking his beautiful head.

"Maybe she visited Grandpa first, then went to Iran, and got herself caught? But what am I saying here?"

"Did she ever get to see your grandpa?" The question was a breakthrough moment. Michael and I exchanged a look that mirrored our now shared confusion and concern.

"But why would she lie like this? She's never..." My voice broke, as a tremor of fear and confusion took hold, shaking me to the core.

"It has to be some kind of misunderstanding," I start convincing myself.

I try to deny it all.

I must try harder to convince myself.

I must repel all the doubts.

I must.

But.

I can't.

"But then, if she never visited Grandpa, could it somehow make sense? That she was on some sort of... really secret mission?"

Michael's gaze met mine, heavy with unspoken thoughts. After a moment's hesitation, he spoke.

He locked eyes with me, his expression a mix of concern and skepticism.

"Jumping to conclusions won't help us here," he finally said. "It's all murky, and for all we know, the reality might be far different from anything we're imagining. But, jeez, what am I even rambling about here?"

Feeling a surge of emotion, I retreated to the balcony, pressing my hands against my face as if to block out the world. The tears came then, unrestrained, a reflection of the turmoil inside me. I felt like my entire reality was crumbling away.

Mikey was there, encouraging me to express all the pent-up emotions. "It's okay to let it out," he insisted. So, I cried, releasing every bit of pent-up sadness and frustration, until I got tired. In my exhaustion, I surrendered to sleep, but it was a restless, haunted sleep. As the tears dried down my cheeks, a deep weariness took hold, pulling me down into a fitful slumber where the day's turmoil continued to echo and stay. My dreams were fragmented, filled with shadows of my confusion and grief, not offering solace, but only a continuation of my waking state. This wasn't the restorative sleep one longs for; it was but a pause in a terrible storm, a brief interlude in the ongoing narrative of my distress.

When I woke, the world seemed altered, now imbued with a stark, heavy truth. I knew I had to act, to seek answers, but I felt utterly stuck, my energy totally sapped.

I reached out to everyone connected to my mom, from her friends to her colleagues, hoping for any shred of clarity or comfort, but to no avail. The responses I received were vague, filled with generic words of sympathy. Linda, though, remained unreachable, fueling my suspicions even further.

Why do the closest people to one just vanish when someone is struck by tragedy?

****

The days that followed were the bleakest I'd ever experienced. Michael and Derek stepped in to handle the ongoing projects, including storytelling sessions, interviews, and managing lingerie shipments. My ability to engage in work, or anything for that matter, had vanished, drained by the overwhelming situation and my fears about Mom.

On the third day, a chilling discovery online sent me spiraling again. A news report detailed the arrest of spies in Iran and mentioned three individuals, including my mother. The report was explicit, discussing potential death sentences, an idea that horrified me and reignited my tears.

I could not swallow freely.

Every gulp felt heavy.

What was happening?

It was then that Michael brought up a crucial detail I had overlooked. the concept of a "spy swap." That term, unfamiliar to me until now, was mentioned by Linda. It referred to a diplomatic negotiation where countries exchange prisoners, often spies. It was a beacon of hope, suggesting that my mother could be returned home safely, avoiding any severe personal penalty.

Swap or trade whatever it is.
GIVE MY MOM
BACK!!!

However, this glimmer of hope was quickly dimmed by the reality that such exchanges are complex and time-consuming. The possibility of my mother's return, while a relief at first, was soon marred by the knowledge that it could take months, if not years, to materialize.

Dealing with a shock usually takes about a week before our brains start to reboot and think somewhat straight again. During this time, everything else that had me worried, like Ben and Logan's drama, seemed trivial. Derrek's attempt at writing job interview stories, sprinkled with my advice, didn't hit the mark. About 50-60 of these fictional interviews just didn't sparkle like before, and my crew gently hinted that without me at the helm, we might see this project sink. Yet, I couldn't muster the energy or motivation to dive back into it. My days were consumed with digging up anything I could find on my mom, her job. I barely clocked three hours of sleep a night.

Then it clicked. I hadn't found anything out of the ordinary about my mom's work or her colleagues, but her last words to me echoed in my mind. "Stay away from Verbas or Weisser," she'd said before darting off, supposedly to Islamabad. Now, given all this chaos, her warning seemed even more strange. Was there a link? I bolted to my room, fired up my laptop, and plunged into the depths of the Internet once more, searching for clues.

The first search term I punched in was "Verbas," which didn't turn up anything recently. Instead, it catapulted me back seven or eight years, to a time when Verbas was a buzzword in tech circles. It appeared to have been a tech behemoth until around 2016 or 2017, after which it dissolved amid a scandal involving the arrest of its executives and the vanishing of its CEO. Reading through the articles felt like unraveling a science fiction plot, with Verbas embroiled in an artificial intelligence project tied to some highly controversial surveillance ambitions.

Artificial intelligence?

I believed it was a thing in 2022 and beyond and back in 2016?

What?

Okay, I had to keep digging.

But why had my mom warned me about it? The pieces didn't quite fit together until I searched and stumbled upon the name "Weisser." It was a breakthrough: *Weisser had escaped the U.S. This individual had been deeply entangled in the Verbas fiasco,*

So, this person named Weisser was also involved with Verbas.

My further digging into "Weisser and Verbas" unearthed two startling revelations. Weisser was not just any criminal. She was a woman named Ellen, ranking sixth on the FBI's top ten Most Wanted List as of 2024. More astonishingly, she had allegedly stolen military-grade drone technology from some kind of Army base and vanished, supposedly to China. Beyond that point, the trail went cold. The realization that Ellen Weisser, a woman of such infamy, was potentially connected to my current predicament left me utterly dumbfounded. I tried to digest this whole mess, then realized my brain felt like it was trying to solve a Rubik's Cube in the dark. Sitting there with Michael and Derrek, pouring over all the clues I'd gathered, felt like we were trying to piece together a jigsaw puzzle with half the pieces missing. When Mikey stepped out for the bathroom, Derrek leaned in close and dropped a bombshell that nearly knocked me out of my chair.

"Shh, keep it down before Mikey catches on to the whole Fedora guy thing."

"Holy.... okay."

He'd connected the dots.

The dots between "Ellen" mentioned by Logan and his mysterious fedora friend, and the Ellen Weisser wrapped up in all those tech scandals and the FBI lists I'd just been reading about. It felt like someone had just flipped the script of my life into a spy novel.

"Is it the same Ellen?" I interrupted, my mind racing faster than a sports car. He nodded, and suddenly, my room felt too small, like the walls were closing in on me.

"So, you're telling me," I said, trying to keep my voice steady, "that this Ellen Weisser, who's basically a ghost according to the Internet, and is on the global watch hunt, is the same person behind Logan, Ben, and the mysterious fedora guy? And she's also the one who wants to meet me in Venezuela? And somehow, all of this is linked to what we did to Brad and his creepy friend?"

Derrek just looked at me, and I saw his confirmation. The pieces clicked into place, but knowing didn't make me feel any better. I felt like I was standing on the edge of a cliff, looking down into an abyss.

As a desperate alternative, I tried to laugh it off, "So, now, I'm in some international intrigue because we exposed a couple of local creeps?" Then the laugh died in my throat. This was no joke. This was my life turning into a thriller movie plot, and I wasn't sure I was ready for the action.

Waiting for Michael to come back, I felt a mix of fear, excitement, and a hundred other emotions I couldn't name. One thing was clear, however—M: I needed to do something, and I needed to do it fast.

Chapter XXXIV: Code: Family

Ever caught yourself doing bizarre stuff when you're stressed out? Or noticed how your noggin' kicks into overdrive, getting your body to do all sorts of things? Yep, it's all linked. Stress gets a bad rap, and I'm not here to say it's all sunshine and rainbows, but sometimes, the chatter about its downsides is a tad overblown. Sure, stress can mess with our bodies in not-so-great ways, but hit that fight-or-flight mode, and bam! Your survival instincts kick in big time. That's when you might just surprise yourself, pulling off things you never thought you could. They say, under the right pressure, diamonds are formed, and strengths are revealed.

I was just doing my thing, like any other person—maybe a bit more or less. Yet there I was, my mind in overdrive, juggling the chaos of stress from dealing with my mom, my friends, my own business, and the looming shadow of the criminal world. How did I land in this mess? Where did I miss the warning signs? Was it a series of my own blunders, or were some of my mom's past actions catching up with me? No matter what, I was determined not to let these thoughts throw me off track.

I attempted to focus on prepping for job interviews (the fictional kind, you know), but it was a no-go. Most of my time was spent trying to piece together the puzzle, attempting to see the bigger picture in this muddle, which felt like an impossible mission.

On an unusually scorching summer day, I stuck to my routine, relentlessly searching for any clue that might pop into my mind. I devoured articles about Verbas, delved into everything about

Ellen, and more. I was convinced there was a sign somewhere why else would my mom reach out like that? The thought looped through my head endlessly.

Derrek and Mikey popped in now and then, each visit unfolding its own narrative. I was tight-lipped with Mikey, though, bound by a promise to Martha that tied into this whole mess I'd found myself in. That morning, rummaging through my mom's belongings, everything seemed typical until one item stood out—a book not belonging to her but to Michael. My heart raced when I spotted a book with a soft pink cover. Sure, I'd always known it was there, but that day, it struck a different chord with me.

The book, "The Language of Flowers" by Vanessa Diffenbaugh, wasn't new to me—I'd read it some five or six years back. And Michael, he'd once shared that it was a favorite of his, one he'd returned to often.

I yanked the book from its spot and began poring over the essential chapters, refreshing my memory of the storyline and my initial reactions to it. "Victoria Jones... She had this unique talent for using flowers to talk," I mused, absorbed in the narrative.

"Symbols, expressions - her way of weaving her emotions and messages through floral language!"

After absorbing the insights, I slammed the book shut and slumped into a chair, my breathing growing heavier as I drummed my fingers anxiously on the table.

"Messages..."

"Secret meanings...."

"Stay away... Stay away."

I murmured, echoing the phrase repeatedly until a crucial memory clicked into place.

"Stay away" was more than a warning; it was a special name my mom used for a hidden spot near Amador city, meant for emergencies. It wasn't just about dodging trouble; it was a sign for me to go to this safe place she set up to keep me safe from my dad's threats.

Now, my dad wasn't a factor in the current situation, but there was something else nagging at me—the phone call and its transcript. The one where my mom called me before she supposedly flew to Islamabad. I bet that call's been played back a bunch since she got nabbed on espionage charges, with the authorities and who knows who else dissecting every word. But I was sure that they all missed something—a detail that only just clicked for me.

"If you ever come across the names Verbas or Miss Weisser, stay away from anything related to them. Okay?"

"Stay away from them..."

"Stay away..."

I turned everything inside out, hunting for a hint or anything out of the ordinary, but came up empty-handed.

But this one?

It had to be this then. If there was a clue to be found, it must be linked to what I just remembered — it's the only explanation. I was sure of it. And with that realization, my mind was flooded with a fresh wave of stress.

That hidden spot my mom set up, back when she thought I was in danger from my dad's connections, which was key. She had drilled the name into my memory, and every time she said, "Stay away," it was my cue to head there. Though I only had to use it three times, and each was a false alarm, nobody ever showed up to cause harm.

Her car was nowhere in sight, and I hadn't gotten around to buying mine yet, so my only option was to hustle for the public transport to make my way to Amador City. Getting there was a hassle–it's mostly served by tourist routes, not regular public transport, so I ended up hopping from one ride to another. I left my phone, turned back to Sacramento, opting for paper maps to guide me, marking the spot the old-fashioned way.

I packed a knife, flashlight, an electric shock device, and a few other essentials in my bag. By the time I reached my destination, night had fallen. It took me about an hour to scout the area.

The place, an old garage, looked like a forsaken hut from the outside, battered by storms and wear. But on the inside, it was a different story.

Breathe!

The place greeted me with an air of nostalgia; it had been almost a decade since my last visit, yet everything remained untouched, frozen in time. The same flimsy locker was there, its vulnerability unchanged—you just needed to reach through a broken window to flick it open from the inside. Without any light inside, my flashlight became my guide, casting beams across the familiar yet unchanged interior. A quick survey revealed the usual old knick-knacks, each potentially meaningful in its own right. Yet I was on the hunt for something more substantial.

And there it was, justifying my instincts. Tucked in the corner of a modest table sat a box, cloaked in dark grey, with a lock that demanded a five-character code, any combination from the Latin alphabet. At that moment, my emotions were on pause, overtaken by a surge of focused determination. My stress wasn't just a burden; it sharpened my senses, channeling all my energy into cracking open that enigmatic box.

BUT WHAT? Seriously, the stress of trying to unlock something crucial without a clue where to start is next-level intense. Then it hit me: electronic locks often have a self-destruct feature after a few wrong attempts. I figured maybe I had three tries, but who knows? I punched in "Ellen" first, thinking about the warning she gave me, and how it all tied to Verbas. It seemed like a solid guess, but nope, that wasn't it. In my mind, one chance down, two to go.

I was on the verge of pressing "A," for my next guess when I paused. *"Hold up. This isn't going to be that simple. Nothing ever is, especially not with my mom. Her clues, her games, as it turns out, they've always had layers. This isn't just about the hints she dropped; it's about something deeper, some cryptic way of communicating, especially if she really is a spy! God fuckin damn it. What's the real message here?"*

'Hina. Remember! The warning she gave me.'

Think.

Think.

My childhood toys?

No!

Think!!!

My birthday? Her? Benjamin's?

How many thoughts can waltz into my mind?

Caught up in the riddle of the warning she'd left me–to stay away from Verbas and Miss Weisser–I'd been racking my brain, but after "Ellen" didn't cut it, I was stumped. Then it hit me, what she mentioned earlier about jetting off to Islamabad to visit my sick granddad. That's got to be a clue, right?

Right

Rewind to original transcript. Mom, what did you tell me?...

GRANDPA!

"He is ill," my ass!

Now my brain was in overdrive, producing the quickest analytical work I'd ever done.

His name is Iqbal, my grandpa. He was the one my mom said was ill in her last phone call, but that call wasn't just a simple phone call, was it? It was an encrypted message. His name is Iqbal which has five letters! It seemed the obvious choice, and I almost entered it, but paused. Too easy. If my mom, tangled in global intrigue, was sending a covert message, she'd be subtler.

The message had layers. "Stay away" pointed to this location. I get it; Islamabad was a red herring; nothing to point at. My grandfather's name, while fitting the letter count, was too public. Then it registered in my mind - But his nickname? Known only in

Afghanistan and among close circles in Pakistan, he was a shadowy figure, a "Ghost." But in Urdu, he wasn't a ghost; he was "Bhoot."

It has five characters!

That's it. It wasn't straightforward, just as my mom was never straightforward.

Deep breathing.

Fingers twitching.

So, "Bhoot" it was.

I typed it in,

My heart racing.

Click.

The lock disengages.

Inside the box were just two pieces of paper.

Chapter XXXV:

Adrianna Fiore

Fast forward 17 hours, and there I was, having hit redial on Adrianna's number eleven times, only to be buddy-buddy with her voicemail each time. I spaced out the calls, anywhere from five to fifteen minutes apart, my fingers jittering like they were zapped with electricity, teeth on edge, all the way to the office of Based on Stories of Belle & Envy. By the time I got there, I'd already buzzed Derrek twice, and he was en route to join me.

The evening was oddly serene, everything unusually peaceful, except for one element: me. I went through three packs of chewing gum, swapping them out every ten minutes as my irritation hit the roof. I had sent Tyrese home, craving solitude to prep for what felt more like a showdown than a chat with Derrek.

Then came the buzz at the door. I took a deep breath, stood, and after a brief pause to gather myself, I opened the door to greet Derrek.

"Sit," I directed him, my tone more command than invitation.

"Hey, sorry, I'm a tad late. You sounded off on the phone. Everything cool?" he inquired.

"Just sit, please," I insisted, turning to face him once I was back at my desk. He looked a tad taken aback but complied.

"Alright, what's up? You seem tense," he ventured.

Now seated myself, I glanced at two photos on my desk, my grip on a pen so tight it was nearly snapping.

"Look, the last thing I want is for what I'm about to say to be true," I began, "But you need to stay silent until I've said my piece. Don't interrupt, don't agree verbally, don't make any unnecessary movements, just nod. Got it?"

He looked like he wanted to say something, but then just nodded quietly. Before getting into the next scenes, I need to explain what happened seventeen hours ago.

****

Inside the locker box, I found a mix of papers — some with designs and others with just text. Among them, one was a photo, another just a block of words. With my flashlight in hand, I illuminated them. But that creepy, dark place wasn't where I could think straight or analyze anything. I decided to wait until dawn to make my exit.

And that's what I did.

As morning broke, I wandered through the forest, eventually hitting a tourist trail. I passed by some old cottages, making my way back.

I'd glance at the photo and the text, trying to make sense of them, but my mind was a jumble. The photo showed two girls, seemingly around the same age, but beyond that, I couldn't piece together anything more–not at that time yet.

By 11 AM, I had made it back to the office, freshened up and ready to dive into the papers I'd retrieved. Settling at my desk, I began my investigative deep dive.

Identifying the first girl in the photo didn't take long. I recognized Ellen Weisser from the online images. The picture was old, probably a decade, showing her as a teen or in her early twenties. It was clear: Ellen was one of the girls, unchanged by time.

However, figuring out the identity of the girl next to her was a whole different ballgame. It took me over five hours, a breakthrough only came after I decoded the message on the second paper. That was the key.

With this new understanding, my next steps became clear. I started making calls, and now, with Derrek stepping into my office, I was geared up to launch my interrogation phase 2.

"When did you start at Golden State?"

"What?"

"Just answer me, Derrek. When did you first step into Golden State University?"

"We kicked off the same year, both of us freshmen. Why are you asking this?"

"And before that?" I pressed on.

"I was stuck helping my dad on the farm, like you know."

"Ever hit up any big cities, maybe toured the East Coast?"

"No, not until I became a student..." Small pause. "But why are you digging into this?"

I didn't respond. Instead, I stood up, clutching the two papers, and a hidden item from the desk, out of Derrek's view. I approached him, unfolding the photos.

"Recognize anyone here?" I asked as he peered at the images.

He scrutinized them, then shook his head, a mix of confusion and rising anger in his eyes. But before he could voice his thoughts, I cut in.

"Check out Google. This Ellen here, now look at the photo. Spot the resemblance?"

He paused, connecting the dots.

"Yes, that's Ellen, the one on the most-wanted list, the same person linked to the mess with Logan and you, right?"

I remain silent for a moment, then affirmed with a nod. "Correct."

"Do you recognize the other girl in the photo?" I asked, focusing on the second figure in the image.

The photo captured two girls—one slightly taller with long, somewhat curly brown hair that blended dark and light shades. Her face radiated natural beauty, almost stunning, with large round eyes, pronounced eyebrows, and lips touched by light red lipstick. She donned a red dress paired with a black corset, suggesting a medieval flair. That was Ellen. My inquiry, however, concerned her companion: a girl with short hair, a hint of yellow to her skin, slightly narrow eyes, a delicate chin, and nose, clad in jean shorts, posing in front of a fence with an indistinct building in the backdrop.

"No, I don't recognize her. Can we find her on Google too?"

"There's no Google trail for her; she's not that famous. But take a closer look; you might find something familiar," I urged.

He leaned in, scrutinizing the image, yet no spark of recognition appeared. "I've got nothing."

"Alright then," I said, pulling a chair to sit directly in front of him, the photo in hand. I pointed to the upper arm of the girl in the picture. "Notice this tattoo?"

We sat in silence for a good fifteen seconds.

"Yes?"

"Do you know what it is?"

"No idea,"

"It's the Zia sun symbol, typically associated with Native American cultures. Various tribes have used it, or variations of it. And notice, her arm is bandaged—she was injured, recently wounded when this photo was taken."

Derrek leaned in for a closer look, his surprise evident, yet he still seemed lost.

"Okay, here's the thing," I continued, "I did some research, and this girl was part of the Meysee tribe, now a federally recognized group. They govern their land, their towns... She was from a respected family there, but severed ties over a dozen years ago left and started anew. I suspect she had some trouble; maybe she broke some tribal rules and faced consequences. That's just my guess, but clearly, she was trying to break free."

"Whoa, slow down," Derrek interjected, his confusion clear. "I'm lost. The fuck this have to do anything with me?"

I continue "Think back—when Adrianna first showed up in Sacramento, what did everyone notice? What stood out about her?"

"What are you getting at?"

"Derrek..."

"Alright, alright," he concedes. "She was stylish, right? And yeah, her tattoos... they were a talking point, weren't they?"

"I'm not sure if you remember, but she has several tattoos on her left upper arm, and one of them looks exactly like this," I say, pointing at the photo. "Even Mikey and I noticed it back then. But here's the kicker–it's clear that other tattoos were added on top to disguise it as something different. However, the Zia sun symbol is still noticeable. And the scar? It's also on the left arm, just below the Zia sun, clearly visible because it's one area without any tattoos. I'm guessing she couldn't get inked there."

Derrek looks at the photo and then at me, clearly puzzled. He closes his eyes, shakes his head, and starts to speak, still not seeing the connection.

"I know this isn't conclusive evidence that this is Adrianna" I continue, "but here's where the second paper comes in.

Showing him with full text inked on it that reads:

" To E, whose quiet strength did impart,
A grateful song in my freed heart.

Your subtle nudge, my liberty's start,
In silence, thanks, you're my art.
A. F"

"Is that...?"

"Yes, Derrek, yes." I affirm, stepping back slightly while sliding one hand into my back pocket.

"The 'E' clearly refers to Ellen. And here's the proof." I gesture to the photo showing the two women, identifying Ellen. "This girl's initials are A.F. She has the same tattoo, a similar appearance, though she looks a bit different here, and there's a similar scar. And remember, Adrianna's last name is Fiore. That means Derrek, Adrianna has known Ellen for nearly half her life. She looks up to her, works for her. That's how Logan and the Fedora hat guy knew about Jesse and Brad, what I did to them and everything else. Adrianna has been in cahoots with Ellen the whole time. That's how she knew about everything. It all leads back to Logan and Ben. There's no other way to see it, right?"

"Fuck me" he says.

I shake my head, my thoughts racing. "My mom discovered something, tried to warn me with this message. And now she's imprisoned, far away. There's a link here, do you see it? and I won't ignore her warning."

"Hina... I..." Derrek starts.

I interrupted him sharply. Closing the gap between us, I step forward until I'm almost touching him.

"I've got one question for you, just one. And I want the truth, nothing else. Trust me, I'll know if you're lying—I've got my ways."

His gaze meets mine; no longer confused, just firm and determined.

I pull a knife from my back pocket, the one I took from the "Stay away" hideout and press it lightly against his throat as he sits there.

"Tell me, Derrek, have you ever had any dealings with Adrianna, Ellen, or Logan? Are you, in any small way, linked to them?" Internally, I remind myself to trust no one. Everyone I've trusted has let me down, harbored secrets. Now, Derrek might just be another one on that list, he connected me to Adrianna!

I press on, my voice steady: "Your honesty here decides what happens next. If you're truthful, I'll let you walk away, no matter how much the truth hurts. But if you lie... trust me, only one of us is leaving this office alive."

Right then, I felt something stir inside me, a sensation I'd never encountered before. Was it anger? A sense of power? Maybe a hint of revenge? I couldn't pin it down, but the energy was palpable, coursing through me, making me feel like there was another part of me awakening, one I hadn't met before.

He doesn't move, just blinks a few times, taking it all in.

Then he looks up, casual as if we're discussing the weather, not life and death.

"If I end up dying at the hands of the one person I adore most, well, that's okay... I guess that's my modern-day Agamemnon moment..."

He pauses, then looking straight in my face.

"But before you decide anything, I've got something to say. If you can sense the truth in it, even better."

I can feel my eyebrows arching, and the hand gripping the knife starts to tremble. I try to steady it, to hide the shake.

"I'm not sure who's your friend or foe anymore, what secrets are swirling around. I don't have your knack for sifting through mysteries, digging up secrets, and deciphering things, so I don't know how much weight my words carry; they might not be as useful as you expect. But I will still say them, regardless. — here's my truth: I love you, Hina. That's everything I've got to offer."

Steady.

Don't shake.

Keep your breath even.

Stay still.

My gaze locks onto him, every muscle in my face fighting not to twitch.

Ten seconds tick by. Abruptly, I remove the knife from his neck, snap it closed, and slide it into my back pocket. I take a step back, pivot, and stride back to my seat. I sit down, fingers drumming rapidly on the table. Then I halt and begin to speak.

"You know, launching Belle Epoch Envy felt like a gamble. Two months in, I found my rhythm, envisioned myself in a business suit. Hina, the independent spirit, crafting something heartfelt, diving headfirst into entrepreneurship. I saw myself among business folks, retaining an employee's empathy but stepping into an employer's shoes. But now? That vision, that dream, it's blurry. I've heard there are countless worlds spinning at once, worlds I never knew existed. And here I am, on the brink, trying to figure out which of those worlds is mine. Where does Belle Epoch Envy fit in? What's happening with my mom? Where am I?!! Fuck... Anyway..."

He places his hand over his face, concealing it entirely, and remains still.

I keep talking. "Here's the hotline for RexTV, the network where Adrianna's supposed to work, along with the extension for her department. Please call them and ask for Adrianna."

After a brief pause, he utters, "Hina," then takes the number, makes the call, and speaks with someone for a couple of minutes before returning.

"They said there's no journalist or reporter there by the name of Adrianna Fiore," he reports.

"Right, I got the same answer," I acknowledge. "But when I inquired about the Sacramento project, the live broadcast focusing on plants and related issues, and who the leading reporter was, they mentioned, 'Oh yes, Emily Hathaway.' Emily Hathaway? Seriously? That's Adrianna for you. She's been using a false identity for years at RexTV. 'Adrianna' might not even be her real name; it's likely one she adopted when she began her new life. But now, she's vanished, gone off the radar... unreachable, that bitch was lying to me this whole time."

"And she's been lying to me for over 5 years."

I glanced at him. He shakes his head.

"And now she's gone, I can't even see or reach her, fuck...fuck...fuck" I slam my fist on the table, repeating myself out of frustration.

"She's not gone; we just can't see her at this moment." Derrek corrects me.

"What do you mean she's not gone?" I ask.

"She still has to go to court for the case with Brad, right? Sooner or later, she'll have to show up for a hearing. We can see her then. All we need to do is find out when the next hearing is... and don't forget... I've got my scores with her."

I clearly hadn't thought of that, and suddenly, I feel a flicker of hope. He has the point, and it's an opportunity we can't miss.

The day ends with us saying goodbye like it was just another day, even though so much had happened.

I know it sounds like, what? Just that easy after I almost killed him? But yes. After so much stress, we decided that way.

It felt odd, like suddenly nothing mattered. I wonder if I'm being naïve for trusting him. Anyone close could be lying, after all. But I know one thing for sure: the Hina I was during my college days is long gone. I'm deep into something big now, and I'm not sure if I'm proud because of what I've learned or sad because my carefree life is over. All I knew was I had to keep MOVING FORWARD. How I decided that I'll tell you in the final chapter.

Chapter XXXVI:

The Last Interview

Even now, to this day, m left wondering if my mom was ever really a spy. It's a tangled thought. If she was traded back to us in a spy swap, that meant she had been living this double life all along, a life I was completely blind to knowing. Part of me felt betrayed, scared even at the thought of her being a spy. But then, the bigger part of just wanted her back, no matter what she was — spy, writer, surgeon, or pole dancer. She was my mom first and foremost.

The whole ordeal left me in knots. I was a total wreck until I had a long heart-to-heart with Michael. We went back and forth over everything, but it was his words toward the end that really hit home for me. He said something like.

"Hina, I can't pretend to understand exactly how you feel. Your situation is uniquely yours, and it's heavy. But here's the truth— no amount of sadness or despair is going to change your mom's situation. Not right now. But do think about the future when it's time to make some tough decisions. Who do you want to be? Someone who crumbled under pressure, or someone who rose above it, achieving things that might actually give you some leverage, some way to help your mom success isn't about forgetting the bad stuff. It's about building yourself up further, so when the time comes, you can make a real difference, especially for your mom."

That conversation with Michael didn't solve everything, but it gave me a different way to look at my mess of feelings.

Ben tried visiting me twice, but I wasn't having any of it. To clear my head, I just hit the gym with Abby, hunting for a hit of that good old dopamine. I even found myself outside Logan and Ben's shop, Belle Epoch Envy, staring through the window at what used to be my dream. Later, in a moment of solitude in front of my bathroom mirror, I did something drastic. I made a tiny cut on my finger and swore an oath to myself: "*No more distractions, no more emotional oorphysical detours. I was going to keep moving forward, no matter what. And about Mom? I had to come to terms with her being a spy, even if just to keep myself from falling apart. It was my coping mechanism, and yet I was able to convince myself she knew the risks and she'd be okay. "She is a strong woman.*"

She will survive!

She will come back.

She is a fighter.

She raised me in an unknown world.

She's fought.

She will fight.

She'll win.

Still, to really make a difference, I needed to be successful, be someone with influence and truly effect change... realized I needed more than just good intentions. Success was the key—a position of influence could amplify my voice and actions a lot.

It was a bitter pill to swallow to recognize that wealth and connections can dramatically elevate one's ability to make a difference. The world is an uneven playing field, but it's the world we live in.

Determined, I pledged to myself to stay the course, persist in my unique blend of reality and fiction in job interviews, continually apply for real ones, and pour my heart into creating lingerie that resonated with my customers, lingerie that carried a message and a meaning-—empowering women.

Each application I sent, every design I sketched, was a step toward building that influence, a step toward becoming a force for change. I knew the road would be long, fraught with challenges and setbacks, but the vision of what could be if I succeeded fueled my determination.

So, I wrote with purpose, applied with hope, and designed with passion, all the while keeping my eyes on the larger goal. It wasn't just about landing a job or selling a product; it was about building a platform from where I could advocate for the causes I believed in, be a voice for those who might not have one or were never heard.

This path I was on wasn't merely for my own accolades or accomplishments. It was about using any success I achieved as a lever to lift myself and 'others' up, turn any spotlight that I found myself in on issues that mattered. Every tiny win, every accepted application or well-received lingerie piece wasn't just a notch on my belt. It was a step toward a bigger dream where success wasn't an end, but a means to contribute, stir the pot and shake the status quo, thereby crafting not just a career, but a legacy that echoed beyond my own personal story.

So, here's what I did: I wrote and prepared a handwritten paper for my book, but this page wasn't destined for the book. It went to my bedroom door, hanging there. It was crafted to be a personal beacon, a reminder for any future version of me who might glance back, riddled with doubts, to reignite the spark of my empowering journey and become a guide to steer me right whenever the path got murky. This page, etched with my calligraphy, declared,

"Think job interviews are just for getting a job? You are mistaken.

I am not like you. I don't go to interviews just to be hired, to be liked, or to earn more.

They're part of a bigger vision, a larger ambition, a passion, if you will.

To understand this vision, you need to go through countless job interviews. Then, perhaps, you'll awaken to the realization that the world isn't as straightforward or as daunting as it appears. You'll see there's a thin line between laughter and tears and realize there's more to this world than meets the eye. You'll likely realize that there are multiple worlds that exist simultaneously where you dwell, cleverly hidden from each other, not just one world.

I don't do interviews to impress anyone else. I do them to prove something, to hit something.

I am Hina Strubel.

And this is my book. "

I also shut Logan and Ben out of my life for good. I approached Lilly and laid out everything I had discovered about Logan, Ben, their murky connection to Venezuela, Ellen, and the man with the fedora. I didn't pause for her to react. Instead, I left her with these words: "Take your time to process all this. When you're ready, and you've made a decision that you can stand by years from now, come find me. I'll be here, always ready to listen, as your friend, the best friend." With that, I walked away, leaving her to mull over the revelations and deliberately keeping my distance for a while.

In a bid for a fresh start, I ditched Mikey's couch for my own little corner of the world-—a new, cozy apartment. Still, Mikey and I were still thick as thieves, chatting and catching up.

As July's heat cranked up, I found my groove again, buried in a mountain of work. Abby and Mikey, bless their hearts, kept popping over, making sure I didn't turn into a complete hermit from my writing frenzy and my pretend job interview marathon. Yeah, I only actually went to five real interviews. The rest? Let's just say I have a vivid imagination, as I clocked in at 999 total ones. I was saving the grand 1,000th for something real, something big... whenever that might show up.

****

"Did you hear about Joshua?" Mikey bellowed over the gushing of the kitchen tap while I was scrubbing plates and Abby was glued to her screen.

"Me?" I called back, turning off the tap and drying my hands.

"Yeah, it's the talk of the town."

"Alright, spill it."

"Joshua's at it again with his skatepark shenanigans."

I stopped mid-dish drying. "We're actually revisiting that disaster?"

"Yep," Mikey leaned in, "It's like the sequel we didn't know we needed."

Abby perked up, a glint of glee in her eyes. "Guess what? He finally asked Louise out, and for their big date, he decided to impress her with a stunt at the skatepark, right on the old factory ramp."

Ah, Louise, that very one—my former flat mate, cloaked in a veneer of friendship.

"He wiped out, didn't he?"

"Worse," Abby said, barely containing her laughter. "He went for this crazy move, something straight out of an action movie. And... bam! Not only did he have a faceplant, but he also got it all on camera."

What a teen drama!

I couldn't help but laugh, imagining Joshua trying to show off for Louise and ending up as the Internet's latest joke.

"So, what did Louise do?"

"She was there, saw the whole thing," Mikey chimed in. "She rushed over to make sure he was okay, but you could tell she was trying hard not to laugh. Poor guy tried to win her heart and ended up winning the Internet's pity instead."

"Seriously?" I shook my head, still chuckling.

"Dead serious," Mikey confirmed. "Joshua's now the Evel Knievel of bails and fails. And Louise? Well, she's obviously got quite the story to tell."

Things had really started to look up. I was beginning to shake off the shadows of the past, and my name was buzzing around everywhere more than ever. Derrek had even dubbed me the "queen of interviews." It gave me a push to aim higher, be more than just a voice behind the stories. I wanted to inspire others, especially girls who were looking to carve their own paths in life. I had this growing sense that my upcoming book could really make a difference, show folks the why and how of my journey. Not that I was hung up on being liked—it was more about aligning my work with my bigger mission.

Our team had expanded way beyond my initial dreams. Morning briefings became a big thing, with a crew of over six diving into marketing, sales, and editing. The investor couple, courtesy of Abby, saw something in us called bigger potential! They were ready to throw in another hefty sum, $85,000, to be exact, for the next quarter, but not now. They were impressed but had one request -—make the 1000th job interview unforgettable. I didn't blink at the challenge. Not at all Deep down, I had a hunch about how to make it happen, even if the details were still fuzzy. My gut told me this interview was going to be something big. Real big!

Given this new frame of mind, my approach to life took on a more comedic hue. I wasn't weighed down by anxiety or sadness anymore, nor was I bubbling with joy. I felt like I'd used up whatever chemicals in my brain that allowed me to feel anything deeply. My focus turned to my business. That newfound perspective also influenced my work, and I created a video titled "How to Master Interviews and Wear the Classy Bra," which unexpectedly went viral. My sales and the popularity of my stories saw a significant uptick within just a couple of weeks.

In between all of these activities, I reached out to Tyrese for an update on the publishing house that was teetering on the edge of bankruptcy. They had gone into debt and were shutting down, desperately searching for a lifeline. I inquired if they were still open to partnership opportunities. Tyrese said he'd look into it. Surprisingly, I learned they had tried to contact me twice for a potential collaboration, but I had been too wrapped up in my mother's situation to notice or respond.

In my quest to hit that landmark 1000th job interview, I thought that any of the next three I attended could potentially be "The One." Yet as fate would have it, none of them felt right. The first was at a start-up, so disorganized that the interviewer forgot my name halfway through. It was more comical than inspiring. The second was a corporate giant where the interview felt so cold and impersonal, I might as well have been talking to a wall. The third, a quirky local business, was where the owner's dog, obviously more interested in my shoes than me, interrupted us every five minutes.

Each experience was unique, but none had the magic I was searching for and needed. It didn't feel right to label any of these as my grand 1000th. So, I decided against including them. It felt dishonest, but I still had to do it. They were just not special enough; not worthy of the milestone I had envisioned. It might've looked like I was holding out for perfection, but in my heart, I knew the right moment would come and I would recognize it. I just had to be patient.

I began tuning into TV news, something I'd never really been into before, holding out hope for some announcement about a government spy swap with Iran that might include my mom. But as the days turned into weeks with no such news, I started to accept the situation, now constantly wondering how I could reach out to her.

The whole coffee habit was another thing I reassessed. It dawned on me that the energy boost from my morning cup was just a loan that I'd have to repay with interest as increased fatigue later in the day. My morning briefs started to feel the impact of this realization. My wardrobe took a turn toward more professional attire; high heels became my go-to, paired with chic suits and classier, albeit short, dresses that managed to be both stylish and yet a bit loose.

My beauty routine shifted too. My nails went from red and pink to consistently black, and I settled on a lipstick shade that was nearly invisible, just a hint of subtle pink. My hair? I figured that if I was going to be remembered, I needed a signature look. So, I opted for a medium cut, styled in softly waving lines down the middle, and I decided against wearing any earrings.

There was one moment when I sensed Mikey might be nudging me to reconsider things with Derrek, but my life was now too crammed with romantic entanglements. Deep down, I still acknowledged that if I were ever to entertain the idea of a relationship, Derrek would be at the top of my list. However, I had firmly closed the door on that path, at least for the foreseeable future.

In a post-meeting with a shipping company to negotiate a renewal of our special contract, Tyrese hit me up with news about that publishing house I had asked about, more precisely, a printing house. It had been on the brink of shutting down but was now eager for a fresh start with us, especially since we were branching into publishing. The prospect sounded promising, but it demanded careful consideration. They proposed creating a new department within our business, a suggestion that initially gave me pause. Instead of immediately agreeing to a partnership, I countered with an alternative. They could join us as employees, contributing to the company and sharing in the profits from sales. The arrangement would require them to undergo job interviews with us, a process I felt uniquely qualified to oversee, given my extensive experience on both sides of the interview table. Tyrese floated the idea of bringing in an HR manager for this effort, but I dismissed it, confident in my ability to manage the hiring process.

In five days, we came to an agreement.

They decided to come to our office.

They consented to an interview.

They sat down in our office.

They were ready to be heard.

I was ready to make the decision.

On the crisp morning of August 2nd, I woke up, doused my face with cold water, stretched out the sleep, and whipped up a smoothie—ginger, cocoa powder, chia seeds, and almond milk. My makeup routine took a solid fifteen to twenty minutes, and I dressed in ten. My phone kept buzzing, but I only took two calls:

One from Tyrese and another from Tifanny, our young, but incredibly talented, editor. Her vast reading and writing experience at just 19 impressed me, so I trusted her with editing my stories and intertwining them with our lingerie line. I'd already introduced her in my stories as the "Iowa girl"—the one who swapped emails with me, brimming with brilliant ideas. We hit it off instantly. It took quite some persuasion, but eventually, she made the bold decision to join our crew. Packing up and moving from Iowa to California all by herself at 19? That's not just a bold move; it's a leap into a whole new world... They say true vision can bridge any distance.

Each lingerie piece was to tell a story, inspired by job interviews turned fictional, aiming to empower women. Michael had moved out to live with Dan and was off to a conference. That day, a sleek black sedan pulled up to my place—a driver ready to take me to the office. I'd arranged for this luxury, well knowing that the moment I'd been waiting for was finally upon us.

Right outside the office, I hesitated, realizing I was already running ten minutes late, but I was deliberately so. My team was inside, probably getting restless. Tiffany texted me that they'd all arrived, expecting my leadership. The thought of grabbing a quick cappuccino crossed my mind —a little caffeine boost before facing the day's challenges. Then, I remembered my rule against relying on borrowed energy. Coffee, like any quick fix, comes at its own cost, and today, I needed to rely on my own resolve.

Just as I was about to make my grand entrance, Abby's sudden tap on my shoulder spun me around.

"Seriously, Abby?"

"Yeah, sorry for the ambush. You've been MIA in texts and calls, so I figured I'd catch you here. Got something kinda bizarre to share before I jet off to JFK tomorrow," she said, her voice a strange mix of amusement and hesitancy.

"Now's not great, Abby, I'm late for a meeting. What's up?"

She dove right in. "You know how we all thought Martha had finally moved on from Brad?"

"Wait, what do you mean "we all thought?""

"Exactly my point. Martha's still head over heels for him,"

I shook my head twice.

"No way,"

"Yep way. Yes" Abby insisted.

"And how would you know again?"

"Okay, Jake, my distant cousin you've never met, works at the prison or jail where they're keeping Brad."

"Never heard of him but go on."

"Well, Jake says Martha's been trying to get in touch with Brad. Letters, gifts, the whole nine yards, but obviously, they don't just let that stuff through."

"You are not real."

"As real as it gets," she confirmed. "Marthas still hung up on him, even with the assault charges hanging over his head and all that stuff."

Silence took over, as I turned back towards the entrance, letting her words sink in.

Abby was absorbed in her phone,

While I momentarily found myself in another world.

Clearly not the one I had known moments before.

This world was stark, devoid of emotions, a realm where light scarcely penetrated and dominated by shadows and grey.

I realized I'd glimpsed this place before, perhaps in childhood, but I'd never delved this deep or stayed this long. Now, I remained immersed, exploring its depths, feeling like an eternity had passed when it was only minutes.

When I came back to reality, my gaze found Abby again.

What I had experienced there didn't stay behind; it followed me, altering my perception subtly, but indelibly. Something within me had shifted, transformed by my brief sojourn in that other, darker world.

As I wrapped up, and started moving, Abby's voice stopped me in my tracks, "So, Hina, what's your plan? You going to shake some sense into Martha?"

I didn't pause, just kept on walking toward the entrance, but a smile crept across my face. A deep, knowing smile. I wasn't about to unpack all my feelings right then and there, but a thought had crossed my mind, clear as day:

"*Not everyone wants to be saved.*" And with that realization, I retreated to my sanctuary, more precisely, to the entrance.

Reflecting on it all now, Martha and almost everything about her kind of slipped away from my thoughts; it's like my brain didn't hold on to her memory for too long, it just faded, faded away.

Despite my usual anticipation of pain, it wasn't as uncomfortable as I thought it would be. In fact, it almost felt like nothing happened at all.

Heading to the hall, I reached into my bag, grabbed my black cap, and pulled it down low over my face just as I bumped into Tyrese. He paused for a brief chat before we headed inside.

"They've been waiting for twenty minutes," he said.

"They're still there. Right?"

"Yes, they are,"

"What do you think?"

"They seem really into it,"

"Even if we're thinking of hiring them, not making them partners?"

"Yeah, they wouldn't be here otherwise,"

"Okay, let's go iin.

"Just so you know," Tyrese added as we were about to enter, these guys have been doing this for over 16 years. They know their stuff. Let's keep it short; we're the newbies here."

"Hush, and let's just go," I said, and we walked in.

The meeting room was cozy, bathed in warm brown tones that gave off a welcoming vibe despite the dim lighting.

The table was packed with Tiffany seated in the middle between Tyrese and me. On the other side sat a well-dressed couple, with the woman on one end and the man on the other. They were easily in their mid-thirties or beyond. Leaning forward, I greeted them, "Hello, glad I made it on time despite the downtown circus and dodging a few eager journalists." My cap hid half my face, but they caught my smile as I nodded to them in greeting. They returned the hello, standing briefly in respect before sitting back down, signaling we were all set to start.

Tyrese kicked off the meeting, setting the stage before introducing Tiffany as the genius behind all my edits.

"The blend of writing with fashion that you've achieved is not just unique; it's downright inspiring," the woman commented, her partner nodding in agreement.

"That uniqueness is exactly what drew us here," the man chimed in.

Flattered, I jumped in "Tyrese mentioned you've been in the publishing game for over fifteen years. Right?"

"That's correct, howev..."

I didn't let him finish, now jumping in with, "But I heard your last gig wrapped up due to financial troubles?"

He confirmed it with a nod, adding, "It's a bit more complicated, but yes, that's the gist of it."

"It seems like the world doesn't quite know what to do with seasoned pros," I mused, glancing at Tiffany, who offered a supportive smile.

"We're thrilled at the prospect of working together, of course assuming we're all looking in the same direction."

I paused, letting the silence hang for a moment before diving in.

"Mr. Elison, Ms. Lubeau," I said, reading their surnames on paper and lifting my cap slightly to see them better. "I won't pretend I've got more experience than you both. But what we do have is our own vision. And, if you don't mind me asking, what were your three most significant publications? We're talking novels here."

They exchanged a quick glance before Mr. Elison listed their hits, "Blue and Orange Sky, Candle Me Away, and... Nua Rosa's Black Empathy," ending with a proud smile. The woman seemed to agree, nodding along.

"Candle Me Away was my jam!" I couldn't help but grin.

"And I adored Black Empathy," Tiffany chimed in, all smiles.

Turning to Elison, I asked, "How do you feel about diving into a mixed industry? Is it a thrilling challenge?"

He pondered for a moment, "Creatively, it's a fresh field, but the business end is familiar territory. We've got the publishing know-how, which should ease the transition, I believe."

"And I'd add," Lubeau began, but I cut in, excited.

"Exactly what I was thinking! Nothing less is expected from an experienced field worker like you!" I said, beaming.

I excused myself to grab some tea, leaving my cap aside and letting my hair down. Coming back with the drinks, I handed Tiffany some papers,

My face was fully visible to them now.

Ready to lead to the next topic, I caught Ms. Lubeau's gaze on me. She whispered something to Elison, breaking eye contact.

"Mr. Elison" I started.

"Do you think women's lingerie should be mixed with publishing, like having their own stories? Sounds a bit odd, doesn't it?" I ended my sentence as Mr. Elison prepared his response.

"In the realm of innovation, what's considered weird often draws more attention than we might initially think," Mr. Elison began, his smile broadening. "To innovate is to craft the new, whether from scratch or by blending existing elements. Denying this concept's uniqueness would be dishonest on my part. It's the essence of innovation, after all."

He smiles.

But she does not.

Ms. Lubeau does not smile at all.

I take my moment, however, and smile back.

"Ms. Lubeau?"

"Yes?"

"Do you agree with your colleague?"

She flashes a smile, but it's clearly forced. Adjusting her glasses as if bracing herself, she takes a deep breath and begins to speak.

"Definitely, my colleague made valid points. We've worked together for so long that we often understand each other's thoughts without our needing to say anything."

"Great then! To make a real difference, we must embrace new ideas. Each of us, in our own way, is learning to accept something new - new beginnings – you with your methods, and we with ours."

"New things. New beginnings," I say again.

"Yes, we're all about embracing new beginnings," I continue, settling back into my chair. "Our approach is to innovate, introduce fresh starts that people will value down the line. With us, your expertise in publishing won't just survive; it'll thrive. You'll have the freedom to handle external projects and pursue your own, all within a framework that benefits us both—kinda unique partnership, but formally under the employer & employee contract."

I pause, giving my words more weight.

"And"" I start again after a moment, "we're all stepping into a journey toward success. Do you believe your transition will smoothly integrate with our team?"

Familiar, huh?

Huh? I'm repeating in my head.

Mr. Elison, ever the composed gentleman, cleared his throat and assured us confidently, "Our experience will undoubtedly be a strong asset to you." Meanwhile, the woman beside him remained silent, her expression hinting at some underlying concern.

"Awesome!" I said, shaking off any uncertainty. "This partnership is all about growth for both of us. I love tackling new challenges and helping others do the same. Success as we move forward together. From my view, it's somewhat endearing..."

Small pause.

Their heads up.

Eyes directed to their side.

"...Like watching a child clutching their favorite toy on the first day of school, uncertain of the bigger playground."

Small pause

Head down to table.

Head up again.

Eyes interlocking with each other.

"But you know what? A bigger playground means bigger adventures. And without those, there's no real taste of success or survival, is there?"

Small pause.

They are looking at each other.

Their eyes, blinking.

Eyes on me again.

I am smiling.

They also start smiling because it's formal here, and they have to.

We announce agreement and there's excitement, then headshakes and smiles again. Excitement is in the air again, and finally we escort them out.

As I wrapped up the meeting, promising to circle back in a couple of days, there was a moment. Ms. Lebeau's gaze lingered on me, like she was trying to read an unsolved mystery. We exchanged goodbyes, her look still puzzlingly intense.

"So, are they part of the crew now?" Tyrese threw at me as soon as the door closed behind them.

"We will see."

"Huh?" His eyebrow lifted.

I left him with that, stepping out into the streets, my mind racing with thoughts. It felt like everything was clicking into place, as I stepped out of the office and paused on the sidewalk. I quickly checked my emails on my phone, then pocketed it and took a moment to appreciate the day. It was sunny and hot, but I felt a refreshing breeze of excitement rather than the heat. The issues that had been pressing on me didn't weigh as heavy anymore. My resolve felt like it had reset everything. I had no idea that "a resolve" could solve so much. I found myself thinking about my friends, how it would continue between us, about my mom, how long it would be until I could see her again, About Derrek, where things stood with him, and finally, how long before my business would really take off making me extremely successful, especially with Ms. Lebeau and Mr. Elison potentially on board.

What a day, right? The bright sun and gentle breezes made it perfect for me.

The only thing missing was the perfect background music to match the mood.

 imagine Lilly's cello filling the air—that would have made it absolutely perfect.

The streets were becoming more and more colorful.

Grey thoughts came my way.

But now I could immediately repel them.

It was a nice day,

Something to start with,

Something to live with,

Something to be challenged by.

Things did not work before, but now they did,

Two failures did not predicate a third,

Plan C really, really works, if you still wonder.

And oh, just in case you hadn't caught on,

Mr. Elison and Ms. Lebeau?

They were indeed Mr. Knowitall and Ms. Sharpnose, personified.

www.ingramcontent.com/pod-product-compliance
Lightning Source LLC
Chambersburg PA
CBHW032143010726
47494CB00002B/336